A RETURN *of* DEVOTION

Books by Kristi Ann Hunter

Hawthorne House

A Lady of Esteem: A Hawthorne House *Novella* from *All for Love Novella Collection*

A Noble Masquerade

An Elegant Façade

An Uncommon Courtship

An Inconvenient Beauty

Haven Manor

A Search for Refuge: A Haven Manor *Novella*

A Defense of Honor

Legacy of Love: A Haven Manor *Novella* from *The Christmas Heirloom Novella Collection*

A Return of Devotion

HAVEN MANOR • 2

A RETURN *of* DEVOTION

KRISTI ANN HUNTER

BETHANYHOUSE
a division of Baker Publishing Group
Minneapolis, Minnesota

Published by Bethany House Publishers
11400 Hampshire Avenue South
Bloomington, Minnesota 55438
www.bethanyhouse.com

Bethany House Publishers is a division of
Baker Publishing Group, Grand Rapids, Michigan

Printed in the United States of America

Library of Congress Cataloging-in-Publication Data
Names: Hunter, Kristi Ann, author.
Title: A return of devotion / Kristi Ann Hunter.
Description: Minneapolis, Minnesota : Bethany House Publishers, a division of Baker Publishing Group, [2019] | Series: Haven manor ; #2
Identifiers: LCCN 2018033953| ISBN 9780764230769 (trade paper) | ISBN 9780764233128 (cloth) | ISBN 9781493417193 (e-book)
Subjects: | GSAFD: Love stories.
Classification: LCC PS3608.U5935 R48 2019 | DDC 813/.6—dc23
LC record available at https://lccn.loc.gov/2018033953

This is a work of fiction. Names, characters, incidents, and dialogues are products of the author's imagination and are not to be construed as real. Any resemblance to actual events or persons, living or dead, is entirely coincidental.

Scripture quotations are from the King James Version of the Bible.

Cover design by LOOK Design Studio

Cover photography by William Graf, New York

Author represented by Natasha Kern Literary Agency

19 20 21 22 23 24 25 7 6 5 4 3 2 1

To the Giver of New Beginnings
2 Corinthians 5:7

And to Jacob,
who always reminds me
that every day is a fresh chance
to try again.

CHAPTER ONE

MARLBOROUGH, ENGLAND
1816

She should have been prepared. After all, she'd had two months to imagine this moment, to brace herself for someone new to enter her life. In truth, she'd done little else besides imagine all the possible scenarios, each one worse than the last.

But she hadn't imagined this.

Daphne Blakemoor stared at the man in front of her and blinked. Repeatedly. Quick, slow, one eyelid at a time, every variation she could think of because it was simply not possible that the man in front of her existed. At least, not for another twenty years or so.

The dark blond hair, straight nose, angled jawline, and deep-set blue eyes in an almost overly symmetrical face were all too familiar. She'd seen the younger version every day for the past thirteen years in the face of a boy on the cusp of becoming a man. At that moment, he was three rooms away, replacing the final section of chipped and scarred dado rail in the saloon.

Discreetly, she pinched her leg through her skirt. She tried to picture a pony standing next to the man, just to see if she was lost in her imagination.

Nothing changed the scene on the porch just outside the front door. The man was still there, his mouth pressed into a stern line while a pucker formed between drawn eyebrows.

She'd seen a similar look on Benedict's face whenever something confused him. It wasn't as direct as this man's—or as disconcerting. In twenty years, though, who could say? The boy was going to look just like this. Well, without the expensively tailored clothing and probably boasting a few more muscles. He was going to be a laborer, after all, not an aristocratic gentleman. The similarity was enough, though, that anyone would think this man was the boy's father.

He wasn't, though. Daphne knew. She'd been there.

And while there was a lot she'd forgotten—whether by accident or on purpose—the face of the man who'd fathered her son wasn't one of those things.

All Daphne's carefully thought-out plans, all her encouraging talks in the mirror—silent, of course, so her friend Jess didn't tease her for it—all the practice she'd done getting a speech ready for this moment, all of those things were worthless because in that instant, Daphne couldn't recall a single word.

What she wanted to do was shut the door solidly in this man's face and scamper away to hide in the quietest, darkest corner she could find.

What she did was stand there. In the doorway. Doing nothing. Because if this man was the new owner of her home, she had no idea what the proper course of action was.

The man's head tilted to the side and the pucker between his brows grew deeper.

Daphne gulped. No one stumbled across Haven Manor. That's what had made it such a wonderful place to hide for the past twelve years.

This man had to be in possession of explicit directions on how to get here. Since those would have been given to only one person, there was no *if* about it. This man was the new owner and she was blocking the entrance to the house, staring at him like a goose.

But what else was she to do? Benedict, the brightest spot in her life and the boy who wore a younger version of this man's face, was inside, and she simply couldn't let them see each other. Not until she'd come up with a plan and a well-rehearsed speech.

Speech or no speech, she should probably introduce herself. Minutes of silent gawking didn't do much to recommend her as an employee. The man was about to speak first and he was starting to look like he was seriously considering having those first words be her dismissal.

The woman was a simpleton.

She looked normal enough for a country lass, with brown hair swept up into a loose knot, brown eyes, and a touch of color to her skin from living in a place where people could actually feel the sun on occasion.

However, she'd yet to say a word. She'd yet to do anything besides stare at him and blink a lot.

Who was she? Obviously a part of the basic caretaking staff that had supposedly been here for years. William hoped she wasn't the cook he'd asked the solicitor to hire in preparation for William's arrival. The process of answering the door usually included some form of greeting, but she was taking so long to perform that portion he rather thought anything she tried to cook would end up burned.

A maid, then? Her dress was a nicer quality than he expected for a maid, though it certainly looked like it had been around for years. Was it possible she was the housekeeper?

He couldn't imagine a housekeeper without any wits, but then again, the house was in the middle of nowhere. His coachman had barely found it even with precise directions. A house such as this would be the perfect place for someone competent but unable to communicate.

Tension eased from his shoulders and face. The woman must be mute. As long as she wasn't deaf as well, they should be able to muddle along, though he would mention to the housekeeper that perhaps someone who couldn't speak shouldn't be answering the door.

He took in a breath and opened his mouth to speak, but she beat him to it, breaking the silence and sending all his calming conclusions crashing to the stone porch.

"I'm afraid there's no one home just now, sir. You'll have to come visit later."

William forgot to shut his mouth. Not mute. He was going to have to return to the idea that she was a bit light in the head, then.

"I'm not here for a visit," he said slowly and with particular care for his enunciation. "I am Lord Chemsford."

The title still felt strange on his tongue. After spending thirty-three years introducing himself as Lord Kettlewell and his father as the Marquis of Chemsford, now he was Lord Chemsford and there was no Viscount Kettlewell. It was enough to leave a man feeling a bit like he didn't know himself.

"My lord." The woman bobbed a perfect curtsy but didn't move out of the way or introduce herself.

She did know who he was, didn't she? Yes, his instructions to the managing solicitor had been brief, but surely she knew who she worked for. Then again, this woman might not know what to do with that information even if she knew it.

He cleared his throat and set his mind on giving her a chance. It wasn't as if he planned on spending his evenings sitting about the drawing room, chatting with his servants. If they could get past this moment, he could reserve judgment until he saw how she did the rest of her job.

Whatever that might happen to be.

"I own this estate," he said slowly.

She blinked at him again but still nothing happened. She didn't step aside, didn't introduce herself, didn't so much as say *welcome.*

Wind rustled the limbs of the trees surrounding the property, birds twittered amongst themselves, and a thick blanket of peace seemed to surround the entire neglected estate. Behind him, at the foot of the stairs leading up to the porch, the horses shifted their weight, causing the carriage harness to creak, but even that didn't break the calm feel of the place. He'd have to make sure that peace remained as he renovated the house and restored the grounds.

Peace was something his life had been lacking for a rather long while.

He had been right to select this property as his home out of the many he'd inherited from his father—along with a title, a reputation, and a slew of relatives of varying closeness who wanted to live off the marquisette.

They'd never look for him in the middle of the fields of Wiltshire at a run-down property his father had won in a card game.

It was the perfect place to live.

If he could ever get in the door.

"Perhaps we, or you, could . . ." William faltered on his sentence. What was the correct request in this instance? Step aside? Go into the house? He was already regretting his decision of mere seconds ago not to send her to pack her bags.

He slowly tensed and then relaxed the muscles in his body, starting with his shoulders and working down to his toes. He wasn't a man given to rash decisions, and dismissing a woman from his employ while he was still on the porch seemed rash no matter how odd the circumstances, but he was at a complete loss as to what to do next. He could push past her easily, given that she was an average-sized woman and he was, well, a rather average-sized man.

Finding a different door might be a more prudent choice at the moment, though. The thud of one of those other distant doors closing broke the awkward but peaceful silence, followed by the jangle of harness and the rattle of wagon wheels. Entering his house for the first time via the service entrance was hardly ideal, but he did want to gain access to his new home before nightfall without having to bodily move a woman.

Then she moved herself.

A wide smile split her round face and she stepped backward into the house, sweeping the front door open with a flourish. "Welcome home, my lord."

Well.

That was unexpected.

Or rather, that was what he'd initially expected but then she'd blocked the door and . . . Honestly, it wasn't worth puzzling out. He should simply take the opportunity before she changed her mind again.

William took a large step into the front hall, his gaze narrowing on the smiling woman. It was a forced smile, tight and unnatural. She had the presence of mind to put on a bit of a façade now but not to actually let him in the door earlier?

"I'm allowed entrance now?" he couldn't resist asking.

She blinked, and the smile grew wider and tighter. "But of course, my lord. It is your home, after all."

"I was beginning to wonder," he murmured. He cleared his throat. "And you are?"

"The housekeeper." She clenched her hands together in front of her and executed a smooth curtsy. "Mrs., er, Brightmoor at your service."

She curtsied like a gentlewoman and stumbled over her name like a street urchin. And she was in charge of his house? That might have done well enough when the only thing she had to do was keep the roof from caving in, but she might be rather difficult to live with.

Yet she was here so he'd have to make do, at least for a few days. As long as she didn't poison his tea she was better than no housekeeper at all. He sighed. "Have we a footman to bring in my bags and show my man where to bed down the horses?"

The woman poked her head out the door and looked to the graveled drive where his coach was sitting. Pasley, William's driver and head groom, was standing by the two horses' heads while his valet, Morris, was standing by the door of the carriage. If either of them found the farce that had played out on the porch of the house to be strange or even entertaining, they weren't showing it. Like proper servants.

"No," the housekeeper said, dragging the word out a good bit longer than necessary as she buried her hands in her apron. "But we've a boy who lives . . . nearby . . . who helps with the garden, goats, and chickens."

He shook away a sudden burst of dizziness as he attempted to wrap his mind around what the woman had said. His abandoned estate had a garden? And livestock? "We've goats and chickens? But not footmen?"

"We haven't had need for a footman, but food is something else entirely." Her tone—considerably more cultured than he would have expected for a woman living in what was essentially the middle of nowhere—was chiding enough that he had to swallow an instinctive apology.

She did have a point, though. He hadn't seen many nearby farms on his drive in, just a lot of trees. If they were to have daily food or items such as eggs or milk, a small plot and a handful of animals were probably necessary to provide for herself and whoever else was part of the *we*.

"Reuben is rather capable with horses," Mrs. Brightmoor continued, still rolling her hands in her apron. "But your bags look quite large. Can your man carry them? Or perhaps you could help him and carry in your own?"

It wasn't that William had never carried anything in his life. There had been a time or two he'd had to carry his own bag or even help lift a trunk, but that she would suggest such a thing was a bit shocking. Despite his capability, he rather thought that if he were going to hire people to do a job, he ought to let them do it.

And he tended to hire a lot of people.

It was ironic the number of people he employed when all he really wanted was to be left alone. Still, hiring an extra servant or two was a far better use of his money than two more finely tailored suits of clothing that he had no need of.

Yet here he was with a staff of what appeared to be three, assuming the cook he had requested was around somewhere. He should have asked what the solicitor meant by a basic staff. Their definitions were obviously not aligned, and until they were, it looked like William would have to do a bit for himself.

His heart pounded a bit harder as he stepped one foot back over the threshold. His gaze flickered back and forth from the carriage to the housekeeper. Would she let him back in when he returned, or would there once more be a human blockade in his way?

Since there was no way to cross a ten-foot porch and go down a dozen stone steps without actually departing, William left the house and returned to the carriage, where he pulled out the leather bag he'd kept inside the carriage with him.

"My lord!" Morris protested, stepping closer to the remaining baggage strapped to the back of the carriage.

William shook his head and adjusted his grip on the bag. "Go with Pasley. Once the horses are unhitched, the two of you can carry the trunks in."

Morris looked back and forth. "Go with him where?"

William glanced around as well. Not a single outbuilding was visible. The house had been carefully placed on a slight rise to look like the only thing around. Trees extended out to the sides, presumably blocking the view of whatever was down the other side of the hill.

There was a rutted path, however, and a set of tracks leading around one side of the house. William was about to suggest they try that direction when a boy came loping around the corner. He looked to be mostly arms and legs—thin ones that Mrs. Brightmoor had accurately assumed wouldn't be much help with carrying trunks, and the neck extending out of his once-white work shirt barely looked big enough around to hold up his head.

There was a brief glimpse of something that might have been spectacles before the head dropped and the boy watched his toes as he walked, leaving William looking at a mop of auburn curls that would require half a tin of hair wax to tame.

Morris's thinned lips indicated he didn't particularly care for the idea of following a boy who looked at his toes, but he didn't say anything so William left him to it. It wasn't like they had much choice.

William slid the smallest of the bags from beneath the strap holding the baggage onto the carriage and turned back toward the stairs before Morris could protest again.

The door to the house stood open, with the enigmatic Mrs. Brightmoor nowhere in sight. He crossed into the front hall once more and nudged the door closed with his foot.

Then he stared.

He'd been too focused on his housekeeper to look at the room earlier, and if asked, he wasn't sure he could have said what he expected it to look like.

But whatever it was, it hadn't been this.

The large room, nearly devoid of furniture, was still impressive, especially when one considered how long the house had been empty. A scattering of intricate tables so small they couldn't hold anything and equally useless delicately carved chairs lined the tall walls. Bright red wall coverings that had clearly seen a better day made a stark contrast to the white trim and wainscoting.

But the part that most took his breath away was the art. Painting upon painting covered the walls. Statues stood like sentinels in the corners. A glance through the open doors on all three walls revealed that the abundance of art was not confined to the front hall.

And every last bit of it, even under closer inspection, appeared clean and meticulously cared for. His housekeeper might not be able to speak well, but she—or someone else lurking around the house—could certainly wield a cleaning cloth.

As if his thoughts had conjured her, the woman appeared in the large open archway across from the front door. The smile had returned, though it seemed more natural now, changing the shape of her round, sun-kissed face into a charming combination of hills and valleys. She looked entirely too young to be the housekeeper of anything. Perhaps she merely felt intimidated by him? It was understandable. He might be the only nobleman she'd ever encountered.

"There you are," she said in her quiet, cultured, and entirely non-subservient tone.

So, she'd gotten prettier while he went to get his bags, but not much else had changed. He sighed. "Yes. I'm here. Perhaps you could direct me to my rooms?"

She blinked. "Of course. The stairs are right this way."

Of course. Because everything else had gone as expected in this encounter.

He strode after her, entering a room equally as large as the hall he'd just left but with two grand staircases climbing up the side walls and framed by even more artwork.

She was already halfway up the stairs, impressing him with the pace she seemed to achieve despite her shorter stature. It was a pleasure to walk somewhere with someone without having to alter his normally brisk pace. Not that he walked places with servants, except occasionally Morris.

He caught up with her on the first-story landing as she approached a door and flung it open with a wave of her hand that was disconcertingly different from the discreet easing open of doors he was accustomed to servants doing.

It might be worth keeping Mrs. Brightmoor around simply for the plethora of surprises that came along with her.

CHAPTER TWO

"Your rooms, my lord." Confidence wasn't something Daphne felt anywhere outside her comfortable little routine, which the imposing Lord Chemsford certainly didn't fit into, but she knew she'd done a good job preparing these rooms. Well, as good a job as could be done.

There was a certain disrepair that came from twelve years of hard use. Not on the furniture, of course. Daphne and her friend Kit had been sure to have all the valuable and ornate furniture stored away carefully before converting the room into a bedchamber for all the boys in their care.

Boys who no longer lived here. Only Reuben remained. Benedict was living with Mr. Leighton, the master woodworker he was apprenticed to, and all the others, now living with families who'd taken them in as their own, were much better off with secure futures and a place to belong. Most of the girls Daphne had once cared for had been placed with families as well, but they'd stayed in the room on the other side of the landing.

This room had been for the boys, and it was evident on the walls and the floors. She couldn't blame them for the watermarks on the ceiling, though. That was simply evidence of a roof in need of much repair.

Daphne stepped farther into the room, making sure Lord

Chemsford could easily enter and set the bags he carried on the floor.

Bags she had suggested he carry.

It would be a miracle if she stayed employed through dinner. So many years of living away from anything considered polite society had obviously made her forget what was acceptable and what wasn't.

She cleared her throat. "I've been airing it out frequently and changing the linens every few days so it would be ready when you arrived."

After setting the bags down, he strolled about the large chamber.

An enormous bed sat in the center of one wall, with ornately carved posts extending nearly to the ceiling. It was an exceptionally heavy bed, and they'd nearly taken out the banister bringing it back up to the house, but hopefully it and the plush Turkish rug in front of the hearth were eye-catching enough that he wouldn't notice the waist-high marks that lined the wall from where the iron beds the boys had slept in had rubbed over the years.

No such luck.

He crossed to the wall and rubbed a hand along one of the faint grey lines before looking up, his gaze tracking from one spot of water damage to another.

"They're old," she said, since it was obvious she wasn't going to be able to pretend they weren't there. "Nothing is going to drip on you should it rain tonight." Not unless there was a new leak she didn't know about, which was entirely possible. The roof certainly had been showing its age of late, and there was more than one bucket strategically positioned in the upper garret rooms. The roof above this room, however, had been carefully repaired.

"This will do," he said.

Daphne didn't realize how tightly she'd been holding herself until he uttered those words. She'd grown up in London, on the fringes of the *ton*. She'd held up enough drawing room walls in her short, first, and only Season to know more than one aristocratic gentleman who would have been outraged to be given rooms this shabby, even though as far as he knew the house had been sitting practically empty for decades.

Yet, here was a man, a marquis, who was willing to carry his own bags and wasn't going to squawk about the reasonable shabbiness of the room.

How different life would have been if *he* had been the man she'd met on that one night she'd tried to be someone other than herself. What would have happened if her one devastating adventure in life had been with a man who wouldn't set out to ruin a girl's honor and reputation? What if she'd met a gentleman who would come to her rescue instead?

The man in front of her certainly looked enough like the man who had devastated her and changed her life that it was easy to imagine the marquis as a better, more noble version.

Except he wasn't. Regardless of what he looked like or how practical he seemed to be, she had no business imagining him in the role of rescuer. He wasn't here to love her in spite of her past and love her child as his own—particularly since Benedict didn't even know he was hers but thought he was just another unwanted child she'd taken in to care for . . . and honestly her life was so much more complicated than it felt when she really stopped to think about it.

No man in his right mind, and particularly not a nobleman, was going to want to be involved with her.

She shook her head and brought her focus back to the man who was now looking at her rather expectantly.

Oh dear. What had she missed?

She was going to offer to have hot water brought up, wasn't she? Perhaps tea and refreshments? There might not be footmen but surely there were maids? Someone? She couldn't be caring for this entire house on her own.

But she simply stood there, eyes wide as she stared back at him, occasionally blinking slowly.

He had to allow that she might never have cared for a guest. She couldn't be much past five and twenty, though the solicitor had indicated the current housekeeper had been working at the house for many years. This woman must have spent the bulk of her adult life practically alone. Though inconvenient, he had to remember that her lack of personal interaction skills were understandable.

Hopefully she wouldn't mind much when he had a competent housekeeper hired and moved her to the position of parlor maid, which, if the cleanliness of the parts of the house he'd seen thus far was any indication, would be more in line with her skills.

"Have hot water delivered," he said with a sigh. "And perhaps—"

"Tea?"

William cut his sentence short as another woman walked into the room. While there could be some debate as to whether or not the housekeeper was shorter than average, there was no question this woman was. Was there something in the water in Wiltshire that stunted its women's growth? The new woman's blond hair was scraped back into a tight bun, a contrast to the slightly fuzzy brown halo caused by the housekeeper's looser hair configuration.

In the new woman's hands was a tray. Steam rose from the teapot that sat in the center, surrounded by a cup, saucer, and an assortment of small sandwiches and biscuits.

"Er, yes." William cleared his throat. "Tea."

The blonde inclined her head at the housekeeper. "I've brought up the refreshments you ordered. Water is heating as you asked. Reuben will bring it up after he finishes caring for the horses."

William's attention pulled from the tray his apparently not-as-incompetent-as-he'd-thought housekeeper had requested. Those long, skinny limbs on that boy he'd seen earlier were going to haul his water up? He'd be lucky to have a bath by morning.

"Yes," Mrs. Brightmoor said in that same slow, stilted way in which she'd talked about his bags earlier. "Thank you. Good." She nodded and blinked a bit more as she watched the little blonde deposit the tray on a small writing desk in the corner.

Once everything was arranged, the petite woman gave a small curtsy and moved toward the door.

As she walked past, she plucked at the housekeeper's sleeve. William would have missed it if he'd blinked. Even now he wasn't sure he'd actually seen it, but the strange little jump the housekeeper gave was proof the incident had, indeed, occurred.

Mrs. Brightmoor gave her own elegant curtsy. "We'll leave you to . . . it."

She smiled again and followed the other woman out the door, shutting it firmly behind her.

Something wasn't right here, but he wasn't sure if it was the remoteness of the house or an indication of a bigger problem. The growl in his stomach reminded him that while he couldn't answer that question right now, he could solve the problem of the gnawing hunger in his belly and the throat parched from travel dust.

As he bit into a biscuit, an explosion of flavors he couldn't identify but refused to live the rest of his life without filled his mouth. In the quiet solitude of his room he allowed himself to groan in pleasure and drop down onto a large upholstered chair. Not a speck of dust drifted into the air. He took another bite, savoring the taste on his tongue as he chewed. For food this good and a house this clean, he'd be willing to put up with a considerable number of oddities in his servants. The fact that it gave him one more excuse not to have any guests at the house was simply an additional benefit.

Daphne made it down the stairs to the ground floor before her trembling body refused to go another step and she collapsed against the wall.

Instead of boys she'd loved and raised from infancy, the room upstairs was now occupied by a stranger. Daphne didn't handle strangers very well most of the time, and she certainly wasn't managing this one. This man could crush her with a word and was somehow painfully connected to the most grievous mistake in judgment she had ever made.

What was she going to do?

A strong, small hand snagged her elbow and hauled her toward the stairs that dropped down into the servants' domain. It wasn't a grip Daphne could easily break, given the strength Jess had earned in the several years she'd spent working as a spy for England. Jess had come to the house three years ago as a stranger, too, but she'd been a stranger in need of care, and nothing got past Daphne's defenses faster than that. Over the years, they'd become friends.

Although forcibly propelling her down a small stone staircase wasn't exactly friendly.

As opposed to the grand steps she'd nearly tripped down moments before, these were worn and plain and devoid of the grandeur of the rest of the house. Daphne had been down these stairs countless times in the past twelve years and the difference had never bothered her.

Today it did. Until fifteen minutes ago, no one living in this house had ever been subordinate to anyone else. They'd been a family, working together to maintain the building, produce enough food, and make enough money to survive.

For the past twelve years, the plain stone stairwell had simply been the way to the kitchens. Now it was a threshold, a passageway that denoted the people who used it were of a lower class than the people who didn't.

Daphne had been raised above those stairs. Well, not these particular stairs, but ones that were very similar. But when she'd moved here, there'd been no distinction. Everyone in the house belonged everywhere.

Not anymore.

Now Daphne's status had changed, and her comfort and security depended upon serving the man upstairs. Keeping her position was hardly her greatest concern anymore, though.

Jess kept her grip on Daphne's elbow until they'd moved all the way in to the kitchen, then she let her go with a little push.

Daphne stumbled toward the worktable and groped her way to one of the stools next to it. She breathed in until her lungs burned from the stretch and focused on a deep gouge in the surface of the table. There was no way of knowing what had made that gouge, but there was something comforting in its existence.

Unlike nearly every room upstairs, this table was the same as it had been for years. It was comfortable. She could pretend nothing had changed.

But it had.

He was here now, and he was a problem.

Jess moved about the room, going on with her business as she usually did. The woman was always unruffled, but wasn't she at least a little bit worried about their current situation?

"Did you see him?" Daphne asked in a harsh whisper.

Jess paused and looked at Daphne, one delicate, pale eyebrow arched high. "Of course I did. You think I'd enter a room and not look around?"

"Yes, yes." Daphne sprawled her upper body across the table. "But did you *see* him?"

Jess set down the onion she'd pulled from a box and crossed the kitchen to wrap her hands around Daphne's cold fingers. "I know what you're thinking."

Daphne rather doubted that. By the time Kit had brought Jess to Haven Manor three years ago, Daphne had learned how to, for the most part, suppress the tendency she'd had as a young woman to drift into imagined scenarios and detailed fantasies. With the responsibility of raising a dozen children, losing track of reality during the day could be dangerous, so she'd waited until she was alone washing the dishes, going to bed, or rocking a sleeping toddler to indulge in such daydreams.

But with only three nearly grown children remaining in her care, Daphne occasionally lapsed back into old habits. Such as now. There was no way for Jess to know that currently a part of Daphne's mind was busy coming up with all sorts of possibilities, including wondering if the man she'd tried so hard to forget had somehow over the past fourteen years turned into the man residing in the master chamber.

Never mind the fact that Benedict's father had brown eyes and this man had blue and Daphne had never heard of a man's eyes changing color like that.

"You're thinking," Jess continued, seemingly oblivious to the fact that nearly half of Daphne's attention was turned inward, "that our new employer looks remarkably like Benedict."

Silence fell between the two women as they looked at each other. And while that hadn't been exactly what Daphne was thinking, it was certainly close enough, though she'd hoped perhaps the striking similarity was only in her mind.

Jess gave Daphne's fingers a squeeze, and a renewed energy surged through her. If anyone had a solution to this problem, it would be Jess. The mysterious woman may have entered the home looking a bit like a lost puppy that had been backed into a corner, but she was a survivor.

The blond woman gave a short, sharp nod. "And you would be correct. They look identical." She let go of Daphne's hand and turned back to the onion, sliding a knife from the wooden block on the table near the wall. "Since you didn't faint dead away in the middle of the front door, I'm assuming he's not the father. How are they related?"

Daphne propped her elbows on the worktable and dropped her head into her hands with a groan. She didn't want to think about Mr. Maxwell Oswald, didn't want to remember the details of that night, but they were burned into her memory with a branding iron. Recalling those memories created so many conflicted emotions—guilt and shame certainly, but also joy because of Benedict and her new life purpose. She couldn't imagine her life without those. She'd much rather think about the good that had come from her bad decision than to think about the decision itself.

She'd been caught up in the moment, pretending to be her friend Kit, who was vivacious and popular and not terrified of moving more than two feet from the wall in a room full of people.

If she were honest, she'd been more engrossed in the idea of what could be than with the man himself. She'd never had a *tendre* for Mr. Oswald, had barely even known him by more than sight and reputation.

The idea of being wanted, though, had been intoxicating. For once she'd been the center of someone's attention. She'd been seen and hadn't felt a burning need to run away because she wasn't herself. She'd been completely covered from head to toe in a masquerade costume, including wig and mask.

But that wasn't what she needed to remember now. She didn't need to remember that she'd not only compromised herself but also betrayed her nearest and dearest friend in the process. This wasn't about remembering her. It was about remembering him.

A blush crept up Daphne's cheeks as she realized how little she actually knew about Maxwell Oswald. "Cousin, perhaps?" Daphne trudged through her mind, trying to remember all the times Kit had gone on about what a brilliant match Mr. Oswald was. "His father was the second son of a marquis, though I'm not sure I knew which one." Daphne swallowed. "Right now I'm willing to place a great deal of money on it being Chemsford."

CHAPTER THREE

Jess chopped the onion with smooth motions of the sharp knife. Finally she scooped the pieces of onion into a pot and looked at Daphne. "What do you want us to do?"

The next breath slid into Daphne's lungs just a bit more easily than the one before. *Us.* Jess wasn't leaving. Part of Daphne was always waiting for her to leave, to run, to decide Daphne and everything that came with what remained of Haven Manor were too much hassle.

Running was always still an option. After all, Jess had come here to hide from something, or perhaps someone, and the house was much more vulnerable now that people were coming and going from the property. It sounded like for now, at least, she didn't plan on packing her bags and disappearing.

Daphne was willing to take now and let someday wait for later.

"He can't be allowed to see Benedict. Ever."

Jess snorted. "You do remember that the boy is Mr. Leighton's apprentice, don't you? The man who was hired to make repairs and updates to this entire house? Benedict is going to be crawling all over the place for the next year at least. It's not possible."

"Why not?" Daphne said. "He's an apprentice. Lord Chemsford will have no reason to seek him out, nor any need to be in a room where the work is being done. He's a nobleman. The woodwork would get dust on his boots. It shouldn't be too difficult to ensure they are never in the same room."

Jess pulled a turnip from a nearby basket and rolled it from hand to hand as she considered Daphne. "With or without Benedict's help?"

Daphne bit her lip. That was the other difficulty in this situation. Benedict knew he was illegitimate, just as all the children who'd lived here were. He also knew his parents, or in this case his father, were nobility of some kind because all the children had come from such situations. None of the children had been told who those parents were.

Having grown up knowing what it was like to feel different from her peers, to wonder why no one else started to shake when meeting someone new or feel the burning desire to hide under the bed instead of go to any sort of social event, Daphne had wanted Benedict to feel as normal as possible. To feel like he belonged.

So she hadn't told him.

He didn't know he was hers.

Since she'd loved all the children as if they were her own, she'd thought it would never matter. He'd be the same as his pseudo-siblings being raised in secret to protect them from the ridicule of society and shielded from the horrors of possibly ending up dead in a workhouse.

If she told him now that she'd lied to him his entire life . . . would he forgive her? She couldn't risk the close relationship they had, the mother-son connection they'd created despite his never being able to address her as such.

"Without," Daphne said quietly. "It has to be done without his knowledge."

Jess didn't agree or disagree, simply moved forward with her food preparations. "It's not possible."

Daphne sat up taller on the stool and crossed her arms over her chest. "Why not?"

"Aside from the logistic impossibility of keeping two people apart in a building for more than a year? What about the fact that

Mr. Leighton is certainly going to have interactions with Lord Chemsford? And yes, he will also notice the similarity." Jess crossed her own arms and lifted her brows. "What do you intend to tell Sarah, Reuben, and Eugenia?"

Daphne groaned and dropped her head to the table.

All three children remaining at Haven Manor worked for the estate in some capacity to explain their continued presence. They all viewed each other as family, and they still thought of Benedict as an older brother, despite the fact that he now lived with Mr. Leighton. Keeping them all away from their new employer wasn't going to be possible. What would they think? What would they say?

Another groan ripped through Daphne's chest as a sharp throbbing began in the middle of her forehead. How was it possible for two people to look as similar as Benedict and Lord Chemsford? No one would believe they weren't father and son. No one. And if it became public knowledge that Benedict wasn't legitimate, the life he was trying so very hard to build could be destroyed.

Perhaps Benedict could move north. People in Scotland appreciated skilled woodworking, didn't they? And the possibility was small that anyone there would know Lord Chemsford.

That didn't solve the problem of all the people who already knew Benedict. What if someone said something to Lord Chemsford? Would he demand answers from Daphne? Would he dismiss her when she didn't give them?

If he did, she'd be forced to go to the workhouse. She'd never see Benedict again. Perhaps she could live off the sympathies of Mrs. Lancaster, the kind old shopkeeper from nearby Marlborough who had helped her when she'd first arrived in the area all those years ago. The woman was getting old. She needed someone to leave her shop to, didn't she? Daphne could be a grocer. Well, except for the fact that running a shop required her to interact with people she didn't know well.

"Daphne? Daphne?"

Jess's voice cut through Daphne's mental wanderings, bringing her crashing back into the kitchen of the secluded manor.

She raised her head slowly and swallowed. "Yes?"

One golden eyebrow arched and Jess's blue eyes crinkled in humor. "Really?"

Oh dear, had there been a question? What had Jess asked? Apparently not something she expected Daphne to agree to. "Er, no?"

Jess laughed and shook her head as she added more ingredients to the pot in the fireplace.

Daphne grimaced. Spending the past two months dusting and cleaning on her own had gotten her out of the practice of suppressing those flights of fancy her imagination liked to take.

Jess gave a pointed look over her shoulder. "The children?"

Daphne opened her mouth to try to come up with a way to keep everyone away from their new arrival, but Jess cut her off.

"Reuben is going to see the man in a matter of moments when he takes that water upstairs." Jess nodded to the multiple pots and buckets of water heating over the fire.

"I'll think of something," Daphne muttered. She had time. Since Benedict didn't live with the rest of them in the little cottage down beyond the garden, he didn't see the other children every day. She had a day or two to create a plan.

"You won't," Jess said quietly, "but if you want to buy yourself some time to admit that, you need to make a few things happen."

Jess was wrong. Daphne was a desperate mother trying to protect the well-being of her child—and herself, but mostly her child. She was capable of anything.

A little more time to come up with a plan would be nice, though. "What things?"

"Mr. Leighton and Benedict finished the work in the saloon today. Tomorrow they're moving into the parlor. That was my old room. It won't require a great deal of work, but they'll be in it for a few days. You need to give Lord Chemsford a tour and show him those rooms tonight."

"Why?" Daphne knew the house was his now and he had the right to go wherever he wished, but she didn't like the idea of taking him through it on a tour.

"Because he's moved into a new house, Daphne. He's going to want to see it. If not tonight, then tomorrow, when those rooms will be occupied with workers." Jess hacked a knife through more vegetables with a speed that made Daphne tuck her fingers away.

"A tour. I can do that." She could. Hadn't she just concluded that a desperate mother could do anything? "What next?"

"If you want more than a day or two, it's going to be difficult. You could convince him to send the work crew up to the garret rooms so the staff can move back into the house. Then have him move his living quarters down to the main floor, into the parlor. If he has no reason to go upstairs, he is less likely to run into Benedict. That's a lot of things that have to happen, though. You'll have to work hard to make all that a possibility."

"Me?" Daphne's voice cracked. Somehow she'd pictured Jess performing the required manipulation. After all, she was good at it.

"Yes, you." Jess stabbed the cooking knife into a block on the table by the hearth. "You are the housekeeper. He's hardly going to sit down and have tea with his cook. Or would you rather we tell him his only parlor maid is a twelve-year-old girl and have Sarah ask him his plans? She'll probably get a good look at him while she does that."

Daphne groped for the edges of the stool she was already sitting on, afraid she was about to tumble off it. "This is a bad idea. You be the housekeeper. I obviously don't know what I'm doing."

The other woman didn't say anything, simply stood with her hands on her hips, head cocked to the side, and eyebrows raised in expectation, waiting for Daphne to think through what she'd just said and realize it was utterly ridiculous.

"Oh." Daphne winced. "That wouldn't really work, would it? Now that he's already met me and I told him I was the housekeeper?"

"Not to mention you can't cook much besides mashed turnips and boiled rabbit."

"A perfectly filling meal, that."

"For a band of ruffians, maybe. But you don't put that on the table of a marquis, no matter how reclusive he is." Jess grabbed another pot off a hook and started gathering ingredients.

Daphne bit her lip. She hadn't considered that. Gone were the days of easy, simple fare. Lord Chemsford was going to expect meals that took hours to prepare. Jess likely wouldn't see anything but the kitchens for hours each day.

"Do you know how to make fare fit for a marquis's table?" Daphne held her breath. If Jess said no, what would they do?

"I wouldn't have volunteered for the position if I couldn't," Jess said.

"Of course not," Daphne mumbled. "I'm going to be on my own upstairs."

"Not completely." Jess set the pot over the fire and pulled out a bowl to begin making some sort of bread dough. "He's going to hire more servants."

"That is not exactly comforting," Daphne moaned. "I'll be expected to oversee those servants."

"It can't be much different than managing the chores for a dozen children. In all likelihood, it's easier." Jess looked at Daphne, then sighed and slid the bowl to the side. "Sarah is a fine parlor maid. Eugenia is doing well helping me in the scullery. They aren't going to be enough, though. There's a good chance he'll have you do the hiring. We can make sure that everyone hired is someone who supported Haven Manor when it was a refuge. They might even help you with whatever futile scheme you come up with for the Benedict situation."

Jess shrugged as she slid the bowl in front of her once more. "Of course, they'll all assume Lord Chemsford is Benedict's father, but that will simply make them more protective."

"And more inclined to hate their employer," Daphne murmured. "Anyone who helped us with the children before wouldn't take too kindly to one of the men who dumped his illegitimate child on our doorstep."

Jess sighed and braced both hands on the table to spear Daphne with her blue gaze. "Then tell them. Don't tell them. Hire them.

Don't hire them. Tell Benedict. Don't tell Benedict. There is not a perfect solution in this scenario that doesn't cause you some bit of discomfort. Pick your poison and drink it."

"Well, that's not nice," Daphne grumbled.

"I'm not nice," Jess returned. "I'm realistic."

As much as Daphne hated to admit it, Jess was right. Daphne's comfortable life away from the prying eyes of society and people in general was over. It had been nice while it lasted. "You're going to have to tell me what to do."

"I already told you what to do." Jess buried her hands in the dough and began to mix it. "Tell Benedict the truth. Then if he wants to stay out of the marquis's path, he can."

No. There had to be a way to solve this that allowed Benedict to maintain what little shred of childhood innocence remained. Daphne frowned. "I meant, tell me what to do with the house and the servants."

"Weren't you raised to be the woman of the house one day? Just find a mirror and pretend you're talking to your housekeeper."

Daphne's frown deepened. Most of the time, Jess's frankness didn't bother her, even when it was framed as a jibe in Daphne's direction, but right now she found it frustrating.

Yes, Daphne knew she tended to be a little bit scatterbrained, but *she* knew it had more to do with her imagination than any lack of intelligence. There were times when it felt like Jess assumed the lack of attention could be laid at the door of a lack of mental substance. It was usually easier to ignore those moments, but today they were just a bit too much.

"I believe I've rather forgotten all those lady-of-the-manor lessons, Jess. Fourteen years of fending for myself has made them rather faint."

"Fair enough." Jess wiped her hands on her apron and grabbed a pencil and a scrap of brown paper from the side table. She scribbled for several minutes, then shoved the paper across the table. "Does that help?"

Daphne glanced down at the paper.

1. Assign living quarters to the valet and groom. (Grooms live beside the stable. That's why they built two rooms when they renovated the barn.)

2. Make sure Sarah knows not to clean upstairs without your permission anymore. (Don't send her up there while he's abed or changing.)

And on it went. A smile bloomed as Daphne read all eight items on the list. She could follow a list. Even a sarcastic one. "Yes. This helps immensely."

"Good." Jess paused for a moment, remaining so still Daphne would have thought she'd left the room if not for the fact that she could still see her.

"You know," Jess finally said, "it's okay to not be good at something. It's okay to ask for help."

Maybe. Probably. But Daphne wasn't really good at anything. At least, not anything that was actually useful. She could play the piano and draw, two skills that provided absolutely nothing when it came to survival. She possessed not a single tangible skill that was better than what any other average person could accomplish.

Admitting that out loud, though, would make her sound pitiable and self-conscious. She knew she wasn't a horrible person or even an unworthy person. She just wasn't all that remarkable anywhere except her imagination.

CHAPTER FOUR

William slowly nibbled on the last biscuit as he took in the view of the estate from his bedchamber window. For as far as he could see, there was nothing but grass and trees. All the outbuildings, non-ornamental gardens, and service areas must have been carefully placed to not disturb the tranquility on this side of the house. It was more peaceful than he'd dared to hope.

Behind him, Morris and Pasley shuffled by, carrying the largest of the trunks into the dressing room. William hadn't made it that far yet. It didn't particularly matter what the dressing room looked like, as he was having the entire house refurbished. No matter what state the house was in, everything in it was more than twenty years old. At the very least, it needed a new coat of paint.

He ran a hand along one of the grey marks on the wall. What on earth had the previous owners done in here?

"Mrs. Brightmoor has informed me there is a room for me off your dressing area," Morris said as he emerged from the dressing room. "We've another trunk to bring up and then I shall retrieve my own."

William nodded and picked up his tea. It didn't matter when Morris got William's clothing unpacked and pressed. There was no one here for him to see, no one waiting on him or expecting him to do anything. No one to tell him what he could and couldn't do. He was blissfully alone. "Take your time. Your throat must be as parched as mine, if not more so."

Morris bowed and slid silently out of the room.

William returned to the window with his teacup, allowing himself the luxury of a deep sigh that eased one more bit of tension from his shoulders as he drank in the view along with the tea. The place where he'd been living in Ireland for the past several years had a gorgeous view, but it was full of people and buildings. This peaceful nature was exactly what he'd been hoping for when he chose this place. All his life his father had talked about people. Who he knew, who he refused to know, who he liked.

Who he hated.

William had nothing against people, but right now, as he was trying to determine what sort of marquis he was going to be, people were the last thing he wanted to deal with.

The door opening behind him pulled his attention from the window. The boy he'd seen earlier sidled into the room with a large bucket. He didn't appear any less gangly when he was inside the building. His neck was scrawny and his arms didn't look strong enough to carry the bucket of water he was hauling, yet nothing spilled out over the edge.

This close, William could confirm the boy was wearing spectacles, but he still seemed to only want to use them to look at his toes.

William didn't have the heart to make this boy—and he really was nothing but a boy—haul up enough water to fill a proper bath, even the small hip bath in the corner near the hearth. He couldn't hire a proper footman tonight, but he could have Pasley bring the water up later or perhaps even take his bath belowstairs, closer to where the water was being warmed.

With a nod to the dressing room—not that the boy could see it—William said, "A basinful will do."

As the boy moved toward the dressing room and the washstand visible through the door, his shoulders sagged a bit. William thought it was probably more due to relief than the weight of the bucket, but it didn't matter. William couldn't stand there and watch him bring up bucket after bucket in painful, slow agony.

Despite the order, though, the boy crossed the room to stand by the hip bath after filling the washstand basin, as if he wasn't sure whether or not to actually leave the bath empty.

"If it helps," William said, trying to keep his voice low and steady, the way he would with a skittish horse, "you may leave the bucket."

The boy swallowed, his Adam's apple jerking in his skinny neck. "As you wish, my, er, your, um, graceship?"

William gouged his front teeth into his tongue and sucked his cheeks in until they pressed against his teeth. *Do not laugh. Do not laugh. This is not an appropriate time to laugh, especially when you aren't even sure why you want to laugh.*

There was humor, yes, in the boy's fumbling statement, but it also inspired a bit of despair. This was what he'd chosen to subject himself to in the name of privacy, peace, and reputation? He darted a glance at the view behind him, free of avaricious family and peers intent on wasting their lives in between seeing to their responsibilities.

Yes, it was worth putting up with a great deal for that.

He wasn't overly accustomed to feeling humor, so while the despair was easily pushed away to be considered later, the humor lingered, tempting him to grin. He managed a solemn nod in the boy's direction, though. "I'm a marquis, lad. *My lord* will do."

"Of course." The boy licked his lips. "Will that be all, *my lord*?" He lifted his head and his eyes finally connected with William's.

Then they widened, growing until they seemed to fill the round silver spectacle frames. He shuffled his feet and banged his knee on the half-empty bucket, inducing a small wince. His throat jumped as he swallowed once more before running his free hand across his face and dropping his gaze back to his toes.

"All the stable renovations were completed last week, and your horses have been settled. I'm afraid the only feed we have is what we give the chickens and goats. I can go into town and make arrangements for more tomorrow," he said quickly.

Town, assuming Marlborough was indeed the closest town to this place, was at least two miles away on rather remote pathways that could barely be called roads. William had seen nothing but trees and the occasional animal pasture or farm field for at least a mile. Was this boy the only protection and manual labor around? "How old are you, boy?"

"Nine, sir, er, my lord. I'll be ten in a little over a month."

The ridiculousness of a nine-year-old being the highest-ranking male on staff made William want to laugh again, though this time without the tinge of humor. He couldn't have been working here long, so what had the women done before that? Surely Mrs. Brightmoor hadn't been seeing to the care of this entire estate completely on her own. "Are you the only, um, man working here now?"

The lad's chin shot up as his chest puffed out as much as it could. His face was a bit harder this time, the eyes a bit more narrowed. The swollen pride in his chest made his arms and legs look even thinner. If God was gracious, the boy would one day grow into the length of his limbs and become a rather imposing specimen. Right now, he just looked awkward. Determined, yes, but also very awkward.

"Yes, my lord. I help see to the garden and animals. And I chop all the firewood."

Thus far his house had been in the hands of two young women—one rather slow-witted and the other barely taller than a child—and a boy who didn't yet need a razor. That was assuming, of course, that the shorter woman was a maid and not the cook he'd had hired in preparation for his arrival.

The thought was rather terrifying. "Who else works here aside from Mrs. Brightmoor?"

William moved toward the dressing room to splash a bit of water onto his face, hoping the lad would feel more at ease if William were doing something other than staring at him. The boy had yet to answer, though, when William returned to the bedchamber.

In fact, he looked confused, mouthing *Mrs. Brightmoor* to himself repeatedly. "Oh! Mrs.—yes. Well." He cleared his throat. "My, er, um, sisters. They work here as well. Sarah helps with the house and Eugenia works in the scullery."

"Are your sisters older than you?" *Please, please let them be older.* Employing a nine-year-old stable boy was one thing. But an eight-year-old parlor maid? It felt . . . He wasn't entirely sure how to put words to what it felt like, but it made his skin itch and his stomach threaten to reject the tea he'd recently finished.

"Yes, sir."

William relaxed, and his stomach settled. Older. Good. That made sense if the older sisters were maids here and the younger brother came along.

But the boy kept speaking. "Sarah is twelve and Eugenia is eleven, my lord."

Desperate to buy himself a moment to cover his reaction, William buried his face in the linen towel he'd grabbed from beside the washstand. He was employing two women and a family of children? That was what the solicitor claimed was a basic caretaking staff? While, granted, William had yet to see proof that they weren't capable of taking care of the estate, the idea didn't sit well with him. These servants had been under the care of the marquisette and they'd been left defenseless.

A lot could happen to women and children who were this isolated with no protection, especially as young as Mrs. Brightmoor must have been when she came to work here. Who had helped her? Because it certainly hadn't been this boy, who hadn't even been born when William's father had won the house in a card game. "Do your parents work here as well?"

The bravery that had come along with the boy's defiance and pride slid away and the awkward young lad returned. He shuffled sideways toward the door, grasping the handle of the bucket. "I've animals to see to, my lord. Will you be needing anything else?"

Yes. Answers. Answers to lots of questions he'd have never

dreamed needed asking. But William wasn't about to press a nine-year-old boy for them. The housekeeper he'd met earlier, though, he was perfectly willing to interrogate.

"Thank you for the water . . . what was your name?"

"Reuben, my lord."

"Thank you for the water, Reuben. That will be all."

The boy nodded and loped his way toward the door.

"Oh, and Reuben?"

The boy stopped with one foot across the threshold, snapping his head around so quickly that his spectacles slid down his nose.

William let the smile through this time, might have even pushed it a bit. "You don't have to say *my lord* every time. *Sir* will do after the first. And remember to leave the bucket."

Another throat-spasming swallow preceded the boy's solemn nod as he set the bucket on the floor. He looked serious, as if William were imparting a wisdom far greater than a social norm that had been taught to everyone else of William's acquaintance since childhood. Did that say something telling about the boy's upbringing or about the company William kept?

The entire encounter replayed in William's mind as he crossed to retrieve the bucket of water near the door. There was something strange about it. He shook his head. This entire experience was strange. Never had he walked into a house that wasn't entirely staffed—usually they were overly staffed—with people trained and ready to do their jobs. He tried to remember to thank them—mostly because his father never had—but more often than not they were in and gone before he had the chance.

When was the last time he'd had an actual conversation with one of his servants?

The remaining baggage was soon delivered to the room, and Morris set on the task of scrubbing the travel dust and debris from William's skin.

"A bath would be considerably more expedient, my lord," the man said, his mouth set in a thin line. Displeasure was the only emotion the man ever let show.

"Arrange for one to be set up belowstairs until more staff is hired. For now, though, the dust in my hair is making my head itch."

Despite the hat he'd worn while traveling, dirt had worked its way through the thick strands. Morris brushed as much dirt out as possible before leaning William over the hip bath and pouring the bucket of remaining water over the hair.

It wasn't ideal, but it would do. William shook the wet hair out of his eyes with a sigh, already beginning to feel reenergized.

"Will you be dressing for dinner, sir?"

"No," William answered, the freedom in making such a statement leaving him a bit more relaxed. "My normal day clothing will do."

Thirty minutes later, he was dressed in comfortable trousers, a linen shirt, jacket, and a simply tied cravat. It was an outfit he'd never have dared go to dinner in anywhere else, but if the house's footboy—he refused to call Reuben a footman—didn't even know proper forms of address, no one was likely to mention the master's clothing.

They might not even notice it.

He ran a hand along the wall in the nearly empty dressing room before departing. The strange markings were on one of the walls in here as well. Scratches accompanied the dark grey streaks. They were rather evenly spaced across the walls of each room. Were there marks like this in other rooms?

William didn't know much about the house. His father had won it from the son of the man who'd built it. The man claimed his father had been strange, eccentric to a fault. Thus far, William was inclined to agree. The man had built himself a showplace, an oasis of calm far away from absolutely everything. Either he had thrown elaborate house parties or he'd spent his days wandering alone through his own personal art museum.

Outside the bedchamber, a large glass dome allowed light to flood the square two-story gallery. He'd been so focused on following his housekeeper earlier that he hadn't had time to give more than a glance to the enormous paintings decorating the tall white walls. The two staircases from the floor below met and entered the gallery in front of a set of plain wooden double doors. The middle of the gallery was open to the floor below, and across the span was another door William presumed led to another bedchamber and dressing room.

He circled the gallery on the side away from the double doors, running his hand along the wall but finding no more grooves or markings of note. The solid wall across from the double doors sported an enormous painting of some sort of battle victory. He didn't know enough about history to be able to determine the scene, but he appreciated the energy and vibrancy of the painting.

The door directly across from his own did indeed open into another bedchamber, but this one was almost nondescript. Plain furniture sat on a bare floor and very little decoration covered the room.

Considering that every other room he'd seen so far had been crowded with artwork, the starkness of the room was jarring.

Two beds filled the bedchamber. Not mirroring sets of rooms for the mistress and master of the house, then. He could also discount the idea of elaborate house parties. It would seem the man hadn't even wanted family to feel overly welcome.

Odd.

Not as odd as the chapel he found beyond the double doors, though. Benches sat in three short, neat rows in front of a carved wooden altar. A few straight-backed wooden chairs sat against the wall on either side of the doors.

It wasn't unheard of for older country manors to have chapels, of course. Dawnview Hall, the seat for the marquisette that sat just outside of Birmingham in Warwickshire, had a chapel, but it had been built at least a century, if not two, before this house. It also wasn't still used as a chapel. Throughout his childhood, his mother had claimed it as her private salon, escaping there to read or do her needlework. Toward the end of her life, she retreated there to simply sit and stare at the alcove that had once held the altar.

William wasn't sure what the new Lady Chemsford had done

to the space. The few times he'd returned to Dawnview since his father's remarriage a mere three months after the death of his first wife, he had kept his visits short and wandered through the house as little as possible.

This house, which he didn't even know the name of, wasn't even one hundred years old yet and was within two miles of a town that boasted two churches. Yet it had a chapel that was still set up as a place of worship.

Just how reclusive had the previous owner been? Had he been a nonconformist who worshiped in here alone? Or perhaps with whomever used the beds in the starkly unadorned room? Perhaps one of those traveling preachers who went from small town to small town bestowing sermons and enlightenment on those who didn't otherwise have spiritual guidance had stopped here and spoken to an intimate and limited audience.

There was something serene and comforting about the thought, but also something unsettling. It made the house seem cut off from the world. As much as William craved privacy and a bit of distance, he wasn't sure he wanted to be completely removed from *everything*.

He shook his head as he ran a hand along the edge of one of the benches. Just because the house was built for isolation didn't mean he had to accommodate the feature. Marlborough was an easy walk from here, an even easier ride, and the roads between there and London were in excellent condition.

There was absolutely no reason he couldn't manage the marquisette from here instead of the family seat. At least for a while. A desk was a desk, after all, and he wanted one that didn't have proximity to his father's second wife, Araminta, and her son, Edmond. William simply couldn't bring himself to live under the same roof as the family his father had planned for even as his first wife wasted away from illness. The family his father had loved.

William left the chapel and quickly explored the remainder of the first floor. Two more small bedchambers sat in the back corners of the house, each as austere and sparse as the first guest chamber.

While the decor was a bit lacking, it appeared William had plenty of beds to offer anyone whom he wished to do business with at the house. There was more than enough art on the ground floor walls to improve the atmosphere of the guest rooms, but the house was also lacking in amenities. It hadn't seen any of the new developments of the past sixty years. Even the chairs looked less comfortable than anything he'd sat in recently.

He'd yet to see signs of the woodworking crew he'd instructed the solicitor to hire, so they must not have made it to this floor yet. It would be easy enough to turn the project into a more extensive refurbishment. Perhaps a bit more of a remodel. If he started making extensive renovations, though, it would be an indication he intended to live here for a very long time.

As that had been his original intent, the sick feeling that accompanied the thought surprised him. Perhaps he wasn't as ready to throw convention away as he'd assumed.

Statues and paintings accompanied William's journey down the stairs. There was no rhyme or reason to the layout that he could see, no similarity in style or theme. Just art. Stuffed in every corner and plastered across every wall.

Well, every wall the master of the house was likely to see.

Was any of it valuable? He hadn't any idea. Nor did he think his father ever knew he'd won a hidden museum. If he had, anything of value would have been stripped from the walls and taken to Dawnview Hall. Perhaps one of William's first guests should be an expert of some sort who could tell him what exactly he'd inherited.

At the bottom of the stairs, he tilted his head back, looking up and up into the glass dome and the light streaming through it. The emptiness of the cavernous rooms hit him harder than he'd expected, or perhaps it was simply the quietness. He'd never lived anywhere that didn't have a full staff. Though they all tried to be quiet as they went about their work, simply breathing would stir the air and bring a sense of life to a place.

Yes, once there were servants roaming the halls, the distant sounds of footsteps or creaking floors, a door closing, or even the hum of a servant working in the yard, this place would feel more like a home. Once William knew all the nooks and crannies, recognized some of the art, became familiar with which floorboards creaked, he would feel comfortable.

There was something freeing about the quiet, though. No one was expecting anything of him—whether good or bad.

There wasn't the reputation of his father looming over one shoulder while the expectations of his mother dangled on the other.

He could and would make a home here. At least, a temporary one. Eventually he would have to marry and decide where to start a family, and that may or may not be Dawnview Hall. The place was big and dark, with guilt and sorrow worked into the very stones and mortar that made its sturdy walls.

A pleasant smell tickled his nose and distracted him from wandering the rest of the rooms on the ground floor. Instead, he tried to follow the aroma and found himself standing in front of a door beneath one of the main staircases in the central hall. It stood open, revealing smooth stone steps and plain white walls.

The undefined rules of society William had grown up with dictated he stay on this side of the door that obviously led into the servants' domain. But in a house that boasted not a single bell pull and didn't have servants stationed at convenient intervals to run messages, the rules, by necessity, had to change. If he wanted to know when he could eat whatever he was smelling, he was either going to have to return to his room and interrupt Morris's industrious unpacking or go down the stairs himself.

It was odd how disturbing and yet exciting he found the idea of stepping over this threshold. He'd wanted stillness. He'd wanted to be a more modern sort of aristocrat than most of the ones he'd known. If those two things came with a bit of newness and discomfort, so be it. The result would be worth it.

A clench of his stomach preceded a low grumble and he grinned. One thing was the same no matter where he went or whom he was with:

Good food made everything better.

CHAPTER FIVE

The air of dishevelment at the bottom of the stairs was surprising. Of course, William wasn't sure what he'd been expecting. The cleanliness of the rest of the house—despite the fact that there was a group of workmen supposedly somewhere on the premises—led him to expect the same below-stairs. There wasn't any dirt or dust visible, but a crumpled pile of linen sat in one corner while a stack of buckets and a broom rested in another.

Several doors opened off two walls and an opening on the third wall extended off into a corridor.

It was the large archway on the fourth wall that grabbed his interest. He could see the main kitchen through it and, along with the rich smell of food, two hushed but determined female voices drifted on the air.

"Why would I go up there? Reuben took him *bath water*. I'm hardly going to risk walking in on *that*."

"If you don't go up there, we won't know when to serve dinner. What do you expect him to do? Yell down the stairs?"

There was quiet for a moment, and William shifted closer to the archway to be able to make out the women facing each other over a scarred wooden worktable. Their short statures meant neither of them could lean very far over the table, making their intense conversation look a bit humorous.

Mrs. Brightmoor was blinking at the little blonde, who didn't appear remotely as timid as she had in his rooms earlier.

"I don't suppose that would be very appropriate, would it?" the housekeeper finally asked.

"No." The woman he now assumed was the cook pushed away from the table with a nod. "But seeing as he made his way down the steps and is currently standing right over there, I'd say it's a moot point."

She swung her blue gaze over to William, staring him down for a few heartbeats before turning her attention to a pot hanging over the open flame in the fireplace. Mrs. Brightmoor's eyes shifted his way as well, though she looked a great deal more surprised than the cook had. Her gaze did not flit away immediately. Instead, it stayed locked on him, slowly widening as her face lost color, despite the warmth of the kitchen.

"My lord," she finally said, moving away from the table to perform a slight curtsy. She glanced at Cook before licking her lips nervously and turning back to him. "The meal isn't quite ready yet. Er, perhaps a tour?" She took a step away from the table and gestured toward the stairs behind William.

Was she trying to get rid of him?

He braced his feet apart and lifted his eyebrows as he observed the room, resisting the urge to cross his arms over his chest despite the ornery mood he found himself in. "We can start with the kitchen."

She turned around, face scrunching up in confusion as she looked at the various tables and utensils that crowded the simple room. Cook ignored them both, efficiently moving about and finishing her food preparations. "I, well, here it is. This is the kitchen." Mrs. Brightmoor pointed to the doors that lined the wall behind him. "Larder, pantry, and washroom are through there. The scullery is over here."

"So I see," William muttered and felt like an utter fool. What had he expected? A detailed showing of where they stored the pots and pans? He'd hardly be interested in it even if she'd offered.

"Oh." Her mouth pressed together and she turned toward the stairs. Once her back was to him, she mumbled, "You hardly need a tour of the kitchens, then."

"I suppose not." William fell into step beside her, pulling in his cheeks to keep from grinning at his own stubbornness. He might be playing the fool, but it had befuddled the woman who'd so far managed to do nothing but confuse him, so perhaps it was worth it. "I'd be happy to tour the dining room, though, and make my way through a plate of food."

"I'll have it brought up directly, my lord," Cook said as she uncovered a basket piled with golden rolls.

William desperately wanted to be a five-year-old boy and snag one of the crusty breads to carry with him on his short journey to the dining room, but he'd thrown his decorum aside enough for one evening.

Leaving the plain stone stairwell to step into the opulence of the main rooms was a shock all over again, as he still wasn't accustomed to being surrounded by such an abundance of . . . of . . . things. Each room Mrs. Brightmoor led him through was more of a gallery than a functioning space.

He stumbled to a halt in the doorway to the dining room as his gaze landed on what had to be the most ostentatious and unusable piece of furniture ever created.

It was a table of some sort, made of dark, heavy wood and held up by enormous intricately carved gargoyles on each corner. Their bodies and wings spread out in such a way that the very act of sitting at the table was going to be a bit of an adventure. The accompanying chairs looked equally deadly, more resembling gothic thrones than simple dining chairs.

Mrs. Brightmoor curtsied again and left the room, leaving him to make an attempt at seating himself without the embarrassment of an audience. It took a few tries and a bit of maneuvering, but he managed to sit without hurting himself before the food appeared. To his surprise, it was being carried by the housekeeper herself.

Then again, who else was going to carry it? He employed two women and a trio of children. She didn't pour his wine but instead left the bottle on the table for him to handle himself. If the variety in front of him was any indication, he'd received all the courses at once.

The stillness of the room—in fact, the stillness of the entire house—weighed down on him as he began to eat while trying not to impale himself on a gargoyle wing. It wasn't that dining alone was all that new of an experience, as he'd been living on his own and socializing with only a handful of friends with any sort of regularity. Still, he found himself scraping his knife against the plate more frequently than necessary just to create a noise to break the suffocating quiet.

Fabric rubbed against fabric as he moved his arm to reach for his wine, disturbing the silence once more. Never had he been more aware of every move he made while eating. It was fascinating and unnerving at the same time.

The new sound of footsteps approaching the room had him setting down his glass and watching the door.

His strange little housekeeper entered the room, placed a pudding on the table in front of him, and then slid out, leaving him once again free to watch the flickering flames of the candelabra and wonder if they were crackling like tiny fireplaces.

Part of him wanted to call her back so he could hear something besides his own breathing.

Being alone had advantages, though. There was no one to witness the way he scraped the bowl clean of every last taste of bread-and-butter pudding.

He looked down at the empty plate and bowl with a bit of consternation. What was he supposed to do now? Normally the dishes would have been whisked away by servants who had been standing quietly to the side, waiting to perform the task.

Should he just depart and leave the dishes on the table?

He was still contemplating his options when Mrs. Brightmoor returned, her very existence charging the room with questions far more complex than how his dirty plate was going to find its way down to the dishwater in the scullery.

Perhaps a pressing quiet wasn't so bad after all.

The last thing Daphne wanted to do was reenter the presence of Lord Chemsford. Interacting with strangers in general was a struggle for her, and this man held control over her future and that of those she loved.

It was the children who gave her the courage to enter the room. All of them, but Benedict in particular, were relying on her, whether they knew it or not.

"If you've finished," she said, picking a vase over his left shoulder to address so she didn't have to actually look at him or those blue eyes that seemed to be picking her apart, "our parlor maid can clear the table while I show you about the house."

The marquis moved to stand and banged his knee against the head of one of the gargoyles. Daphne winced in sympathy as air hissed sharply between the man's teeth. As he finished standing upright with a grimace, he said, "No need for a tour. I'll have plenty of time to wander through the house tomorrow."

That was precisely what she was worried about. "You'll sleep better if it feels like home, my lord, and it won't feel like home until you know where you live."

Daphne nearly rolled her own eyes at the insipidness of her comment. In her experience, no matter how welcoming a place seemed, it took actually living in it for a while for it to feel like home.

To her surprise, though, he seemed to consider her statement. She'd been spewing desperate nonsense. Did he actually think it would matter?

Apparently he did. "Show me the house, then." He waved a hand at the door she'd entered through.

Daphne swallowed and pasted a smile on her face. While she'd never admit it, Daphne feared Jess was right and keeping the marquis and Benedict apart in the house indefinitely was impossible.

If she used Jess's suggestions to buy a bit of time, though, she just might be able to come up with something.

Or at least think of a way to explain to Benedict that he wasn't directly related to a man who looked exactly like him, and no, she couldn't tell him why she was so absolutely certain.

Daphne walked from room to room, trying to remember how a professional housekeeper sounded and acted. She'd lived in this house for twelve years. It was home in the way nowhere else had managed to be. Even the caretaker's cottage still felt a bit cold and uncomfortable, and she'd been living in it for two months now. These walls, though, where she'd learned to treat each day with its own value and ignore the past and the future, they still gave her a feeling of belonging.

It didn't seem to matter that all the paintings and treasures as well as the intricate, expensive furniture had been stored away while she, Kit, Jess, and the children lived here. She knew the walls, knew how the giggles echoed through the house when the children slid across the polished marble floor of the front hall in their stockinged feet, knew which steps to avoid when going up or down the stairs at night so as not to wake the children.

As she moved from the drawing room to the front hall, she slid a hand along the doorframe, her finger finding a shallow gouge in the wood, a result of John deciding to chase Blake through the house with a fireplace poker.

From the front hall, she led the marquis into the music room. She resisted the urge to run a hand lovingly over the keys of the large pianoforte sitting in the center of the room. The old harpsichord down in the caretaker's cottage simply wasn't the same, though she and Sarah took turns playing on it most evenings. It had three broken keys and a tendency to fall out of tune, whereas this instrument was as close to perfection as any Daphne had ever played. And she'd played on pianofortes in some of the nicest drawing rooms in London before leaving the city became a necessity.

She managed to keep her fingers off the instrument, but her gaze was another story. Longing swelled in her as she moved around the gleaming wood casing, and a melody slipped into her head, making her fingers itch to give it life. She bit her tongue to keep from humming. The instrument, like the house, had been borrowed. Without permission. Their unknowing benefactor had no idea he'd provided a refuge for her and a home for many discarded children over the years.

Probably best if he remained ignorant.

"This is the portrait room through here," Daphne said, leading him through a short corridor that jutted off from the music room. "Have you any ancestors on these walls?"

There. That was the perfect impersonal but polite question. She wasn't supposed to know the history of the house, was she?

"No," he said slowly, with his head cocked and eyebrows raised, as if he were perplexed by her question. "I've no relatives on these walls."

She waited for him to say more, to offer an explanation, but he fell silent as he strolled into the room, hands clasped lightly behind him. Her own frown touched her face. He wasn't going to tell her that his family had never even set foot in the place? She could see not telling her he'd inherited it by way of a card game, but to offer nothing? Wasn't that how proper conversations went?

Of course it was. But this wasn't a proper conversation. He had no idea that she wasn't merely a servant but was, in fact, a gentlewoman—of a lower class than he was to be sure—and she was perfectly proper to converse with and high enough to expect a modicum of politeness from him.

Probably something else it would be best he not learn.

He walked the room, looking from portrait to portrait, sculpture to sculpture. It was a useless room, built onto the house for no purpose other than to display art and treasures. There was no indication that the man who'd built the place ever entertained, so the cavernous room, though perfect for a small assembly or country dance, had been for his enjoyment alone.

A waste. But one God had used in those mysterious ways of His. Though the young children were now able to run and play with the other children in their new families, when they'd lived in this house this empty room had been the place where she and Kit had them expend their energy when the weather prevented them from going outside.

But Kit wasn't here anymore. She'd married a man who shared her passion of providing for unwanted children, and when they returned from their wedding trip, they would travel the country, seeking families to take in more children.

And Daphne would remain here. Watching over the last few remaining charges and helping them forge their own future.

It was good work, if a bit lonely. Especially since she didn't know what her role was going to be moving forward. When there were no more children to care for, what would Daphne do?

The marquis meandered his way around the room, oblivious of the philosophical wanderings of his housekeeper standing awkwardly in the doorway. He was across the room now, nearing one of her favorite pieces. It wasn't a treasure that had been collected by the original owner, but one of the few items that remained in the house from when the women and children had lived here.

It was a game table, designed and built by Benedict. He'd made two of them, the cruder of which was now in the caretaker's cottage.

Perhaps leaving it here in the gallery was Daphne's way of leaving a mark, of remaining a part of the house's history. There were a few of his other creations about the house as well as two of the paper filigree–covered boxes they'd made to sell at the town market. One of the tea boxes sat in the newly finished saloon and another in the dining room. Small reminders for Daphne that this place had once been a home, not just a house.

Lord Chemsford ran a hand over the game table, jerking backward when he accidentally tripped the catch that swung the inlaid chessboard around to reveal an inlaid backgammon board. He knelt and poked around the table until he found the compartments that stored away the hand-carved chess pieces and backgammon discs.

"Mrs. Brightmoor," he called across the room, "where did this table come from?"

The pride and security the piece had brought her moments earlier faded into trepidation. "I'm sure I wouldn't know, my lord." Her voice was shaky as the fear of discovery wrapped around her throat. "The house was abandoned when I came to work here."

"Yes," he murmured. "No one has lived here for more than twenty years as I understand it."

"So I've heard," Daphne agreed.

He pushed up from the table and faced her, clasping his hands loosely behind his back again. "It was empty when you came to care for it?"

"It had been quite left to the elements when I, er, started."

He looked back at the table, eyebrows pulled together. "I see."

Daphne shifted her weight from foot to foot. Mr. Leighton claimed Benedict was extremely modern and innovative with his wood designs. Was it possible the table looked too modern for the house? "There's quite a bit more art to see," she blurted out. "The house is full of it."

"The house is a mausoleum of art." He frowned at one of the paintings. "Some of it is rather questionable."

"The glass parlor is rather impressive," she said, hoping to distract him from whatever path his thoughts were taking.

It seemed to work as his attention drifted from the walls to her. "Glass parlor?"

"This way." She led him back through the music room and into a drawing room so ornate she held her breath every time she entered it to clean. There was glass everywhere. Beyond what one might expect such as vases, candelabras, and figurines, there were items that begged to question the sanity of the creators. Never could Daphne have imagined someone needing a fake writing quill made of glass, yet there it was. And the glass strands that made up the fringe on the small footstool? They were the definition of frivolous.

There was nothing of the women and children in this room. It had, in fact, been the first room they'd carefully packed away, taking turns to keep Benedict's inquisitive fingers from finding the delicate creations. This was the room that felt the most foreign now, where Daphne went when she needed to remember that she didn't live here anymore.

The saloon at the back of the house was a different story, and as Lord Chemsford took the lead and entered that room, it was all Daphne could do not to call him back, to try to convince him that wasn't a part of the house he needed to see tonight. Or ever.

Despite the fact that Mr. Leighton and Benedict had repaired and repainted everything in this room, restoring it to a glory it hadn't seen in a long time, Daphne still thought of it as a large dining room. Instead of red sofas and curved-leg chairs, she saw a large wooden table taking up most of the room, providing a place to eat, work, and bond as a family.

Lord Chemsford went straight to the glass-paned double doors and threw them open, taking in the view beyond. Daphne knew what he was seeing. She'd stood on that porch every evening and looked at the moon reflected on the lake. Everything had been discussed out on that back porch. The doors had been used so much that one of them had broken and they'd replaced it with a large wooden plank. That was why the saloon had been the first room to be refurbished. There'd been an awful lot of life to erase from in here.

An awful lot of *her* life to erase from in here.

Suddenly Daphne was incredibly tired. Weary to the point of wondering how she'd manage to walk down to the cottage and ready herself for bed.

"That's most of the ground floor," Daphne said with a forced smile. "I'm sure you're tired."

He turned to her with eyebrows raised. "I thought you said I needed to get to know a house so that I could sleep well in it."

"That was before I realized how late it was. You couldn't possibly have time to inspect the entire house this evening. Best to spend some time in your rooms so you feel fully settled."

His only answer was to stare at her. All the things he could be thinking about her flew through her mind. Few of them were flattering and most probably questioned her sanity or intelligence, but she couldn't worry about that right now. Right now she needed him to accept her excuses and retire.

Finally, he nodded. "Have water brought up first thing in the morning so I can shave."

She gave a small curtsy and held her breath as he left the saloon and climbed the stairs to the bedchambers above. Then she scurried down to the kitchens, where Jess was preparing for tomorrow.

"How did you do this every day?" Daphne asked, bracing herself on the wooden table. "My heart is in my throat and about to choke me from the fear he'll find out everything that once went on in this house. There's no way for him to discover that, and Benedict isn't even in the house right now so there isn't any real danger at the moment, but I just can't help feeling that it's going to fall on my head."

Jess finished stacking the clean plates. "Oh, it's going to come crashing down on our heads." She pushed a tray toward Daphne so it could be placed on the rack with the others. "Your only hope is to delay it until we can shore up the defenses. Just try to stay out of his way as much as possible. If he can't talk to you, you can't accidentally say anything wrong."

Daphne took the tray with a frown. "You always did know how to comfort a girl," she said dryly. But what Jess lacked in tact, she made up for in practicality. Daphne would stay far away from the marquis unless household duties or distraction from Benedict required she do otherwise.

Keeping them apart was going to be a full-time job. And she still had to take care of the house. And come up with a plan that would work long term.

This was going to be a very long few weeks.

CHAPTER SIX

There was irony to be found somewhere in his current predicament. Despite buying a modicum of merit in the housekeeper's idea that touring the house would make him feel at home and let him sleep better, he found himself staring at the ceiling, sleep knocked away by the pain pounding against his skull.

This was part of the reason he didn't travel extensively like many of his peers. New places tended to give him a headache. New surroundings, new beds, new sounds and smells. It wasn't unheard of for it to take him a week to completely adjust and relax. A week's worth of mild headaches every time he went anywhere tended to keep him well rooted.

Normally, he could focus on breathing and ignore the pain long enough for sleep to claim him and in the morning he would feel better. Not tonight. Tonight the pain was threatening to make him ill as it seemed to roll down his spine and land with a *thunk* in his stomach.

He rolled over. Perhaps lying on his side would alleviate some of the agony slicing through his temples. Instead, it pulled a rough, low groan from his chest. His stomach seized at the increased pain, and he pushed himself to a sitting position, trying to breathe through the nausea, but instead inducing a wave of hacking coughs that had him gripping his head between his hands. If he squeezed hard enough, would the pain ooze out through his ears?

The ruckus brought Morris into the room, wrapped in one of the dressing robes William had passed on to him last year. His hair was matted to one side of his head while the other remained perfectly styled. The lantern he held aloft sent a flickering glow over the bed, and William lifted a hand to shield his eyes from the light.

"My lord?" the valet asked. "Is it your head, sir?"

William grunted. Any more of a response was too much work.

"Shall I summon the housekeeper, sir? Even with the barest of staff, they must keep a stillroom with some medical supplies." The valet was much too professional and stoic to wear a sneer on his face in William's presence, but it was clear in his voice.

"Yes," William said as quietly as possible so as not to disturb his head further. "Wake the housekeeper."

The valet left and William slid his eyes closed before attempting to gently ease himself back down to the pillow.

Five minutes later, Morris was back in the room, but the only thing in his hands was the lantern.

"What's wrong?" William asked, pushing himself up.

"I cannot find Mrs. Brightmoor."

"She's not in her room?"

He cleared his throat. "I don't believe she has a room, my lord."

"What?" The pounding in his head made it hard to think, but it sounded as if his valet had just said that his housekeeper didn't have a room in the house.

"I'm afraid you and I are the only ones in the house, sir. The garret rooms are empty and the downstairs rooms are stacked with beds. There is no indication anyone is using them for anything other than storage."

William hauled himself from the bed, his first instinct to go verify the valet's outlandish claims himself. They couldn't possibly be true. Except Morris didn't make jokes about such things. Morris didn't joke at all.

Standing upright surprisingly settled his insides, though. Even the pounding in his temples eased enough for him to be able to think. He ran a hand across his forehead. "She has to be somewhere."

The house was far enough from everything that it wasn't possible she traveled here every day. The children might travel from some nearby farm, but right now he didn't care if they slept on the drawing room couch unless they knew the location of the stillroom and whether or not it contained medicine that would help his head.

"I believe I saw a cottage down past the garden." He could send Morris, but if standing had helped, perhaps walking would do even more. "Get me boots, trousers, and a jacket."

"Right away, my lord."

William looked a wreck, but he didn't care as he took the lantern and stepped out into the darkened gardens. The coolness of the night took the edge off of what remained of his pain, and a few deep breaths left his insides feeling almost normal.

Maybe he'd just bring a pallet out onto the lawn and sleep under the stars.

The cottage had the same air of maintained negligence that seemed to hang over the rest of the property. Cared for so that it didn't fall into disrepair, but not kept in prime condition.

After a moment's hesitation, he knocked on the door of the cottage. He was going to feel incredibly foolish if this house was empty, but then again, there'd be no one to see him, so the embarrassment would be limited.

There was no immediate answer, but the bedchambers were likely upstairs so he knocked again, a bit firmer than before.

A great deal of scrambling and scuffling could be heard through the door before it finally eased open to reveal Mrs. Brightmoor, her brown hair pulled back into a braid that reached the middle of her back and a threadbare pink robe wrapped tightly around her. She rubbed a hand across her eyes as if she were still half asleep. "My . . . My lord?"

"Why are you down here?"

"I live here." She glanced over her shoulder and then turned back to him, one hand pulling the door a bit closer to her side.

It was so reminiscent of that afternoon on the porch of his own home that William was suddenly determined to get inside the cottage. What he'd do when he got there, he didn't know, but his head hurt, so he wasn't going to care about the fact that all his thoughts weren't precisely logical.

He wanted in the house and he wanted a headache remedy. There was no reason why he couldn't have both. Perhaps one might even give him the other. If she lived down here, it might be where the medicine was too.

"While I admit it sounds like a paltry reason to wake the house, I'm afraid I have an aching head. If I do nothing to make it abate, I won't sleep and I'll be ill for the next two days."

Her eyes widened and everything about her posture softened. She let go of the door, and it eased open a few inches. "That sounds dreadful. There's several treatments in the stillroom up in the house you can try for relieving a pain in the head." With a glance down, she pulled her wrap tighter. "Let me . . . Give me a moment and I'll get what you need."

He nodded and waited for her to let him in, but she didn't. Instead, she gripped the door as if she planned to shut him outside.

"The night air is cool, Mrs. Brightmoor, and the grass is wet." In truth, the night air was doing him a great deal more good than harm and his boots could more than handle the bit of dew collecting on the grass. But she didn't need to know that.

"Quite so." She glanced behind her once more and then pushed the door open wider. "Would you like to step inside? I won't be but a moment."

He stepped over the threshold without a word, and she scampered up the stairs that cut through the middle of the room. There was a door to the right of the stairs with a large empty area in front of it. Closer to him, a small table and chairs were pushed into the corner.

On his left was a small sitting area. A harpsichord that looked as if it had been pulled from the rubbish heap was pushed against the back wall. A small collection of chairs created a circle in the middle, but against the wall nearest the door was a strange oval table. It appeared to have a chair attached to one of the long edges.

William wandered over to it but paused when a noise came from the door on the other side of the room that presumably led to a small kitchen. When he heard nothing else, he continued toward the oval table that had caught his attention.

Even if poking around didn't teach him anything about his housekeeper, it would distract him from the throbbing behind his eyes.

"What is he doing here?" Jess asked as Daphne returned to the room the two women shared and threw a pelisse on over her dressing robe and night rail.

"Looking for the stillroom," Daphne answered, scooping up her boots from beneath her bed. "He needs medicine for a sore head." Heart in her throat at the thought of all that could go wrong with that man in the cottage where they'd done little, if anything, to hide the history of the property or the presence of the remaining children, she tried to pull on her boots and walk to the door at the same time.

It wasn't a very successful endeavor.

"He thinks the stillroom is down here in the cottage?" Jess rolled her eyes and reached for her own coat.

"No, he thinks his housekeeper is down here in the cottage." Daphne paused long enough to finally secure her boots to her feet. "Stay here. We don't need him knowing you and the children sleep down here, too. He might put together what we've been doing."

She turned toward the door but paused with her hand on the latch. "You might need to help Reuben pull his bed out of the kitchen after we leave. It flipped over as we shoved it in there. He's sitting against the door right now so Lord Chemsford can't enter."

Jess tilted her head and looked at Daphne. "You think he hasn't already checked all the sleeping areas in the house and realized none of us are there?" She shook her head and waved Daphne out the door. "Never mind. I'll help Reuben. You're better with the nurturing and medication anyway."

Daphne frowned but stepped back out onto the small landing between her and Jess's room and the room Sarah and Eugenia shared. No matter what Jess thought, Daphne knew there was a difference between speculating about something and knowing something.

And no man was going to take kindly to learning that three women and a dozen children had been crowded into his house. It wouldn't matter why they'd done it. At least, she didn't think it would.

But wouldn't it be nice if it did?

She could say, "*Did you know for the past twelve years, Haven Manor has been a refuge for children who would otherwise likely lose their lives as their mothers were forced into poorhouses?*"

"*What a fascinating use for an empty building,*" he would say.

"*Yes,*" she would continue, "*and with the children here, their mothers were able to claim some of the future that would have been denied them. They were able to build lives, and most of them used that second chance to do great work helping other people.*"

"*And here I was thinking it would simply make me a fine home. Your plan is much better. You take the house and I'll live in the cottage.*"

She would laugh. "*No need. My friend Kit is now married to Lord Wharton and they've been traveling around England locating farming families willing to take unwanted children in as their own. The older ones will probably still have to find work and make their own path in the world, but it's not so bad. We've only three left—four, if you count Benedict.*"

Daphne nearly tripped on the last step, as even imagining talking to Lord Chemsford about Benedict was enough to frighten her out of the perfect little world in her head.

She took a deep breath as she stepped into the room downstairs and back into a reality where telling the marquis what they'd been doing in the house even four months ago would probably get them all thrown off the property and bring an end to Nash's ability to work as a solicitor.

As far as Lord Chemsford knew, Nash was simply the solicitor overseeing the minimal care of an abandoned estate.

But he was so much more than that.

Daphne and Kit had been floundering in the charity of kind Mrs. Lancaster during Benedict's first months. Still, they'd decided to do what they could to help Margaretta, an old friend who was on the run and in a delicate condition. But then Nash had fallen in love with Margaretta and they'd all embarked on a mission to save other women and children who had nowhere to turn.

Noble, yes, but not what the marquis had been paying him to do.

The marquis wasn't watching the stairs for her return as she'd feared. Instead, he was inspecting the writing table near the door. It was one of Benedict's creations. The chair pushed in and fit solidly into the table, creating a perfectly smooth oval. When the chair was pulled out, the top would slide open, revealing an inkwell and quill tray, and the middle portion of the tabletop would angle upward to provide an excellent surface for drawing or writing.

"This is a fascinating piece of furniture." He slid the chair out and back in.

"Yes." Daphne cleared her throat. "Your head? We'll need to go up to the house to get what you need. There's nothing down here." She tried to smile brightly as she whisked through the drawing room and out into the night. Hopefully the darkness made her cheer appear more real.

He fell into step beside her, holding his lantern steady as they crossed the lawn. "Why *are* you down here?"

Her mind had churned for an answer to this question since she'd let him in the house, but she wasn't having much luck. Dew was already settling on the grass and dampening the hem of her robe, proving that making such a commute every day was a bit ridiculous.

Without a believable excuse, she decided to stick as close to reality as possible. She could keep it vague and let him fill in the holes as he pleased. Whatever he came up with was better than the truth. "There's a limited number of usable servants' rooms in the house right now. The garret rooms had fallen into neglected disrepair before I came here and have since suffered a bit of water damage as well."

See? Complete truth. Only the rooms belowstairs near the kitchens were in livable shape. The servants' beds that had once lined the first-floor bedchambers for use by the children were now stacked two high across the belowstairs rooms. She didn't volunteer the whereabouts of Jess and the others. Hopefully he would assume they were somewhere in the house or possibly even the barn while only she was making use of the cottage.

Although, her using the cottage was awfully presumptuous of her. It would normally have been reserved for an estate manager or other higher-level employee.

He didn't say any more about it, though, so she didn't either.

CHAPTER SEVEN

She entered the house through the door that led straight into the main kitchen. He followed and once again she found herself sweating over his presence. She'd gotten him out of the cottage, yes, but now he was in the servants' domain, an area they'd thought safe. How much of themselves had they left evidence of? These rooms had been well used when they should have barely been touched for more than two decades.

If she took him into the stillroom, with its shelves packed full of the myriad tonics, herbs, and remedies needed in a house full of children, he was going to have questions.

Questions she really couldn't answer.

"Why don't you sit here?" She patted a stool by the kitchen worktable and gently pried the lantern from his hand. "I'll retrieve the quinine and ingredients for willow bark tea."

She kept moving through the room, hoping he would listen to her, but the footsteps that continued behind her proved otherwise.

The only thing that was going to keep everything from falling down around her ears tonight was the fact that the stillroom door hung a bit crooked. Opening it wider than a few inches was difficult and made a horrendous scraping noise. She knew exactly where the items she needed were. It should be easy enough to slip in before him.

But if he stuck his head in after her? Was there a possible believable explanation? She sighed. No wonder she enjoyed making up stories in her head. Misleading and lying in real life were exhausting and more than a little stressful.

The scrape of the door against the floor was louder and more horrendous than she'd remembered, echoing through the stone passageway loud enough to make her wince, and she wasn't nursing an aching head.

A moan ripped from her companion as he collapsed against the wall, eyes closed, hands pressed to his head. Her heart went out to the poor man's obvious agony, but his moment of distress was her golden opportunity.

She'd already opened the door enough for her to squeeze through it, so she slid into the room and quickly retrieved what she needed. Despite the fact that she hated causing anyone distress or pain, she closed the door behind her, sending another grating noise straight to his lordship's pounding head and making him moan again.

"I'm sorry," she said gently before nudging him back toward the kitchen.

He lowered himself carefully to the stool, then folded his arms along the top of the table and dropped his head down on them. Dark blond hair fell in messy waves about his head, curling at the ends as it stuck up in various directions. That was slightly different than Benedict. Her son's hair was completely straight, even when it was in need of a cut.

Daphne set the lantern on the table and pushed her son out of her mind, along with everything else other than the task at hand. With all immediate threats averted, she was able to focus on taking care of another human being. It was the easiest she'd been able to breathe since he'd arrived. She knew how to do this. After all, she'd been the one to clean scraped knees and kiss smashed fingers. She'd been the one to hug away tantrums and sit up through the night to offer aid and comfort.

The fact that this was a grown man who could send her life

into ruin—again—and not one of her children didn't change what needed to be done.

She bustled about the room, stoking the banked fire and setting the kettle on to heat, then dipping a rag in the bucket of cool water by the door so she could place the damp cloth across the back of his neck before preparing the medicinal treatments.

A bit of willow bark tea had been used to aid many an aching head in this house, along with a dose of quinine for particularly painful cases. The tea took a while to steep, though, which left her fretting for something more to do, something that would start him on the path to recovery.

When the children had suffered such pain, she would always hold their heads in her lap and run her hand through their hair.

That didn't seem quite appropriate in this instance.

Thinking about it made her fingers itch to run through his hair, though. Would it feel the same as Benedict's? Or did William being a handsome man change the way it would feel?

And he was handsome. She hadn't been willing to admit that earlier, even to herself, but the dark, quiet night was made for silent confessions. There was a seriousness to his face that drew her. The angles were strong and defined, catching the light of the lantern in interesting ways as he lifted his head and moved the cloth to his forehead.

His eyes slowly blinked open and met hers, turning the reflected lantern flames into a mesmerizing blue fire. Even in pain, he didn't seem like the type of man to run away from responsibility, to shirk his duties, to deliberately set out to ruin a woman's reputation.

How different would her life be if she'd met such a man on that dance floor all those years ago? Someone who would have swept her away to a quiet country life on a secluded estate. She could have been mistress of a place such as Haven Manor instead of its housekeeper.

He tilted his head to the side, lifting a brow in inquiry as she stood there, staring at him, falling into the imagination that had caused her so much trouble over the years. The imagination that needed to be safely locked away in the back of her mind. Only once had she let it mingle with reality. That had ended with her fleeing London with her best friend at her side, a ruined reputation at her back.

Her future had been questionable then. It wasn't much better now.

She slid the dose of quinine toward him and busied herself with the tea.

"This isn't what I normally use to ease pain," he mumbled after swallowing the quinine.

She set the tea in front of him, carefully avoiding any additional eye contact. "Drink this."

Obediently, he took a large gulp before setting the mug on the table in front of him and spinning it slowly as he stared into the murky liquid. "What is the real reason you don't live in the house?"

"It's a rather large place for someone to live on their own, isn't it?" she asked before realizing that he, essentially, lived in it alone. Or he would think he did. Did he consider himself to be alone or did he count his servants? Although at the moment there was only Mr. Morris under the roof.

"Hmmm." One hand lifted the mug to his lips again and he took another gulp as his other hand reached for the medicine bottle and rolled it around in his long fingers. "I'm glad you had this."

She started to tell him they had the means to handle just about any minor illness or injury, but she clamped her mouth shut at the last moment and simply smiled. It had been a long time since she'd had servants in her life, but she remembered they'd been expected to be silent and unseen. She'd been envious of that sometimes when she'd been forced to attend one social situation or another.

Despite learning how to do a great deal of manual labor over the past few years, Daphne didn't really feel like a servant. She had been raised to make polite conversation. The two ideas warred in her mind even as she opened her mouth to speak. "Does your head pain you often?"

"When I travel. Mostly when I'm sleeping in a new place.

Something about the air, I suppose, though getting up and walking around has seemed to ease the pain a great deal tonight." His voice was quiet. Because of the night or the pain, she didn't know.

Once again she wondered if she should slip away and leave him to drink the tea in silence as a proper servant would do. It seemed rude, though. When she was miserable she didn't want to be alone. She wanted someone to coddle her and tell her she'd feel better soon.

She couldn't do that for him, but she could keep him company. If he wanted it. Which she couldn't really ask him.

She also couldn't leave. Now that the fire was more than warm coals she'd have to wait until Jess arrived to start cooking, then return to the cottage to dress properly for the day.

So she would compromise. She sat on another stool, the one farthest from him on the opposite side of the worktable, and watched the fire crackle. She would be present but silent. If he wanted conversation, he could be the one to start it.

He didn't. He simply sat in silence, watching the fire as well.

Daphne let her mind drift away.

If she'd married a country squire or a clergyman like she'd always assumed she would, this could be a normal evening. Her and him, sitting before a dying fire as she took care of whatever ailed him.

Or maybe he would be taking care of her. What if it were her head that was aching? What if her country-bred husband fixed her tea and took the pins from her hair?

It would be nice to take care of someone who could potentially take care of her in return. Children were wonderful and Daphne loved them dearly, but there was a definite direction of care in that relationship. And while Kit had always been closer than a sister and Jess had become a very dear friend, neither had ever been overly nurturing.

A sigh escaped her before she remembered she wasn't alone with her imagination.

"Thank you."

"You're welcome." She turned to him in automatic response to find his direct gaze pinning her in place. How long had he been watching? Did he wonder what she was thinking? Did he wonder about her at all? Did she want him to? She cleared her throat and dropped her gaze to the lantern. "Is it helping?"

"Yes." He ran a hand through his hair and across the back of his neck. "Better than anything I've tried before, actually. I'll turn in now. If I need anything else, I'll know where to send Morris."

"I'll leave the medicine out for a few days so it's easy to find." She was not letting that valet anywhere near her stillroom. It was obvious he didn't care to be in a house without sufficient staff and cut off from what he probably considered to be the civilized world. He hadn't spoken a word to anyone when he'd come down to collect his dinner and take it back to his rooms.

Daphne forced a smile in Lord Chemsford's direction as he rose from the stool. Her issues with his valet weren't his problem. Neither was the fact that she was going to have to stay up in the kitchen and keep an eye on the fire. Those were the types of comments servants didn't share with the master of the house. "Good night."

He nodded, scooped the lantern from the table, and left the kitchen.

And then she was alone.

Gentle noises pierced Daphne's sleep, prodding her back into the real world. She blinked as she lifted her head, the various aches and pains caused by sleeping bent over the kitchen worktable making themselves known with screaming intensity. A groan rumbled up her throat as she stretched before mumbling a greeting in the direction of Jess and Eugenia.

The young girl bounded over, her dark gold braid swinging behind her, and wrapped her arms around Daphne. "Mama Jess said to let you sleep even though it had to be mighty uncomfortable."

Daphne smoothed back a curl that had escaped the girl's thick braid. "Sometimes comfort isn't the most important thing."

Eugenia nodded, a serious pucker to her mouth, before her

expression cleared and she returned to collecting the cooking implements Jess needed to prepare breakfast. "That makes sense. I don't always like how hot Mama Jess heats the dishwater, but it does make the pots come clean easier."

"Exactly." Daphne smothered a grin as she peeked over at Jess, who was shaking her head as she sliced bread and slid it onto the rack to toast.

"His lordship is still abed, so he won't be going for a ride this morning."

All three women turned their heads to the kitchen doorway where Mr. Morris stood. Despite the early hour, he had on a perfectly pressed, discreet set of clothing, immaculately groomed hair, and boots so shiny Daphne was sure she could see herself in them from across the room. It was enough to make her very aware that she was in a robe that had nearly worn through at the seams and dull leather boots that hadn't quite gotten laced correctly the night before.

"That's interesting," Jess said, not slowing her movements. "What would you like us to do with that information?"

"The stable lad needs to be notified. I'm sure he would have been charged with morning preparations." The man's mouth turned down at the corners, his face settling into displeased grooves so easily it was testament to the fact that this was probably his natural state.

Daphne half rose to deliver the message. She needed to go down to the cottage anyway and the barn was only a bit out of her way. Besides, it would get her out of this room and away from one of the new people in her life whom she still wasn't quite sure what to do with.

The cutting look Jess sent her had Daphne plopping her bottom back down on the stool. The frayed edge of Daphne's robe, peeking out from beneath the pelisse she'd thrown on the night before, was suddenly fascinating. She looped a loose thread around her fingers and hoped it wasn't obvious she was breaking out in a cold sweat.

"Reuben is more of a boy-of-all-work than a stable lad, but I'm sure Mr. Pasley would like to know of Lord Chemsford's change of plans." Jess pointed her knife at the door that led outside. "The fastest way to the stable is through that door and down the path to the right. Take a left at the fork."

The valet straightened his jacket and sniffed, curling his lip into a sneer. Was he actually going to argue with Jess? No one argued with Jess. Well, they might once, but no one argued with her twice because she usually ended the argument by tossing a knife into the woodwork on the other side of the room. Daphne had once seen her slice a feather off a boot at twenty paces. So far she'd never actually thrown a knife *at* anyone—the boot had been wearer-free at the time of its defeathering—but this morning she looked like she was considering it.

Daphne couldn't help feeling a little bit of sympathy for the man. He was certainly accustomed to different working conditions. Still, he didn't have to be quite so stiff-necked about it.

She held her breath as he opened his mouth, but all he asked was, "When are the dining times?"

"I'll serve his lordship whenever he wishes," Jess said, not pausing in her food preparations. "The staff eats at half past nine unless Lord Chemsford is in need of something."

The man's upper lip curled even farther as he glanced at Eugenia, who grinned and waved before hauling a bucket of warmed water off to the scullery. "*All* the staff?"

"Yes." Jess dropped her spoon onto the table and braced her hands on the wooden work surface, a bit too close to the knife she'd used on the bread for Daphne's liking. Jess didn't pick the knife up, though, simply leaned into the table a bit to better glare at the valet. "*All* the staff. I'm already having to keep food warm and ready for two different serving times. I'm not adding a third."

"But—" Mr. Morris started to protest, clearly affronted at the idea of an upper servant dining with lowly maids and groomsmen. He was actually going to argue with her.

Daphne tried to shrink into a slightly smaller ball while Eugenia peeped out of the open doorway to the scullery, eyes wide as she took in the scene.

Jess grabbed the knife and the remainder of the loaf she'd been cutting earlier, despite the fact that she'd already cooked toast. She emphasized every word with a swift slice through the bread. "Not. Doing. It."

Daphne bit her lips to keep from smiling. She certainly hadn't gotten a favorable first impression of the man the day before, but it would seem he'd crossed Jess even more at some point.

The man swallowed and walked to the door with brisk steps. "I believe I'll take my message to Mr. Pasley."

"Tell him half past nine, would you?" Jess asked with a sickly sweet smile. "And if you could have Lord Chemsford ready to dine by nine, I'll be able to serve his food at its freshest."

The man sneered once more. He was really quite good at creating the ugly expression. "His lordship will be down when he wishes. And if I am not down at the nebulous half past nine you dictated, I expect my meal to be ready after Lord Chemsford's."

Daphne eased around the worktable, making sure there was nothing between Jess and the pockmarked wooden beams across the room. Jess had a great deal of control over her temper, but she let it loose to make a point when it served her. It would go off like a well-aimed gun. If a gun could shoot knives that sliced with precision. Daphne shook her head. That was a terrible analogy.

Jess shrugged and continued slicing bread. There was apparently going to be a great deal of toast this morning. "Your plate will be on the servants' dining table at half past nine. When you eat it is up to you."

He gave another frown but said nothing else as he wrenched open the door and stomped through it.

Jess slid the knife back into the block and then tilted her head to look at the mound of sliced bread. "Looks like another evening of bread pudding, then."

Before she realized it, Daphne was doubled over laughing. Bright, solid, cleansing laughter. The kind she wasn't sure she'd indulged in since they'd learned that the owner of their beloved refuge intended to actually claim it for his own. Once she'd caught her breath, she snagged one of the already cooked pieces of toast and left the kitchen to dress for the day.

As she walked down the path to the cottage, she couldn't help feeling a spark of hope. Maybe, just maybe, everything was going to turn out well.

CHAPTER EIGHT

The sun was shining through the windows when William finally woke considerably later than normal and with a remarkably clear head. Whatever Mrs. Brightmoor had given him last night had allowed him to sleep better than he had in ages, which, in turn, eased his head more than usual.

Morris had everything laid out in the dressing room, ready to prepare William for the day. He'd even arranged for William's daily ride to be postponed until the afternoon, not that William intended to ride today. Walk outside and let the fresh air clear the last of the tension from his head, maybe, but not ride.

Within an hour, William was trailing his hand along the banister as he made his way down the stairs, craning his neck this way and that to take in pieces of art he'd somehow missed the day before. There was too much to actually appreciate any of it. If this were going to be any sort of comfortable home, the collection would have to be pared down.

And the staff was going to have to be bulked up.

There was no one to send belowstairs to request that his breakfast be served and there was no bell in the dining room. That meant he had to wait, go upstairs and send Morris down, or go down himself the way he had yesterday. None of those were a good precedent to set.

As it turned out, though, his light staff was apparently efficient.

Even as he stood beside the ridiculous table, contemplating his options, Mrs. Brightmoor appeared, tray in hand. She arranged the plate of food, teacup, and teapot with steam curling from the spout at the head of the table while he carefully arranged himself in the chair.

"It's a beautiful morning," she said as she turned his plate so it was presented to him in as appealing a form as possible. "Have you plans for today?"

His fingers fumbled across the edge of his toast. While it was somewhat normal for the housekeeper to know the schedule for the master of the house, the exchange of information usually wasn't handled as breakfast chitchat. "I . . . I'm not sure."

"I see." Her smile drooped a bit but then punched back up, looking a little stiffer than it had before.

He picked up the toast and reached for the small container of marmalade, moving slowly and darting several quick looks in his housekeeper's direction. "I'm . . . going to eat now."

She didn't move.

He cleared his throat. "Alone."

Her brown eyes disappeared as her lashes lowered and she stepped back before executing a perfect curtsy and then scrambling awkwardly from the room. He suspected she hadn't gone far, but at least she wasn't hovering over his breakfast anymore.

The food was perfection. Surprising considering the light staff and the outdated kitchens. He didn't know a great deal about kitchens, but he knew that what he'd seen downstairs would have had most London chefs quitting on sight.

After savoring the last bite, he set his fork on his plate and leaned back in the chair with a sigh.

"How does your head feel?"

William jerked in his chair, barely avoiding connecting his knee with an obnoxious gargoyle again. He blinked up at Mrs. Brightmoor, standing by the table once more. Had she been watching him eat? How else could she possibly have known the instant he'd finished his food? "Ah . . . better. Thank you." He pushed the chair back and stood, careful to keep as much distance between them as possible. "I will probably spend the day outside. I've found the best thing for recovery is fresh air and light exercise. If I sit too much, the pain returns more often."

"Oh!" Her shoulders relaxed and the tension eased from around her smile, leaving a blinding curve of happiness behind. "You should take a tour!"

"I thought we did that yesterday."

"We've a lot of grounds here and most of them are overgrown. If you wander outside without a guide you might get lost."

There were so many issues with her statement, starting with the *we* that claimed some sort of joint ownership and ending with the implication that he was a naïve child who couldn't walk in the woods without getting lost. William wasn't entirely sure where to begin. Perhaps it was best to simply cut off her concerns. "I'll be sure to keep the house in sight."

Her smile drooped into a frown as she gathered dishes onto her tray. "But then you won't see much. There are a great deal of trees about and they are all fully covered in leaves right now. You won't be able to see enough of your new home. A home isn't only made of brick and wood, after all. Everything and everyone is a part of it."

William rubbed his bottom lip between his thumb and forefinger. His own mother hadn't badgered him like this. Of course, by the time he'd been old enough to be lectured about this sort of thing, she'd been too weak to do so. Those last years had been difficult for him, being away and out of reach while she suffered alone. He'd gone back to visit whenever he could but it wasn't enough. It could never have been enough.

Had she felt alone rattling about in that house every day without companionship?

All of a sudden he didn't want to be in the house anymore. He wanted people, connections, a reminder that even though he was by himself he wasn't actually alone.

"Perhaps I'll ride into town. Then I won't have to worry about getting lost on the footpaths."

"You can do both if you walk. There's a path toward Marlborough that cuts through much of the grounds." She frowned at the window. "We should leave soon, though, if your head feels up to it. Rain tends to come with no warning in the afternoon."

He coughed. "We?"

"Yes, we. I've assigned myself the duty of seeing that you settle in properly. If this place and town are to be your home, you should know every bit of it. I won't leave your side until you've discovered everything you need to know."

That was what William was afraid of.

"The barn, or I suppose it's the stable now, with the renovations you had done to it over the past two months, is over there. The animals as well." Mrs. Brightmoor gestured with one hand toward a path that led to a wooden building that was a strange mix of old and new. He'd sent instructions that a proper functioning stable be built, and it appeared he'd gotten just that. A functioning stable. If he wanted it to match the house one day, he'd have to build a completely new one.

He turned his attention from the stable to find Mrs. Brightmoor was already five steps away from the path leading to the stable. She gestured in the opposite direction to where a wide expanse of lawn ran down from the house toward the lake and a small rise across the way blocked the view of whatever outbuildings were on the opposite side of the house. "We hang the laundry just over that dip in the hill."

She kept moving forward. "And the lake is this way."

William ambled along after her, keeping his pace slow, both to actually see what they were passing and to prevent overexertion from affecting his head. She never complained about his speed, never even huffed an impatient sigh, simply slowed her stride or even stopped occasionally until he was within a step or two and then she'd be off again.

For someone who had been so very insistent that he be shown

the estate he'd elected to call home, she was moving awfully fast. They'd traveled in a fairly straight line since departing the house.

It made him more curious about her than the buildings around him. Curiosity over a servant was a new experience for him, but something about her, about the house, about the entire situation, didn't seem to make sense.

William liked when things made sense.

Perhaps it was simply that terrified sort of curiosity that kept people watching horrific situations just to see what was going to happen next. Not that he thought she was going to do anything terribly horrific. She was a fairly small person, so unless there was a band of ruffians waiting in the woods they were fast approaching, he didn't have reason to worry for his safety.

His sanity, however, might be in imminent danger. This woman, who shouldn't have drawn a second thought from his mind, had inspired more questions than any gently bred woman of his acquaintance.

The way her pace quickened the slightest bit as she circled the lake and entered a path cutting into the woods gave him pause and made him reconsider the idea of ruffians. William paused at the tree line.

It took her about seven paces to realize he wasn't close behind her. She paused and turned to wait for him but frowned when she saw he'd stopped completely. "Are you well? Is it your head? This walk could be a bit much after spending the evening with an aching head. Perhaps you'd be more comfortable spending the day in your room? Or the library? I could make you more willow bark tea."

William took a deep breath, letting the clean fresh air fill his lungs and clear his head. No, he did not wish to go back in the house, but did his housekeeper truly not understand how strange her behavior had been since his arrival? Maybe he'd learn something if he stopped evading her and actually engaged in the strange conversations she kept attempting.

He cleared his throat and leaned one shoulder against a tree, crossing one booted foot over the other. "I'm simply wondering where you are trying to take me."

"To the town, of course."

"To the . . ." His voice trailed off, unable to completely repeat the sentence. "You were serious about that? Walking through the woods to the town?"

She glanced at her toes. "It would let you walk in the fresh air but not be in the direct sun. Too much sun occasionally inspires a bit of a pounding in my own head." She pried a stick out of the ground with her toe and then her head popped back up with a beaming smile. "Besides, a house takes its character from its surroundings. If you don't know the town, how will you be able to know the house?"

William cleared his throat and glanced over his shoulder to the house up on the hill. He could see the figures of the workmen unloading something from a wagon and taking it into the house to continue their work on the back parlor. "You do know the house isn't alive, don't you? The rafters aren't likely to come join me for tea, berating me for not understanding them. Besides, wouldn't I learn more about the house by staying within its walls than wandering about outside?"

"Walls are simply barriers." Her smile became tight as she looked up at the house as well. "And you don't really think a house is nothing but brick and mortar."

The house? Yes, actually. Add a bit of timber and that was all it was. She probably meant the life lived within it should be more, but he wasn't about to give her the satisfaction of agreeing with her. "You don't know the first thing about me."

"I know you are Lord Chemsford"—she held up one finger—"and your favorite color is blue." She held up a second finger, smiling in triumph. "That's the first and second thing."

He blinked at her. "How do you know my favorite color is blue?"

She shrugged. "It's your first day in a new home so you'd likely choose to surround yourself with what you know and care for. You're wearing a blue jacket."

William glanced at his sleeve, which was, indeed, a deep blue. "That's . . . rather amazing of you."

And more than a touch frightening.

"It could also have something to do with Mr. Morris yelling at all of us not to spill anything on your favorite coat while he brushed it out this morning."

A grin busted through William's growing concern before he could stop it. "Don't let Morris know, but my other blue coat is actually my favorite one."

They stood, her in a subservient silence that didn't seem quite right and him with a sense of peace he hadn't experienced in a very long time. He didn't really care about going back to the town today, but unraveling the mystery of his housekeeper was more appealing than anything else he could think to do.

Besides, he still had to decide whether or not to dismiss her once he'd found a suitable replacement or see if having a full staff to manage would make her somewhat normal. "Very well," he said with a nod at the path beyond her. "We'll go to town."

They walked in silence for the most part, with her marching past grand trees, jumping over thin streams of water so small they couldn't even be called brooks, and occasionally lifting a hand to let her fingers glide against a bit of hanging moss or a tall clump of flowers. Every so often she would hum, a little fragment of a tune that wasn't there long enough for him to catch what song it was.

William followed behind, cataloguing the path in his head so he could return home again, but also so he could take this same path on his own at a later date. The beauty of the woods was something he wouldn't mind taking in at a slower pace someday, perhaps on horseback so he didn't have to be quite so concerned with where his boots landed.

They broke out of the trees and joined a rutted country lane. Just ahead of them was a stone bridge arching over a narrow river.

He remembered the bridge from yesterday, which gave him a better idea of where the path cut through and how the house stood in relation to their current position. Coming through the woods trimmed at least half an hour off the trip, perhaps more.

"You're a quiet tour guide," he observed. Silently touring the countryside with her wasn't going to tell him anything other than how much stamina she had when it came to walking.

She paused and glanced around. "Um, well, this is the bridge into town."

"And that is the path back to the house?" He pointed to the break in the trees they'd recently exited.

"Well, yes."

"I see." He considered her for a moment. When he'd been a child he'd learned early on how to read his father's mood. The man had never been violent, at least not with his fists, but it was easy to tell when he'd had a bad day or gotten into yet another disagreement with William's mother because his shoulders would pull in and every movement would show a tension, as if his arms and legs were being pulled back by some invisible harness.

Mrs. Brightmoor had looked like that yesterday. And this morning. But last night and ever since they'd started walking in the woods, she'd seemed peaceful and at ease. What would the town bring? Was it solitude that eased her? If so, she wasn't going to be able to manage well when he hired more servants.

Answers required they continue their journey, so he waved a hand at the bridge. "Shall we be on our way?"

CHAPTER NINE

Daphne considered kicking herself as the buildings around them became more substantial and closer together.

She'd have never considered the idea on her own, but as soon as he'd mentioned leaving the house and going for a walk it had seemed the perfect distraction. With Lord Chemsford away from the house, he wouldn't see Benedict or Mr. Leighton while they were working.

Of course, since she was with him she wasn't able to use this perfect time to come up with any sort of long-term plan, but still, bringing him into Marlborough had seemed brilliant.

Except for one thing.

There were people in Marlborough. Lots of people. Most of whom she'd gone out of her way to have little to no dealings with. She'd seen the local people, of course. One couldn't live anywhere for more than a decade and never see anyone, but her wallflower tendencies from London had flourished in the need for secrecy. Unless she was amongst the handful of people she knew, she did her best to disappear.

Benedict was different. He liked talking to people. How many of these people did he know now that he was living in town with Mr. Leighton and attending church services every Sunday instead of simply once every few months? How many people had seen him occasionally visiting Mrs. Lancaster's shop?

Despite the fact that the children were meant to be secret, Kit and Daphne had risked bringing them to town on occasion. After all, people tended not to see what they weren't looking for. None of them were blind, though. Well, except for Agatha, who sat on the side of the road near St. Mary's selling flowers.

The question became, then, were people gaping and gawking at them because they realized Lord Chemsford looked like Benedict or because an aristocratic nobleman with a fussy valet and a very talented tailor walked alongside a woman who resembled the local milkmaid? Daphne had a large patch near the hem of her cloak, and her dress was simple, grey, and fashioned so a woman could dress without aid of a maid to help her fasten everything together.

Nothing said upper-class lady quite like a set of tapes between the shoulder blades.

Daphne wedged the sides of her lips up into a smile as yet another person slowed down to stare at her walking into town with a man at her side. There was no turning back now. She was simply going to have to muddle through and pray for the best. A miracle would be very welcome right about now.

She cleared her throat and gestured to her left. "There's St. Mary's. We've two parishes in Marlborough. St. Peter's sits at the other end of High Street."

The marquis nodded. "And the household? Which do they attend?"

How to answer that? Until a few months ago, Daphne hadn't ventured into town for Sunday services more than once a month, and even then she'd alternated between the two churches so as not to allow anyone to see her too much or become overly curious about why she had two different children with her every time.

"Mrs. Brightmoor?"

"Oh, yes, church." Daphne cleared her throat. "We aren't really part of either parish, so we let the household attend whichever church they wish." That sounded good, didn't it? It even kept her from lying while not admitting that more often than not they had their own private service at the house.

She mentally begged him not to remember that the household had, until yesterday, consisted of two women and three children. As far as he knew, it had consisted of her alone for much of the time before that.

It would have been nice to know exactly what had been conveyed to him about the current care and upkeep of the house. Nash had tried to communicate as little as possible over the years so as to keep anyone from giving too much thought to the property. He'd had to tell them something, though, especially when the place had changed hands from father to son.

They crossed onto High Street and walked through the middle of the town in the bright light of morning as people bustled about.

This had been a foolish decision. Daphne took deep breaths in through her nose, trying to calm her racing heart as her gaze darted from one person to the next. What would she do if someone asked after Benedict? If someone mentioned the resemblance? Her middle squeezed in on itself and she pressed a hand to her stomach. What she wouldn't give to be back at Haven Manor, quietly setting her home to rights.

Only it wasn't her home anymore. It was Lord Chemsford's.

"This is one of our inns," she said, waving an arm toward the building that was fairly quiet at the moment but would become a riotous center of activity when a stage arrived. "We have a lot of inns. People of all stations like to pass through Marlborough, so we've some very nice ones."

That was the perfect solution. She cleared her throat. "You may find those accommodations more to your liking while the house is being worked on. It tends to get rather noisy and will surely be inconvenient as the workers move from room to room."

Yes, she would still have to worry about a local person saying something, but if she could convince Lord Chemsford to stay at an inn, she'd persuade Benedict to stay at the cottage, and everything would be good.

"No more inconvenient than spending weeks on end in a room not truly your own," the marquis said, dashing Daphne's hopes.

"I may have to change rooms from time to time as the work shifts, but I would much rather deal with the inconveniences of my own home than reside at an inn."

"Oh."

Daphne stopped and stared down the wide, cobblestoned street. Tile and brick buildings lined the road with porticoed storefronts ready to become part of the weekly market. That would be another day she could get him out and away from the house. Anyone living near Marlborough should experience the market.

Also, there were places a tourist would like to see: the white chalk horse carved into the hill, the stone circles in nearby Avebury. It wasn't as if he'd like to go to all of those places with *her*. In fact, she would prefer he departed the house while she stayed in it.

But even if he did everything she could think of, that only took up a matter of days. The inn had been her first and so far only long-term solution, and he'd crushed it before she'd even had a chance to imagine how it could work.

"Carry on, Mrs. Brightmoor." His voice was tinged with exasperation as Daphne blinked away her mental list of places that might entice the marquis away from Haven Manor.

"Carry on?" she asked.

He tilted his head to give her a quizzical stare. The directness of his blue gaze had her pulling her cloak a bit more tightly around her. She didn't like being the focus of anyone's attention, much less someone she didn't really know. It didn't matter how similar the faces, Benedict had never possessed the power and confidence to turn his gaze into a lethal weapon like this man could.

"With the tour?" he replied. "You said it was vital I understand the town if I was going to live here."

"Right. Yes." She twisted her hands in her cloak and searched the area. Where to take him? She couldn't turn around, so onward into town was the only way to go. Hopefully she'd come up with something soon. "This way."

What did she really have to show an aristocrat? There was a

reason they used Marlborough as a resting stop on their way to somewhere more exciting. Cheese factories weren't especially interesting, and he was hardly going to care about the location of the poorhouse. The common field where the local children played was of no matter to him either.

Really, the only places Daphne ever went in town were Nash's office—and taking the marquis there when the solicitor wasn't expecting him seemed cruel—and Mrs. Lancaster's. Many people found the unique store interesting, but would Lord Chemsford want to see it? He wasn't going to be doing the shopping.

"We've a few schools." A sense of accomplishment filled her as she waved in the general direction of the other end of town. Aristocrats were always interested in education and such, weren't they? Of course, The Ivy House, which housed the Marlborough Academy, couldn't be seen from their current location. The other schools weren't even on this street. Should she walk him in that direction?

"I've no children, Mrs. Brightmoor. And if I did, my sons would be attending Harrow, as I did." His gaze narrowed as he looked around the town.

Was it from the sun or was his head paining him again? Only a few hours ago his head had hurt enough to keep him awake. Perhaps such a long walk wasn't such a great idea.

Daphne's palms grew sticky with sweat, and she tried to discreetly wipe them on the inside of her cloak. She should get him indoors. If the sun was bothering his head, the shade and coolness inside a building would help. But where?

She looked up and down the street. Would any of it interest a peer of the realm?

No. Inns and taverns were the only places in Marlborough catering to his kind. That left Nash and the grocer as her only options. Just once, she'd love to have a decision laid before her that wasn't about selecting the better of two terrible options.

She guided him to the side of the road shaded from the morning sun, gesturing occasionally at one building or another. As they approached the multi-paned window of Nash's office, she strained her neck to peer inside.

Empty. Well, empty of people. She was a bit relieved that she didn't have to introduce Lord Chemsford to Nash quite yet. Even though the solicitor was more than able to handle a surprise or two, it did seem polite to warn him of the previously unknown connection first. She also wanted the marquis to be in a better mood so his first instructions to Nash weren't to find Daphne's replacement.

She needed to make him so happy that he would forget her rather questionable antics since his arrival.

"Do you like licorice?" she gasped out.

"Licorice?" he asked with a lifted brow.

"Yes." Daphne swallowed and took off marching down the pavement. "Lancaster's has the best licorice around."

That might be a complete and total fabrication. Daphne hadn't any idea if anyone else in town even sold licorice, much less if it was any better. What she did know was that Mrs. Lancaster had some and it was good because whenever she slipped a piece to the children, they closed their eyes in bliss and floated about the rest of the day. More importantly, the old woman never let anyone leave her store unhappy.

Daphne hadn't a clue how old Mrs. Lancaster actually was. For as long as they had been acquainted, the grocer had possessed a bit of grey hair and wrinkles. Lots of wrinkles. Wrinkles formed from an excessive amount of time smiling at neighbors and guests. Her husband had died years before Daphne had come to town, and she'd been running the store ever since.

She'd been meddling in the lives of everyone in town since she could talk. Or so she claimed.

Mrs. Lancaster was also one of the very few people who knew Daphne was Benedict's mother. She'd taken in Daphne and Kit when they ran away from London, cared for them, gave them a temporary place to live, and taught them how to survive on their own. She'd held Daphne's hand through the birth of her son. There was no one in town Daphne trusted more.

Now she only had to hope the woman wasn't so old that she would keel over after one look at the marquis.

"This," Daphne said as she pushed open the door to the shop, "is where we buy our supplies and foodstuffs."

He stepped in after her, sighing at the slight relief from the sun and heat, but he turned immediately back to the window. "Is that a saddlebag?"

"Yes." Daphne shifted her weight from foot to foot. How to explain Lancaster's? In addition to food, spices, and other edible products, she stocked a selection of market wares, allowing the townspeople to work their own stalls during the market and purchase other items during the week.

Over the years it had become a place for townspeople to gather and work out their woes as much as a place to shop. Whatever one needed, Mrs. Lancaster could probably find it.

Fortunately, the shop was currently empty, aside from the proprietor. Mrs. Lancaster bustled about behind the counter, filling bins and checking shelves as she hummed to herself.

"Good morning, Mrs. Lancaster," Daphne said.

"Greetings, dear." The woman turned around, a kind smile splitting her face into grooves made all the deeper by the lines and wrinkles of age. When her gaze landed on Lord Chemsford, her eyes widened, and for the first time Daphne could remember, the open smile was replaced by a look of complete surprise that quickly gave way to a stern scowl. One wrinkled hand reached back and curled around the handle of her broom as if she were prepared to shoo the marquis right back out the door.

Daphne surged up to the counter, heart in her throat. If Mrs. Lancaster kicked them out, she had no idea where to take the marquis next or how to handle his questions about the incident. "This is Lord Chemsford. He's newly moved to the area. He has *no connection* to it."

He cleared his throat and frowned, not at the store or the scowling old woman, but at her. "If that is how you intend to introduce me, Mrs. Brightmoor, I'd thank you to leave me to my own devices."

At the fake name, Mrs. Lancaster's eyes narrowed further. She looked back and forth between Daphne and Lord Chemsford. "No," she said slowly as her face cleared of disgust and her normal smile returned, "believe me, it's a more proper introduction than you would believe." A bit of a glint entered her eye. "It's a quirk of small towns, you know. We've our own language."

"Oh?" He looked at the grocer and then back at Daphne. The irritation had faded and something suspiciously close to a glimmer of humor softened the hardness.

Daphne swallowed. How could he possibly find this amusing? She was very much concerned her heart was going to explode and cause her to expire right then and there.

He leaned a bit closer to Mrs. Lancaster. "What is the hidden message my guide has just relayed?"

"If I told you it wouldn't be very hidden, would it?" Mrs. Lancaster bustled around the counter, her right foot dragging slightly with each step. "We can't be sharing the town's secrets with every handsome newcomer who wanders in the door."

Daphne blushed as if she'd been the one to declare the marquis handsome instead of the shopkeeper. Not that she could deny the statement. She hadn't lost her head with his cousin because she found him ugly, and the marquis was definitely the better looking of the two.

Still, she could do without the opinion being announced while she was in his presence. It was difficult enough to ignore the fact that she could all too easily imagine him in another time and another place, whisking her onto the dance floor without a single intent to ruin her.

Yes, if the world would just conspire to help her ignore his appearance, she would be exceedingly grateful.

"I've every intention of staying in the area for a while," the marquis was saying, head inclined toward Mrs. Lancaster. "I've an estate just over the river."

Mrs. Lancaster's eyes widened, and she jerked a glance at Daphne. "Have you now? I thought there was nothing that way but farms and forests."

"It's been empty for a while now, but I intend to change that. How long until I become a local and earn my way into the inner circle of knowledge?"

"It's not so much about time, my lord." Mrs. Lancaster reached her hand into a bin on the wall. "It's about knowing you'll do your part to protect us." She pulled her hand out and held up a piece of candy. "Licorice?"

CHAPTER TEN

William was fairly certain he'd never been inside a grocer's shop. He was completely certain he'd never visited a grocer's shop like this one. There probably didn't exist another grocer's shop such as this. He slipped the licorice into his mouth and chewed carefully. He couldn't remember the last time he'd eaten the candy, but he recalled not caring for it.

He still didn't care for it.

But as he'd already been declared something of an interloper, he wasn't about to turn down the offered treat.

While he wasn't entirely sure how his housekeeper had convinced him to let her take him on a tour of the town or why it vaguely felt like it had even been his idea, he liked Marlborough. It was comfortable and clean without the pretentiousness he often encountered in London or even the stately homes where he'd been staying in Ireland. There was nothing bold about it or even all that remarkable. It simply was.

"What can I get for you today?" the old woman asked his housekeeper.

Mrs. Brightmoor blushed a bit and dropped her gaze to the ground. "Um, nothing. I'm . . . giving Lord Chemsford a tour of town."

The shopkeeper blinked at her and then at him. "You brought him all the way to town for no reason?"

William officially liked this woman. She may be strange, but she was smart, and she wasn't afraid to speak her mind in front of him. He had a feeling she'd just as openly berate him as she had the housekeeper, who was now crossing her arms and setting her mouth in a determined, flat line.

"It's important for a man to know his town."

"And when the town gets to know the man?" Mrs. Lancaster asked.

It was yet another cryptic conversation passing between the two women. Would they speak plainer if they thought he wasn't listening? It was worth a try. He turned his back and strolled away from them a bit to peruse some of the goods that were almost unusual enough to actually distract him from the conversation at the counter.

"Are you sure about him?" the shopkeeper whispered.

William examined a teacup and tilted his ear toward the women while he held his breath.

"Mrs. Lancaster, of course I'm certain."

"Yes, yes, you wouldn't make a mistake about that." A long, shaky sigh. "Why bring him here?"

"Where else would I take him?"

Where else, indeed. Why did she need to take him anywhere, though? Was there something back at the house she was trying to hide? Something being hidden even now?

"I'll make him a bag of sweets," the old woman said, her voice a bit louder as she moved back behind the counter. "That will keep him happy as you walk around."

"But I don't know where to take him," the housekeeper said. Well, that's what he thought she said. She'd moved to the end of the counter with the shopkeeper, so it was a bit more difficult to make out the sentences.

"Take him to Nash's . . . talk business all day."

William cocked his head. The solicitor in charge of the house's care was named Nash Banfield. Was that whom they were referring to? Their knowing him wasn't a surprise, as Mrs. Brightmoor worked at the house and the town itself was fairly small. But to refer to him by his Christian name?

His housekeeper's response was too quiet for him to hear, but it made the old woman chuckle and pat her on the head, causing her to reach up and adjust the fuzzy brown topknot.

He wandered the store a bit more, unsure how long to leave the women to their conversation. The shopkeeper seemed to be a voice of reason, so perhaps she could calm whatever had gotten under the skin of his housekeeper. Then they could return to—or perhaps create—a normal working relationship. One where she quietly went about her job and he was able to forget she was there.

When phrased like that, the normal social system sounded a bit pompous. If he were to start treating the servants as equals, though, his house would fall into chaos. He employed them, paid fair wages, and didn't expect an undue amount of labor.

In fact, if he began paying attention to his servants it likely would be as awkward for them as it was for him. Just picturing asking Morris to sit down for tea and a chat made William chuckle. The valet likely would faint on the spot.

William circled back around to the front of the store, as fascinated by the place as he'd been when he first walked in. The shopkeeper gave him another face-splitting grin and beckoned him over to the counter.

"What do you do, my lord?"

From the time he was very young, William had learned it was best not to show surprise. Over the years he'd gotten a great deal of practice with this, as people had delighted in sharing with him the latest gossip and exploits, particularly those of his father. He used every bit of that ability now to keep his face impassive. A glance at his housekeeper revealed she didn't think the older woman insane. As far as he'd noticed, Mrs. Brightmoor wore every emotion known to man plain on her face.

She appeared nothing but curious now.

Perhaps both women had a few attics to let.

"What do you mean?" he asked carefully. "I'm a peer of the

realm. What do you expect I do?" He did what all the other peers did—or at least the responsible ones. He managed his estates and investments, considered politics, and did what he could to improve the community around him by providing employment and occasional structure improvements. He had visions of modernizing the marquisette so it would continue to perform those duties for years to come.

Those responsibilities usually demanded a bit of respect, but all he was getting from the shopkeeper was a frown. William wasn't accustomed to being frowned at. People didn't often frown at a marquis.

The frown was gone as quickly as it appeared, though, replaced once more by an engaging smile as the woman held out a paper bag. "You're a human being before you're a peer, aren't you? Take these as a welcome present. Sweeten up your day a bit."

He took the bag and the question to save for later. The bag slid easily enough into his coat pocket, but the question about his humanity lingered in the back of his mind.

All his life, he'd been the heir apparent, the man who would be the marquis, who would help rule the country, who would provide the livelihoods of hundreds, but he'd never given much thought to who *he* was because he'd always assumed that *was* who he was. While he wasn't entirely sure anymore, he did know he wasn't his father, and that might have to be enough.

His housekeeper was ridiculous. Or maybe William was ridiculous because he was still following her. When they left the shop, she took him on a circle of town. So far he'd seen a white horse carved into a hillside, a few empty stalls ready for use at Saturday's market, and the green where the town children played on sunny afternoons.

And he still didn't know why he'd needed to see any of it.

Perhaps, to a woman such as she, these were important and meaningful places. It was possible the woman had never been farther away from Marlborough than the house where she now worked and, in her eyes, the oldest house in town that had somehow managed to avoid the fire hundreds of years ago was truly an impressive sight to behold.

But he'd seen the ocean, the cliff country, and London. While he appreciated the simplicity of Marlborough for the retreat it brought him, he didn't find it extraordinary.

"There's an interesting well down this street —"

"No." William held out his hand. They'd finally made it back onto High Street, and he was putting an end to this farce. "We're stopping at that inn for something to eat."

He gestured to one of the nicer-looking establishments he'd seen on their walk. Their very, very long walk. He was so tired of walking.

And he was hungry.

"Why?" Mrs. Brightmoor asked. She'd gotten bolder as the day wore on, almost as if she didn't see herself as his servant but as his peer. It was impertinent, to say the least, and uncomfortable because there were moments when she'd made him forget as well, when he'd simply walked along, finding her to be pleasant company.

Until he'd remembered who she was and the entire business became awkward.

Perhaps it was time to remind her they each had a role and a place and that stepping out of those roles made the world messy. "Because I'm hungry, Mrs. Brightmoor, and the aroma indicates they serve food there."

The flustered version of the woman reappeared, and he almost wished he'd gone to see the well. She glanced at him, then at the inn, and back again, looking lost and perhaps even a bit frightened.

Then she sucked in a deep breath and gave him a triumphant smile. "But you haven't seen Mr. Banfield yet."

William jerked at the outburst. He couldn't help it. She'd been looking so small that the last thing he'd expected was a bold outburst, as if the idea were going to run away if she didn't pounce on it.

"No," he said slowly. "I haven't. What has one to do with the other?"

"It's getting late. Na—er, Mr. Banfield doesn't always keep regular hours. We should see if he's there. He's the man your father hired to oversee the care of the estate, you know."

"I do know. But does he have food?" William asked in a clipped tone. Yes, he was being rather abrupt in a way his mother always warned him not to be, but in this case he had to think even she would find it acceptable.

"No," Mrs. Brightmoor bit back. "But if you wish to speak with him awhile, I can have food from the inn brought to you."

Hadn't she, just a few hours earlier, been trying to get him to take a room at that very inn? Now she was insisting he stay out of it?

He'd never met anyone so unpredictable. Throughout the entire tour, in which he was supposed to get to know the town and how it worked, she'd studiously avoided introducing him to anyone other than the grocer. Now he simply had to meet the solicitor?

Once again, curiosity welled up in him. She was a fascinating conundrum. What was going to happen next? "Very well. Lead me to Mr. Banfield."

She nodded, walked briskly up High Street to a building with a large multi-paned window overlooking the main part of town, and opened the door.

Inside was a man of medium build with dark hair showing a bit of grey at the temples and sticking out as if he'd run his hand through it so often that the strands had given up the idea of falling back into place.

Newspapers, books, and documents were everywhere. It was probably some sort of organized chaos, but William had never seen anything like it. His solicitor in Birmingham kept his office neat as a pin and furnished with luxurious dark wood tables and deep-cushioned upholstered chairs.

"Mr. Banfield," Mrs. Brightmoor said with distinct enunciation, "I don't believe you've met Lord Chemsford."

William wasn't sure if the man had heard her. He was too busy staring at William with eyes that had pulled tight at the temples and lips pressed into a near frown.

The solicitor turned to Mrs. Brightmoor. "Have *you* met Lord Chemsford?"

William was well accustomed to people keeping secrets around him. The aristocracy was forever trying to control who knew what and barter one piece of gossip for another. His father had done it, threatening people if they told his first wife what he did in London or buying silence if the threats wouldn't work. It had made William's childhood home even worse over the years until now William found the very idea of a secret under his own roof distasteful. Now a secret was being kept right under his nose and everyone involved was doing a poor job of pretending otherwise.

The smile Mrs. Brightmoor gave the solicitor was wide and tight and so obviously fake it was laughable. "Of course! I met him yesterday when he arrived at Ha—er, the house."

Whatever unspoken message was relayed with that sentence seemed enough to relax the solicitor a bit. William rolled the words through his head and picked them apart, but he couldn't make sense of what could have been hidden in them. So he stepped into the middle of the enigma and extended a hand toward the solicitor. "A pleasure to meet you on something other than paper, Mr. Banfield."

"Indeed." The man walked around the desk and shook his hand. He then scooped a large stack of newspapers from a chair and set them on a nearby table. "Please have a seat. I'm sorry I wasn't at the house to welcome you. No one told us when you planned to take up residence."

William eased into the chair, pleasantly surprised when it was more comfortable than it looked. "I wasn't sure how long it would take to complete the business I was attending to in London."

"I understand." The man shuffled a few papers around on his desk. "I trust everything was satisfactory upon arrival?"

Had it been? His rooms had been ready, food had been available, and the barn had been adequately altered to house the horses, carriage, and groom. That was everything he'd asked for.

But then there was the fact his housekeeper didn't actually live in the house and the vague sense of his being the unwanted visitor the servants watched to make sure he didn't abscond with the silver.

"It was satisfactory," he finally landed on. Because it had been. Not exemplary and not without question, but satisfactory. "More staff will need to be hired, of course."

The solicitor nodded. "Yes. It's a while before the next mop fair, but I know the local people. We can fill any positions quickly."

William nodded. "I'll prepare a list." He should probably decide whether or not he was keeping his housekeeper first. It would certainly go smoother if she was a part of selecting the maids and the belowstairs staff. He glanced toward the current housekeeper, who was simply standing to the side of the room, hands clasped in front of her, lip clenched between her teeth. "The food, Mrs. Brightmoor?"

Mr. Banfield's eyebrows shot up as he, too, looked over at the housekeeper, but he said nothing.

"Right away, my lord," she said, bobbing a curtsy in William's direction but holding Mr. Banfield's gaze with her own. She scurried from the room, and William watched her through the window as she scampered across the street and into a redbrick inn.

The solicitor cleared his throat. "Is everything at the house to your liking? I confess, I'd hoped we would have a bit more of the updating you'd requested done before you arrived. There are several accommodation options I can arrange if you'd like to stay elsewhere during the work."

Both Mr. Banfield and Mrs. Brightmoor seemed very concerned about how put out William would be with having a bit of construction done in a home that was plenty large enough to avoid the mess and noise. Especially since, as far as he'd noticed, the work was cosmetic in nature, though the signs of water damage indicated work might need to be done on the roof. Why had it been allowed to deteriorate? Had additional funds been requested and denied, or was the solicitor as strange as the housekeeper?

"I've no complaints on what little I've seen. The cabinetmaker you hired to do the interior work seems to do an excellent job, if a bit of a slow one."

Mr. Banfield ran a hand along the edge of his feather quill. "Yes. It's only him and his apprentice at the moment. There's no finer craftsman in the area, though."

They discussed the more significant work, including the unusable garret rooms that needed to be addressed before he could bring in more staff. He wasn't even sure where the cook and the maids he'd heard about were living. Did they all sleep in the cottage?

That made him think of the outbuildings and the other renovations he'd like to see done to modernize the estate. Whether he lived there long term, rented the home, or sold it, the work still needed to be done. As the solicitor took notes and asked questions, the conversation slid away from the house and into business. Mr. Banfield displayed a good head for the details as William made testing requests of him.

If William was indeed going to stay here for a long time, he would need a local solicitor to help him, perhaps even take the place of the one he'd inherited from his father. Hopefully Mr. Banfield would prove efficient and competent, despite the appearance of his office.

The food came, and the men ate as they talked. The solicitor's intelligence continued to reveal itself, and William felt even more confident that he could, at least for a time, run the marquisette from Marlborough.

Another thread of tension released from William's body. His need to get away wasn't going to require him to sacrifice his responsibility to fulfill his marquis's duties.

How had Mrs. Brightmoor gotten her current position with this smart and observant man in charge? It was one more piece of information that didn't quite fit.

William waited until the housekeeper left the room again to

return the dishes to the inn before asking, "How long has Mrs. Brightmoor been seeing to the house?"

"Years," Mr. Banfield answered. "She's worked there since your father's solicitors asked me to oversee the place."

That couldn't be right. William's father had won the house almost fifteen years ago. Even if he'd taken his time arranging someone to watch over the house, that would mean Mrs. Brightmoor had been there more than ten years. She didn't look old enough unless she, too, had started working there as a child.

Mr. Banfield steepled his fingers beneath his chin. "My wife helped set the house to rights when we first took over the care of it, but Mrs., ahem, Brightmoor has been in charge of the actual caring for the house for many years."

That was a bit more palatable. If she'd started there as a young woman of fourteen or so and been groomed to take over as housekeeper, it would explain why she knew how to care for a house but not for people within it. It wouldn't be fair to dismiss her without giving her the chance to learn.

Though he hadn't any idea how one went about acquiring housekeeper lessons.

Other questions burned in his mind, but he didn't give voice to them. While he felt he could trust this man with his business dealings, there was still something in the secretive conversations and speaking looks that made William feel he couldn't trust any answers he didn't uncover for himself. He needed to keep his questions to facts.

"And the rest of the staff? How long have the maids and the cook worked there?"

Mr. Banfield ran the quill through his fingers. "All were hired recently. The children grew up locally, helping occasionally at the house. When we needed a bit more staff to prepare for your arrival, it was natural to hire them, despite them being a bit young."

It made sense. So why did it still bother him?

The sun was beginning to sink in the sky as William led Mrs. Brightmoor out of town, back across the bridge, and onto the path back to the house. He knew the way now and would be able to return—without his housekeeper—whenever he wished.

He was beginning to wish he'd found a way to leave her in town, because while the journey this morning had been quiet, the walk home was anything but. Her commentary wasn't about trees, flowers, birds, or even the deer that scattered when they came around a corner.

She wanted to know his plans. What was he going to do with the estate? How often did he intend to travel to London?

It was an inquisition, and he was more than capable of putting up a resistance. It irritated him greatly that he had to, though, and it wore through the patience he'd earlier been determined to offer her. As they broke through the trees near the lake, the final thread of patience gave way. He'd been more than polite with her today, exceedingly so if one included yesterday. It was time to remind her that he was the peer and she the housekeeper. It could be her first lesson in appropriate behavior.

"Mrs. Brightmoor," he said through gritted teeth, turning to face her as a slight breeze wafted across them and sent escaped strands of hair streaming across her face. "Kindly recall that you work for me, not the other way around."

"Of course," she said with wide eyes. "But if I don't know what you are going to do, I don't know what I need to do."

"You need to do whatever I tell you to do, and right now I am telling you to leave me alone," he growled.

Her mouth dropped open and then clicked shut.

Finally. Silence.

Wanting to take the win before he said anything cruel, William turned on his heel and stalked across the yard. If he saw her hovering again this evening, he just might end up with nightmares.

CHAPTER ELEVEN

Daphne stayed out of Lord Chemsford's way for the remainder of the evening. It was a task made easier by the fact that Benedict and Mr. Leighton had returned to town to work on a few pieces of moulding in the workshop. Neither of them would be at the house for at least the next two days.

She even pulled Reuben in from the stable to act as footman and deliver the man's dinner.

All the children were quiet as they gathered for their own meal. Of course, Daphne didn't really expect them to be comfortable around the contemptuous Mr. Morris. The groomsman, Mr. Pasley, seemed a much more congenial fellow. He was at least happy to take Reuben under his wing and teach him how to care for animals a bit more complicated than goats and chickens.

It was only a matter of time, though, before the children would ask Daphne about Lord Chemsford. Eugenia hadn't seen the man yet, but Sarah and Reuben both had. Perhaps they'd decided they didn't want to know. As long as they kept any speculations to themselves, Daphne was more than happy to put off the conversation for a while.

As they cleaned up at the house and moved to the cottage to prepare for bed, Daphne did her best to laugh and joke as normal, to pretend their routine hadn't changed a jot just because there was a new master in the house.

All the while, her heart was pounding, as if she were literally trying to outrun the clock she knew was ticking away behind her. Everything was going to fall apart—likely sooner rather than later—and she didn't yet have a plan for how to handle it.

As all of them gathered in the girls' bedchamber for the nightly Bible reading, Daphne fell back on an old favorite to try and ease her fears. She smoothed the pages of a well-read passage in Deuteronomy as she settled into her perch on the edge of the bed the girls shared. Eugenia snuggled in on her left while Sarah sat on the right. Reuben was sprawled across the floor, and Jess leaned against the doorway.

"Why aren't we reading the next part of John?" Eugenia asked around a yawn.

"Because sometimes . . ." Daphne stopped in the middle of her sentence and took a deep, shuddering breath. She didn't need to pretend here. This was family. And she'd always tried to show the children it was good to be open, honest, and even vulnerable with those you love, even when it was too dangerous to be so elsewhere.

Such as up at the house.

She cleared her throat. "I find myself needing certain reminders from God sometimes. It's good to do that, you know, to fall back on a promise when life demands it."

The children all nodded, happy to follow wherever Daphne led, especially when it came to the Bible reading. It had been the only part of their lives where Daphne had led the way. She'd discovered the comfort of daily Bible study when she'd been trapped in a small house on the edge of Marlborough while carrying Benedict, afraid to go anywhere lest someone see her condition and the sin that had brought it about.

She'd read this story in Deuteronomy so often she could quote parts of it.

Moses had made a muck of things, and while God in all His grace had forgiven the man, he who had led the Israelites out of Egypt hadn't been allowed to step foot in the Promised Land.

He had, however, been allowed to raise up the next generation of leaders who would take God's people where they needed to go.

Daphne related to that all the way to her bones. One moment, one decision, one mistake had left her ruined, but here she had been given an opportunity to raise children to be better and do more than she ever could have. If she'd stayed in London, holding up ballroom walls and lurking behind drawing room pianofortes, she never would have discovered the existence of a place where she felt comfortable in her own skin, where she felt useful.

She would never possess the ability or courage to guide anyone anywhere, but she could raise up a Joshua just as Moses had done. These children, including Benedict and all the ones now living with families of their own, were her next generation. They were the ones God was preparing to go forth into the world and live for Him.

Daphne's measure of grace and forgiveness allowed her to be part of their precious, innocent lives.

"'Be strong and of a good courage,'" Daphne said from memory as she looked around at the three upturned faces. "'Fear not, nor be afraid of them: for the Lord thy God, he it is that doth go with thee; he will not fail thee, nor forsake thee.'"

How very much she hoped to instill such courage in these children. They were going to need it. Life wasn't kind to people without connections, with questionable origins. They would have to fight for everything, and she wanted them to do it with integrity and the assurance of God's love.

She would do whatever it took to keep them with her long enough to truly feel secure in that love. It felt a bit presumptuous to say she wanted to be their Moses, but it was a strong idea to cling to, to put her own hope in. If at all possible, she would help raise up a generation with a bit more courage and reliance on God than she'd had.

And it would be enough.

It would have to be.

Because anything more would require her to step outside of this home she'd created. Her wilderness.

"Mama Daphne," Sarah said as she poked at a hole in the hem of her night rail, "is Lord Chemsford Benedict's father? Is that why he's here?"

Eugenia, who didn't look at all surprised by the question, added, "Is he going to give Benedict a home like the other children got?"

Pain bloomed through Daphne's chest as her heart broke into a dozen pieces at the girl's quiet words. A few tears dripped down her cheeks and Daphne didn't try to stop them. She never tried to stop them. That only ever made it worse. Letting them come meant they were out of the way all the sooner.

Ignoring the tears tracking down her cheeks, Daphne forced a small smile and ran a hand over Eugenia's hair. "No. Lord Chemsford is not Benedict's father. It's simply a very strange coincidence that they look alike. There's no reason for either of them to be concerned with the other."

A soft snort came from the direction of the door, but Daphne didn't let her smile falter. As much as she wanted to place an outright ban on any further discussion of the remarkably similar appearances—and especially discourage anyone mentioning it to Benedict—she didn't want to handle the questions such a declaration would bring. So she ignored the frown on Sarah's face and the confusion on Reuben's, and she gave Eugenia's head a loud, smacking kiss. "It's late and none of us are quite accustomed to the amount of work we have to do now. It's time for bed."

No one said anything more than murmured good-nights as they settled down. Reuben retreated to his cot in the drawing room, while Eugenia and Sarah snuggled together under the quilt on the double bed they shared. Then Daphne took her lantern across the landing to the room she shared with Jess.

The other woman was already in her night rail and brushing out her hair. She was wearing the sly, impish grin that always preceded a hefty dose of teasing. "Did the marquis enjoy his tour?"

"Of course," Daphne muttered. "It's every aristocrat's dream to have their housekeeper trick them into walking for miles the day after having a tremendous pain in the head. It's the best way to meet a slew of people so common they normally wouldn't be close enough to him to describe his shoe buckles."

Jess's grin widened. She always seemed so proud of Daphne when she managed to strike back a bit.

Truth be told, it made Daphne a bit proud herself.

"Did you have any problems?"

"No," Daphne said quickly as she slipped beneath the covers. She was more than ready to escape reality for a while.

The reality was Nash had thrown irritated frowns at Daphne when Lord Chemsford wasn't looking. She couldn't really blame him. He'd done so much for her over the years and she'd never told him the identity of Benedict's father. Even when he'd worked with them to manage the finances of the manor, arranged for trusted workmen to donate a portion of their time to maintaining the house, and helped them stay hidden from those who would rather have the children disappear than grow up quietly in the country, still she'd kept that information from him.

And now he was faced with working for a man who was obviously somehow connected to Benedict and he didn't even know what secret he was trying to keep. It wasn't fair to Nash, since he'd invested as much of his life into saving the mothers and children as she had, but Daphne hadn't had any way of telling him more today.

"You won't be able to keep it up much longer, you know," Jess said as she climbed into her own bed. "Have you determined a new plan?"

Daphne punched and squished her pillow until it was the shape she wanted. "All I have to do is keep them apart for another week. Then he won't notice any of us. People like him don't notice the staff."

"That's a bit delusional," Jess murmured before changing the subject. "Do you think he's up there, talking to that horrid man he calls a valet about 'people like you'?"

Daphne popped up on her elbows. "What do you mean, 'people like me'?"

"What did you mean by 'people like him'?"

"Aristocrats. The wealthy people who are accustomed to a house crawling with servants."

When Jess only gave another mildly agreeing murmur, Daphne pressed. "Jess, who are people like me?"

A white slash in the darkness revealed Jess's grin as she answered, "Touched in the head."

"I'm not touched!" Daphne flopped back on her pillow.

"Daphne," the other woman said through a chuckle, "you all but abducted our employer on his second day in the house. That's not a great marker for sanity."

"Oh, go to sleep," Daphne grumbled.

Jess laughed but rolled over and lapsed into silence, leaving Daphne to go into her own pre-sleep routine. The one where she drifted away to a life other than the one she had. It was the only time she allowed herself to admit she wouldn't mind an escape from the regret and the consequences. Had Moses ever done something similar? Had he laid awake at night wondering what would have happened if he'd just remembered the difference between talking to a rock and striking it? Had he imagined what he might have done?

Probably not. But Daphne did.

She closed her eyes and let her mind wander where it would. Sometimes she imagined what would have happened if she'd never botched up, if she'd stayed in London and done what she should have. Of course, those imaginings always included the impossible existence of Benedict. She couldn't imagine her life without Benedict.

Other times she thought about what she would do with the children if there were endless amounts of money and time.

Most of the time, though, she imagined herself as someone else entirely—though, of course, still with Benedict in tow. Sometimes she was bold like Jess or personable like Kit. Sometimes she pictured herself walking into a crowd of people and not instantly gravitating to the back corner to brace herself against the wall as her knees trembled.

Tonight was one of the rare times she imagined herself back in

London, though. She was young and dressed in her finest gown, which was still considerably simpler than most of the dresses surrounding her. Daphne knew the dress. Remembered humming as she'd pulled it apart and turned it into church dresses for Sarah and Eugenia years ago.

But as sleep crowded in, that memory faded and all Daphne saw was herself, standing in a corner with a cup of punch. It was almost a real memory, a slice of happiness as she watched Kit smile up at her dance partner.

A dance partner who looked remarkably like Lord Chemsford.

Had he been at any of those parties all those years ago? He'd have been Lord Kettlewell then, preparing to step out into adulthood.

He'd been nice today—well, nicer than he'd had to be. Had he been as nice then? Would he have been as kind, patient, and polite to the young girl holding up the wall as he'd been to the frenetic and eccentric housekeeper?

She imagined he would. She imagined that he brought her a fresh cup of punch and stood in the corner all evening, talking to her about Benedict's woodworking skills or puppies or something equally as pleasant. How much more fun an evening like that would have been for her.

With a happy sigh she burrowed deeper into her pillow and let the dream carry her away.

William absolutely refused to be apprehended by his highwayman of a housekeeper today. He'd fallen asleep the night before with nothing but a slight nagging pulse in the back of his head that he'd easily managed to ignore. Then he'd risen at his normal time and gone for a ride, investigating some of the woods he'd seen yesterday from the comfort of horseback and solitude.

Upon his return, he'd slunk into the house and deliberately sought out the young parlourmaid he'd seen only in passing the previous two days. She always seemed a bit frightened when she saw him, but perhaps that was simply the way her face looked. It was a bit of an odd shape, with a pointed chin and large eyes.

"Sarah, isn't it?"

"Yes, my lord," she said quietly, clutching the rag in her hand to her chest.

"Have the kitchen prepare my breakfast on a tray. I'll, uh, have Morris come down and retrieve it when I'm ready for it."

Her curtsy was shallow but graceful, and her gaze remained intent on his face. "Right away, my lord."

William nodded and turned away from her, retreating to his rooms before Mrs. Brightmoor could waylay him. With some maneuvering and a bit of luck, he could dress for the day, eat his breakfast, and slip back out of the house to inspect the grounds and outbuildings on foot without his housekeeper suggesting he take a detailed look at the local tree bark or visit every farm within a five-mile radius.

She was unlike any servant he had ever met. He should, by rights, feel like the only person in the house, but he found himself peeking around corners before he left the house after breakfast just in case she was lying in wait.

Successfully escaping the house put a bit of a spring in his step and a smile on his face. His horse had been brought round to the front door this morning and the young boy had been waiting to collect the horse upon his return, so he had yet to get a good look at the stable and other buildings.

There were definitely signs the stable had once been a smaller, older barn before the recent renovations. Mr. Pasley had never been shy about requesting what the horses needed, so the adjustments must have been adequate, at least for the time being.

The sound and smell of animals greeted him as he approached. Ah, yes, Mrs. Brightmoor had been maintaining a collection of goats and chickens for her personal food.

A large pen jutted out from the side of the barn. The fence was a bit low for a horse corral, though. He peered over the edge and saw the pen wasn't for horses, but for chickens. Lots and lots of chickens. The mass of scratching fowl numbered at least two dozen, perhaps more. Another larger pen beyond this one contained an equally stunning number of goats.

How many chickens and goats were required to provide food for a small handful of people? This was enough to feed a large farming family. Several large farming families. Perhaps a small militia.

A low rectangular house ran along one side of the chicken pen. It didn't look particularly new and neither did the fence. Perhaps the original owner had run some sort of egg business and they'd assumed he would want to as well? It was rather presumptuous, but he couldn't explain a village worth of chickens any other way. Who was supposed to buy them, though? Anyone in a close vicinity would have their own chickens.

A lever on one side caught his eye and he poked it, jumping when the house itself shifted, the back board angling out in such a way that one could easily retrieve the eggs without ever stepping foot in the chicken enclosure.

Ingenious. And something William had never seen before. Not that he had much to do with farming or egg collecting, but if his other estates had such a device, he'd have heard about it, wouldn't he?

The question of the number of chickens was surpassed by curiosity over how the chicken house worked. He bent to look underneath and became absorbed in yet another mystery. Beside the lever was scratched out the same bold B with an S looping through it that he'd seen on the desk in the cottage. The year 1813 was carved beneath it.

A year when the estate had, supposedly, been all but abandoned. Had it been built here or moved here?

Was there anything else from the clever furniture maker hiding on the estate? He glanced around the property, noticing several roofs popping out of the trees around the lake. Mrs. Brightmoor had briefly pointed out the scattering of small buildings yesterday but had mentioned that all of them were empty and unfurnished. While there were several less-than-pleasant words William could use to describe his housekeeper, he didn't get the impression that *liar* was one of them.

She was hiding something, yes, but if she were willing to lie in order to keep it protected, she'd have done so already, and their encounters should have been considerably less awkward.

There was furniture in the cottage, though. At least one piece of it with the same maker's mark. He strolled back to the point where the path from the house split, with one side going toward the stable and a well-tended garden that looked far too large, and the other down to the cottage. It seemed like an invasion to go down there. If she'd had a room in the house like a normal housekeeper, he'd have been loath to search it without a good reason. It seemed the cottage deserved the same treatment. At least for now.

Which left the main house. Did he dare? Would he be able to stroll through the rooms at his leisure or would she pop out from behind the curtains and insist he inspect the new moulding?

The bang of a closing door had him scrambling back down the path to the stable and ducking in the open doorway before peering back up at the main house. The action stirred a bit of anger at himself. This was *his* house, *his* property, *his* life. If he wanted to go into his own home and wander around, he was going to do it.

Particularly since he could see a little figure in a small-patterned muslin dress and brown spencer moving in the direction of the laundry-drying lines.

CHAPTER TWELVE

As William circled around the side of the house to the front door, he passed a large wall of glass. White curtains blocked the view through a set of large glazed panels and the windowed double doors that sat between them. An intricate half circle of stained glass arched over the expanse. He hadn't seen such a wall on his tour of the house.

The latch lifted easily, and the door swung open on silent, well-oiled hinges, granting him access to a glorious library.

While he could do without the profusion of art that seemed to be plastered on the walls, the abundance in this room was more than welcome.

Like the portrait gallery, this room had obviously been added later, attached to the main block of the house by a short corridor. Bookshelves were built into the two long walls, creating panels of leather bindings from the floor to the ceiling. A large plain desk sat on one end of the room near the windows, while clusters of sofas and chairs took up the other half. He ran his hand over a large globe in a carved three-legged stand and it spun on its axis in a colorful swirl of geography.

The room was almost marvelous enough to distract him from his goal. Treasures surrounded him, but there was nothing in here that looked like the unique creations he'd seen at the cottage and the chicken pen.

With one last look over his shoulder, he moved into the drawing room. While he wasn't entirely sure what he was looking for, he was confident he'd know it when he saw it. Or perhaps he'd already seen it and hadn't noticed. Like the game table in the portrait gallery.

He moved through the front hall and the music room, pausing to look at the chair by the piano that seemed to be fitted with a shelf for holding sheet music. An interesting idea, but wouldn't the music fall off every time the chair was moved?

Once in the portrait room, he made a point of not looking at the myriad of unrelated faces staring down on him as he crossed to the table to kneel beside the game table. He had to hunt for a while, as much of the table was taken up by the turning tabletop and the clever storage compartments, but near one of the legs, he finally saw it. *B S 1815*. A more recent creation, then.

Next, he spent a great deal of time carefully searching what was supposed to be another drawing room but couldn't really be seen as anything other than a gallery. There was glass and art everywhere, with plenty of shelves and tables to display it all. Nothing looked creatively practical.

In the saloon, he peered intently at every shelf and table until he began to feel a bit absurd. Fortunately, there was no one of consequence in the house to witness his search.

The saloon bore a marked difference from the rest of the house, thanks to the as-yet-unmet Mr. Leighton. The fresh paint and modern trim were beautiful and understated, proving the solicitor had indeed chosen a good workman for the job. The furniture in here also had been restored and appeared to be some of the best in the house. The clean lines worked, despite their age. The air of comfort instead of ostentatious display meant this room likely had been one of the few the previous owner had actually used.

William moved about the room, trying to appreciate each item for its own value but becoming rather disappointed when the tea table was nothing but a surface with four legs. Finally, on a table near the far wall, he found another piece: a box, covered in intricate paper filigree that made it a distinctly different piece of art than the items filling the rest of the house.

It was beautiful but not classic or refined. He picked it up and opened it, revealing multiple bins with a removable tray that created several sections for storing different types of tea.

He closed the box and flipped it over. There was the same B and S along with the year 1811.

A search of the remainder of the house yielded even more instances of the same logo, each bearing years when the house had, supposedly, been empty: a small bookshelf built at a slant to hold a collection of brown hymnals in the chapel, a crude lantern hook near the bed in one of the smaller bedchambers. A dressing table in the austere chambers across from his own had a hook for holding the pitcher so it could be easily tipped with one hand.

Some of the pieces were less sophisticated than others, with more recent dates on the more intricate ones, but all of them showed a unique and appealing eye for practical design. Some of them, like the writing desk in the cottage and the game table in the portrait room, showed a refinement and skill that would be prized by most furniture makers.

Were there even more practical contraptions down in the working areas of the house? Perhaps a washtub that did the scrubbing or a bread bowl that made kneading easier? He wasn't sure what either of those tasks actually required, but they both seemed rather laborious.

He returned to the library and dropped into the chair behind the desk.

A desk that, while not nearly as ridiculous as the dining table, didn't really inspire productivity. It was as dull as the dining table was intricate. He had a feeling the entire time his estate books were open on it he'd feel the urge to leave them behind and sit on the far sofa with a book instead.

It was possible that was what the previous owner had done. Why else would he not have created a working study separate from the distracting grandeur of the library?

The solution was obvious. Whoever had made the game table and the writing desk needed to be commissioned to build him a new desk, perhaps even a full study worth of furniture, with the same elements of creativity and usefulness.

There couldn't be too many cabinetmakers in the area. Mr. Leighton would surely know who the B S was. Or possibly S B. The letters were intertwined, so he wasn't entirely sure.

One thing he knew, though, was he would never be satisfied with a normal desk until he could see what the man could design.

Daphne couldn't do it.

For the last two days, while Benedict and Mr. Leighton had worked at the shop in Marlborough, Daphne had tried to be the perfect housekeeper. Mostly, she just tried to stay as out of the way as possible, be silent while delivering his meals, and avoid eye contact at all cost.

It had been exhausting.

Through it all, though, she'd thought and planned and schemed and now, with the pounding of hammers resuming in the parlor, she was forced to admit she was not going to be able to keep Lord Chemsford away from Benedict. Not by herself.

There was nothing else to do but let Mr. Leighton know what was going on and maybe, hopefully, the man could manage the work in such a way that Benedict and the master of the house never crossed paths.

Unfortunately, she was not the only person determined to talk to Mr. Leighton this morning.

"Lord Chemsford!" she called as she moved toward the sounds of construction, not knowing what she'd say when she got the man's attention but needing to stop him nevertheless.

He nearly jumped out of his boots before spinning about so fast he nearly fell over. "Mrs. Brightmoor," he said in a tight, flat tone.

"Have you had a chance to see all of the grounds?" Daphne almost groaned and dropped her head into her hands. Of course the man had seen the grounds. He went riding across them in the morning and spent yesterday afternoon walking about with the two men who were going to be designing new plans for the overgrown landscaping. Still, she needed him out of the house, just for a few moments, so she could talk to Mr. Leighton. She plunged ahead. "There's an interesting grotto down by the lake."

He shook his head and opened his mouth before snapping it shut on a sigh. After shifting his weight to face her more squarely, he frowned. "I've seen as much of the grounds as I need to at the moment. When the new landscaping plans arrive, I shall walk them again so I can visualize the changes."

"Oh," Daphne said, the overly bright smile she'd plastered onto her face falling a bit. She pushed her shoulders back and forced the corners of her mouth a little higher. "What can I do for you, then?"

"I wasn't seeking you out," he said through gritted teeth.

Daphne gulped. Her turning back into her meddlesome self after two days of perfectly dreadful servant decorum seemed to have inspired a bit of anger. This was yet another reason to be grateful most of the children she'd been raising were now in a comfortable home situation. She'd been able to teach them the skills for an eventual life of service, but she was obviously lacking the ability to demonstrate the necessary deference.

If he would grant her a few more minutes of grace without dismissing her, she would return to being neither seen nor heard and pummeling her frustration out on her pillow every night. Just a few more minutes.

The man sighed once more and seemed to deflate a bit as his frown slid from his face and his tone turned more congenial. "I am, however, seeking Mr. Leighton. If you'll pardon me."

He blinked as he asked her pardon—she was rather taken aback by it as well—but then he shook his head and turned back toward the direction he'd been walking in the first place.

"Mr. Leighton?" Daphne trotted forward, hand outstretched as if she'd have the nerve to grab the man's coat in order to keep him in place. She pulled her fist to her chest to keep herself from making such a blunder. "What do you want with Mr. Leighton?"

His lordship turned halfway back around, eyebrows lifted high. "What does it matter what I want with Mr. Leighton? The man works for me, or so I've heard, and I wish to speak to him."

"Of course." Daphne scooted around him and put herself between the marquis and the parlor, nearly knocking over a bright orange vase on a spindly decorative table. "I'll let him know you wish to see him directly."

"I'll simply tell him myself."

He took a step forward and Daphne scampered backward until she was practically throwing herself across the door.

"You don't want to do that."

His gaze narrowed. "Whyever not, Mrs. Brightmoor?"

Why not, why not, why not? Daphne bit her lip as she tried to think up a reason—*any* reason. At this point she'd take the most ridiculous one in the world but right then her thoughts were stuck on whether or not oranges had been named for the color or vice versa.

"You'll get dirty!" she cried out in sudden inspiration.

His eyes closed briefly for a moment and then he tilted his head as if he couldn't possibly have heard her correctly. "Dirty?"

"Yes." She nodded emphatically. "There's an incredible amount of dust in the room. If you step in it, Morris will be brushing your jacket for the rest of the day." Of course, this man was an aristocrat. He might not care if his valet had an incredibly arduous and avoidable task to add to his day.

She cleared her throat. "And if Mr. Morris is brushing your jacket he can't see to . . . to . . ." What did the efficient yet stuck-up and annoying valet do all day? "He won't be able to set your dressing room to rights. Sarah and I are barely allowed in there, you know."

Lord Chemsford's teeth clenched, bringing an even sharper line to his jaw. "I wish to speak to Mr. Leighton. If a bit of dust should land on my boot while I arrange this meeting, I assure you that Morris is more than capable of seeing to its removal."

Daphne threw away whatever modicum of pride remained within her—which honestly wasn't much—and draped herself across the door to the parlor, drooping against one of the doorframes in a fashion dramatic enough to make anyone on Drury Lane wince. "I simply cannot, my lord. What if you were to track the dust all over my house? It's only myself and Sarah here to do the cleaning."

"I'll hire another maid."

"Not in the next hour." Twenty minutes. All she needed was twenty minutes. And whatever time Mr. Leighton needed to stash Benedict away in a corner somewhere.

She crossed her arms and tried to look imposing, remembering the way the housekeeper in her father's London house had laid down the law about Daphne eating biscuits in bed. "If you'd like to hie off to Marlborough and hire one, I'll let you in as soon as you return."

"You'll *let* me in?"

Perhaps that hadn't been Daphne's best choice of words.

He looked from her to the door, behind which steady bursts of pounding kept the occupants oblivious to the scene at the door. "Just how do you know it's dusty in there?"

Daphne blinked. He believed her? He was giving her ridiculous claim merit? "I, er, uh, I delivered them refreshments earlier."

He looked her up and down. "You don't look especially dirty. That's the same dress you were wearing when you brought out my breakfast this morning."

"Yes, but you can't see the dirt. That's the beauty of patterned muslin. Hides everything."

She had no idea if that was true or not. Her wardrobe was a very dated and worn combination of clothing altered from her fourteen-year-old London wardrobe and dresses made from fabric Mrs. Lancaster had pushed on them over the years. She had six dresses now, and they held up well to the rigors of country life, but she'd maintained some of her old habits of personal cleanliness so she had no idea if the dresses held up to country dirt.

"And patterned muslin doesn't drop a speck of it as you move through the house?" He shook his head. "Washing day must be miserably difficult."

Drat the man. Why did he have to see the continuation of logic in everything? Couldn't he, just once, take what she said as truth?

They stood there, staring at each other for what seemed like hours but was probably no more than a few seconds.

Finally, he clasped his hands behind his back and inclined his head. "What solution do you have for this problem, Mrs. Brightmoor?"

"Solution? Me?" No one ever asked her for solutions. Her way of dealing with problems was to imagine them away.

"Yes. Since you find my plan of walking into a room of the house I own in order to speak to a man I employ so abhorrent, I assume that means you can provide another one."

"Mr. Leighton can come to you. In the library." It was perfect. She'd get her twenty minutes and then Mr. Leighton could give Benedict instructions to get out of the way while the older woodworker then kept the marquis occupied with their meeting.

Lord Chemsford ran a hand over his jaw. "But won't that—"

"I'll let him know." Daphne opened the door behind her just enough to stick her head inside and let Mr. Leighton know to see Lord Chemsford in the library at his earliest convenience.

The lanky man gave her a grin and a nod before hammering a nail into the dado rail Benedict was holding against the wall. For the past dozen years that room had been a bedchamber instead of a private parlor. Life had left a few more dings and dents than one would expect of a small sitting room.

Daphne closed the door with a triumphant smile.

"Won't *he* bring dust into the house?"

"Of course not," Daphne said with an emphatic frown. "He knows to clean himself off first."

Not that he needed to. There were hardly enough woodchips in the room at the moment to merit a broom.

Her stomach clenched. Desperation had turned her into a complete and total liar.

"Very well," Lord Chemsford said slowly. "I shall return to the library and await the arrival of a cleaned-off Mr. Leighton."

As he turned and left the room, Daphne took the first deep breath she'd taken in what felt like hours. What was that verse from Hosea? *For they have sown the wind, and they shall reap the whirlwind.* She had a bad feeling that she was on the verge of seeing just how big a whirlwind this house could handle.

No. Soon it was going to be over because she wasn't going to have to do this on her own anymore. With her mouth set in a grim line, she opened the parlor door once more and stepped inside.

CHAPTER THIRTEEN

William stalked away from the parlor, wondering how in the world he'd managed to lose control of that situation. He'd grown up knowing he was going to be the marquis, learning how to manage the people and the places that came beneath him because of that title, and generally trying to find the delicate balance between wielding power effectively and being a pompous clodpate.

He had a sinking feeling he'd lost that balance just now.

When faced with Mrs. Brightmoor's desperate-looking smile, which was as obviously fake as a seaman's wooden leg, he'd deigned to explain himself to her in an attempt to make her more comfortable. Given that her job was to see to the comfort and livability of his home, it was an unexpected concession.

He didn't want to dismiss her, though. She'd obviously given a great deal of care to the house and had been a solid employee from the looks of it. It was doubtful she had an excessive amount of savings. She might not even have anywhere to go. If she had, she likely would have found a less isolated position a long time ago.

Still, he couldn't have his housekeeper making him feel like a heel in his own home simply because he'd been seeking out another employee.

As he strode through the breakfast room, a box on the sideboard caught his eye. He'd missed it the other day in his wanderings of the home, probably because it was so difficult to look at anything aside from the hideous gargoyles when he was in here. It bore a marked resemblance to the box in the saloon, though. The paper-filigree design on this one was a great deal more intricate, the loops and swirls of paper forming an image of this very house.

He poked at it until he found how it opened, flipping a mechanism that made several trays swing out. As the other box had, this one cleverly provided a way to store multiple types of tea in accessible ways. Flipping the box revealed the B and S he knew he was going to find, along with the year. 1816.

This year.

William's head snapped up as the parlor door opened. Footsteps moved to the saloon before the door clicked shut again.

"I'm afraid I don't understand, Miss Daphne."

William frowned. *Miss Daphne*? An edge of Irish lilt curved around the name, making it sound soft and gentle. Yet, at the same time, it sounded common and approachable. Somehow Miss Daphne fit her better than the stuffy-sounding Mrs. Brightmoor. It was considerably easier to imagine a Miss Daphne throwing herself across a man's path than a Mrs. Brightmoor.

Of course, William didn't have to imagine such a thing, did he?

"I'll explain everything," Mrs. Brightmoor answered. "You can come downstairs and listen while I prepare a tray for your meeting. Perhaps if he's eating he won't rush you out of there."

Rush him out . . . ? An inkling of an idea began to form, and yet it was too incredibly farfetched to be true. Then again, Mrs. Brightmoor had proven capable of attempting the impossible.

Was there a chance she'd been trying to keep him away from Mr. Leighton?

If so, he had to admire her dedication and, to a point, her ingenuity, even though it was clear she didn't think matters through before she acted upon them. Perhaps once William uncovered what she was trying to hide about Mr. Leighton, life could return to the way it had been the past couple of days.

Peaceful. Quiet. With servants acting in the manner they were supposed to.

He set the box aside and made his way down the stairs to the kitchens. It was time to put an end to his housekeeper's scheming. Whatever she was worried about, he'd show her it was nothing. Or, if it was indeed something, he'd take care of it and then chide her for hiding it. If there actually was something bad about Mr. Leighton, and she and Mr. Banfield and everyone else he'd worked with had let it slide, William was going to show them all he knew how to wield the aristocratic power he'd inherited.

Laughter met him at the bottom of the stairs, but it cut off as he walked into the kitchen.

The cook stood at a table, removing meat from a skewer. Mrs. Brightmoor was placing a tea tray on the worktable while a man picked his way through a bowl full of biscuits. He was tall and lanky with a shock of wild, curly red hair beneath a plain brown cap.

"Mr. Leighton, I presume?"

The man looked up and his eyes widened as he took in William from head to toe. His gaze flitted from William to Mrs. Brightmoor, where it stayed for a moment or two before coming slowly back to William. "Yes, my lord."

The voice was as stiff as the man. In fact, everyone in the room seemed to be stiff. Holding their breath. Watching. Waiting.

Finally, the man grabbed the cap off his head with one hand and ran the other through the crop of curls that seemed to spring in every possible direction.

Was it because the man was so obviously Irish? Did they think William would dismiss him because of it? He had to admit it was a possibility. There were plenty of men in his position who wouldn't hesitate to do just that. It was rather admirable, really, that Mrs. Brightmoor was willing to risk losing her job so Mr. Leighton didn't lose his.

Perhaps William could right everything in his house by simply being welcoming and nice to the man. "A pleasure to meet you,

Mr. Leighton. I was admiring your work in the saloon. I'm Lord Chemsford."

Mrs. Brightmoor coughed. "No relation."

William narrowed his gaze at the housekeeper, who was giving a great deal of attention to the perfect placement of an empty teapot in the center of the tray. The little blond cook across from her looked as if she were considering running the housekeeper through with the skewer.

"Er, of no relation to whom?" William asked.

That bright, ridiculous fake smile popped back on to Mrs. Brightmoor's face. "Why, anyone Mr. Leighton would know. Small towns, remember? In Marlborough we like to know how, er, business connects to other people. Support the area, so to speak. I was just letting Mr. Leighton know that you're new."

Cook stabbed the skewer back into the meat she'd just pulled from it.

Perhaps his friendly greeting of Mr. Leighton wasn't going to set everything on the path to normal. Unless this was normal. In which case he was glad he didn't usually have a reason to visit the kitchens.

William gave his attention back to the woodworker, who, in spite of the fact that he still hadn't moved except to put his cap back atop his head, appeared the most levelheaded one in the room. "I'd like to discuss a desk."

"A desk?" the man asked.

"A desk?" the housekeeper parroted.

William didn't look but the slap of skin on skin led him to believe that the cook might just have smacked her hand over Mrs. Brightmoor's mouth.

"Perhaps you'd like to come up to the library so we can discuss it?" William had phrased it as a question but he turned back to the door without waiting for an answer.

There was the rough sound of a clearing throat, and then heavy footsteps fell in behind him as he went up the stairs.

William made a point of not looking back. He refused to give in to the curiosity that made him want to watch what his housekeeper would do next, like some fascinating country fair attraction.

Once they were in the library, William sat behind the boring desk and offered Mr. Leighton the chair opposite. "You've done all the woodwork in the house?"

The man nodded, adjusting the soft brown cap on his head, making red curls stick out in odd directions. He scratched at his chin beneath a scraggly beard that was as red as his curls. "For the past ten years."

William released a sigh of relief. If the man had been doing work around the place for ten years, more than likely he knew where the new items had come from. "I've come across some items in the house—intriguing items. They're marked with a B and an S. Would you know about them?"

"Came out of my shop." Mr. Leighton's gaze dropped, and he plucked at a rough patch on the leg of his trousers.

"Excellent." William would work his way up to getting more information about who the designer actually was. Making a small bit of progress felt like a massive accomplishment today. "I'd like a desk of similar design."

Mr. Leighton's head came up, eyebrows drawn together and deep grooves across the bridge of his nose. "Similar to what?"

"The chicken house, the tea boxes, the game table. I like the ingenuity and the use of space."

The man scratched his head beneath the cap. "I've got a design at my shop. It's just a sketch on paper, but I can bring it to you. We haven't built one yet, but the idea is sound."

Even better. "I'd like to see it tomorrow."

"Uh, yes." The man shifted in the chair, as if it didn't quite fit him correctly. "I'll do that. I, uh, wouldn't mind taking a look at it again, maybe working it a bit before bringing it in to you. Perhaps my apprentice and I could leave a bit early today so you aren't delayed."

William nodded and sat back in his chair. "Understandable." He paused for a moment. "Did you know I lived in Ireland for several years?" He nearly groaned. Of course the man didn't know.

William had made a point of not letting many people know. If his father had known his son was that close he might have become even more of a nuisance.

The woodworker simply nodded. "It's a beautiful country, my lord."

"That it is. In nature and in people." William looked Mr. Leighton in the eye, hoping the man understood William couldn't care two farthings whether or not the man was from Ireland as long as he did a good, honest job.

"Indeed, sir." The man nodded and swallowed. "Till the morning, then, my lord."

William nodded. "Till the morning."

As the woodworker left, William heaved a sigh. Now, finally, his peaceful country home was going to become just that.

The desk design was magnificent. Mr. Leighton had delivered it as promised and then let William know that he would be measuring and pulling moulding from a few rooms today and then working in his workshop for a while to make the necessary pieces.

William had been staring at the paper ever since.

It was a work of art. Designed to go against the wall instead of standing free in the middle of the room, the desk was an intricate combination of bins, drawers, and shelves that made William want to pick up a quill and answer all the correspondence he found trivial and annoying simply so there would be more things to stick in all the little nooks.

It was a bit of a shame that such an impressive work—if indeed the real thing could live up to its presence on paper—was going to be hidden away in an isolated country house.

William would just have to commission more pieces from Mr. Leighton. Was the B and S a tribute to someone? It made matters a bit confusing, but the craftsmanship he'd seen developing in the pieces dated most recently made up for the eccentricity. If the desk was as impressive as the drawing indicated, William might even ask for a second one he could take to London with him when he went up for the parliamentary session next year.

The only thing missing from the desk was a place to store his various estate ledgers. If they could be close at hand but not on the work surface itself, he'd be able to work more efficiently.

He left the library and followed the noise to the dining room, where he found Mr. Leighton with his back to the door, standing on a ladder and pulling down a section of carved moulding. William waited patiently for the man to come down, not wanting to startle him into falling off the ladder.

"Benedict, my boy, we may have to carve more new pieces than we thought." The Irishman, still balanced near the top of the ladder, frowned as he poked at the back of the wood he'd just removed. "Looking at the state of this wood, I'm guessing it was damaged before it even went up. Putting paint on inferior wood is like putting a silk dress on a cow."

There was a laugh from the other room, followed by, "She may make it into the ball, but she'll ruin every dance."

Apparently the nonsensical statement was something the woodworker said often.

The young voice—most likely the apprentice William had yet to meet—continued speaking as Mr. Leighton made his way down the ladder, the section of wood tucked under his arm. "It shouldn't be a problem. Do you want me to come measure and sketch it out now? I've just finished sketching the proportions of the flowers for the doorpost."

Leighton got to the bottom of the ladder and froze, one foot still on the rungs, eyes wide above his bushy red beard as he saw William standing there. He swallowed hard enough that the bob of his throat was visible even through the beard. "No," he called out. "We'll just take the piece with us. You can, er, finish that rose and then, uh, go out and get some water from the pump."

"I can bring you refreshments." William's eyebrows shot up as his housekeeper's voice emerged from the parlor where the apprentice was working.

The click of shoes on bare floor drifted away even as Mr. Leighton called after her, "No, that won't be—"

"She's already gone, Mr. Leighton," the boy answered.

Mr. Leighton flipped the piece of wood over and over in his hands, shifting his weight as he glanced from William to the parlor door and back again. Why was he so nervous? Hadn't William's commissioning more work from the man eased his fears about William's acceptance?

Perhaps something had gone wrong and he didn't want to tell William about it. Everything in the room looked as it should, though, perhaps even better since the atrociously ugly furniture had been pushed to the side and covered with a sheet.

"You've been doing exceptional work from what I've seen," William began, attempting once more to put the man's mind at ease. "And you're working quickly, which I appreciate." The pace was quite impressive, given there were only two of them. When they got to the more structural portions, such as the garret rooms, more help would probably be needed.

"Thank you, my lord." The woodworker flipped the wood around one more time. "What can I do for you?"

William nodded, assuming his compliments had settled the concern in the other man's mind, and held up the sketch of the desk. "These plans. Is it possible to turn this cabinet part here into drawers similar to this section over here? Also, I'd like to be able to store five or six ledgers somewhere easily accessible."

Leighton set the wood moulding on the floor before lifting his brown woolen cap off his head and running a hand through the riot of curls. "Well, uh, let's see here."

The man's voice had dropped low, almost to a whisper as he took the sketch from William.

He cleared his throat and ran a finger along the paper. "The ledgers shouldn't be a problem, here in the middle." Another anxious glance drifted toward the parlor before the man cleared his throat and continued. "As for the drawers, well, it depends on where the mechanisms for all the other openings and compartments need to be."

William's eyebrows shot up. The sketch was incredibly detailed, with seemingly every square inch of space carefully allotted to serve a purpose, and the man who was going to build it didn't know how that worked? "Shouldn't you know that already? You said those other pieces came out of your shop."

"They did. It's simply that . . ." The man's shoulders deflated as the longest sigh William had ever heard from a man's chest fluttered over the sketch. "The thing is, my lord, this isn't my design."

William's eyes narrowed. "Whose is it, then?"

The woodworker swallowed. "My apprentice."

The young voice he'd heard from the other room had designed this desk? Created the other pieces he'd seen throughout the house? It would explain the advancement in quality over the years. "Well then," William said slowly, "why don't we ask him? I think you called him Benedict earlier, yes? Maybe he'd be interested to know you've been telling me his work is yours."

Leighton pulled himself up to his full wiry height. "I did no such thing, my lord. I told you those pieces were made out of my shop and that's the truth. The wood, the tools all came from my shop. Benedict's been working with me for years, even before his apprenticeship became official. I'm still the master woodworker here, and I'm still the one who will be taking orders and payments."

"But you are not the one designing my new desk, apparently," William countered coldly. He raised the volume of his voice slightly as he called, "Benedict?"

"You don't need to do that, my lord." Leighton shifted his weight back and forth. "It's really best if you work this with me."

William narrowed his gaze, watching the woodworker while continuing to call for the apprentice. "Benedict, I would like to discuss an alteration to my desk design."

"Of course, my lord!" Whereas Leighton had gone from nervous to looking nearly frightened, the apprentice sounded almost excited. Tools clattered in the other room and then footsteps approached the door before William could see a shadowy figure in the corner of his vision.

"I . . ." The figure stopped moving. "Oh my giddy goat."

William blinked, breaking his stare with Leighton. The woodworker appeared about to faint as the boy's voice changed from excited to cold. Not just cold. Icehouse cold. Frozen-over-Thames cold.

A curl of anger unfurled in William's throat. This must be who they'd all been trying to hide from him. He set his mouth in a grim line, preparing to do whatever was necessary with the finally exposed secret. He turned.

And then he, too, stood completely still. Was he even breathing? Did someone in the house possess smelling salts? There was a possibility they were all about to need them.

It was like looking in a mirror. An old mirror. The nose. The eyes—both shape and color. The hair—even the way it was a slightly darker color on one side of the head than the other. This boy was him twenty years ago.

How was that even possible?

"Who are you?" William demanded.

"Benedict Sutton." The boy squared shoulders that were only beginning to broaden and lifted his chin. "If you don't mind, my lord, I'd like to ask the same question of you."

Name and title were probably not what the boy was looking for, but William didn't have anything else to give him. "I am the Marquis of Chemsford."

"Dear Lord, save us all," whispered Leighton.

While William could certainly appreciate the man's sentiments, it seemed a strange thing to pray at the moment, unless he knew more about the situation than he was letting on. "Do you have something to add, Mr. Leighton? The boy and I both appear to be at a loss."

"Well, I, that is to say, I . . ."

The woodworker was saved by the entrance of yet another person into this farce. Mrs. Brightmoor came striding in, a tray of lemonade and sandwiches in her hands. She stumbled to a halt, looking from William to the boy and back again.

"I know who you are," the boy said, the ice in his voice turning to shards that threatened to pierce William's chest.

William's stomach clenched as he began to get an idea that he, too, knew who he was to the boy. By nature, he was private and discreet, but there'd been a time for a few months after his mother's death and his father's sudden remarriage that William had lost control. He'd made more than one poor choice before coming out of his emotional stupor and righting his life, and he'd always been thankful that God had allowed him to come through that time unscathed.

Or so he'd thought.

"No," Mrs. Brightmoor said as she rushed to put the tray down on the sheet-covered table. "No, you don't."

"He doesn't?" William asked at the same time the boy added, "I don't?"

William didn't wait for the housekeeper to answer. He spoke directly to the boy. "How old are you?"

"Thirteen."

Thirteen. William swallowed hard. That was the same age as his half brother Edmond, who didn't look half as much like William as this boy did.

The age was right. It was possible. William's knees threatened to give way.

"It doesn't matter how old he is." Mrs. Brightmoor stepped between them, face pulled into a determined grimace as she looked from boy to man and back again. "He's not . . ." She paused, took a deep breath. "He's not your father."

"Are you certain?" the boy asked, echoing the question bouncing through William's brain.

"I am very certain."

"Then who is?" William asked. "Who is the boy's father? If you are so very positive that it isn't me, you must know who it is, and as the current head of the Oswald family, I demand to know his identity because the lad is sprung from somewhere on my family tree."

Of that William was absolutely certain. It wasn't possible for the boy to so closely resemble William and not be somehow related. Since there hadn't been a female cousin born in decades, his connection with this boy was certainly through the paternal line.

Mrs. Brightmoor backed away a step. What sort of emotion was she seeing on his face to elicit such an action? He wasn't entirely sure what he was feeling at that moment.

He'd never cared much for his family. In fact, hadn't liked a great deal of the aristocracy he'd met. When Edmond had been born, William briefly dreamed of finding a way to convince the Clerk of the Crown that he'd died so the title could pass to Edmond and William wouldn't have anything more to do with it.

Since proof of death generally required a dead body, he decided to make the best use of his money and power instead and simply put as much distance as he could between himself and the frivolous immaturity of the rest of his peers.

Apparently someone in his family had decided to distance himself from responsibility in another way.

"I made a promise," Daphne said quietly. "I'm so sorry." But she wasn't talking to William—wasn't paying William much attention at all. She stood in front of the boy, wringing her hands and looking for all the world like she wanted to wrap him in her arms and shield him from all the bad news coming his way.

And he looked like he wanted to let her.

Was it possible . . . ? It couldn't be. But she was so adamant that William hadn't fathered this boy. He blurted the question out before he could stop himself. "Are you his mother?"

CHAPTER FOURTEEN

Despite the fact that Daphne had resorted to fabrications yesterday in an attempt to prevent this very meeting, she really wasn't a good liar. Nor did she want to lie in front of her son. Even if she'd never acknowledged his true parentage, she'd raised him—was still raising him in a way—and she wanted to set a good example.

Then again, she also didn't want to let him learn her secret.

But oh how she wanted to answer yes, to claim Benedict as her own. Not being able to do so hadn't been as difficult when there'd been a houseful of children. With a dozen young lives to care for and love, she could tell herself it was better for Benedict to feel like he was the same as the others, that he belonged. He was already different from the rest of the world. There'd been no need to make him different from his family, too.

Now that the house was nearly empty and would only grow emptier in the next few years, she felt like she'd lost something. She couldn't risk telling Benedict the truth and losing even more. She was already his mother in everything but name. It was enough.

She'd have to contemplate how to handle the questions already forming in her boy's pain-filled blue eyes later. Right now she needed to manage the marquis.

Somehow.

She took a deep breath and set her shoulders, turning to face him and picking a point over his left shoulder to focus on. "I raised him," she said, lifting her chin a bit and trying not to let it tremble.

"You raised him?" the marquis asked. "Then who is his mother?"

"I promised not to share that either." And she had. She'd promised Benedict, even though he didn't know it. She'd promised to help him feel as normal as possible, to not hurt him any more than life already had. She'd promised to love him like a mother but never tie him to her with the knowledge of their relationship.

"As you are the only person in this room who seems to know anything, I suggest you tell me something," Lord Chemsford said. "I think we can all agree the resemblance between two people in this room is a little more than coincidental."

Daphne's heart broke as she looked back at her son.

Benedict, who had always been so mature, so determined to be the man of the house and protect them all, wrapped his arms around his middle and looked from adult to adult like a child lost in the market crowd. He didn't look like a scrawny adult, didn't even look like a young man of thirteen. His world was threatening to crash around him and he looked ready to crumble with it.

She wasn't about to let that happen.

Telling herself to look the marquis in the eye even though it made her stomach jump and her knees tremble beneath her skirts, Daphne racked her brain to find the words that would make this right. Or if not right then at least not detrimental to Benedict.

The stickiness of sweat made her palms itch, but she refused to wipe them on her skirts. Not one sign of weakness could be allowed. She had to be strong for Benedict.

"I don't see why anyone has to tell you anything." She swallowed. "My lord."

He lifted an eyebrow. "You don't?"

"You've no problem with his work, obviously." She tried to swallow again, but there was no moisture in her mouth. Instead, it was pooling in her stockings, making her feet wiggle within her boots as the spark of nerves worked its way to the tips of her toes. "I see no reason why you need know about his, er, private affairs."

The marquis's eyebrows lifted even higher and Daphne tried not to wince. *Affairs* was probably not the best word to use in this instance.

The fact that Lord Chemsford believed he could be the father meant that he was familiar with the word as more than just a term. That alone should be enough to kill off any more fantasies about riding through the glen together on horseback. They'd been ridiculous fantasies anyway. Daphne didn't even ride.

"Mrs. Brightmoor," Lord Chemsford said slowly, "I am not in the habit of shirking the responsibilities of a man of honor."

Daphne nearly choked on her tongue. What would Kit say? No, Kit would attack him. What would Jess say? "Admirable, I'm sure." Daphne almost grinned at the droll tone she managed. "But in this case you've no responsibility to take."

Lord Chemsford glared at Daphne for a few more moments before seeming to dismiss her as he stepped to the side to have an unencumbered view of Benedict. His gaze was steady and unwavering, even as his mouth tightened at the corners. "Being the marquis means I have a responsibility to the title beyond what I do personally. I've no intention of shirking that duty, even if it means accepting the repercussions of the previous title-bearer."

Daphne's mouth dropped open a bit in confusion. What was the man talking about? She sorted through his sentence, which sounded exceptionally formal and perhaps a bit muddled, despite the confidence with which it had been delivered.

Oh no. He couldn't possibly be thinking Benedict was his brother, could he? That William's father was also Benedict's father? The very idea made Daphne shudder a bit in revulsion.

Benedict made a choked noise, and Daphne turned from the marquis to see that her son's shoulders had slumped forward and his blue eyes glistened with unshed tears. He wasn't watching the marquis. He was watching her.

She wanted to go to him so badly and hold him tight as she'd done when he was a young lad with a splinter from his latest woodworking attempt. This was so much more than a splinter, though. This was probably his worst nightmare come to life—his identity dragged into the light and examined with ruthless scrutiny.

Her feet refused to do more than wiggle in her boots. If she took one step it would lead to running from the room, because it wasn't only Benedict having to face the shadows of his past.

It was Daphne, too.

The accusations and questions about Benedict's parentage fell on her like boulders. Every statement made her see her father's disappointed face once more, made her feel the desperation that sent her and Kit fleeing from London, made her choke on the notions of worthlessness and regret that had only been alleviated by holding her precious baby boy and seeing there was, indeed, still some reason to keep living.

She couldn't fall apart now. Later, she could cry into her pillow. Later, she could escape by imagining life was still the way it had been six months ago.

Of course, first she would torture herself by imagining all the ways she could have handled this situation better than she was currently doing.

"You've nothing to worry about, my lord. Your title remains untainted, at least in this instance." She had no idea what else he or his father had done, and she didn't want to think about it. She'd managed to separate the sin from the children she'd raised, including her own, and she needed to be able to do the same with her employer if she wanted to continue working here.

"I am the head of the Oswald family." Lord Chemsford's gaze swung back over to Daphne. "And you're going to have to do an awful lot of talking to convince me this boy doesn't fall beneath that authority."

Another guttural moan drifted from Benedict as he pulled himself out of his slump, but he said nothing.

"And what if he does?" Daphne was stunned to discover her

feet did indeed know how to move. She stomped across the floor until she was close enough to stab the marquis in the chest. It was difficult to say who was more surprised when she actually poked him, but surprise didn't stop the words from continuing. "What do you intend to do? Wrap him in fine tailoring such as yours and present him to society? Perhaps hide him away? I'll not allow you to drag him off to the wild country so he can conveniently disappear."

A muffled squeak sounded from the corner where Benedict was standing.

Mr. Leighton cleared his throat.

Daphne's cheeks grew hot. She'd forgotten the man was in the room.

The woodworker crammed his cap onto his curls. "I think the lad and I should step out and leave you two to, er, come to terms here."

"No." Benedict's voice was small but the shake of his head was strong, almost violent. "I want to know. We've never asked who our parents were. It seemed easier not to know, but I don't like this feeling, Mama Daphne. I don't like being here like this and not knowing."

The glare of superiority Lord Chemsford gave Daphne made her want to poke him again, but he stepped around her and approached Benedict. "Where did you grow up, lad?"

"Here," Benedict said on a rush of air.

Daphne knew how he felt. All her air rushed out, too, as she gazed at their similar faces now only inches apart.

What did he think? Did he believe her when she said this man wasn't his father? Frankly, if Daphne hadn't been there for his conception, she'd be thinking the mother had lied, too.

"Here?" The marquis glanced around the room. "At the manor? And who is 'we'? You said 'we've never asked.'"

"I, uh, well." Benedict shifted his gaze from the marquis looming over him to Daphne. There was terror on his face. He knew he'd let information slip out that was not meant to be shared.

It was too late now. Daphne tried to give him a reassuring smile even as she fought for a new idea. She could leave the room. But would the marquis follow her? Probably only if she'd managed to attract his attention back to her somehow.

She couldn't think of anything to say, though. But then she didn't have to because the man turned back around to spear her with his gaze. "Has my father been inadvertently running a charity house on this property?"

That was uncomfortably close to the truth.

The marquis didn't seem angry anymore. A cold neutrality had taken the place of the earlier heated emotions. Did that mean he found the idea intriguing? Or even good? Or did it mean he'd gone so far past angry that he moved into some sort of controlled rage?

"I'm sure you've seen the books, my lord. This was not, nor has it ever been, a charity." It had been a home, and Daphne refused to think of it as anything else. Besides, they'd never taken a penny of the upkeep allowance for the children. It had all been used exactly as it was allotted.

Lord Chemsford rolled his shoulders back and braced his feet. "The boy's father. Who is he?"

His name and his face formed in Daphne's mind, but she couldn't have wrapped her tongue around the words even if she'd wanted to. Never had she spoken of that night to anyone other than Kit. Jess only knew the generalities of the situation.

Now, as Daphne stood there, she was overwhelmed by every memory—not just that night but all the days and years that followed. The myriad of emotions attached to those memories curled through her. Despair, shame, and fear . . . but also joy and love and hope. All of it melded together in a massive lump in her throat that threatened to choke her.

She *knew* God had forgiven her. She *knew* she was a valuable person, that she'd gone on to do something good with her life. She *knew* that while parts of that evening had been her fault and she'd made poor choices, she'd also been taken advantage of and manipulated.

She knew all of that but right then, at that moment, not a single statement felt true. Loneliness and exhaustion washed over her, chilling her, while guilt and shame battled within her for the role of foremost emotion. Armies of memories stabbed her heart until Daphne rather wished she was one of those women who could faint on command.

Darkness crept into the edges of Daphne's gaze, threatening to make her wish come true.

"Mama Daphne?" Benedict's voice punched through her cloud of misery. Arms, so thin yet so strong from the years of woodworking and farm labor, wrapped around her. "It's okay. I don't have to know."

"But I do," Lord Chemsworth said.

"Why?" Daphne choked out. "If you give me a good reason why, I'll tell you who his father is." But not the mother. Never the mother. Benedict would never forgive her for keeping that a secret.

She prepared herself for a lecture on honor and responsibility, on maintaining reputation and name. As if she wasn't acutely aware of their importance. Instead, he held up the drawing of the desk.

"Would you have him hide this here? Restrict his talent to making fancy egg-retrieval systems for chicken coops instead of spreading wide his ability to design something like this? The boy is thirteen. Imagine what he'll be able to do in ten years. Do you wish to hold him back?"

Daphne wrapped her arms around Benedict and sputtered, "Of course not!"

"Then you have to know he's going to encounter more people like me—more people who *know* me. If we are not properly prepared, the obvious unacknowledged connection will be the end of whatever success he could have."

She blinked. Of all the things he could have said, all the reasons he could have named, he'd chosen Benedict's future. It was the one thing she couldn't fight against, the one thing she'd do anything to secure. She took a deep breath and intertwined her fingers with Benedict's. For him, she could conquer the fear threatening to weaken her knees.

Still, the words wouldn't form. The stern expression of Lord Chemsford, filled with thoughts she couldn't begin to guess, stole her ability to breathe, much less speak. She shifted her gaze to her son, standing so close she could see how much taller than her he'd grown. Tears still shimmered in his eyes, and he seemed terrified and excited at the same time.

What would happen to him? Was his obvious connection to the marquis going to limit his future?

"He's right. I need to know." Benedict's jaw clenched until the lines of his neck stood out.

As much as Daphne didn't want to admit it, at some point it was better to be prepared than protected.

Benedict pulled back a little, not letting go but not holding her close either, as if he wanted to offer comfort but wasn't sure about receiving it. "I never really thought about you knowing details of my life that I didn't, and I don't particularly care to be in that position with anyone else. I don't know where I came from, but you do. You know my father." He swallowed. "And my mother."

"What happened to his mother?" Lord Chemsford asked, his voice still strong but a bit softer on her ears.

She couldn't look at them, either of them, or she would be ill. Already her stomach was trying to crawl out of her throat, trying to swallow the words she was attempting to force out. She could do this. She could tell them who had fathered Benedict, but nothing more.

"His mother is living a good life." Well, she had been. Daphne was reserving judgment on her current situation. "There's nothing either of you can do for her."

Benedict pulled away a bit more, his arms slipping to his sides. She risked a glance at his face and saw something she'd never seen before. He'd closed himself off from her, and it hurt. It hurt more than she could have imagined. If he felt this way now, knowing the truth would make him hate her.

One step at a time, she whispered in her mind. They would deal with the father's identity now because they had no choice.

Hopefully soon Benedict would move on from wanting to know who his mother was and everything would be the way it had been.

With her eyes shut tightly enough to block out every vestige of sunlight, Daphne licked her lips and took another deep breath. "His father's name is Maxwell Oswald."

CHAPTER FIFTEEN

William had cut himself off from his family so much over the past ten years that it took him a moment to sift through his memories and find the man. Maxwell Oswald. The son of his father's younger brother.

As boys they'd spent quite a bit of time together, but when William had gone to attend Harrow, they'd become two people who occasionally had a reason to be in the same room rather than any sort of friends. Their appearances were similar, he supposed, but he wouldn't have thought the other man could father a child who looked so remarkably like William. Then again, Maxwell's father had looked enough like William's father that the two could have easily passed for twins.

This was an instance of "blood will tell" if ever there was one.

William cleared his throat and dropped his gaze from the housekeeper. It wasn't difficult to do. She looked utterly broken and miserable and somewhat accusing, as if he'd caused her harm in getting her to reveal a secret everyone in the room—well, excluding the master woodworker—should have already known.

No, he didn't feel any guilt when looking at Mrs. Brightmoor. Looking at the boy was another story entirely.

The young man's teeth were clenched, defining his jawline and making him look even more like the man he was becoming.

William curled his hand in a fist to resist the urge to run a hand across his own face, measuring the similarities and seeking the differences. He should do something. He just wasn't sure what.

If this had come to light thirteen years ago, there would have been no question as to the appropriate path to take. There was also no question the men who had headed the family at the time wouldn't have taken it.

None of that mattered now, as the boy was nearly grown. They couldn't slip him into the family as a ward or cousin, couldn't pretend his birth was something other than what it was. Even admitting his existence would be problematic now. The boy hadn't been raised to face the scrutiny or the questions, wouldn't possess the refinement to be brought into the family.

It wasn't as if the boy was seeking a life of leisure anyway. He obviously enjoyed the work of the path he was on, was settled into a good position, and had a future in front of him. If William fled the room now and hoped no one ever had the gumption to broach the topic with him, the boy would likely lead a fine life.

So perhaps that was what he should do. The idea of shirking his duties made William cringe—that had always been his father's inclination, after all—but in this case he simply didn't know what else to do.

It appeared no one else did either. Probably because it was one of those impossible situations where there was nothing to be done, there was no way to change the course they were on.

Yet, at the same time, how could they all continue forward?

William's gaze dropped to the paper in his hands, the desk plans that had spurred this encounter in the first place.

It was as good a subject change as any. William needed a way out of this conversation and he rather thought the boy could use an escape as well.

"You designed the desk?" William asked, holding the paper aloft.

Benedict nodded, the tendons of his neck stretched tight by his clenched jaw.

"It's ingenious." And it was. William had been impressed when he'd thought it was designed by Mr. Leighton. Knowing a mere apprentice—an incredibly young apprentice—had done it, well, he couldn't help but be a bit fascinated.

"Thank you," the boy choked out. He glanced to Mrs. Brightmoor and then back to William. "I like making pieces where all the space is usable and easy to access."

William's grip tightened a bit on the paper as he fought for a way to have some form of control. He avoided personal situations such as these, as they always tended to become messy. He'd rather handle a problem with the marquisette or one of his estates any day. After all, he'd been preparing for those his entire life. But this . . .

"When you've time, we should meet. I've some points of discussion that might require an alteration in the design to make it function better for me."

He felt a bit ridiculous speaking in such a tone to a thirteen-year-old boy, but maybe treating Benedict like a man was the only way forward here. William hadn't felt like a boy at the age of thirteen, having already come face-to-face with his father's lack of regard for anything or anyone other than himself. Perhaps granting the boy some credibility would give him back the dignity that had just been taken from him.

And he did appear as if something had been taken from him. William had seen a similar look on men who suddenly realized their purse had been stolen sometime during the evening and they were going to have to ask someone to pay their tavern account for them. Only this was worse.

It was the look of a man whose purse had been stolen and there was no one he could ask to pay for him.

The boy looked at the paper and nodded, his weight shifting back and forth on his feet as a bit of the tension left his body. "I can do that."

"Excellent."

William wasn't out of the situation yet, though, because they all still stood there. Staring at one another.

Well, William was staring at the other two. Mrs. Brightmoor wasn't staring anywhere but at Benedict, and the boy refused to take his eyes off William. They were just as stuck as they'd been ten minutes ago.

He could simply leave. No one would stop him. But it felt wrong. Maxwell had already turned his back on the boy, knowingly or not, and William couldn't bring himself to do the same.

"We could look at it now," the boy croaked out. He licked his lips and swallowed, but it was obvious the words had come rattling through a mouth dry as dust.

William had to admire Benedict. He could have turned and run and no one would have blamed him. He, too, was seeking the escape that maintained his dignity while still getting him out of this room.

"Right, then," William said slowly, wishing they shared the trait of wanting to be completely alone in the face of emotional turmoil. He glanced at Mrs. Brightmoor but quickly returned his gaze to Benedict. The boy's attempt at stoicism was far easier to manage than the agony in his housekeeper's face. "The library?"

Benedict nodded and preceded William from the room.

The walk to the library seemed much farther than a house of this size could accommodate.

The library was just as silent as the dining room had been, but it was immeasurably more peaceful. William had expected being alone with the boy to be worse. Instead, he felt somewhat of a camaraderie with him. Neither of them had known a confrontation such as this one could occur. Both had been surprised, hit from nowhere by the sense of betrayal and confusion. Somehow, being unified in that stupefaction made it easier to be in the room together, even if looking at him was still more than a little disconcerting.

William glanced at the plans in his hand once more. It was as good a place to begin moving forward as anywhere. He crossed the room and spread the plans out on the desk. "I'd like a place to hold my ledger books. Perhaps somewhere in this vicinity."

Benedict was slow to cross the room, so William stayed braced on the desk, looking down at the paper. He could wait. He even welcomed the few moments to better prepare himself before looking at his own younger face again.

A smooth hand with long, thin fingers came into view. Rough calluses were visible as one finger extended to point to a particular area of the desk. "It would be easy enough to make individual spaces for them. They could be shelves or vertical slots. If you put it in the middle of the upright portion it won't, um, it won't take away the space needed for these side cabinets."

William had initially thought of only two other requests for the desk, but as they talked he found himself coming up with more. Not only because the more the boy talked about furniture the more confident and relaxed he appeared, but because his unique and creative ideas kept spurring more fascinating options until William was ready to have the boy redesign the office at every single estate the marquisette owned.

Eventually there was nothing else to discuss on the desk. As Benedict straightened from the design, a bit of that lost, shattered look crept back across his features.

So William blurted out a request for a new sideboard in the dining room.

Young blue eyes blinked at him for a moment. "A sideboard."

"Yes." William swallowed. Did the boy suspect the request had been born of some sense of guilt or pity? Perhaps it had, but there was no question that William had to replace the furniture in the dining room. Why not give the commission to the boy and Mr. Leighton? They were local, skilled, and a project may be just the thing to help everyone find a way to live with their new knowledge.

"Yes," William said again, a bit firmer. "Have you seen the furniture in there? It's atrocious."

"And heavy," the boy murmured. He then reached for a piece of paper and slid a pencil from his pocket. His hands moved across the paper in sure strokes, sketching the lines of an elegant sideboard and asking William questions that no sane man could answer about something intended to hold cutlery, plates, and food.

William simply murmured in agreement after every suggestion

Benedict made. Honestly, even if the piece turned out unusable, William wouldn't mind paying for it. The image being revealed on the paper, though, was magnificent. A bit much for a small country dining room, perhaps, but magnificent nevertheless.

By the time they shook hands and discussed wood selections for both pieces of furniture, the boy was actually smiling.

Benedict was likely to remember later that he felt gutted, but for now, his life was good, and William felt a bit like a conquering hero for helping him find that peace, if only for a moment.

Daphne paced beside Mr. Leighton's wagon, waiting for her son to emerge from the house. He'd been in the library with Lord Chemsford for almost an hour now. What were they doing? What were they saying? She wanted more than anything to go after Benedict and hold him like she'd done when he was a boy and scraped his knee climbing a tree.

But he wasn't a boy anymore.

And this was far from being as simple as a scraped knee.

Finally, a door banged closed, but it wasn't the servants' entrance into the kitchen that he normally used. He'd come out the back door of the house, out onto the porch overlooking the lake and grounds.

He'd been avoiding her.

Not just her, but everyone in the house. Jess and Eugenia would surely have been in the kitchen, and at this hour, it was possible Sarah or Reuben would have been there as well.

He shuffled around the corner of the house and stopped when he saw her standing there. His gaze met hers for only a moment before sliding away to stare at the ground.

Daphne held her breath, waiting for him to make a move. Would he turn away from her? Choose the long walk back to town instead of coming near her?

Relief made her limp as he finally continued walking toward the wagon. Mr. Leighton had already hitched up the donkey and sat on the simple plank seat. He hadn't said much after Benedict and Lord Chemsford departed the dining room, simply set about packing up his tools for the day.

Daphne had stuck to his side, helping him carry the tools to the wagon, knowing eventually Benedict would seek out the Irishman. She wished she had as much confidence that he would come to her for comfort, but she didn't. If the way he was currently not looking at her was anything to go by, her instincts had been correct.

He said nothing as he climbed into the wagon and sat beside his master. "I appreciate you being willing to stop work a bit early today."

"Sometimes a man just needs to rest his hands so his mind can do the work," Mr. Leighton said softly.

Benedict nodded. "He's commissioned a sideboard as well as the desk. I'll have to do some work in the shop in order to complete those."

"We can hire a man or two to help with the basic labor."

Daphne couldn't take it anymore. She placed a hand on the wagon and leaned a bit into it. "Benedict, are you all right?"

He sighed and looked at her, his eyes flatter and more lifeless than she'd ever seen them. "I'll have to be, won't I? It might take me a day or two, though. I'm not . . ." He ran his hands across his trouser legs and nodded to where she was gripping the wagon. "You might want to step back. I don't want you getting a splinter when the wagon moves forward."

Daphne snatched her hand back and pressed it into her chest. She could give him that day or two. That was a fair request. He'd learned something very difficult today and he wanted to think about it. Whatever pain it caused her was nothing she didn't deserve.

That didn't mean it hurt any less as the wagon rattled away.

CHAPTER SIXTEEN

Three days later, her son still wasn't speaking to her.

Daphne clutched the sheet she'd pulled from the drying line to her chest and buried her face in it. For nearly half of her life, Benedict had been the spot of sunshine in her day. From the moment he first stirred and she felt his presence, he'd made her happy simply by being in her life.

Each morning when she had peered over the edge of his bassinet, he had smiled at her. Every time she'd washed out a scrape or accepted a ragged flower, he'd smiled at her. Over breakfast, or after caring for the animals, or when she handed him a stack of freshly washed linens, he would smile. There hadn't been a day in almost thirteen years her heart hadn't been fed by the joy of the boy she couldn't completely claim.

She'd thought the loss of his daily smiles when he went to work with Mr. Leighton would be the worst thing that could ever happen.

Oh, how wrong she was.

The worst thing was having him here, in the house, and her not receiving those smiles. In fact, since she'd watched him drive away, she'd seen nothing but the back of his head. He didn't stroll through the kitchen to greet her and didn't seek her out when he took a break. She tried to be grateful that he was still working, perhaps more than ever, and that Mr. Leighton hadn't sent him away or confined him to the shop.

But her selfish desire for his joyful smiles limited the thankfulness she was capable of feeling. Her worry for him trampled the rest. She'd thought once he had a day or two he'd come talk to her, but he hadn't. Should she send Jess? One of the other children? Perhaps ask Mr. Leighton if he'd talked to Benedict?

"Mama Daphne?" Sarah asked quietly as she tugged a bit on the fabric being crushed in Daphne's arms. "Shouldn't we be folding that? It will be much harder to press if you keep squashing it."

Daphne looked at the young girl, so like her she could have been Daphne's daughter. Not in appearance, of course, as Sarah resembled a lithe woodland nymph while Daphne had been born with the shorter, stockier build of a good country lass. But they shared many other traits, such as love of music and insistence on seeing the good around them—or, in Daphne's case at least, ignoring the bad.

"Yes." Daphne swallowed and carefully unwrapped her arms from the bundled sheet. "We should fold it."

She forced herself to focus on turning the sheet into a neat square of folded linen and then moved on to the next one.

As they brought the corners together, Daphne cleared her throat and allowed her desperation to know how Benedict was doing drown out her need to not concern the other children. "I don't suppose you've spoken to Benedict today?"

The young girl seemed a bit confused but nodded. "Of course I did. He came in with Mr. Leighton this morning."

So it was only Daphne he was avoiding, then. And, she had to assume, Jess. Her friend would tell her if Benedict had said anything, wouldn't she?

With the last of the sheets lying neatly in the basket, Sarah set about pulling down the smaller lengths of toweling and pillowcases, talking without looking up. "He's been a bit touchy lately. He told me he'd finally met the new owner and asked me why I hadn't warned him." Sarah dropped the towel into the basket and folded her arms around her as she looked up at Daphne, eyebrows drawn close together. "I didn't know what to say, so I told him the truth—that I wasn't sure if he wanted to know where he came from."

Agony swept from Daphne's heart to her toes and out to her fingers. It was almost painful enough to send her to the ground beneath the fluttering strips of linen. "What did he say?"

"That I was right. He didn't want to know. And that if I spent any time and energy wondering about where I came from I should try to forget it. I was better off not knowing."

Daphne's eyes slid closed, trying to block out the pain as easily as she blocked out the sun. What sort of thoughts were going through Benedict's mind? He'd always been confident, so sure of his abilities and what he wanted to do with them. From the first time he'd realized a knife could cut into a piece of wood, he'd been fascinated.

That first wood had been the kitchen worktable, and sometimes Daphne still ran a finger over the gouged-out corner and smiled.

From that point on, simply holding a piece of wood and considering the potential had brought him joy.

Had the confrontation with Lord Chemsford stolen that? Or was it having to face the fact that Daphne knew so much more than she'd ever told him—that she'd deliberately kept him from knowing any of it? Perhaps it was simply having to face the specifics of something he'd only ever known in a vague, general sense.

Whatever it was must be torturing him for him to say what he'd said to Sarah.

"Mama Daphne?" Sarah broke into the fog surrounding Daphne's brain. "Why would he say I was better off not knowing?"

"I suppose," Daphne said through a dry throat, "he meant you shouldn't worry about it. The past isn't what matters, it's the future."

"But you've always told us the past can be the stone that weighs you down or the foundation you build upon."

She did say that. And she meant it. Daphne had built this patchwork family of children on the firm belief that something good could come from her mistake, that God's grace could still pour out on her life and let her do a good work for Him in spite of everything else.

Only now those good works seemed to be falling apart around her.

Had she used up the grace God had given her? Or somewhere along the way had she veered from the path once more and thrown a new stone at her rebuilt life? She had been lying to her son for more than twelve years. Perhaps God was now calling that sin into account.

"Are you sure Lord Chemsford isn't Benedict's father?" Sarah asked with a matter-of-fact lightness Daphne couldn't quite grasp.

"What?"

"I know you said he wasn't and Benedict says the same thing, but . . ." Sarah bit her lip. "If he's truly not, then looking so much alike must be uncomfortable. For both of them."

"I am entirely sure," Daphne rushed to assure her. "He's not Benedict's father."

"Oh." Sarah was quiet for a moment and their folding was accompanied by nothing but rustling breeze and birdsong.

As they piled the laundry into the baskets, though, Sarah said in a small voice, "We wonder, you know? We used to talk about it, back before . . . before those families were found for the younger ones. We'd talk about what we thought our families were like."

How had Daphne not known about this? She'd been surrounded by children for years. She'd slept between their rooms. When had they had such serious discussions? "I didn't know."

Sarah nodded and picked at the edge of the towel still in her hands. "It's natural, isn't it? Because somewhere out there we all had—or have—a mother and a father, but life didn't work out for them. At least, not in a way that would include us. That's why we stayed hidden. Because life hadn't gone the way it was supposed to and we had to grow up a bit and try again from a different point."

Daphne didn't remember saying that to the children, but she supposed at some time she probably had. She'd certainly thought something similar many times. It had been necessary to hide the children and to impress upon them the need for secrecy back when she and Kit were taking care of the children and forcing their parents to pay for their upkeep and disappearance.

In the ways of children who've been told something from birth, they didn't question it for years.

As Benedict and Sarah had gotten older, they'd pressed Daphne for more. Eventually, she'd been forced to share part of the truth—that they were illegitimate and that the world wasn't kind to those born outside of society's expectations.

Of course, once the secret was out, all the children soon knew. Since they'd never known anything different, they'd simply accepted it as normal. But now they weren't as sheltered, weren't as cut off from the world, they would all know that it was anything but normal.

"Did, um, Benedict say anything else?" Had he said anything about Daphne?

Sarah shook her head and hefted one of the baskets onto her hip. "Not really. He said when we'd thought the wondering would be more agonizing than the knowing, we were wrong. He said knowing that someone else knew more about us than we did was worse."

Daphne made a noise in the realm between a grunt, a moan, and some sort of wounded animal dying a slow, painful death in the middle of the woods.

Sarah took it as a sound of agreement. "I suppose that's true. It would feel like a lie, wouldn't it? If someone knew something about you but never told you."

"What if they wanted to protect you?" Daphne choked out.

"At some point, I suppose I'd hope they thought I was strong enough to handle it."

Daphne stopped and set her basket down before she dropped all the clean linen in the dirt. Sarah walked a few paces and then turned around, a question on her face.

"Do you want to know?" Daphne asked the young girl who was so quickly turning into a woman. Soon Sarah would be making her own life.

"No." She smiled at Daphne. "But thank you for letting me decide."

Sarah turned and walked the rest of the way to the house, leaving Daphne standing alone on the lawn. Was that what Benedict was wanting? Was he hoping Daphne would let him decide if he wanted to know where he came from . . . and who his mother was?

She'd made the offer to Sarah, but making it to Benedict was so much more difficult. Because in this case, the answer would only make the situation worse. He would see it as a betrayal. And in a way, he was probably right.

But Daphne couldn't live wishing she'd made other decisions. She couldn't. If she did, she'd spend her entire life imagining a different past and it would become the weight that dragged her to the bottom. She would sink and never come up for air.

So she would look to the future. It wasn't as if today could get much worse.

"I'm expecting guests this afternoon."

Daphne clutched the freshly ironed sheet to her chest, filling it with wrinkles once more.

The day had just gotten worse.

Of all the reasons Lord Chemsford could have summoned her to the library, this was not on the list of things she'd expected.

He narrowed his gaze at her. "You are familiar with the concept of guests, are you not?"

"Of course I understand the concept," she bit out. "But I don't understand how you could bring them here while the place is a shambles."

It wasn't truly a shambles, but in addition to Benedict and Mr. Leighton, a crew had arrived that morning to begin work on the roof and garret rooms. Surely that, combined with how horribly out of date the house was, would be enough to discourage him from having visitors. It didn't matter that people of his class were accustomed to ignoring the staff, they still expected a certain level of comfort.

They still interacted with the housekeeper.

She couldn't face his guests. She had to convince him the last thing he wanted to do was entertain.

"I'm not entertaining."

Daphne blinked. She hadn't spoken out loud, had she? No, his entertaining guests was just a common expectation. He was simply drawing the correct conclusions. She hadn't blurted out something ridiculous and uncomfortable.

Again.

The marquis continued, "We've plenty of usable bedchambers upstairs, and the library is in entirely adequate condition to discuss business matters. I don't think they'll be here more than two days at the most."

Daphne blinked as surprise and the slight hope of relief flooded her. Businessmen wouldn't care about the housekeeper as long as food was plentiful. "Two days? That seems a rather short trip."

He shrugged. "They're free to stay in Marlborough if they wish to extend their sojourn in the country, but my business with them shouldn't take more than a day or so. The house is hardly in the condition for an extended visit."

Words formed on her tongue, but she managed to stop herself before uttering them. She'd acted without thought in her attempts to keep him and Benedict away from each other, and look where that had gotten her. Did she dare make a suggestion? Yes. Yes, she did. Because even though the secret was out and Benedict's parentage, or at least his paternal pedigree, had been revealed, no one in the house was any more relaxed than they'd been before.

If anything, the tension was worse.

What they needed was time and space away from each other. Of course, Daphne always felt better when she was away from people she didn't know well, but it stood to reason they could all do without a daily reminder of that difficult discussion.

Of course, she wouldn't be reminded of it so often if she didn't lurk around corners, watching both the marquis and Benedict to see if either of them did anything with their new knowledge.

She took a deep breath and plunged on. "Why don't you simply go to them, my lord? Wouldn't that be easier?"

He sighed and rolled his shoulders, looking oddly vulnerable for a man with no one to really answer to. "There are benefits to being a marquis, Mrs. Brightmoor. Aside from the many laborious obligations that come along with the title, I don't have to do anything I don't want to do. That includes travel. As you'll soon learn, I like to be home."

She swallowed. Her father had been a gentleman, a man of considerably lower class than the man who sat before her, and yet there'd been a steady stream of other gentlemen through his study. If Lord Chemsford stayed here . . . How many more people did a marquis have dealings with? How many people were about to invade her quiet, secluded life? "So we're to expect a great deal of these occasional guests, then?"

He picked up a pile of papers from the corner of his desk. "I suppose. I find it easier to do business in my own home." He glanced at one of the papers, a personal letter by the look of it, and frowned. "It's not a great concern to you. Men with business on their minds don't tend to require many amusements. A healthy negotiation and spirited discussion during the day, a good book and a brandy in the evenings. You'll need to provide nothing but aired-out chambers and a bit more food."

"Right, then." Daphne swallowed hard and wiped her hands on her skirt, her callused fingers scraping against fabric soft from an abundance of washings.

Please, God, do not let any of the men coming now or ever know who I am. It was unlikely, even if she knew them, that they would remember her. People hadn't tended to remember her when she was standing in the same room.

He'd said they were men of business. As long as that was all it was, she would be able to manage.

"I don't expect any of my family."

She blinked. No, she hadn't spoken out loud this time either. He was simply reading her mind. "Oh."

"That's not something I would normally tell you, as it truly isn't a concern my housekeeper should have, but—" he sighed and pointed at the paper he'd recently been frowning at—"the fact that my cousin is trying to get himself in my good graces in exchange for use of some of the properties in my care brings to mind the fact that this is not exactly a normal situation."

He ran a hand along the edge of the desk as he looked from the letter up to Daphne. "Should Maxwell become persistent in his intentions to renew our childhood closeness, I will be sure to make arrangements for Benedict to be elsewhere first."

Daphne nodded, knowing she should be grateful for the concession, but the fact that Maxwell Oswald coming here was even a mere possibility was going to give her nightmares.

Not that it really mattered if he saw her. He didn't know her, would have no reason to remember her. She'd been wearing a mask and costume that night and pretending to be Kit. There was no danger for her.

Just a great deal of remembered shame.

"Have Mr. Pasley prepare the stable. They'll be arriving by carriage." Lord Chemsford turned his attention to an open ledger, effectively dismissing her, but his thumb tapped against the edge of the book and his gaze didn't move across the page.

Not that his idleness was Daphne's concern, of course. He was a marquis. He could stare at dust drifting in a sunbeam if he wanted to.

She, however, had a house to prepare. Already sweat had pooled at the small of her back, making her dress stick to her skin. Working for someone else was so much more difficult and irksome than she'd expected. When there'd been a dozen children under the roof along with Daphne, Kit, and Jess, it had seemed like there were always linens to change, wash, or fold. Her current workload was less than half of what it used to be, but it felt ten times more tedious.

But the lord of the manor had expressed his wishes and, for at least the time being, she and Sarah had no choice but to see them through. She couldn't even pull Eugenia in to help. Between his lordship, his guests, and the household staff, both Jess and Eugenia were going to be working hard on the meal preparation.

She turned and took a step toward the door.

"Mrs. Brightmoor."

His low voice brought her to a halt as effectively as a shout. He continued speaking before she could turn back around, though.

"Perhaps, in the interest of concentration, it would be best if the construction on the house paused while the men are here."

Conflicted emotions rolled through Daphne. Was he ashamed of Benedict or merely trying to protect him?

Did it matter?

"Of course," she said softly and left the room.

Sarah and Daphne rushed to prepare the bedchambers. They didn't even know how many men were coming, or if they were bringing servants or other staff with them. Just in case, Daphne set about preparing every possible bed.

Then she walked through every room, making sure each one was ready for the guests of a marquis. In the upstairs sitting room that had once been her bedroom, she paused to lean against the frame of the open window and try to catch her breath. The peaceful birdsong she'd enjoyed so often was broken by the sound of a carriage coming through the trees at the front edge of the property.

She and Sarah had finished preparing the rooms none too soon it would seem.

"Time to go downstairs," Daphne said to Sarah, pushing away from the window and tucking the dustrag she'd been using into the pocket of her apron. "Since we're light on footmen, we'll have to see to escorting the guests ourselves."

It would have been nice to change, since her wrinkled apron and wilted dress hardly made the best first impression, but there was nothing Daphne could do about it now. Morris sneered at her, looking her clothing up and down when she entered the front hall a few moments after he did. Daphne simply squared her shoulders and stuck her nose up a bit more in response.

She refused to be ashamed of hard work, especially work that had been dumped on her with little notice. What had Morris been required to do in preparation? Press another neckcloth?

Daphne waited just inside the front hall, near the door that led to the central hall and the two grand staircases. Sarah stood behind her, squaring her little twelve-year-old shoulders in an attempt at mimicking Daphne's stance.

There should be some encouragement in the young girl's faith and imitation, but Daphne could only think about the fact that more unknown people were about to invade her broken sanctuary. Not to mention the fact that this was her first true test as housekeeper. Sarah was destined for a life of service, and if she was going to succeed, Daphne needed to get this right.

Everything was as ready as she could make it. Now all she needed was for the men who walked through that door to be ones she'd never laid eyes on.

CHAPTER SEVENTEEN

William had never had the desire to be eccentric or be thought of as anything other than noble and honorable. If he were going to shock society, he'd rather do it by taking the marquisette in a visionary new direction than with a strange household or a tactless demeanor. He didn't want anyone talking about him at all, really, unless it was to say what an amazingly distinguished contrast he made to his philandering father.

Accomplishing such a distinction, though, required conforming to every societal norm. For the past ten years he'd distanced himself from all but a small group of people who valued intellectual discourse and a quiet dinner over balls and operas.

He liked his quiet life, where he could breathe without some beady-eyed matron watching for the first sign that he intended to act like his father or make waves like his mother. But he couldn't achieve his goals in such isolation.

Having two rankless businessmen about to walk through William's door felt like the first step back toward the world he'd been all too happy to leave behind.

The clatter of horse hooves broke the silence, and William left the library to greet his guests in the front hall. A sigh built up in his chest as he looked about the room, but he didn't release it. It would seem he was destined to look at least a little eccentric.

His valet, whom he'd pressed into service as a temporary butler as well, stood ready at the door. Mrs. Brightmoor stood meekly on the side, and William hoped she was prepared to show the gentlemen to their rooms. She chewed her lips and generally resembled a skittish horse ready to bolt for the barn.

He really should do something about his housekeeper.

Dismissing her came to mind once more, but he rejected the thought just as quickly. With all that had transpired over the past few days, he couldn't simply dismiss her on a whim.

The revelation of Benedict's existence had provided as many questions as it had answers, perhaps even more. Curiosity plagued William. Thirty minutes where he could ask Mrs. Brightmoor any question he wanted and be assured of an honest answer would go a long way toward clearing his mind.

He wasn't likely to get that, though, and it was another reason not to dismiss her out of hand. He'd wonder about it the rest of his life if he made her leave.

Morris swung the door open as the scuff of boots on gravel gave way to the tap of shoes on the stone of the front steps.

Mrs. Brightmoor sank further into the woodwork. She actually managed to blend her faded orange printed muslin partially into the glaringly red wallpaper. It was a rather amazing feat.

This would be a good test for her, as the men, though utterly respectable gentlemen, were of little importance in English society. They were of great importance to William, however, as what the men had managed to do was pool their limited resources into an exceptionally well-producing modern manufactory in Manchester. He'd invited them here to learn how they'd done it.

Technology was the future, and William had a desire to expand and modernize manufacturing on his own lands. He refused to let the marquisette drown while he was at the helm.

The two men strode in with confidence, easing William's trepidations. He wanted solid knowledge and advice, not pandering and attempts to tell him what they thought he wanted to hear. By all appearances, these two men knew they possessed a certain amount of expertise.

William appreciated confidence.

"Good afternoon, Mr. Gherkins." He then shook the taller man's hand. "Mr. Blakemoor."

After William had greeted each man, he glanced toward Mrs. Brightmoor, but she was nowhere to be found. Suddenly the parlor maid, Sarah, stumbled into the room as if she'd been pushed through the doorway. Her eyes were enormous in her pointed elfin face. She blinked rapidly before executing an awkward curtsy.

William cleared his throat. Another mystery was not what he needed just then. "Gentlemen, my, er, maid will see you up to your rooms, and I'll have your bags sent up directly."

He kept his smile in place until the men disappeared into the inner chamber to climb the stairs, then he ran a frustrated hand across his chin.

He really was going to have to do something about his housekeeper.

Daphne tripped over nothing and almost went sprawling across the smooth marble floor of the tall central hall.

Breath rattled in and out of her lungs so quickly her lips were beginning to tingle. If she could, she'd have reached into her chest and smashed her heart flat so it couldn't pound against her ribs anymore. She could actually feel the blood pulse through her brain, hear it crackle in her ears, so hard and loud she could barely think.

And right now she really, really needed to think.

Her father was here.

Here.

In this house.

Where she'd lived for the past twelve years without the knowledge of the owner. Where she'd raised her child and many others whose very existence he would find reprehensible.

Where she now worked as a lowly housekeeper.

And she'd thought having total strangers invade what had once been her home was the worst that was going to happen today.

Having someone she knew walk through those doors was ever so much worse.

She darted through the strange little sitting room full of glass and into the music room. Simply pacing around the large grand piano grounded her a bit, helped her breathe.

The clicks and taps she could hear over her pulse were probably footsteps echoing through the front hall as her father and a man she hadn't recognized—nor really taken much time to look at—presumably followed Sarah up the stairs.

It hadn't been well done of Daphne to shove Sarah into the room to handle the hostess duties. Were they hostess duties? They were housekeeper duties. It was dangerous to start thinking of herself as the hostess of anything.

The Marquis of Chemsford was not about to elevate her status above that of servant, and she would do well to remember it.

Not even when she'd circulated on the fringes of London's upper crust had she entertained visions of becoming titled. Imagining herself a marchioness now was beyond ludicrous.

How nice would it be, though? To greet her father from a position of power, having risen from the ashes of her past? Perhaps his eyes would fill with admiration and even a bit of regret. Maybe he would grab her hand and beg her forgiveness, ask her to come home for a visit, express a desire to meet Benedict and then greet him with the love and care of family.

She would, of course, grant all of those wishes. Forgiveness had been granted him long ago. Daphne understood the choices he'd made. What good did it do for both of them to sink into poverty and despair? Besides, look how far she'd come. She was sitting on top of the world now. Even though Lord Chemsford was rather reclusive, no one in London would dare to shun his wife.

Daphne blinked and pinched herself hard on the arm. She was *not* the man's wife. She hardly even knew him—was still not sure if she even liked him.

Her imagination was the last thing that could help her right now. Reality was crashing in. She had nothing to show her father beyond her ability to manage to survive without him. That was hardly going to earn his admiration.

She forced slow, deep breaths into her body, and the roar of blood in her ears receded enough that she could make out other footsteps. These weren't going in the direction of the grand staircase, though. They were coming through the glass sitting room toward the music room.

Toward her.

And since Mr. Morris had yet to show an inclination for the pianoforte, she could only assume it was Lord Chemsford, come to see why she'd suddenly disappeared.

She couldn't face him. Not right now. Not until she decided what to do about her father.

Daphne abandoned the pianoforte, dragging her hand across the surface in a bit of longing as she went. This was not the time to linger over what she missed, not with her past threatening to swallow her whole.

She scurried into the short passage off the music room and into the grand portrait gallery. Probably not her best choice of direction, as she was now well and truly trapped. The only way in or out of the portrait gallery was the passage to the music room.

Unless she dropped out of one of the windows.

It wasn't far, at least not far enough to cause any damage other than a few bumps and bruises. Right now, that was a more-than-acceptable price to pay for a few moments of solitude.

There was no time to consider the prudence of such an idea. She went to the farthest window and shoved open the sash. Well, she tried to. The windows in this room hadn't been opened in ages, since the children had only used this room if the weather outside was poor.

With considerable effort, she managed to wedge the window open enough to duck through. She pulled her skirt up a bit and hiked one leg over the window ledge before sitting on it and folding over to duck her head through.

"Are we going to pretend this is a new method for washing

windows, or can we simply skip that part and go straight to you telling me why you are running away from my guests?"

Daphne froze, bent in half, straddling a windowsill, skirt pulled up in such a way that she had to be showing an extremely indecent amount of leg.

She could do it. Roll right on over and continue her escape. But where would she go? The cottage? The kitchens? Maybe she should just keep walking until she reached Marlborough and find some way to start over completely. That was the inevitable outcome once he learned her true identity. At least if she went on her own she could fool herself into thinking it was by choice and not another personal failure.

This time, though, there would be no Kit to help her out.

Kit had wanted to stay after her marriage, wanted to be here for Daphne as the house transitioned from a haven to a proper estate, but Daphne had insisted that was no way for her friend to start her new marriage. She'd sent Kit away on her wedding trip, assuring her everything would be fine. What could Daphne possibly do to cause a problem out in the middle of nowhere? Haven Manor was her home and she could handle anything that happened there.

She'd been wrong.

So very, very wrong.

Daphne folded her hands onto the wood in front of her, dropped her forehead on top of them, and cried. They weren't noisy tears, as Daphne didn't do noisy weeping and sobbing, so to anyone looking—or rather, to Lord Chemsford, since he was the only one in the room—she probably looked like a collapsed marionette or a forgotten doll. Her shoulders didn't even shake much. Daphne was capable of crying a bucketful of tears with three children snugged into a bed around her and not disturbing a single soul.

It was a strange talent, but one of the few she could claim with confidence. It helped that she didn't cry often. She was usually capable of seeing the positives in an awfully bad situation. When she got to the point of tears it was nigh on hopeless.

Just like now.

Lord Chemsford was going to kick her out.

She'd be left to scramble for work. She might even have to leave Marlborough to find it.

She would never see Benedict again.

Kit wouldn't know where to find her when she returned from her wedding trip.

Jess would leave, and Sarah and Reuben and Eugenia would end up in the poorhouse.

The tears came faster, pooling against her fingers and running down them to drip onto the floor.

Something soft fluttered against her cheek.

Daphne slowly lifted her head enough to see what it was, only to find a snow-white handkerchief dangling in front of her. It was held in masculine fingers attached to a silent and serious-looking marquis.

She turned her hand over and accepted the cloth. "Thank you," she murmured.

He nodded his acknowledgment but said nothing as she dabbed at her eyes to dry them. There would be a bit of red around the edges, but if she didn't scrub at her face, that should be the only evidence. The trick to crying silently was to let the tears flow freely. Usually once a tear or two escaped the urge to cry faded, but as long as she didn't try to stop it she could usually avoid the unpleasantness of sniffles and hiccups.

Face dry, she crumpled the fabric in her fist and prepared to face her fate.

Then she promptly smacked her head against the window frame as she tried to sit up. Her instinctive jerk sent her tumbling from her precarious perch onto the floor below. While she should probably be thankful she'd tumbled into the room instead of out into the hedges, the embarrassment of showing the marquis a great deal more leg than she already had sent the redness she'd been trying to avoid surging across her face. Jess could cook dinner on Daphne's cheeks.

She pushed her way to her feet and shoved her chin into the air, trying to claim any possible remnants of her dignity.

Lord Chemsford wasn't looking at her, though. He was staring out her recently vacated window, giving her time to right herself after her spill.

That was rather nice of him, actually. All things considered, it was more than she had expected.

"I'm presentable now." At least, her skirts were in order. Her face still flamed, and her voice sounded as if someone had shoved wool down her throat, but neither of those were going away any time soon.

He turned toward her, the stern, chiseled lines of his face betraying nothing of what he was thinking but all of the power he was accustomed to wielding. "Would you care to explain now?"

Oh, this man. Was it any wonder she'd woven dreams around him? How many other men of his station would even wait to hear a servant's story before dismissing them?

Daphne had never been much of a liar, so her choices right now were to either stay silent or spill the truth. Neither was going to make her look very good.

But one would at least make her look strong.

She cleared her throat. "I know—that is, I knew—one of your guests, and I'm afraid I wasn't quite ready for him to see me."

Perhaps she wasn't quite as ready to be honest as she'd thought.

"Which guest?"

"Mr. Blakemoor," she whispered.

How it hurt to call him that. He'd been *Papa* to her while growing up. It'd been just the two of them. *"A pair of aces against the world,"* he'd said. Until she wasn't an ace anymore.

"How do you know him?"

She took a deep breath and closed her eyes, unwilling to watch what little respect Lord Chemsford had for her die. "He's my father."

CHAPTER EIGHTEEN

So many thoughts crashed into William's brain that focusing on any one observation was a struggle.

Mrs. Brightmoor had been born a Blakemoor and she was willing to jump out of a window to escape seeing her own father.

Even putting that single truth at the front of his mind didn't make everything make sense. How did the daughter of a gentleman end up a housekeeper in the middle of the woods?

She was very young to be a widow, but then again, if she'd been working here as long as Mr. Banfield had said, she hadn't been married.

So Brightmoor was a false name. And not a very good one at that.

He ran a hand along his chin as he watched her. Dark lashes lowered over brown eyes until her gaze was glued to the floor.

Once again, gaining a few answers inspired a number of new questions. The man currently settling in to one of William's guest rooms wasn't the highest class of citizen, but he was more than respectable. He socialized, owned property, and was well liked. While William hadn't been circulating amongst the London clubs and drawing rooms, he hadn't been a complete hermit. Businessmen occasionally indulged in as much gossip as the dandies did, and there'd never been a whisper of scandal about Blakemoor.

How did he have his daughter hidden away as a servant?

Why did he have his daughter hidden away as a servant?

Or did he?

"Is he aware of your current employment?" William asked and then felt like a fool. Of course he wasn't aware. If he was, she wouldn't have been climbing through a window.

But his housekeeper merely shook her head and frowned, pulling her brows together until a groove formed between them, making her nose and mouth look like something of an arrow. "He isn't even aware I live in Wiltshire."

"Where does he think you live?"

A brief shudder of her shoulders preceded the clearing of emotion from her face. He hadn't thought her capable of such a thing. She was always so . . . alive. Everything played across the plane of her face, making it easy to know when he'd perturbed her or worried her. Or, as was more often the case, when she was trying to think of a plan to get him to do something.

But now there was nothing. It was blank.

He rolled his shoulders to adjust the fit of his coat. The blankness was so far removed from what he'd come to expect that it disturbed him.

Her voice was toneless as well. "I don't think he much cares."

Perhaps her face wasn't devoid of emotion. Perhaps blank was simply what pain looked like.

There was information he needed to know, questions he should ask. But the only fragment he could form into a complete thought was that she wasn't who he thought her to be. Everyone in his life had always been and done exactly what he expected.

Until he'd moved here.

What was he going to do? He had guests upstairs who he couldn't exactly kick out. Even if he didn't need their factory knowledge and expertise, he couldn't send them on their way without a good reason.

He also couldn't have a housekeeper climbing out windows or trying to blend into the wallpaper.

But now, even more than before, he couldn't find it in him to lay down an ultimatum and kick *her* out either. Until this moment she'd been a curiosity and a bit of a trial. He'd spent a great deal of time dissecting her movements, but he'd never delved into her motivations. He'd never asked himself *why*.

He'd never truly considered her a person. She'd simply been his housekeeper.

Now she was standing before him with the posture of a lady, despite gripping his handkerchief with all the strength she could muster. Had she always stood with perfect posture and straight shoulders? Had he simply not noticed because he thought her born and raised without the benefit of proper polite instruction?

If he'd barely been able to come to terms with what to do with her before, what was going to happen now that she had wriggled her way out of the box he'd put her in? Granted, it was a box she'd never fit in perfectly, but now he didn't know what to think of her. She was his housekeeper but also a socially acceptable companion. Did he need a chaperon?

The mystery that was his housekeeper grew until he didn't even know where to start unraveling it.

She jabbed the crumpled handkerchief at her eyes one more time and took a deep breath that hissed a bit as it passed through her teeth. "I suppose you'll be wanting me to go now."

He wanted to say yes—he should say yes—but everything in him rebelled at the idea. If she'd had nowhere to go as a country maid, how much fewer were her options as a gentleman's daughter if she'd ended up here in the first place?

"I hardly think that necessary," he replied.

"You . . . you don't?"

"No." Peace flooded him as soon as he confirmed she could stay. "Between Morris and, er, Cook, and the other maid, we should be able to manage anything public. You can still perform your other duties, I assume, as long as you don't encounter your father?"

This was ludicrous, despite the calm within him that assured him it was the right thing to do. If his father could see him from beyond the grave he'd be yelling about how William was besmirching the title and family by going out of his way for a mere servant. The late marquis would have dismissed the entire household before allowing one of them to alter his path. William had handled most of the decisions in his adult life by asking himself what his father would do and then choosing the opposite. It had done him well so far.

Which meant this was possibly an excellent idea.

"You would do that for me?" Her voice was small and her face was no longer blank. It seemed to shine from within.

He frowned. "No. I'm doing it for me. If I dismiss you I'll have to give Morris a dustrag." While he trusted he was making the correct choice, he still didn't trust her, and the hope and gratefulness shining from her face made him uncomfortable. "I have one condition, though."

Her returning nod was quick and the hair that had been knocked askew by her tumble from the window bobbed around her head. "Absolutely."

William pressed his lips together. He was finished with stumbling across surprises, having to guess what was going to happen next in his own home. "When I ask questions, you will answer them. No distractions, no half-truths, no lies."

She bit her lip but nodded again. Since she'd proven to be a rather obvious liar, he had to assume she meant to honor this agreement.

He folded his hands at the small of his back and stood up straight, trying to treat this as he would any other sort of business interview, even though the questions were going to be extremely personal.

"Why doesn't your father know where you live?" On this he hoped—no, expected—there to be a reasonable explanation. Af
all, William's father hadn't known where he'd lived and that s
tion had been by William's choice, for the sake of his sanity
the means to provide a life for himself away from his fath

It would appear that Daphne did not.

"I . . ." She paused and straightened her already
to match his. "I left London many years ago."

"How many?" *Bosh!* This was going to be li

"Fourteen."

"But you couldn't have been more than a child then."

She winced. "I was eighteen."

He did a bit of quick arithmetic. Then did it again. She couldn't possibly be two-and-thirty. At that age, she could indeed have been married and widowed before coming to work here. But then, she'd said she'd raised Benedict. How did he . . . Oh.

"Brightmoor is a false name," she continued. "It's not a very good one, I'll admit, but it was all I could think of when you showed up at the door."

William nodded, though he was barely listening now that he had a new angle to scrutinize.

For days, he'd been thinking about Benedict, considering ways he could rectify his cousin's abandonment. Not once, he was ashamed to admit, had he considered the fact that Maxwell also would have abandoned the boy's mother. He had to have. He'd married Miss Charlotte Rhinehold fourteen years ago, and the woman certainly hadn't been with child at the time. In fact, it had taken them three years to have a daughter.

But William was right about this. It was the only thing that made sense. The timing, the protectiveness, the desire to hide, the loss of family connections, the genteel manners that were more than he'd expected but never completely formed enough to make him reconsider her background.

He was right. He had to be. But he needed her to confirm it.

"Benedict," he said softly. "You ran because of Benedict."

The sudden loss of color in her face was almost enough to verify his guess.

"How did you . . ." She swallowed convulsively, her eyes wide in her round face.

"The timing fits, as does the situation." There had to be more to the story, though. Benedict wasn't the only child working under his roof. What about his maids? Was his cook a lady of good breeding who'd run into precarious circumstances, too? If so, which one was hers? Were any of the others Daphne's as well?

Normally William loved questions. He could lose himself to books and research for days on end until he found the answers he sought without having to subject himself to more human contact than necessary.

But unless Daphne kept a very detailed diary she'd be willing to hand over, these answers weren't going to be found in a book.

He'd been right not to dismiss her a few days ago, and he could thank the Lord he'd listened when instinct told him not to. His family had done this to her—had sent her here. He'd never be able to ask her to leave.

"I need to know everything. Now." His voice was a bit gruffer than he'd intended it to be.

Her chin lifted. "You're not entitled to anything."

"Mrs. Bright—I say, what is your name? Is it still Miss Blakemoor?"

"I just told you it was. But I'd rather you call me Daphne or continue to use Mrs. Brightmoor."

One side of his mouth slid up in a smile despite his current irritation. "You're right. That's not a very good fake name."

"I'm afraid I'm not very good at thinking on my feet in the moment. The decision to use a false name was made rather quickly."

"It was a wise decision." She looked surprised by his praise, but at least it brought a bit of color back into her face. "Very well, then, Daphne." Her name felt strange in his mouth. Never before had he called a woman by her given name. "There are a great many things that don't add up about you, but one thing is now clear: My cousin wronged you. I have an obligation as a gentleman and the head of the Oswald family to rectify that."

"Fourteen years is a long time." Her voice was a bit stronger, a little steadier than it had been before. "It's impossible to know where my life would have gone if we'd never . . . if I'd never met him." She folded her hands primly in front of her once more. "It is, as they say, 'a day after the fair.' There's nothing you can do now. If you help Benedict, maybe sponsor a shop for him after his apprenticeship is complete, that will be enough. That will be more than enough."

"Spoken like a mother," William said softly, clenching his hands together to resist the urge to reach out and offer her some form of comfort. "I assume he doesn't know."

"No. I beg of you, don't tell him. Whatever you ask, I'll do, I'll even leave, just . . . don't let him know I've lied to him all these years."

"Why?" William wasn't in the habit of holding people to foolish emotional pleas—most likely because he wasn't accustomed to being on the receiving end of them—but in this case, he wanted to press whatever advantage he had. She might never be this vulnerable again. "Why would you let him think he wasn't wanted?"

She was quiet for a few moments, and he expected her to quiver and cry her way through whatever answer finally emerged, but she didn't. She spoke confidently when she said, "Because if he knew, then when the time and opportunity came for him to make his own life, he'd have refused to leave me behind."

William rather thought the boy loved her enough not to leave her anyway, but he didn't have time to delve into the topic now. "Very well. We'll say nothing for now. As soon as my guests are gone, though, I want the story. All of it. Nothing left out, nothing skipped over. Then I will decide what to do."

How was William possibly going to behave normally for the next two days?

He had no intention of entertaining the gentlemen, but having children serve their dinner at the ornate, ostentatious table and the decided lack of any mention of a housekeeper or butler made the entire interaction a bit strange. He sat at the table now, trying to pretend there was nothing odd about a young girl in a clean but rather worn-out dress delivering a bowl of soup to the table.

The surface she set it upon gleamed, and William had to admit that Daphne had been holding up her end of the bargain. He wouldn't have thought it possible, but the house seemed even cleaner than it had been before.

Mr. Blakemoor and Mr. Gherkins sat in their respective places in the spired, throne-like chairs, polite smiles on their faces. They probably thought the table as hideous as he did, but they'd never say anything. Despite the fact that he'd invited them here and they held the knowledge he desired, all of the people in the room were aware of who actually held the power.

It would be a lie for William to say he didn't like being in the position of power, but mostly because it did the work of keeping people at arm's length for him. Right then he wished the barrier were a little thinner. He wanted to know more about Mr. Blakemoor personally, not just his wild success with manufactories.

Perhaps he could narrow the divide just a bit.

"Do take care when rising from the table," he said with a crooked grin. "The gargoyles have been known to bite."

"What?" Mr. Blakemoor looked down at one of the potentially offending creatures. "Oh, yes. Of course. Do they, er, bite you often?"

William nodded as he tucked into the food. "The monstrosity came with the house, I'm afraid. I haven't yet had a chance to commission a new one."

"Thomas Sheraton's latest catalog has some fine pieces, all free of gargoyles." Mr. Blakemoor grinned as he ate.

"I considered that," William said, "but I've decided to commission a piece from one of the local cabinetmakers. He has a promising young apprentice. I'm considering investing in the lad's career."

"Quite good of you," Mr. Gherkins said, "even if it means you're dodging gargoyles in the meantime."

So far, so good. William took another bite and swallowed before pushing the conversation on. He needed to learn the character of a man who would let his daughter slink away in shame after an encounter with a marquis's nephew. It didn't seem to fit, given that Mr. Blakemoor appeared to be the sort of man who would express a suggestion without hearing the opinion of the higher-ranking man first. That showed a strength of character William hadn't expected.

Unless the situation hadn't happened the way William was assuming it had. He really needed to find time to sit Daphne down for that uninterrupted talk.

"I trust your journey was pleasant," William said as he cut into the roasted beef.

"Of course," Mr. Blakemoor said. "'Tis an easy ride to Marlborough, after all, though a bit of an adventure to get to your home."

Mr. Gherkins nodded and laughed. "I was beginning to wonder if we were being hoodwinked somehow."

"I am in the process of restoring the estate. I'm afraid we've a long way to go, though, particularly on the grounds."

Conversation continued in idle politeness for several minutes. Eventually the men began sharing the basics of their business strategy. The first course was removed and another took its place. Still the conversation delved into nothing personal.

On a normal day, such a course of events would be a cause for rejoicing. Today William found it frustrating.

"Have you family, Mr. Gherkins?" William asked, the words sounding strange in his voice. He'd never been the one to turn a conversation personal and certainly had never asked about family since he didn't want any similar questions aimed back in his direction. Still, he pressed on. "A son, perhaps, whom you intend to groom for your business?"

A strange glance passed between the two men. William tilted his head so he could more easily see Mr. Blakemoor's expression while Mr. Gherkins answered.

"Yes, I've a son. Two sons, actually. They're a bit young to be involved in the dealings of business just yet, but one day I hope they'll take it over." Mr. Gherkins smiled with a hint of pride.

Unexpected jealousy spiked through William. Had his father ever worn such an expression when speaking of his eldest son? He never had in William's presence. Edmond's presence, yes. His second son could do nothing that wasn't excellent, according to the late marquis. Part of William knew it had nothing to do with either boy and was simply an extension of the man's regard, or disregard, for their respective mothers. Still, it was disconcerting to know his father had never been happy that William would one day take his place.

This wasn't about his father, though. It was about Daphne's.

He swung his gaze over to the man in question. "And you, Mr. Blakemoor? Do you have children who intend to partner with Mr. Gherkins's sons one day?"

The man coughed and became overly interested in the food on his plate. "I'm afraid my wife died many years ago. We were never blessed with any"—cough—"sons. I live near to Mr. Gherkins. Just across the lane, actually. I'll be happy to leave my workings to those young men."

William wanted to ask about daughters, but he didn't. Men hardly discussed daughters at the best of times, unless marriage was on the table. If not for Daphne he'd have never considered asking about daughters. Probably wouldn't have even asked about children. To continue this line of conversation would only make the men wary.

Daphne had promised to tell William everything. He was going to have to be patient.

As the second course was cleared and an artful pudding set before each man, William drove the conversation toward the more comfortable topic of business. If only he could stop wondering what Daphne was doing, he'd be fine.

CHAPTER NINETEEN

"I could put a bit of foxglove in your father's breakfast," Jess murmured as she arranged her laundered clothing in the wardrobe that evening.

Daphne sighed as she ran a brush through her hair. "There's no call for that."

"Not enough to kill him," Jess said as if that had been Daphne's issue, or something she'd even considered. "Just enough to make him rather ill for a while."

It was times like these Daphne had to remind herself that Jess had lived a very different life, and such a suggestion wasn't an indication that the person was bound for Bedlam. She shook her head, left the brush on the dressing table, and wandered over to the window. "If he gets ill, then he'd have to stay longer. I'd rather he see to his business and leave."

"Your father is the taller of the two, isn't he? I never met him when I worked in London."

"Yes." Daphne turned away from the window, a small smile tugging at one corner of her mouth. "But you still aren't poisoning his breakfast."

Jess shrugged but promised nothing.

Daphne had never pried too much into Jess's past. Having her own secrets tended to make her a bit more respectful of the secrets others might be holding. Jess knew most of Daphne's past, of course, since it was the motivation for caring for a dozen illegitimate children. Perhaps now, with Daphne's past so blatantly exposed, Jess would be willing to discuss hers. "You worked for a duke, didn't you? You'd have hardly encountered my father there."

Jess wouldn't meet Daphne's eyes as she arranged the bedcovers. "That's an untrue statement given he's currently the guest of a marquis, but yes, I was the parlor maid for a duke."

"Were you spying on the duke?" Daphne dropped onto the bed, halting Jess's progress with the blankets. She grinned up at the small, delicate blonde. One fact Daphne did know about Jess was that, at one point, despite the slight French lilt that occasionally slipped into her speech, she had worked as a spy for the Crown.

A slight, crooked grin formed on Jess's face. "No. But I did report on his aunt and cousin for a while."

Daphne opened her mouth to ask more, but Jess spoke first. "Are you going to talk to him?"

A click sounded through the room as Daphne clamped her mouth shut hard enough to bang her teeth together. She understood Jess's refusal to discuss her past because Daphne was just as adamant that her father not be a topic of discussion either.

Except she'd promised the marquis they would talk about him, and she hadn't yet come up with a way out of that.

Still, for tonight, she could put it off. She dropped her gaze and cleared her throat. "The marquis? Of course I'll talk to him. I'm his housekeeper, after all."

"And he has questions you have to answer."

Daphne winced. "Yes. Hopefully I can avoid telling him any more than absolutely necessary. I'm not the best prevaricator, though. I wonder if he'd accept hearing the story from you."

Jess snorted and flicked the corner of her blanket so it whacked Daphne in the ear. "Are you going to talk to your father?"

"There's no reason I should."

Daphne picked at a loose thread on her night rail. She didn't like going back in time, thinking about what she'd done, what her father had done. She didn't like remembering what a fool she'd been. Imagining life had gone differently was nearly impossible because she couldn't wish Benedict out of existence. She couldn't picture gaining any amount of health and happiness for herself at the expense of all the children she'd raised or the women she'd helped.

That was the beauty of fantasizing about the future. She could change things, make things good, pretend there was still something good ahead for her.

"Your father might regret sending you away," Jess said, oblivious to Daphne's mental slide into dark despair. "You never gave him a way to contact you."

"I did, actually," Daphne said, her voice calmer than she'd thought it would be. She'd never admitted this, not even to Kit. "On Benedict's first birthday. We'd just taken in Sarah's mother. I was so excited for the future and what Kit and I were going to do. I looked down into Ben's face and I felt, for the first time ever, that I was right where I was supposed to be, that I was capable of doing what was in front of me."

It was a task she no longer had. There would be no more children to raise or women to save in Daphne's future. Soon she would lose the one thing that made her feel useful to God.

Had she not done enough? Was that why it was all coming to an end?

"Within the next year the roof sprung its first leak, Benedict nearly toppled an entire cabinet of vases and sculptures I can only assume have great value, and the enormity of raising more than one baby became an overwhelming reality." Daphne took a deep breath. "But in that moment, I was powerful. So I sent him a letter."

Jess dropped onto the bed beside Daphne. For a while, both women stared at the faded wall coverings, one corner dropping away from the ceiling trim. "He didn't answer."

It was a statement, the obvious result of her attempt at contact, but Daphne confirmed it anyway. "No. For all I know he refused to pay the postage on it or threw it in the fire without reading it."

"What did you tell him?"

Daphne wrapped her hands in her night rail to hide the fine tremble that had crept across her fingers. "That I was safe. That his grandson was beautiful. That I'd found a purpose in life and I thought, hoped, prayed God was going to honor that purpose despite my foolishness. I couldn't bring myself to call it a mistake, not with Benedict sitting right next to me. I've since managed to separate the two in my mind. Acknowledging I made a mistake isn't the same as hating where life went afterward. That would be like getting lost in the woods and breaking your leg and then never walking again because of the scar."

Jess tried to smother her laugh but didn't quite manage it. "That's a terrible analogy."

Daphne gave Jess a quick smile before dropping her gaze to her knees. She knew her mind worked oddly, that she viewed life differently than other people. It wasn't a problem as long as she made sense to herself and didn't have to attempt to explain her thoughts to other people.

She really, really didn't want to have that conversation with Lord Chemsford.

"I'd say it's his loss, but we already knew that, didn't we?" Jess bumped her shoulder into Daphne's. "For what it's worth, I think you're incredible. Strange, but incredible. I've never met anyone like you, Daphne, so determined to see the good and the possibilities in a situation."

"I can't see the good right now," Daphne grumbled. "Benedict hasn't talked to me once since he found out who his father was."

"Maybe he liked pretending you didn't know. He's your son, after all. He may look like his father's family, but you raised him. He's bound to possess a bit of that Daphne-esque imagination." Jess gave Daphne a push. "Now get off my bed. Some of us aren't avoiding the big house tomorrow and have breakfast to cook."

Jess wasn't a hugging person, but Daphne was, so she threw one arm across Jess's shoulder and squeezed before rising from the bed and moving across the room to her own.

She wasn't tired yet, rarely was when she tucked herself beneath the covers, but she knew she needed sleep in order to function the next day.

Tomorrow she would have to remain aware of everything. If she wanted to see to her duties while avoiding the gentlemen, she would have to know where everyone was at any given moment.

Once in her bed, she wriggled and shifted until her head was nestled perfectly in her pillow, the blankets fell just so across her feet, and she had a view of the shadows the moon cast through the uncovered window.

Then she dreamed.

What *would* it be like if her father knew she was here? Without any sort of power or significance or purpose, just working as a housekeeper to survive. Most women of gentility who fell upon hard times were able to find work as a companion or a governess. Few truly had to go into service.

Daphne rubbed her hands together. Those other women wouldn't have calluses on their fingers from hours spent holding a broom or a shovel. They wouldn't know how to plant a garden or efficiently clear a room of dust and debris.

It would be nice, though, if her father didn't care about that. What if he took one look at her and was simply happy she was alive? He could take her in his arms, call her the ace up his sleeve like he did once upon a time, ask to meet Benedict.

How lovely it would be if he wanted to meet Benedict.

It would mean that he, too, had come to the place where he was able to separate the regret of the past from the blessings of the present. He would see that God could do wonders despite the consequences that had befallen her.

Because Benedict was wonderful. He was a blessing. She couldn't be prouder of the man he was becoming. He was going to achieve more than she could have ever dreamed for herself.

And if her father were to join her in that pride, how amazing would that be?

Sleep tugged at Daphne's eyelids. She gave in to it gratefully, visions of her father showing Benedict around one of his new factories dancing through her dreams.

The list of things Daphne should be doing right now was long.

Standing behind a bush wasn't on it.

Yet here she was, back pressed up against the stone foundations of the library wing, eyes closed, enjoying the breeze that ignited a melody in her mind and brushed along her skin as she tilted her head toward the open window to listen to a sound she hadn't heard in years.

Her father's voice.

She didn't have the slightest clue what he was talking about. It had to do with new developments in machinery and the potential of steam engines, but she really didn't care. She could hear his voice again and that was enough.

Over the years her memory had faded a bit, but the patterns and tones of his speech wrapped around her with familiarity, like a favorite blanket that had been forgotten and found one day in the attic.

A few tears rolled silently down her cheeks. She didn't mind them. It was understandable to cry at a time like this. She'd thought to never see her father again. And while they would still likely never embrace or speak, just hearing his voice was a balm she hadn't known she needed.

He was doing well.

She was glad.

And if she enjoyed the brisk tones of the marquis while she was standing here, well, there was no fault in that. It meant two-thirds of the conversation was enjoyable to hear.

Most of the time when she heard Lord Chemsford's voice there was a justifiable edge of incredulity in it. When he wasn't perturbed, though, he was quite nice to listen to. There was power in his voice, a briskness that almost clipped off the ends of his words as if he were in a hurry to get to the next one and make his point. She didn't understand the particulars of the conversation, but there was a noticeable lack of subtleties and prevarications. His questions were direct, his observations stated with boldness.

It was little wonder that he didn't expect this meeting to last more than a couple of days.

But now more than ever, she dreaded the coming conversation. He wasn't going to forget about it, and he wasn't going to let her slide by with a few vague answers.

If she had any secrets left when he was finished she would be astounded.

"What do you say we stretch our legs a bit, gentlemen?" Lord Chemsford's voice drifted through the window, softened a bit from the edge it had born earlier. "I know the grounds are a bit of a shambles, but there's still some fine prospects toward the lake."

"That's a fine idea. I don't suppose you've a bit of fishing gear here?" her father asked. "It's been an age since I've sat along the edge of a beautiful lake and enjoyed the breeze."

The voices moved toward the double doors that led from the library out to the side lawn.

Daphne shrank down a bit lower behind her bush. If they were walking to the lake, there would be no reason for them to come around to the front of the house, yet Daphne didn't trust her luck. She would remain scrunched and hidden until the voices were gone.

But then she faced another dilemma.

The only door on this side of the house was the main front door.

It was a door she'd once used freely but now, if she wanted to be a proper housekeeper, it was a door she should avoid.

Then again, all the men were outside. None of them would see her use the front door, so it didn't actually count, did it?

She pushed through the line of scraggly bushes beneath the library windows and ran up the wide stone steps to the front porch. Feeling a bit like a daring criminal, she pushed open the front door and strode through.

Only to find Mr. Morris walking through the front hall.

With a frown she cast her eyes heavenward. She could have done without the reminder that God could still see what she was doing and had allowed her defiance to produce yet more embarrassing consequences.

The valet said nothing. Then again, he rarely did if he could help it. Instead, he usually conveyed his sentiments through a curled lip, perhaps a bit of a grimace, or, like today, a look of utter, outright disdain.

Daphne gave him her biggest smile in return. "Good morning, Mr. Morris."

"Good morning," the man returned. Despite his derision, she had to allow that the man stuck to a code of manners.

"'Tis a beautiful day," she said, pulling the door closed behind her.

"I wouldn't know," he said, "as I've been acting as valet to all three gentlemen, in addition to being a footman and a butler, since apparently we don't currently have a housekeeper."

Heat rose up Daphne's neck, but she refused to acknowledge it. Instead, she forced her smile a bit wider. "Having a woman in their midst would ruin the professional mood."

He sneered as if she were an idiot and walked toward the stairs to the workrooms below.

On principle she went in the opposite direction and entered the music room.

Sarah was in there dusting, lovingly tracing every nook, cranny, and curve of the grand piano.

Daphne said nothing, even as the girl cleaned an already gleaming portion of the wooden casing. There had to be something Daphne could do, some way she could arrange for Sarah to play the instrument again. Music was in Sarah's blood. Had she been in society, she'd have been praised for her accomplishments. Other girls would be envious of her abilities and her playing would be in such high demand that she . . . that she . . . Daphne frowned. Her playing would land her exactly where it had always landed Daphne. Behind the piano while others frolicked about.

While Daphne had always enjoyed the ability to have something to do while she hid away from the rest of the world, it wasn't something she would exactly wish upon another person.

Still, with the right connections, it was possible Sarah could make a career for herself. There were a few women earning enough to live on from their playing. Not many. It would certainly be easier if she were a man, but it wasn't out of the realm of possibility.

It would take the right people, though. The right connection.

And there was a marquis right here in the house.

Their next conversation was already destined to be awkward, so why not throw a bit more into it? She could broach the topic if it meant establishing a future for one of her beloved charges.

At least that was the speech she gave herself as she moved upstairs to clean.

CHAPTER TWENTY

William rather liked Mr. Blakemoor. If he hadn't known about the daughter, his respect for the man would have been downright admiration. In addition to his business acumen and integrity, every casual interaction indicated he was a decent man. Something didn't quite add up about the entire situation.

Then again, fourteen years could change a person. William considered what he had been like fourteen years ago and shuddered. He'd been blinded by grief after the death of his mother, wracked with anger at his father, and desperate for anything that would make it worth climbing out of bed in the morning.

He'd engaged in some rather foolish behaviors in the name of seeking solace, behaviors he wouldn't even consider doing now if he found himself back in the depths of despair.

Perhaps Mr. Blakemoor was in a similar position. Perhaps he'd made choices all those years ago that he wouldn't make today.

Or maybe he was like William's father, pleasant around his peers and disdainful of his children.

Hiding the man's daughter from him didn't sit well with William, but there were too many unknowns for him to break his silence. He couldn't simply throw Daphne on the mercies of someone who might not have any.

Mr. Blakemoor nibbled on the last of the biscuits that had been delivered earlier as he looked over the plans spread out across the desk. "Our setup in Manchester wouldn't work for your Birmingham facility because you'll be making more artisanal goods, but parts of the process could be done via steam engine. If you split the building you could keep the wooden components separate from the steam."

"I have a friend working on that idea already. He says we'll be near enough to water to make that happen. Then the finished goods will be sent down the channel." William looked over the plans. Every possible bit of space was used, reminding him of Benedict's creations.

His neck itched as he realized he knew more about Mr. Blakemoor's grandson than Mr. Blakemoor did. But hiding Daphne meant hiding Benedict, and since the boy had been the reason she'd had to leave London in the first place . . .

This was why William liked business more than family. Family was tumultuous.

Reuben stepped into the room, holding a cap in his hands and looking only slightly less awkward than he had when William arrived. There was a bit more color to his skin, and he wasn't looking at his toes. William had a suspicion this boy factored into Daphne's past somehow as well.

As he'd said. Tumultuous.

"We found the fishing gear you requested," he said softly before adding a belated "my lord." He cleared his throat. "The poles are outside the stable."

William nodded and dismissed the boy. He quashed the urge to plan on inquiring how the boy was doing at the stable. Mr. Pasley would let him know if it wasn't working out. William had never concerned himself with the lower servants much before. There was no reason to start now. His curiosity would be better aimed at his new factory plans.

"Thank you kindly for arranging that, my lord," Mr. Blakemoor said as he stood and gave William a small bow. "I confess living near our factories has made me miss the sounds of birds."

Mr. Gherkins stood as well, also with a grin. "I completely agree." He gestured to the papers strewn across the desk between them. "As much as I believe factories are the future of this land and that we've created a solid plan, you should know that wherever you put it will disrupt the idyll of the countryside."

Meaning he'd want to put it far away from Dawnview Hall, which he'd already planned on doing. He needed it to be near enough to the town for people to be able to walk to work, but he might not want it to be as short a journey as he originally thought. "Thank you for bringing that to my consideration, gentlemen."

After another round of head bows and handshakes, the gentlemen wandered outside to enjoy the newly provided amenities and William went in search of his housekeeper. He'd been intending to put off their conversation until the men left, but he simply couldn't wait. He told himself it was so he would know how to handle interactions with Mr. Blakemoor, but even he had trouble believing that.

The house wasn't overly large and the layout was rather open. Finding one woman shouldn't have been an issue.

But it was.

It took him nearly twenty minutes to find Daphne, and when he did, he almost wished he hadn't. She was up on a ladder that looked to be as old as he was, dusting frames in the portrait gallery.

"What are you doing up there?" he bit out. Any moment now that ladder was going to give way and Daphne would break her neck cleaning the tops of frames on paintings he didn't care one groat about. He cared about her a sight more than he did any of the people in the portraits.

"Cleaning," she said without pausing her brisk movements, feather duster in hand. "It's what housekeepers do, isn't it?"

"No, actually," he grumbled. "It's what maids do."

She stopped dusting and leaned on the top of the ladder to glare down at him. "I'm hardly about to send Sarah or Eugenia up on this ladder. It wouldn't be safe."

"Which is precisely why I don't want you on it," he said. "Come down here." He paused for a moment, remembering that despite everything, she was the daughter of a gentleman. He still didn't know how he felt about that or what to do about it, but manners warred with habits until he finally added, "Please."

She sighed, made one more swipe across the frame, and then carefully made her way down the ladder.

He held his breath until her feet were back on the floor.

Once back firmly on the ground, she lowered her head and gave him a small curtsy. "What can I do for you, my lord?"

It would be nice if she could go back into the box he'd initially thought she belonged in, but since that wasn't going to happen, he said, "You can tell me what happened with your father."

Her eyes widened and flew to the door behind him. "They've gone already, then?"

"No." He pressed his lips together in a firm line. "I've decided we need to have this conversation while they are still here and I have options available to me."

With a determined frown and mutinous eyes, she said, "With all possible respect, *my lord*, you have no options. We made an agreement, and as you are a gentleman, I expect you to honor it. The fact remains this isn't your decision to make. It's mine."

Was it really? She could claim his honor, but it was his decision whether or not his honor as a gentleman required him to keep a promise made to a servant. A female servant at that.

And that was the sort of logic his father would use when bending situations to his liking. The fact that William could even consider such a line of thinking made him a bit ill. Still, he felt the need to add, "Fourteen years is a long time."

"You have no idea," she murmured.

"Perhaps he's changed."

"I'm sure he has." She ran a hand along the feathers of her duster, sending a puffy grey cloud into the air. "But he has also moved on. Made a life. What good is a spinster daughter to him? What could I do—keep his house?"

He winced. That was true. She wasn't exactly prime marriage material, not if she told someone her true age. But with her smooth skin and gentle face she could certainly pass for someone much younger. Hadn't he thought her twenty-four or twenty-five when he first met her?

"Besides," she said, letting her gaze drop to the floor between them as her voice lowered to just above a whisper, "I wouldn't want to leave Benedict."

Of course she wouldn't. She'd never claimed him openly, but she was still his mother. She might hope to see him leave one day, but she'd never be the one to leave first.

It had seemed so simple while sitting across from a man who seemed such a decent fellow, but now the situation looked like a quagmire in which there was no easy answer. He'd always made decisions based on what was practical, but ever since this woman entered his life, he'd been faced with the human aspect. He now had to consider people and their feelings.

It was dreadfully uncomfortable.

But it was the right thing to do.

"What happened, Daphne?" he asked quietly.

She'd thought she had time to determine a way to tell Lord Chemsford the pertinent parts of the story while leaving out the bits that potentially would get her, Jess, and even Kit and the children in a great deal of trouble. She'd even considered the idea of practicing with Jess that evening so that telling him wouldn't be the first time she uttered the words aloud.

But there was no more time to prepare. If she told him the whole truth, if she told him what she'd actually done, how carried away she'd been, how little she'd thought her actions through, he would lose any and all sympathy for her. Hopefully he would still refrain from telling her father anything, but it would be for that man's protection instead of hers.

No man deserved a daughter who would betray her best and only friend because she was swept away by emotions for a man she didn't even really know.

No man wanted a housekeeper that foolish either.

So she would keep the story simple. Short facts so he would know it had been one lapse in judgment, one foolish night, one moment in history.

Everyone had those moments. Just not all of them ended in such life-changing consequences.

"I met him at a masquerade ball," she said, having to force the words through a suddenly tight throat.

It was a true statement. That night at the ball was the first time she'd ever been face-to-face with Maxwell Oswald. She'd known who he was, of course, since Kit was forever talking about him and pointing him out when they arrived at parties. Until that night, he and Daphne had never spoken.

As far as he knew, they'd still never spoken.

Daphne had been dressed in Kit's costume while the other woman lay in bed, too ill to move. Everyone knew what Kit had been planning to wear, so it was easy enough to pretend to be her when Kit had asked her to do so. At the time, Kit had been sure that if she didn't attend the ball she'd lose her chance to marry Mr. Oswald.

So Daphne went and did everything she could to behave as her bolder friend would have.

But this wasn't really information the marquis needed to know.

"You met Maxwell at a masquerade?" He gestured for her to continue. "What then?"

"We danced." Also true. "Then we stepped over to one of the alcoves to talk." Not quite true, at least not in hindsight.

Looking back, Daphne was well aware Mr. Oswald had chosen that particular alcove because the window overlooked a garden where many people strolled about, taking advantage of the warm night air. And he'd had no intention of merely talking to her.

At the time she'd been lost in the music of the string quartet, listening to the words she'd always wished a man would say to her. Words Mr. Oswald had never actually said.

"And then?" Lord Chemsford bit out, obviously growing impatient.

"He kissed me." True. He'd kissed her in full view of society's most easily offended matrons. And while he'd been calculating Kit's demise, Daphne had been losing her wits. She'd always loved hugs, craved physical connection with those she cared about. Never before, though, had she felt connected to a person like this. It had been glorious. And the way his arms had wrapped around her and held her so tightly, the way they'd shared the same space, the same breath. She'd wanted to hold on to that feeling of belonging forever.

"And?" the marquis nearly growled. "What happened next?"

Daphne frowned at the man. "What do you think happened next? I'm assuming you are aware of how a woman becomes with child, are you not? We left the ballroom. People saw us leave. The rumors were flying while I was still caught up in the romance of it all. I didn't realize what was happening until it was too late and then . . ." She took a shaky breath to steady herself. "And then it was well and truly too late."

His brows drew together. "One night?"

"Yes."

"The night you met?" He sounded completely incredulous.

She winced. That part really did make the parties involved sound bad. And while Daphne had merely been naïve and foolish, Mr. Oswald had been bad. He'd been set on ruining Kit's reputation that night, a sort of betrothal gift to Miss Rhinehold, who had, for some reason, always hated Kit's popularity.

The marquis turned away and began to pace. As the room was rather open since all the furniture was pushed against the walls beneath the portraits, he had quite a bit of room to do so. His legs ate up the floor as he circled the room.

"Does your father know? Does he know who the man was?"

"No," Daphne said quietly. She hadn't told anyone. No one had known besides Kit, because if they had, the already brewing scandal could have become much, much worse. "It didn't matter."

"No, I don't suppose it would," he muttered, making Daphne shrink a bit more into herself.

She had known she was far below the *ton*'s notice and therefore wasn't worth enforcing the normal societal laws. Still, it hurt to have another confirm it. If she'd been someone important, Maxwell could have been made to marry her. The scandal would have been enormous; she would have never been able to walk into a room without whispers and stares, but she'd have been married. She'd have been able to acknowledge her son. He would have grown up with a brighter future.

Instead, she was insignificant. So much so that she wasn't sure anyone other than her father actually knew she'd left town.

Before he could start berating her father for turning on her, she rushed to say, "There was nothing Father could do. I was bearing the consequences while everyone thought—" She clamped her mouth shut. She'd almost admitted everyone thought the sin had been Kit's. "He'd already married someone else. We didn't have the money or power to have another man marry me. So I took the money that had been intended for my dowry and left London."

Daphne's dowry had been a pittance compared to Kit's, which they'd also taken when they left London.

"And that got you to Marlborough, where you found work?"

Close enough. Daphne nodded.

Lord Chemsford stopped and ran a hand along his chin. "Very well. We'll stay as we are for now. They're only here another day."

"Thank you," Daphne said quietly.

The look he gave her stole her breath. It wasn't so much the emotion in it—his face was as unreadable as ever—but it was the fact that he truly seemed to be looking at her. Seeing her. Considering her. As a person. Not as a housekeeper or an annoyance or some strange creature fluttering about his house causing mild havoc.

He took a step toward her, that direct gaze making her want to squirm and fidget.

"What do you think your life would have been like," he asked quietly, "if you'd never met my cousin?"

"It's difficult to say." Daphne broke eye contact. His consideration was something she didn't know what to do with. "I never socialized, not really. That night was the first time I'd actually made it on to the dance floor at a ball."

"So many new experiences," he murmured. "No wonder you lost your way."

That was a nice way of wording it. She'd gotten trapped in her imagination, forgetting about Kit, forgetting even who she was dancing with. It could have been any man, because by the time they'd gone to the alcove, she wasn't picturing anyone real. He was a fantasy she'd conjured. A man who saw her for who she was, enjoyed her imagination, and thought she was beautiful.

Lost her way would have to suffice, though, since trying to explain it further would make her look flighty at best, a bit touched at worst.

"I suppose," she said, determined to push them past the discussion of that night, "I would have married someone from the country. Perhaps a clergyman. I'd have enjoyed helping care for people." Her voice dropped to a whisper. "I like people. Well, I like helping them. They make me nervous unless I have a particular task to do."

He was quiet for a long time. So long she began to wonder if he'd left the room while she wasn't looking, but when she peeked up at him, he was still standing there, those cool blue eyes assessing her, digging through her words for what she left unsaid.

"Well, in whatever task you choose to care for the people in this home, please don't use that ladder anymore. It isn't safe for you either."

Daphne's head popped up, and she blinked at him before turning to look at the ladder. When she faced him once more, she couldn't help smiling.

"As you wish, my lord. I won't use the ladder."

He nodded and turned on his heel to exit the room.

Daphne watched the empty door for a while longer, unable to shake the feeling that something in their relationship had just shifted.

CHAPTER TWENTY-ONE

After three days at the house, there was nothing left to discuss. William could think of nothing to ask that would keep the men there longer. At least, nothing that pertained to the factories.

When they departed, they would take his last distraction with them. Nothing else would be pressing enough to help him push away thoughts of Daphne.

She came into his head at strange times and left him confused and unsure of himself. He didn't know what to think of her, didn't know what to do with her. No matter where he tried to put her, what role he attempted to give her, nothing fit right.

Of course, the obvious title to give her was *housekeeper*, but she'd never quite fit as a typical servant even though she performed the duties of a lowly maid. She was the daughter of a man who was becoming a business colleague and possibly even a partner in this new venture, and she was the mother of his cousin's illegitimate child. Neither of those were titles he could acknowledge openly, so how should he think of her?

William didn't like living in this state of bewilderment. He didn't like not knowing what to think of situations or people.

He really didn't care for the fact that he couldn't stop thinking of her as a person.

Yes, he'd always known his servants were people, but he'd always believed it was better for everyone if their encounters maintained a professional distance. Two weeks with Daphne Blakemoor in his life had proven him right. If he hadn't been thinking of her and her feelings and her future, he'd have dismissed her a long time ago and his life would have been ever so much simpler.

He had to sort this out and that wasn't going to happen here, with the possibility of her showing up around any corner.

"This meeting has been even more productive than I expected." William gathered up the papers and turned to the two gentlemen. While one was a reminder of his current conundrum, they were still the better option at the moment. "I say, if you could spare another few days, come to Birmingham with me and look over the property where I'm considering building this factory. You can talk to the man planning my steam engines. We might both benefit from a visit."

"We'd be happy to," Mr. Blakemoor said with a smile.

"Our factory foreman has things well in hand. My return can certainly be delayed another day or two," Mr. Gherkins agreed.

"Excellent." William kept his smile cool and professional but inside he could already feel himself start to relax, just knowing he was going to get a bit of distance from his current dilemma. Getting away was exactly what he needed.

Once he was no longer immersed in the strange occurrences of this house, everything would shift into perspective. When he returned, he'd set about doing whatever else was needed to make this place into a normal aristocratic estate, as he should have done from the very beginning.

A normal house would bring normal servants and Daphne would find her correct place. He just wished he knew where that was.

Daphne twirled her way through the front hall, skipped across the central hall, and flitted around the saloon to drop onto a sofa with a happy giggle.

Jess followed at a more sedate pace, shaking her head while Reuben, Sarah, and Eugenia trailed behind, grinning.

"You wouldn't possibly be happy to have the house empty, would you?" Jess asked as she sat in one of the chairs.

Daphne dropped her head back to rest on the sofa. "Yes. I am so very happy. And he said they weren't returning for at least a week. An entire week!"

"You know this doesn't change anything, don't you? He's coming back."

Daphne popped her head up. "Of course it changes things. Perhaps not permanently, but for the next few days we'll have our own schedule, without any sneers from grumpy Mr. Morris. The pace will be slower. We'll have more time to visit with one another like we used to." Perhaps she could even convince Benedict to talk to someone. If not her, perhaps Jess or one of the other children. "And"—Daphne pointed a finger at Sarah, trying not to let worry over her son ruin this moment—"we can play the pianoforte in the music room."

Sarah clapped her hands in glee, looking for the first time in a while like a child instead of a young woman. Somehow, Daphne was going to have to find a way to inject moments of joy back into the children's lives, ones that wouldn't disrupt working in the house. Drudgery was going to catch up with them soon enough. She didn't have to rush it.

"Remember there's new people on the grounds," Jess reminded them.

Daphne wanted to stick her tongue out at her friend, but Jess made a good point. There were two men going about the grounds, taming some of the landscaping and creating a plan for his lordship to approve upon his return.

Those men had little to no reason to come into the house, but they were still going to be around. There would be no pretending everything was the way it used to be.

But, oh, what if it were?

What if they'd been able to live in this house with all this glorious furniture?

There were only three children now, where there had once been twelve, but as Sarah, Eugenia, and Reuben ran off to explore the house they'd recently been denied, it was easy to imagine all of them back here.

What if this sofa had been right here instead of tucked away in a storage room? They could have enjoyed the view in comfort while sipping tea and eating biscuits. Life and laughter would have filled the house along with the splendor of the enormous art collection and grand, if occasionally ugly, furniture.

There could be more artwork designed by the children, like the paper filigree–covered box on the side table. The house could be filled top to bottom with beautiful, wonderful items she enjoyed and loved. She'd bring in more children, allowing them to live life a little closer to the way it should have been for them.

Wouldn't that be nice?

"You're drifting again."

Jess's voice pulled Daphne from picturing Eugenia as the daughter of the house instead of the maid. The girl would look lovely in satin.

"I know," Daphne said, pushing up from the sofa. "But there's no harm in it."

Jess looked like she wanted to argue the point but didn't. Instead, she decided to stomp Daphne's popped dream under the boot of reality. "We need a plan."

Daphne frowned at Jess, who stared steadily back until Daphne sighed. Jess was right, of course. Just because Daphne didn't *like* to think about the future didn't mean it wasn't coming at them with the speed of a runaway stagecoach.

"I can't see as we've much else to worry about. He knows about Benedict and he's given me permission to avoid my father." Daphne smoothed her skirts and stared at a particularly worn area of seam. "I don't think anything can go wrong at this point."

"You don't?" Jess arched one eyebrow as she sat back and crossed her arms over her chest. "Try and imagine something."

Daphne frowned again. What good was escaping into one's imagination if the world's problems came along for the ride?

"Try." Jess reached out a foot and nudged Daphne's knee.

With a huff, Daphne crossed her arms. Her eyes slid closed and she pictured herself here, in this room, in this dress, not the way it had been before with children and a comfortable, homely atmosphere, but as it was now. The elegant furniture. The almost daily dread that something horrible was going to happen, that she'd only managed to delay the utter demise of her life by a few years.

She squirmed. This was truly not what she wanted to be doing with her imagination.

"I'm thinking," she murmured, so Jess would know she wasn't sitting here ignoring her.

"There's a knock at the door," Jess said. "Morris is too busy to answer it so you do the honors. Who's there?"

Daphne pictured herself walking through the house and throwing open the door. A wide smile split her face. "Kit and Graham. They've returned from their wedding trip. She's practically glowing. I can't wait to hear about her travels."

"Daphne," Jess groaned. "Fine, fine. Kit and Graham have come and gone, the visit was lovely and such. There's another knock at the door. Who wouldn't be quite as much fun?"

"Anyone from London," Daphne mumbled. She tilted her head as she imagined the most horribly snobbish women she could remember entering the house. "Although," she said more firmly, "that's really only uncomfortable on my side. It's not as if any of them would recognize me. I'd simply be a housekeeper to them."

"True," Jess murmured. "And I could easily avoid anyone who might recognize me. Still, I don't think we've considered every potential bump in the road yet. Try one more time. Close the door."

"This is like a very strange traveling fair game," Daphne said with a grin.

Jess responded by nudging her foot into Daphne's knee again. "Hush. And close that imaginary front door."

Daphne waved a hand in the air in surrender, trying not to take too much pleasure in slamming her fictional door in the face of the horrible women. "It's closed, it's closed."

"There's another knock. This time you feel dread at the sound. You do not want to open that door. Not under any circumstances."

No, Daphne did not want to open that door. Something about Jess's voice, about the tension flowing beneath the words, wrapped around Daphne's throat and took all the fun from the game. It felt real. She pressed a hand to her stomach, hoping she wasn't about to truly be ill.

"You refuse to reach for the door," Jess continued, lowering her voice another notch and letting it become a tense whisper. "But it opens anyway. Who is there?"

Daphne saw, in her mind, the door swinging open even as she reached forward to close it again.

It revealed a man on the front porch.

Her eyelids flung open and she propelled herself off the sofa so fast she sent the furniture skidding backward an inch or two. She paced across the room to stand by the doors looking out over the back lawn and the lake below. With her hands wrapped tightly about her middle, she turned back to Jess. "I don't want to play this game anymore."

Jess's eyes were wide as she stood slowly and eased toward Daphne. "Daph?"

"I thought about it," Daphne said in a rush, "but I never *thought* about it. Even though Lord Chemsford and I discussed the unlikelihood of that man ever coming here, I never thought about what it would actually feel like if he did come, if I saw him. But it would be horrible. It would be so very horrible."

"Daph?" Jess came to her side and laid one hand lightly on her shoulder. "Who did you see?"

Daphne swallowed and forced her gaze to Jess's, if only because she was real and Daphne needed very much right now to remember what was real and what wasn't. After a deep, shaky breath, she said, "Benedict's father."

Silence stretched between as they stared at each other. Whether it was five minutes or five hours, Daphne didn't know. A sudden knock on the door echoed through the center of the house, drawing a muffled scream from Daphne and even a slight jerk from Jess.

"Oh no," Daphne whispered. "No, no, no, no. Jess, if this little game somehow brought him here, I'm going to pick out all the seams in your dresses and make you resew them yourself."

A bubble of laughter escaped Jess's mouth before she clamped her lips shut. Daphne glared at her before leaving the room to answer the door.

It wasn't Mr. Oswald. It was Mrs. Lancaster. Daphne wasn't sure when the last time was she'd been so thankful to see that sweet, smiling, wrinkled face.

"Mrs. Lancaster, what are you doing here?" Daphne wrapped an arm around the woman and ushered her into the house. "You know you can't come to the front door anymore. We don't—well, this isn't our house now."

"Of course it is, my dear." The old woman patted Daphne on the cheek. "It will only stop being yours when you don't care about it anymore."

That wasn't likely to happen. Daphne had too many memories here, had grown too much as a person here to ever not feel connected to this place.

"Besides," she continued as she shuffled past Daphne toward the saloon, "I saw your young man come through town. He rented horses instead of taking his own so that he could change them out and travel faster."

"Oh." Daphne considered taking Mrs. Lancaster to task for referring to the marquis as "your young man," but what was the point? In the fourteen years Daphne had known the older woman, she'd always done precisely as she pleased.

Jess shook her head as she tucked herself in the corner of the saloon near the windows. She'd never been quite comfortable around Mrs. Lancaster, something the woman took delight in.

The children all piled back into the room to get hugs from the shopkeeper.

Mrs. Lancaster plopped a fabric satchel on the sofa and began pulling out small paper packages to hand to the children. "I've brought you each a little bit of your favorites. Don't eat it all at once now."

This was followed by another round of hugs and giggles before the children sat on the floor to peek into their paper bags.

"Did you walk all the way out here?" Daphne asked, helping Mrs. Lancaster to a seat.

"Of course not. These old bones are spry enough to get around town, but that hike is beyond me." She waved a hand toward the window. "Nash is putting his donkey in the barn for a spell."

Reuben pushed up from the floor and folded the top of his bag down before shoving it into his pocket. "I'll go help him. I'm getting to be good in the stable. Mr. Pasley says I have a way with the animals." Pride and confidence puffed up the boy's chest in a way Daphne had never seen before. "I'll milk the goats while I'm out there."

He didn't wait for Daphne's approval before opening the door and trotting down the outside steps. When had he grown so independent? Reuben had always been a bit hesitant and reserved. He waited until being asked and then always tried to go beneath notice. But now he was claiming a skill? Did she even know him anymore?

Jess pushed off the wall. "Girls, since it will be only us for dinner tonight, why don't you see what you can accomplish on your own?"

Sarah and Eugenia skipped off happily, squealing in the stone stairwell to make it echo.

"Handily done," Mrs. Lancaster said with a nod in Jess's direction.

"Why are you here?" Daphne asked. "Not that I'm not happy to see you. You're always a welcome guest, but—"

"You think you can just stop by town with a man who looks like Benedict twice over and get by with a vague remark?" A wrinkly finger pointed in Daphne's face. "No."

Daphne sighed and collapsed back into the sofa while another short laugh escaped Jess's control.

"I know." Daphne eased down into a dejected slump. Why did everyone keep making her relive her mistakes? "Can we at least wait for Nash? I would rather not go through this twice."

CHAPTER TWENTY-TWO

William should have known having Daphne's father with him while he tried to straighten out his head would only make his life more complicated instead of simpler. She had to have gotten the skill from somewhere.

"I don't think you could have asked the good Lord for a better situation," Mr. Gherkins said as the three of them stood atop a hill, looking down at the place they'd settled on to build the factory.

William looked down at the piece of land that was part of his childhood home and nodded in agreement. It was basically perfect. Close to the water, within easy walking distance of town but separated by a large copse of trees and a slight hill, which should keep the noise level down. It was a rather significant distance from Dawnview Hall and even far enough from his sheep pastures to keep from disturbing the animals.

Mr. Blakemoor laughed. "I find myself a bit jealous that this will be your foray into manufacturing, to be honest. It's going to be a considerably easier place to build and start working than our first place."

"Do you still want to be the one to move out here and oversee the start? We could hire someone." As a businessman, William was more than happy to work with the two gentlemen, particularly since his father would never have even given them the time of day, but personally everything felt wrong.

In the two days they'd spent surveying the land and discussing the potential of various sites in Birmingham, a partnership had formed. It was in William's best interest because he was going to have to hire someone to oversee the factory anyway.

The truth was, he had no desire to actually learn the ins and outs of working a factory. He simply wanted to make sure he was keeping the marquisette modern. There were a lot of people depending on him. With this factory, there would be even more.

As beneficial as this partnership was from a business perspective, William didn't think it was going to make hiding the man's daughter from him any easier. It irritated him that he even considered such a thing when making his decisions. He'd left Marlborough so he would stop thinking about his housekeeper, hadn't he?

Mr. Blakemoor nodded, mouth pursed in thought. "Eventually we'll hire someone, but it will go smoother if we start it ourselves and then train our management accordingly. I'll be happy to come out here once the structure is built."

The discussion turned to the construction particulars, including how often one of them should visit the site and whom it should be. Everything was moving faster than William could have hoped.

It should have elated him.

"I'll arrange a set of rooms for you to live in while you're here," William said, "unless you'd rather stay at Dawnview. You're welcome there, of course." He made the offer more out of obligation than any true desire for Mr. Blakemoor to stay in the family home for an extended period of time. William couldn't imagine anyone wanting to stay beyond the few days' visit the gentlemen had already made, but then again, to most outsiders the house was simply a grand estate and the mistress of it a competent hostess.

"I think rooms in town would be preferable," Mr. Blakemoor answered. "I've gotten accustomed to smaller spaces." His usual smile fell away and a look of defeated sadness took its place. "I don't need much. It's only me."

With one last look around the future building site, Mr. Blakemoor began the trek back toward Dawnview Hall. William caught up easily, his mouth suddenly so dry he couldn't even lick his lips. This was the opening he'd been wanting, but what were the right words? Personal discussions were not something with which he had a great deal of practice, although he recently seemed to be making up for lost time. "How long ago did your wife die?"

The older man blinked and then looked at William in surprise. "Oh, years. Elizabeth and I had a good life together. She died so young, though. And I never remarried because I never found anyone who I thought would be the mother she was."

William's pulse picked up and he made a conscious effort to keep his pace long and loose. "You said you hadn't any sons."

"No." The man's steps slowed a bit and William adjusted his accordingly. Mr. Gherkins fell quietly into step beside Mr. Blakemoor but said nothing.

"I have—had—a daughter," Mr. Blakemoor finally said. "But I lost her."

How was William supposed to respond to that? If he hadn't known better he'd have made the obvious interpretation that the girl had died. Perhaps Mr. Blakemoor would rather pretend she had. William's opinion of the man began to spin. "My condolences," he murmured.

After several silent steps, the older man came to a halt and contemplated William with an unflinching but very tired gaze. "I know you outrank me, but I've lived a few more years than you, and your father has passed on. If I may, I'd like to give you a piece of advice I wish I'd learned long ago. Remember that your pride isn't as valuable as you think it is. Keeping it might cost you more than you could imagine."

William was afraid to say anything, even though saying nothing would make him look like he didn't value the experience of an elder, lesser-ranked man. In truth, William couldn't think of anything to say that didn't betray the fact that he knew Mr. Blakemoor was talking about Daphne.

There was still so much he didn't know about the situation. Since leaving Marlborough, he'd come up with at least another dozen questions to ask Daphne, questions he'd love to know the answers to right at that moment.

But as he looked at the man in front of him and thought through what precious little he did know, he came to one conclusion.

This entire situation was a complicated bag of moonshine.

Mr. Gherkins coughed and started walking again. "Your friend Mr. Ramsbury is supposed to be coming by with those steam-engine plans this afternoon, isn't he?"

"Yes," William said, trying to bring his head back around to the more comfortable topic. Calling Harcourt Ramsbury a friend might be a bit of an alteration of the definition most people gave the word, but their interactions had always been pleasant and William kept in fairly regular contact with him. He supposed that made the man as much of a friend as anyone else. "He's probably there now."

"I've asked our driver to have the horses ready to leave in an hour or so. I believe it best if Mr. Blakemoor and I take our leave after we complete our discussions."

William nodded. As late as it would be when they left, the men might not make it farther than an inn in Birmingham, but if they'd noticed even half of the tension he felt in the house, William wouldn't fault their departure.

The situation with Daphne wasn't the only imbroglio in William's life.

The house was just coming into view when he saw a figure in a long black greatcoat striding across the manicured lawn.

"They told me you were at the site so I decided to start walking that way," Ramsbury said as he neared the group of men.

"You could have waited for us at the house," William said.

Ramsbury glanced back over his shoulder, his brown hair that was rather in need of a trim blowing across the stark angles of his face. "It's a beautiful day. No reason to spend it inside."

William sighed. That must mean Araminta, his father's widow, was home. Even if she was ignoring the man, she could make the atmosphere uncomfortable. "I understand."

With a nod, Ramsbury produced a roll of papers from within his coat. "I think you'll find our suggestions to your existing steam engine system well worth investing in. We've put a great deal of effort into improving our valve releases."

Mr. Gherkins accepted the plans and unrolled part of them. Mr. Blakemoor joined him in looking over the partial section of plans and soon both men were grinning.

"That's ingenious," Mr. Blakemoor said. "We'll be in touch very soon, I'm sure."

They discussed the new steam engine for William's factory as they walked to the stable. Once they were there, one of William's grooms held the horses' heads until the driver was ready to take control. With final handshakes all around, the other men were soon off.

"Would you care for tea, Ramsbury?" William asked, gesturing toward the house.

After a brief pause, the other man nodded. "Now that you've returned, I wouldn't mind stepping in for a bit. Lead on, Kettle—oh, I suppose it's Chemsford now. My condolences."

William nodded solemnly because saying that condolences weren't necessary wasn't respectful of the dead. Or the living, for that matter.

They made their way to the house, where the front door swung open as they climbed the steps. A footman in spotless clothing stood beside the open portal. The servant took their hats, gloves, and greatcoats before disappearing quietly through a door near the back of the front hall.

As they made their way upstairs to one of the smaller, more private parlors, they talked of the science society where Ramsbury was a member. The society met frequently to discuss findings and experiments, and some very fine inventions and improvements had come out of the group over the past few years. While William was not intellectual enough to participate in the discussions, he liked knowing about the coming advancements.

A servant bearing a tea tray entered the parlor five steps behind them.

It was all beautifully convenient and a stark contrast to the life he led back at his estate in Marlborough. He rubbed a hand over his face. Did his new estate have a name? If it did he didn't know it. He needed something to call it other than the place where Daphne and a handful of children turned his life into chaos.

"I say, Ramsbury," William began, ignoring the tea tray for the moment and instead wandering over to look out the window, "what do you do when an experiment goes in a completely unexpected direction?"

Ramsbury came to join him, standing a few feet away and looking at the marquis instead of the rolling hills. "It depends. If the new direction is an unexpected result of controlled methods, then I pursue it to see where my assumptions were wrong. If, however, it's apparent that some outside element has changed the results, I toss the whole lot and start fresh."

Well, that wasn't really an option. Yes, William could let the place and move somewhere else—he had more than enough estates—but he had a feeling that out of sight, out of mind wasn't going to work with Daphne. He'd simply worry and wonder how the new occupants had managed when she wouldn't let them into the house.

"What if the element is unexpected but naturally occurring?"

Ramsbury frowned. "I suppose I would start by trying to add more controls. Something that forces the element to be cut off or cease forming."

William nearly choked on his tongue and had to remind himself Ramsbury didn't know William was talking about real people. He was not suggesting William kill Benedict and Daphne to solve the situation.

More controls was an interesting idea, though. He could bring in more servants, should have done so ages ago. Maybe then Daphne's role in his life would be less confusing. Of course, more people brought more complexity to the situation. Believing Benedict wasn't William's child would be a lot to ask of someone new. And if it ever became known that Daphne was his mother . . .

"Don't more controls make the experiment more complicated?" William asked.

Ramsbury's brows pulled together tightly above his straight pointed nose. "Yes," he said slowly. "That is the nature of complex experiments. But the goal is always to have only one variable that you are measuring the effect of."

One variable. Daphne was certainly a variable. William had spent a great deal of time thinking about her and couldn't quite pin down who she was.

A housekeeper he should be essentially ignoring. A gentleman's daughter he could feasibly see socially. A woman of gentle breeding fallen on hard times who he should pity. A strong mother who demanded his respect and compassion.

William sighed. Being in Dawnview Hall, he couldn't help but remember his own mother. She had withstood years of derision from her husband, trying to shield William from it so that he could possibly have a good relationship with his father. It had been a doomed endeavor, but he admired everything she went through to try and make it happen.

Likewise, he admired everything Daphne had gone through to make a life for her son.

"This variable . . ." William trailed off, trying to figure out how to ask advice without revealing the details of his personal life. The most personal conversation he and Ramsbury had ever had before was about where William had his clothes tailored because Ramsbury had torn a jacket while visiting a few friends in Ireland. "Is it ever not what you expected it to be?"

"Only if someone mislabeled the container."

That was a rather fitting description for Daphne if ever there was one.

"Do tell us, Kettlewell, how long you intend to stay this time," his stepmother said as she entered the family parlor, her son Edmond at her side.

When had the boy returned home?

"It's Chemsford now," he reminded her. While Ramsbury's

earlier mistake had been accidental and quickly corrected, William had a feeling Araminta had used his former title intentionally. The brief tightening of her lips as he reminded her that the power of the title wasn't available to her anymore confirmed it. "And I intend to leave within a day or two."

Since being away from Marlborough wasn't fixing his problem, he might as well return and sort it out in person.

In fact, if he left this afternoon, he could possibly make it back to Marlborough tomorrow. There was going to be a night at an inn either way. He crossed the room and gave a quick tug on the bellpull.

"May I present Mr. Harcourt Ramsbury." William refused to present his stepmother to his friend. As he refused to call her by the title that had once belonged to his mother, she was better off breaking with traditional manners and introducing herself. Instead, he turned to his half brother, Edmond. "Shouldn't you be at school?"

Araminta waved her hand in the air. "They sent him down for some ridiculous misunderstanding with another boy. He'll be returning next week." She then poured two cups of tea and fixed them the way she and her son liked them.

William pressed his lips together and avoided looking at Ramsbury. It was one thing for Araminta to be so dismissive of her stepson in his own home. It was something else entirely to be rude to his visitor. His efficient staff would likely be coming in the room any moment with more tea and cups, but that was rather not the point.

Nor was the point that William would have offered the first two cups to his stepmother and half brother if given the chance. The point was that she hadn't even considered for a moment that those cups might have been meant for someone else.

He turned his attention to Edmond. "What happened?"

"It was a bit foolish, I suppose, but I took another boy's—"

"He's having a bit of trouble with his maths," Araminta broke in, "and another boy didn't care to offer him any assistance. As I said, it's a ridiculous misunderstanding."

Edmond shoved a biscuit in his mouth and looked at his toes.

This boy, who couldn't speak for himself, who would steal another boy's paper—because William had no doubt what had actually happened—was the same age as Benedict.

That was rather unbelievable.

Because it also meant Daphne was the same age as his stepmother. Within months of William's mother dying, his father had been scouring London's ballrooms for a young, biddable, sociable wife.

His father and Daphne might even have been at the same parties—not that she would have been the type to draw his eye. She was the exact opposite of Araminta.

And Benedict was the exact opposite of Edmond. What would Edmond be accomplishing now if he had a bit of Benedict's maturity? Then again, who would have taught it to him? Guilt crept in, making William roll his shoulders. It wasn't Edmond's fault their rascal of a father had been the only example he'd had.

"Maths can be particularly tricky for some people," Ramsbury said.

Araminta frowned first at Ramsbury, then at William. "Who is this man?"

"My guest," William bit out because that was all that was truly relevant.

She sniffed and went back to her tea.

"I'm going to take Edmond back myself, so don't worry about staying to escort him," Araminta said, setting the cup of tea down without a single chink of cup against saucer. "I'm withering away here. It was quite unfortunate of your father to pass so near to the Season. I simply can't go to London this soon, but if I don't see *someone*, I'll go mad."

And if he'd needed a reminder of why he had thus far avoided spending time with his half brother, Araminta had just provided it in a neat, easy-to-carry handbasket.

It was the same reason why Edmond was doomed if William didn't do something soon. That was a sobering thought.

"I should probably be going," Ramsbury said, a very understandable declaration after a marchioness had just indirectly declared him not somebody.

"I'll see you out." William stepped from the room, trying to form a proper apology to the man.

As they approached the stairs, though, Ramsbury spoke first. "How long have we known each other?"

William thought back. "Five years, I suppose. We met when you were just out of Cambridge."

Ramsbury nodded. "And in all that time have we discussed family issues?"

"No," William said slowly.

"We should probably keep it that way."

Ramsbury softened his statement with a half-smile and a puff of a chuckle. William gave a low laugh in agreement. His attempt at having a more personal discussion with the man had been a dismal failure.

"I will say, though, if that lad up there is your variable, you need a lot of controls if you want to change the outcome of the experiment."

"And if it's not?" William asked.

"Then you're going to be fortunate if your lab doesn't implode." With that, Ramsbury plopped his hat on his head and walked out the door.

William stared at the closed door for several moments.

Ramsbury was right. Edmond needed controls and William had been too focused on getting away from this place and its memories to provide them. He'd convinced himself that he was devoted to duty, maturity, and responsibility, but he'd been ignoring a prime opportunity to live those qualities out.

Somewhere along the way he'd allowed the sad moments spent in this house—trying to gain his father's notice and approval on his rare visits and watching his mother fade, first as an ignored wife and then as a sick woman the doctors couldn't cure—to overcome the happier memories. He'd forgotten how much his mother had poured into him as a child, how she had guided him.

Someone needed to be that guide for Edmond.

Araminta had a cup of tea waiting for him when he returned to the parlor. The aroma was familiar and sent a stabbing pain through his gut. Did she know she preferred the same blend of tea his mother had? To distract himself, he looked at Edmond. "When this term is over, you can visit me in Wiltshire, if you'd like."

Araminta paused with her cup partway to her mouth. "You're living in Wiltshire?"

"Yes, at a tiny estate Father won in a card game."

"What would I do there?" Edmond asked.

William shrugged. "Whatever you do here, I suppose. Ride, hunt, fish. Visit the town market and the summer fairs."

"With you?" The tinge of excitement in the lad's voice proved William was doing the right thing.

Before he could answer, Araminta cut in. "Of course with him," she said with a frown. "He is the one who invited you. Kettle—ahem, Chemsford may be lacking in social graces, but his manners are impeccable."

Was William supposed to thank her for that?

Ignoring her was probably a better decision. "Yes, with me. I intend to spend at least the whole of the summer there, but probably longer. I see no need to oust your mother from this house before I marry."

"How gracious of you," she murmured.

She probably assumed he intended to marry soon, though she would prefer he die an eccentric old man and leave everything to Edmond.

William had no intention of doing that, even though he had yet to come up with a plan to find a wife without doing the literal social dance most of his class participated in. On second thought, if marrying meant socializing and putting up with people like Araminta, he just might leave the whole lot to Edmond.

Just the idea of multiple Aramintas made his skin itch.

But there were also Daphnes in London, obviously. That gave him a bit of hope.

Not that she was the type of woman he would be looking for, of course. But she was nice. Pretty in a plain sort of way. He couldn't fault her work ethic.

". . . spend my time redoing the public drawing rooms."

William blinked. He'd completely missed what Araminta had said. He never missed what people were saying. Even when they annoyed him he paid attention.

Working with that flighty woman was doing something to his mind.

He pushed thoughts of her aside and focused on what Araminta was saying, boring though it was. How long until Morris could have them ready to go?

CHAPTER TWENTY-THREE

Daphne's idyllic world of pretending everything was as it used to be didn't last very long. Even though Lord Chemsford was gone, work on the estate continued, a constant messy, noisy reminder that everything was changing.

The new groundskeepers snipped away at the hedges beneath the windows, while a steady pounding came from the expanded woodworking crew fixing the roof and making the garret rooms inhabitable.

The lack of living space for servants was likely the only reason that Lord Chemsford had not yet hired a full staff. Once those rooms were completed, having a space of her own would be a thing of Daphne's past.

Once that occurred, learning how to truly manage a household would keep Daphne extremely busy. Right now, though, she wasn't busy. Without anyone in the house, the cleaning was minimal, and for the first time in over a decade she had time on her hands.

Time in which to think.

Time in which to worry.

Time in which to bitterly regret the fact that Benedict had been avoiding her since the revelation of his father's identity.

It also, however, gave her time to deal with the situation. She'd been sending Sarah, Eugenia, and even Reuben to talk to him each day, to try to get a feel for how he was handling everything. He wasn't rude to them, but in what Daphne imagined was typical older sibling fashion, he politely ignored them.

She understood his need to deal with the emotions in his own time, but every glimpse Daphne had gotten and every report from the other children pointed to Benedict being a hollow shell of his usual determined, energetic self.

As his mother, she could not allow that to continue.

She slammed a tray onto the worktable and began scouring the kitchen for items to load on it.

"What are you doing?" Jess asked, jumping out of the way as Daphne cut across the room.

"I'm going upstairs." Daphne dug around in the icebox to find some of the meat and cheese left over from the previous evening's meal and added them to the tray. "Have we any fresh water?"

"No," Jess said slowly as she reached out to stop a small pile of meat slices from toppling onto the table. "I could go pump a pitcher."

Daphne beamed at her friend. "That would be lovely, thank you." She grabbed a loaf of bread, then returned to the table and found a bowl of biscuits underneath a linen cloth. "Aha!"

She placed both of her finds on the tray, rearranging the food so it would be easier to carry. Jess still stood by the table, staring at her as if she'd lost her mind.

Maybe she had, but she wasn't going to lose her son along with it. "Jess? Water?"

"Right." The woman grabbed a pitcher and walked toward the door, still eyeing Daphne carefully. "Water."

Once a pitcher of water and selection of cups had been added to the tray, Daphne hefted it off the table with a grunt. Then she smiled at Jess. "Wish me luck!"

One eyebrow rose, but Jess dutifully said, "Luck."

Daphne nodded in return and slowly climbed the stairs. She hadn't thought through the fact that she would have to carry the loaded tray up three sets of stairs, all the way to the attic. Her arms were shaking by the time she reached the uppermost level of the house.

Perhaps her peace offering hadn't needed to be quite so heavily laden.

Mr. Leighton saw her first and rushed to help her before she dropped the tray.

"Thank you, Mr. Leighton," she said between heavy puffs of air. Her eyes wanted to fly to Benedict and inspect every inch of him for some sign of how he was doing, but she made herself look at each man on the expanded crew in turn. When she finally got to her son, he was inspecting his fingernails, as if the answers to all his problems lay in the dirt and dust that had collected there while he worked.

Daphne forced a smile through the pang of despair. "I thought you might need a bit of refreshment."

"Much appreciated," Mr. Leighton said, gaze flitting from Daphne to Benedict and back again.

"We found a passage that goes out onto the roof earlier." The lanky Irishman ripped off a chunk of bread—of course Daphne had forgotten to bring a knife—and piled a bit of meat and cheese atop it before taking a cup of water in his other hand. "I think I'll take this out there and enjoy the breeze."

The other men, who Daphne had to assume didn't know what had transpired in the dining room a few days ago, looked around a bit before taking the master woodworker's subtle hint and following him out the door with their own refreshments.

Then it was just the two of them in the room. Many years ago it had been just the two of them in Mrs. Lancaster's small bedroom. In some ways it seemed that was when Daphne's life had truly begun, when she'd looked at her son and known she had to find a way to survive.

Looking at him now, she felt a bit of that same determination. She poured a glass of water and held it out.

It was a small victory when Benedict reached out to take it, but her heart jumped anyway.

"Thank you," he said.

She hadn't realized how much she'd missed hearing his voice until he uttered the first words he'd spoken to her in days. Relief made her want to hug him in gratitude, but she kept her arms firmly at her sides.

They stood in silence while he sipped the water. Finally he turned to set the cup on a windowsill.

She took a deep breath, afraid he would leave now that the water was gone. "Benedict, I want you to know—"

Daphne didn't get to finish her sentence because a large blur of nearly grown boy suddenly launched at her and wrapped his arms around her shoulders while burying his face in her neck. Her arms lurched up to return the embrace with all the strength she could muster. Right then, she felt like she could have carried that tray up another hundred flights of stairs if she'd known this was waiting for her at the top.

"I've always known I had a father out there somewhere," he mumbled into her shoulder. "But somehow knowing who he is makes it worse. It makes me wonder who I am."

Daphne's elation melted into a pool of dread and regret. Would telling him the rest make it better or worse? She'd hoped acting as his mother would be enough, that being the same as the other children in the house would give him a sense of normalcy.

But she'd never imagined him doubting who he was simply because of where he came from.

She rubbed a hand over his back, as she'd done every time he'd ever been upset, every time he'd gotten hurt. "You are who you've always been. As you said, it isn't as if the man hasn't always been out there somewhere. He just has a name now."

Benedict pulled back and dragged his sleeve across his eyes. "And a family and . . . and . . . I look just like him, Mama Daphne. There's a man walking around with my face—or I suppose I'm walking around with his since he had his first—but his life is nothing like mine. He's important and I'm . . . I'm . . ."

Daphne grasped Benedict's hands in hers and pulled him around to face her. "You are important, too. Even if you don't have a title or know where you came from, you're important. You matter. You matter to God. You matter to me."

She stopped to swallow down the overwhelming truth of that statement. Benedict had changed her life and she loved where it had gone. The fact that it was changing again didn't matter. He had, in a strange way, given her the best thirteen years of her life. That was more than some people got to enjoy.

She lifted her gaze to his, marveling a bit at how far she had to look up now, and said, "Just because you don't live in this house anymore doesn't mean you get to forget everything I taught you."

One side of his mouth lifted a bit in a shaky grin. "Yes, Mama Daphne. I am created by God and He loves me." He took a deep breath and his voice got a bit steadier. "Jesus didn't come only for the perfect and accepted; He died for the lonely and forgotten, too."

Not exactly the way she always said it to the children, but the meaning was close enough. It was better that he say it in his own words anyway.

"That's right." Daphne squeezed his hands. "And you don't get to go around telling God He made a mistake by creating you. You have a purpose in this world and you're going to live it."

"Yes, Mama Daphne," he said with a full smile. Then his gaze shifted to the tray. "Did you bring up any biscuits?"

"He could be home tomorrow," Daphne said as she ran a brush through her hair. She was still in her day dress, but the pins had been gouging into her head, so she'd taken her hair down as soon as she'd walked into the cottage.

"Could be," Jess said with a yawn. She was already in her night rail with the blankets pulled up to her chin. "Means more cooking."

"Hmmm." Daphne twirled the brush in her hand. "I think his presence changes a bit more than that."

Jess groaned. "He is not Graham and you are not Kit."

Daphne frowned. She was well aware that Graham's unconventional desire to do more than the normal aristocrat and Kit's spunk and heart were a rare combination. Their love story was wonderful, though. It was the thing of fantasies, but it had truly happened. That made it difficult not to, occasionally, plant a spark of hope in her own imaginings.

She'd never expect something like that to actually happen, though. Even when Daphne's reputation had been pristine and she'd trotted about London, she hadn't entertained visions of finding a match above her station. She certainly didn't expect one now. She wasn't Kit.

And Lord Chemsford wasn't Graham. It hadn't escaped her notice that he'd thought, for a moment, that Benedict could be his. It was possible he'd left a woman to pick up the pieces at some point in his life.

There was no evidence that he still behaved in such a manner, so she could hardly hold someone else's past indiscretions against them, but it was more proof that the two of them, with all their flaws, were not the sort of characters found in romantic tales. At least not real-life ones.

And if she found it all too easy to imagine herself as the rightful mistress of Haven Manor, it was simply an attachment to the home and he happened to come with it.

She cleared her throat and tried to sound bored with Jess's observation. "I know that."

"Good," Jess mumbled. "Then all his presence will mean to you is another bed to make."

"Two beds," Daphne said. "Mr. Morris will be returning with him."

Jess propped herself up on her elbows. "You make Mr. Morris's bed? The man's a servant, Daphne! He can tuck his own blankets in."

"Oh." Daphne would know that if she were a true housekeeper. It didn't quite make sense, though. "I always thought the lower servants served the higher servants. You mean valets make their own beds?"

Jess snorted. "I haven't the faintest idea. The Duke of Marshington's valet always did, not that he was a conventional servant either. It proves that it can be managed, though, and it will do the man good." She flopped back onto her pillow with a huff. "And don't take him tea either. He can come down and eat with the rest of the lowly plebeians. In fact, I'm considering making him eat with Reuben in the stable. That will really burn his toast."

Daphne gave a soft chuckle and ran the brush through her hair again. She would never have Jess's gumption, but it was fun to listen to.

Tonight she could pretend that she would have the strength to stand her ground like her friend, but tomorrow, she knew everything was likely to go right back to the way it had been. She would sneak up to the house and try to be a proper servant, hoping that by some miracle Lord Chemsford had had a lapse in memory and forgotten who she was.

Since that wasn't likely to happen, she could at least take comfort in the fact that her relationship with Benedict was on the mend. Work crews were bringing the house she loved so much back to its former glory. Both of those were good things.

But they weren't what she'd had. Living in the cottage instead of the house felt like a loss, but it was really the loss of her freedom that made her feel like the consequences of her past were finally catching up to her.

Her London life hadn't included an abundance of friends or popularity. All anyone had known of her was that she could and would play the piano at any social gathering. But here in the country, she'd been needed. The children had become her family, their relationships had grown slowly and comfortably, and she'd been able to breathe in the space that the country air provided.

She'd been able to find herself. Yes, Haven Manor was a lot of work, but she'd been free to roam it as she wished. Go out or stay inside, eat dessert first if she wanted—as long as she hid it from the children—and play the piano whenever she wished.

She turned on the stool and glanced out the window. From her seat by the dressing table, she couldn't see the house, but she knew it was there. Empty. For one more night.

Jess's breathing was deep and even. Even if she knew Daphne was slipping out of the cottage, she wouldn't have cause to worry.

And it would be nice, just one more time, to do whatever she wished.

CHAPTER TWENTY-FOUR

William startled awake and stared at the ceiling in confusion. It was still dark outside his window and there was little question that he was still tired, so what had woken him?

After the long day of traveling, they'd arrived at the house very late and William had simply told everyone to go to bed. He'd considered going down to the cottage to let Daphne know they were home, but he, Morris, and Pasley were all so exhausted it hadn't seemed worth it.

As the sleep cleared from his brain, he realized that he could hear . . . music?

He squinted at the ceiling, waiting for the shadows in the room to solidify into shapes so he could make his way around them without tripping, then he rose from the bed and reached for his dressing gown. No sounds came from the dressing room or Morris's chamber beyond, so the muted music wasn't disturbing him.

That or the valet was even more tired than William had been.

He didn't feel very sleepy now, though, as he stepped into the gallery and made his way to the grand staircase. The music grew clearer as he walked quietly down the stairs, keeping a hand on the cool wood banister so he didn't trip in the dark room. His steps slowed as he approached the music room, not because he was worried he'd trip over something in the nearly empty front hall but because the music was more powerful than anything he'd ever heard before.

He stopped in the open doorway of the music room. On this side of the house there was hardly any moonlight coming through the windows, so the room was in near complete darkness, except for a halo of light created by a candelabra on top of the piano.

In the center of the glow was Daphne. Her brown hair was tied back at her neck, with a few locks escaping to trail down over her shoulders, her eyes closed as she played the beautiful, mournful tune.

There were moments in life when a man knew he was standing at the precipice of enormity, when he knew his next steps would change the course of his life forever.

This was one of those moments.

Obviously Daphne didn't know he'd returned. She would never have dared play the pianoforte in the middle of the night unless she thought the house empty.

So he had a choice.

He could slip back up the stairs, lie in his bed, and listen to the echoes of music more brilliant and emotional than any he'd ever heard, and in the morning pretend that none of this had ever happened. He and Morris could stage a noisy return without Daphne being any the wiser.

He could do that.

Or he could not.

The alternative was, of course, that he stay where he was, perhaps even ease farther into the room and into one of the chairs behind her. She wouldn't notice. She was lost in a melody so haunting it made William's middle clench. Her head dipped and her shoulders swayed as her fingers traveled back and forth on the keys, willing the mournful tune from the wires within.

If he stayed, though, it would change everything. Rather, it would be an acknowledgment of what had already changed.

If he stayed, he would never be able to move Daphne back into the role of mere servant. He would never be able to dismiss her as someone who simply worked for him and wasn't his concern beyond her health and well-being. He would have to admit that she wasn't a country maiden who'd managed to mimic her betters to sound refined enough to muddle through a high position in service.

She would be exactly who she was: the daughter of a gentleman, a woman who had been raised to excel in speech and music.

To stay would be to experience that, to face the talents she possessed and where they'd come from. To experience that would mean opening himself up to the complexities of her story, a story he barely knew but would feel compelled to explore further. Curiosity would drive him, but treating her with the respect she deserved would mean waiting for her to tell him everything of her own volition.

He wouldn't be able to hold her to the promise that she would tell him everything. That had been a promise made to an employer. And despite the fact that he wasn't going to remove her livelihood, he couldn't quite see himself as merely her employer anymore. The natural societal divide between them had blurred.

Daphne had never really acknowledged that divide, had she? She'd never been one of those who only told him what he wanted to hear. In fact, she almost never told him what he wanted to hear. She'd maneuvered him and ordered him around from the moment he'd arrived, barreling ahead with her ideas and notions and pushing and pulling until he went along. Even knowing that it had all been an effort to hide Benedict from him didn't diminish his respect for it.

Of course, Benedict himself brought another swirl of color into the muddle before him.

No matter which way he looked at it, Daphne Blakemoor did not fit into any of the normal positions in his life. At another time and another place, he'd have simply ignored her. Probably wouldn't have even seen her.

But he could see her now.

And he could hear the heart in the song she played. He would never get to a place of not noticing her again.

It'd taken a week away and a hasty trip to Birmingham to realize that. Now he didn't know what to do with it.

The last notes of the heart-wrenching tune faded as Daphne gently lifted her fingers from the keys.

William held his breath. Was she finished? Depending on which door she left through, she could depart the music room without ever knowing he'd been there. That would be best, obviously. The night and the dark and the unfamiliar twinges of emotion inspired by her uninhibited playing were muddling his thoughts, making him consider actions he never would in the light of day.

Then she lifted one hand and swiped at her cheeks. Just as when she'd cried in the portrait room window, there was no sniffle, no shuddering breath. Just a gentle swipe of fingers beneath each eye. Then she squared her shoulders, set her fingers to the keys, and played again.

Unlike the last tune, this one held a sort of joy. A lilt of hope. The dredges of the previous melody still pulled, but there was something else, something brighter that seemed to light the room beyond the flames of the tapers in the candelabra sitting atop the piano casing.

William slid quietly into the room and eased into a chair.

If she turned her head, she'd see him.

Every now and then he caught a glimpse of shadowed profile, but she never looked over. The circle of light didn't quite reach his toes, so he might not be anything other than a shadow.

Song after song, the tunes got lighter until she looked almost happy. A smile crept onto her face and her sways became more prominent, as if she were dancing to her own music.

A laugh, so light and delicate, joined the notes. William straightened in his seat as her head ducked toward the keys in such a way that he could see the fullness of her smile in the candlelight. Her eyes were closed and a look of pure enjoyment flushed her face as her smile widened and changed her features into something that still might not be called beautiful or striking, but was definitely enticing and attractive.

"Thank you for joining me, my lord," she said softly.

William jerked in his seat, but she still didn't turn to acknowledge him, simply kept playing, filling the room with sounds that would be the envy of any London gathering.

He cleared his throat and adjusted his position. "It is my pleasure, I assure you."

She laughed again, eyes still closed.

William rose carefully from his chair and moved a step closer to the piano. "You play very well."

"Thank you." Her voice was soft around the edges, making the entire scene feel even more like a dream.

He stopped at the corner of the instrument and pressed his leg into the edge until he felt the sharp corner, the small bite of pain assuring him that he was, indeed, experiencing this moment. From this position, there would be no way for her to miss seeing him when she opened her eyes again. "Do you dance?"

Her fingers stumbled and her eyes blinked open slowly. She looked at him, a glassy, dreamy expression still covering her face. The music resumed as she tilted her head and smiled. "They always ask me to play, not to dance."

It had been a while since William had attended a social gathering that entailed a great deal of dancing, but he remembered how the girls behind the piano were ignored in favor of giving attention to the prettier, popular, more readily available dancing partners.

If she was one of those girls, how had she ever encountered Maxwell?

And how could William possibly have been more of a fool than his cousin?

"They left you stuck behind a pianoforte?"

"Always." Her gaze dropped to her fingers. "I don't mind. I enjoy playing. And teaching. I taught Sarah. She'll be better than I am soon. But it is nice to be asked. I always wanted to be asked."

There was something in this conversation that he was missing, something that felt like an important clue, but his mind was too foggy, too caught up in the darkness to find it. Was it the night allowing them to talk in such a way? There was almost a slur to her words. Was it possible she was drunk? He rather doubted it. When he'd first arrived at the estate, the only alcohol to be found in the house was a decanter buried in the back of a cabinet in the library.

A little laugh accompanied a trill of notes. "Well, I've always wanted to be asked by someone who knew I was me."

And that sentence didn't make a crumb of sense. Perhaps she'd gotten into the stash of alcohol he'd had brought in with their first delivery of food and supplies. "Are you drunk?"

Another laugh, another transition into yet another brisk and joyful tune. "No. I never drink. I don't like the way it burns."

William swallowed. He could still walk away. He'd never be able to view her the same again, but if he left now then tomorrow they could at least pretend this had never happened.

He didn't want to leave. The stark contrast between what he wanted and what made sense brought to light how truly cold he'd become. Every decision was calculated, every movement deliberate. He knew what he wanted to be and what he didn't want to deal with in life, and while that was all well and good, it felt chilled compared to Daphne's vibrancy.

"Are you happy?" he asked.

"Here?" She grinned up at him. "With you? Yes. It's the happiest I've been in a while. I don't usually let myself be quite this happy. It's dangerous."

William agreed. For so very many reasons that were hard to remember in their little circle of candlelight. But why would she think so? "Why? What could possibly happen?"

Her head dropped back and she stared at the ceiling, one side of her mouth lifted. Shadow and flame highlighted the dimple that half smile created. "Because you're nice to me. Nicer than any man has ever been—well, besides Nash, but he doesn't particularly signify. Because you make me think things I never thought I'd think about again. Because the sun will come up tomorrow and everything will be just as it was. This will never have happened, but I'll remember it as if it had."

He would remember it, too. Even if they never spoke of it, even if they both buried it beneath formality and routine, he would remember. And if he were already doomed to that torture, he might as well make it a memory worth agonizing over.

"You should dance." William extended his hand.

"But who will play?" she whispered.

"Can you not hear the music in your head?"

"All the time."

"Then we've no need for a piano."

Her beaming smile returned, and her entire face lit up as one hand drifted from the keyboard to place itself in his. She rose gracefully from the chair and rounded the corner of the piano, centering herself in the circle of candlelight.

"What shall we dance?" he asked.

"A cotillion."

He shouldn't have been surprised. She'd been hiding in Wiltshire for a very long time. The last time she'd been around dancing would have been more than a decade ago. "It's been a while since I danced a cotillion. You'll have to remind me."

She giggled. "I barely remember myself."

William took her hand and walked her through the first steps. Remembering the dance was difficult enough. Having to pretend there were other couples in the room to weave amongst was even harder. With no one to pass her off to, he found himself making steps up as he went. She didn't seem to mind, following along wherever he led.

Her eyes slid closed again and she began to hum faintly, making up a few of her own movements as she did.

William found himself grinning as he tried to keep up with her. They curved in and out of the candlelight, which didn't help the confusion of the steps.

It was inevitable that they would eventually stumble into each other, and when they did it inspired a quiet laugh in both of them as William caught her in his arms to keep her from falling.

His laughter faded as he pulled her upright.

He was holding Daphne Blakemoor. He was holding her in his arms and she felt wonderfully welcoming. There were no stiff satins or overly embellished silks to poke through his sleeves, no feathers inducing him to sneeze, no cloying perfume inspiring a desire to open a window. There was just Daphne, wearing one of her faded day dresses that felt smooth and comfortable. There was nothing to distract him from her heart, her warmth, her smile.

She was still chuckling as her head dropped against his chest, pulling her deeper into his arms. She shook her head. "I'm such a terrible dancer. I can't even pretend to be good at it."

William chuckled in return. She really had been rather awful. But then, anyone would be if they hadn't practiced in more than ten years. "I think it was charming."

Her laugh turned into a scoff. "Of course you do. You have to."

"No, I don't," William said softly as he realized it was true. He didn't have to be here, didn't have to be nice, didn't even have to keep Daphne in his employ. He did it because he liked her, and he hadn't liked anyone in a very long time. She was a person he could admire, someone who saw him as a person instead of a title, and at this very moment, she was the only one he could imagine in charge of this house.

She belonged here.

And right now, he felt like he did, too.

He dipped his head toward where hers was buried in his dressing gown. "I don't have to do anything. I choose to be here right now."

Tomorrow could be different—would have to be different—but for right now, he couldn't fathom being anywhere else.

She lifted her head and her temple grazed his cheek. His lips slid across her forehead as her face rose to meet his. He could feel her breath, see the flush in her cheeks and the shadows caused by her lowered lashes.

Those lashes fluttered open slowly, like she was easing awake from the most lovely dream.

He'd never been this close to her, never imagined what intricacies would lie within eyes he'd once thought were merely brown.

They were flecked with gold and amber. Never again would he think them simple.

His heart raced as her eyelids fluttered open and shut over those glorious eyes. He lifted one hand to her neck and slid it up to brace her jaw with his thumb. His pulse hammered in his head as everything but her fell away.

The fluttering stopped as her eyes slid closed once more, and she angled her face closer to his. He felt the sigh as she licked her lips. He was going to kiss her and he had a feeling it was going to be the most glorious moment of his life and somehow he was going to have to go about his day tomorrow as if it had never happened.

"Daphne," he said quietly.

Her eyes snapped open, and the dreamy, hazy glow dropped from her face as quickly as the smile. Her gaze darted all around his face, from eye to mouth and somewhere in the vicinity of his hair.

"Oh, tare an' hounds." She swallowed and blinked. "It's real. You're really here."

She lifted her hands to push against his chest and step away but stumbled as soon as her hands made contact with him. Considering how much they'd touched during their dance, it was unexplainable why he felt that slight press of her hands more than any of the other touches.

William's eyebrows snapped together. Of course he was real. Had she thought she was *imagining* the entire encounter? As flattering as it was to be the one she chose to dream about, the fact that he had struggled and wrestled with the monumental decision to potentially change everything between them while she had simply been living out a fantasy, thinking she was safe in her mind, left him feeling adrift and alone. Perhaps even a bit taken advantage of.

It wasn't a logical feeling, but he couldn't bring himself to care.

She stumbled back another step and pressed her hand to her chest. "Real, real, it was all real," she mumbled.

"No, it wasn't," William answered, surprising himself. But he realized it was true. This wasn't their reality. "It was the night and the candlelight. Neither of us are ourselves."

Her laugh was harsh, sounding even more grating after having listened to the lighthearted joy she'd expressed the past quarter of an hour. "Funny thing about being someone other than myself." She swallowed and coughed before blinking and sending two fat tears gliding down her cheeks, glinting silver in the light from the candles. "I wake up in the morning to find I'm the one living with the consequences."

She fled, stumbling in the dark of the front hall, scratching against the door as she fumbled for the latch.

Every bump made William wince, but he didn't run after her. He was too busy wondering what she'd meant.

CHAPTER TWENTY-FIVE

Daphne's hair flew around her face, obscuring her vision as she ran, heart pounding, down the hill and back to the cottage. With a quick swipe of her hand, she pushed the strands out of the way to keep from inhaling them as she tried to bring her breathing back to normal.

She could hardly charge into the cottage as if the hounds were at her heels. Reuben was sleeping on a cot in the parlor, and while he normally slept like a log at sea, even he was likely to wake if she tripped into the room, breath coming and going fast enough to rattle in her chest.

And even if she got past him, she was sure to wake Jess.

Jess would have questions.

Daphne did not want to answer any questions.

She slumped against the door and slowly slid down until she was sitting on the stone stoop. Burying her head in her knees, she waited for her breathing to slow. She tried counting backward from ten, but she couldn't focus long enough to get past the number eight.

As long as her thoughts stayed in her head, though, and didn't come spilling out of her mouth, everything would be fine.

There'd been more than enough vulnerable moments tonight. She didn't need another.

Lord Chemsford was hardly going to say anything, so all Daphne had to do was treat the evening like any other of her imagined fantasies and banish it to the far reaches of her mind.

If she could convince herself it hadn't been real, nothing would change.

It helped, telling herself that the embarrassment of the night wouldn't last. Bit by bit she regained control of her faculties until she felt it was safe to enter the cottage.

Reuben's soft snores greeted her, and she paused to smile into the dark. One day very soon he wouldn't be there anymore. Maybe he should have already moved into the grooms' quarters in the barn.

Just like Daphne, Jess, and the girls should be in the rooms up in the house.

Living up there wouldn't be like it had been before, though.

It would never be like it was before.

Especially now. Daphne couldn't imagine what Lord Chemsford was going to do with the knowledge that Daphne had been indulging in fantasies about gaining his interest.

Would he think that she'd set her cap for him? Did he think she had plans to entice him into marriage? As if that was even something she could do. Daphne had never had anything to offer a man of his station, especially not now.

Her abilities at the pianoforte were the only skills she had that would be valued by that level of society. Being able to change the linens on a bed with remarkable efficiency wouldn't impress his friends. It would, in fact, do the opposite.

She would act like nothing had ever happened and he would see that tonight didn't matter.

The stairs creaked a bit as Daphne made her way up them, drawing a wince, but the heavy breathing in the room below never paused.

Within minutes Daphne was lying beneath her covers, but it seemed like hours. She stared at the ceiling, willing herself to just go to sleep.

It was a gracious miracle when her eyelids finally became heavy and sleep closed in. It was a restless doze, though, so when Jess rose, her quiet movements were enough to break the light slumber.

Daphne sat up and pushed her hair out of her face before smiling at her friend. "Good morning."

Surprise tinged with a bit of suspicion rolled over Jess's features, but all she did was nod in return. Jess didn't love mornings, so if Daphne was going to get away with anything, it was going to be while the edges of sunlight were threatening to peek over the trees.

Daphne stretched her arms over her head and forced a yawn. Hopefully the gesture didn't look as awkward as it felt.

Jess lifted an eyebrow but continued to coil her hair into a low knot.

Daphne stood and turned her back to Jess, straightening and smoothing her covers with great precision. "Lord Chemsford returned last night, so you'll have to make a bit more breakfast this morning."

The room behind Daphne felt utterly still after her statement. Had Jess already left? Not even the sound of breathing stirred the air.

"And you know that how?" Jess finally asked, her voice toneless.

Daphne wilted and gave serious thought to collapsing back onto her bed and destroying the covers she'd just neatly arranged. When, when, when would she remember to think before she spoke?

Perhaps she could still brazen this out. Jess didn't need to know what had happened up at the house last night. No one did.

Daphne gave a shrug so brittle she wondered that her arms didn't dislodge from her shoulders. "I couldn't sleep so I went up to the house to play the piano. There was evidence they had returned already."

"What sort of evidence?" Jess asked.

Lord Chemsford himself appearing in the music room was fairly irrefutable evidence, but Daphne didn't really care to offer it up.

Unfortunately, she could think of nothing they could have done that would have let her know the house's resident had returned. It wasn't as if the man was going to leave his greatcoat in a pile on the floor of the front hall. Mr. Morris would never allow the garment to be treated in such a way.

"Er . . ."

"Daphne," Jess said warningly. "What happened?"

"Horses!" Daphne cried in triumph, spinning around to face Jess with a smile on her face. "The horses are back in the barn."

"I see." Jess smoothed a loose hair back into her blond knot. "'Tis a good thing you heard the horses before you reached the house. It would have been difficult to explain your presence had he seen you up there."

"Er . . . yes. It definitely would have been," Daphne mumbled.

Jess sighed. "I know how long you were gone, Daphne, and it wasn't a quick jaunt up to the stable to notice it was inhabited again."

It would be nice if her bad decisions would stop having consequences. Daphne sighed. "I played the piano."

Silence filled the room once more as Jess stared at Daphne, eyes a bit clouded but still direct. Obviously she was doing the thinking Daphne never remembered to do before she spoke.

Jess sat and finished hooking her boots. "I'd best get cooking, then. If you could collect the eggs for me, that would expedite breakfast a bit."

Daphne swallowed and nodded, trying to wait until Jess departed to collapse against the wall in relief. Avoiding a chastisement from Jess was certainly worth sending up a prayer of praise. Having Jess so obviously agree that it was best to pretend nothing had happened made Daphne feel a bit better about her plan this morning.

Jess knocked on the door across the passage, letting Sarah and Eugenia know it was time to start the day. Once her footsteps faded down the stairs, Daphne took the first full breath she'd taken since getting up that morning.

She pulled her hair back into a tight knot and selected her

plainest dress. It was a solid brown that had faded into a greyish color over the years. Not that any of her gowns were particularly eye-catching or even fashionable, but the bland dress lacking any sort of print made her less noticeable than the woodwork.

It was the perfect wardrobe choice. Today, the last thing she needed was to draw anyone's attention.

Particularly not Lord Chemsford's.

He'd never been more aware of anyone in his life.

Of course he'd known he would see her when she brought breakfast to the small dining room, but after that he shouldn't have known where she was at all.

Before his trip to Birmingham he'd sometimes had difficulty finding her when he'd needed something. But now he kept track of every noise that echoed through the nearly empty house, knowing that there was a very good chance it was her.

After breakfast she'd cleaned upstairs with Sarah. Their quiet discussion and laughter were amplified by the angles of the two-story central hall, the same way the music had been last night.

Then Sarah had gone to help Eugenia in the washroom while Daphne cleaned the ground floor.

He could sit in the drawing room and know everywhere she went, humming gently, likely without realizing it.

William closed himself in the library to look over the estate books he'd brought back with him from Dawnview Hall, but somehow he still heard her moving about.

Or thought he heard her moving about.

What if he were starting to imagine her, too?

William rubbed his hand over his face and pushed away from the desk to walk over to the double doors. It was as far as he could get from her and still remain in the house.

Was she imagining him now? He couldn't seem to move past that realization that she'd imagined he was there before she'd ever seen him.

And it hadn't been the first time she'd done so.

Everything else could have been blamed on the moment—the secrecy of night, the complexity of their situation, and the emotions pulled from the music she was playing.

Music she had played for an imaginary version of William.

That was difficult to ignore, if not impossible.

They'd nearly kissed by the piano. Had she imagined him doing that before? Was she considering it now? Because he certainly couldn't keep from thinking about what would have happened if she'd come to her senses just a few moments later than she had.

The soft hum he'd heard throughout the house drifted into the drawing room beyond the library corridor.

He recognized the tune as one she'd played the night before. The one that had seemed so full of hope.

Before he could stop them, his feet took two large steps toward the door so he could hear the song better. He pulled himself up short and braced his arm against a bookshelf to keep from going anywhere else.

This was madness.

People. He needed more people in this house. More noises. That would provide the controls Ramsbury had mentioned. Whether Daphne was the variable or his emotions were didn't matter. Both needed to be properly contained.

He needed enough servants that he couldn't distinguish who was doing what. So many servants that she would have no need to do any of the actual cleaning herself. She could stay in the housekeeper's office belowstairs and tell everyone else what to do.

She could even continue living in the cottage. That would add a level of propriety to the situation, should anyone discover it. Not a great deal, but perhaps enough to keep from ruining her further than she already was.

Construction made noise as well. He could hire additional workers.

Noise was what he needed. Maybe the isolation and quiet were getting to him. The sooner the construction was done, the sooner he could bring some of his friends for a visit. They might think it odd when his monthly correspondence included an invitation to visit, but these were desperate times.

He needed people.

The sooner the better.

He pushed open the library double doors with a shove and stepped out into the sunshine to take the most direct path to the stable. With a little bit of luck and some help from Mr. Banfield, he could have the place brimming with people by sundown.

A carving of a goat on a beam over the entrance of the barn caught his eye. He'd missed it the last time he'd come to the stable since the chicken coop had stolen all of his notice.

With one finger, he traced a line over the lifelike carving. He'd never been one to believe that places were haunted by anything other than a person's own memories, but he couldn't help feeling that there was life in this place, life he wouldn't have anticipated given the fact that it had sat empty all those years.

Little things like this goat carving were such a stark contrast to the glorious art inside, but they were just as special and beautiful. When William eventually had this stable torn down in order to have a larger one built, this beam would remain part of the house's collection.

"Would you like your horse saddled, my lord?"

William looked down to find Reuben looking up at him through his round spectacles. The trousers were a bit dirty and the boy was wiping his hands on a rag, but his posture was straight and he was looking William in the eye.

Quite a bit of progress for a lad in only a few short weeks.

William cleared his throat. "Yes. My horse. I'm going to town."

Light-colored eyes glanced down and then back up again. Reuben cleared his throat and shifted his feet. "Begging your pardon, my lord, but are you not going to change first?"

William glanced down and nearly groaned. His head was so

muddled that he'd strolled out to the barn in his trousers and slippers. "Of course. Have my horse ready when I return."

"Yes, my lord." Red curly hair bobbed as the boy gave a nodding bow and then turned to walk into the stable.

William trudged up to the house to change, considering once more the contrast between the goat carved into the stable's crossbeam and the collection at the house.

It was a rather vast collection and probably some of it was valuable.

He just hadn't any idea as to what.

An expert would know, though. At the very least, an expert would help William know what he had. A collection this large should be catalogued somehow, and if one already existed, William had yet to find it.

He knew just the man to do it. He'd first met Derek Thornbury when a friend had brought him in to assess a collection he'd just inherited. William had gotten along splendidly with the art-and-antiquities expert. Since then he'd run into Derek on several occasions. Last he heard, the man's work had taken him to Oxford, a mere forty miles away.

Derek was personable and brilliant and more than a little unobservant when it came to anything other than art. He'd be somewhere between a guest and an employee, with a dash of chaperon thrown in for good measure.

He was the perfect person to bring to the house.

While he dressed to ride into town, William told himself this was a smart decision, not a desperate one. He needed time and distraction so that he could somehow wrap his mind around the complexity that was Daphne.

Once she wasn't such a mystery he'd stop thinking about her all the time and she'd go back to simply being a woman he employed.

Yes, he was being smart, he reminded himself once again as he walked back down to the stable. He was not being a coward.

As soon as his hands stopped shaking, he might even believe that.

CHAPTER TWENTY-SIX

The fire in the kitchen hearth warmed Daphne's toes as it heated the soup in the pot anchored over the flame. Bubbles formed across the surface of the soup, swelling slowly until they popped in a small splash before forming again.

Jess walked up to Daphne and stood shoulder to shoulder with her, staring down into the pot. "Did you lose something in there?"

"I don't have anything to do," Daphne mumbled.

Jess barked a short laugh. "So you decided to stare at a boiling pot? For pity's sake, let me get you a book."

"A book?" Daphne asked.

"Yes, a book. Leather, wood, pages with black ink on them. Similar to piano music but with words." Jess folded her hands in front of her like a book and pretended to read.

"I know what a book is," Daphne sighed. "I just haven't read one in a long time. There's never time to read."

"Apparently there's time to stare at soup. Does reading really take that much longer?"

"I should be busy. I'm always busy." She was. She couldn't remember the last time she'd done something for herself and by herself. There had been plenty of fun to be had in activities she'd shared with the children: going on picnics, reading books aloud, singing songs.

Even Daphne's daily Bible reading habit had been mostly for

the children, so she could tell them the stories and share scripture with them when they couldn't risk taking the whole troop into town for church.

"As you wish," Jess said with a sigh as she leaned against the worktable. "I'll play this game."

Daphne pulled her gaze from the soup and looked at her friend.

The blond woman lifted her hand, one finger extended. "Are the linens fresh?"

"Yes," Daphne said slowly. "Horatia Mason, one of the new maids, took care of that this morning."

"Furniture dusted? Floors swept? Carpets beat?"

Daphne nodded as Jess ticked off task after task. "Sarah and Rachel, Horatia's sister, have the last carpet outside right now. Mary, who got sent over by Nash this morning, is finishing polishing the stair banisters."

"And the downstairs servants' chambers?"

"The new footmen, Cyril and James, finished moving the furniture around an hour ago. It's a bit tight, and at least one of the footmen is going to have to sleep in the stable for a while, but everyone is situated."

"And we both know that if you start trying to manage the kitchen or meals I'm likely to throw something at you," Jess said. "So I suppose you're right. You have nothing to do."

She leaned in and glared at Daphne. "Go read a book. Take a walk. Take a nap, for goodness' sake. Anything, really, besides stare into a pot of boiling soup as if you're contemplating dunking your head in it."

Daphne crossed her arms over her chest. She didn't begrudge Lord Chemsford hiring the maids, or the footmen, or the abundance of groundskeepers, of whom there were now three. She was, however, very unnerved by this feeling of . . . of . . . Well, she wasn't even sure what she felt and she didn't like that. Being in tune with her emotions was what she had done her entire life. To not know herself was as awful as not knowing what to do with herself.

"I don't have a book." Her voice was that of a petulant child, but Daphne couldn't bring herself to care.

Jess walked over to the table in the corner and reached behind two loaves of bread wrapped in linen to pull out a thick brown book. She shoved the tome into Daphne's arms. "Here."

"What is it?" Daphne asked as she turned the book over to look at the cover.

Jess shrugged and started picking through the vegetable bin. "I've no idea. Kit left it in a basket. I haven't had a chance to take it up to the library yet."

Daphne turned the book over and read the title with growing despair before dropping onto a stool at the worktable, banging the book on the table, and letting her head fall on top of it with a loud groan.

Jess cleared her throat. "Obviously not *that* book, then. There's plenty more in the library upstairs."

"This is *The Elements of Universal Mathematics, or Algebra.*" Daphne propped the book up on its end so Jess could see the spine. "This is horrible."

"Not really," Jess said. "We already knew that Kit would read anything and everything she could get her hands on. But at least you've abandoned the soup." She gave a little shudder. "Although burying your head in algebra instead isn't much better."

"There hasn't been a single lesson since Kit left." Daphne flipped the book open. They'd promised themselves that none of the children would lack for education, that ignorance wouldn't limit their future possibilities. And now that was exactly what was in danger of happening to the few who remained.

Algebra couldn't be that difficult to learn, could it? While she'd never been part of the academic lessons Kit gave, she hadn't been terrible at maths growing up.

"Lessons such as those are usually the first to go when you're having to relearn how to survive," Jess said softly. "But if you have time to stare at soup, you have time to prepare lessons. You can teach the children in the evenings."

"Are you sure you don't need help in the kitchen?" Daphne asked, watching as Jess bustled about, preparing even more food for all the additional mouths now in the house. Jess had already refused to allow Daphne to suggest that Lord Chemsford hire an additional kitchen maid. Truthfully, Daphne had been relieved not to have to speak to Lord Chemsford. Hiring a new maid would require seeking him out, and it was obvious he wanted her far, far away from him.

"No," Jess said. "Eugenia and I are functioning well enough. Who knows how much Eugenia would talk if someone was actually answering her?"

The scullery was possibly the worst place for people-loving Eugenia, but Daphne didn't have the faintest idea how to correct that. She could, however, address the issue of the children's education. Besides, algebra had to be less complicated than her life right now.

She dropped her eyes to the book.

"Let the numbers sought be *x*, *y*, and *z* and the Squares mentioned in the Problem *rr*, *ss*, *tt*, *vv*." Daphne blinked. This was well beyond the math she'd learned as a girl. Where were the numbers?

Jess snorted and slid a knife from the block. "Better you than me."

Daphne frowned and slammed the book closed, but she didn't stash it away. She would start at the beginning and figure this out. She would slip more books out of the library, too. Lessons might be different without Kit, but Daphne could manage. "Where are the baskets?"

Jess pointed toward a corner with her knife. "Over there. Why?"

"I'm going to load one up with more books."

"Maths books with numbers, I hope."

Daphne waved the book at Jess. "I'm going to figure this out. And then I'll teach it to Sarah, Eugenia, and Reuben. They may be destined to a life of service, but they will not be doomed to a life of ignorance." Daphne dropped the book in a basket and started to stomp off, but then stopped at the kitchen door, turned back to Jess, and pointed a finger at her. "And I'm going to teach you, too. We'll all be better for it."

Jess's mouth dropped open just a bit, eyes wide as she looked in Daphne's direction.

As much as Daphne would have enjoyed basking in a moment when she'd actually managed to surprise Jess, she needed to take advantage of her current motivation to actually go into Lord Chemsford's area of the house. She could go to the library, load up the basket, and then leave it by the door to pick up when she went to the cottage later that night.

A soft hum vibrated through Daphne as she felt a lightness that she'd lately only been able to find when she closed her eyes and dreamed. A sense of purpose was a beautiful thing.

The number of servants in the house had more than doubled and none of them were doing their job.

Well, he supposed they were doing their *job*. He'd seen them out of the corner of his eye a time or two, discreetly moving about and taking care of the tasks they'd been assigned. Frankly, he'd expected that to look a bit more helter-skelter given that Daphne had been doing almost all of the work herself, but she seemed to have delegated assignments with exceptional efficiency.

In fact, he hadn't seen Daphne since the new maids and footmen arrived.

So why was she constantly creeping into his thoughts? Wasn't he supposed to forget about her if he couldn't see her?

He pushed aside the correspondence he'd been attempting to sort through. It included another letter from Maxwell asking to utilize one of the marquisette estates for an off-season country gathering. William shuffled the letter back to the bottom of the pile. Until he could think clearly about Maxwell's requests and not simply snatch everything possible away from him in retaliation for his past actions, it was probably best that he ignore his cousin's letters entirely.

They made him think of Daphne. And of his own past and his own shortcomings and all of the times he'd failed to consider the lives of other people when making his choices.

He pulled out a ledger book. Numbers always made sense, with their definitive answers and unfailing logic. He would lose his head in the clear-cut world of numbers and forget about Daphne for a while.

Three entries later, Daphne came striding into the room with force and purpose, stumbling to a halt when she saw William seated at the desk.

William looked up at her, unable to pull his eyes away. There was a strength evident in her face that he'd never noticed before. It was in the set of her mouth and the tilt of her eyebrows, low over a narrowed gaze. She was a woman on a mission, and it looked glorious on her.

Until she spotted him, of course, and everything melted away into a murky puddle of expressions that could have meant anything from regret to worry to embarrassment or, really, any other personal, insecure emotion. William had little experience mucking about with such emotions in other people, so he couldn't begin to identify them.

Her eyes darted from him to the basket in her hand to the ornate globe, then the books and the ceiling and the door she'd just entered before making the circle all over again and leaving William just a bit dizzy.

"Daphne," William said, attempting to sound bored and failing miserably. Fortunately, she looked miserable enough herself to completely miss his failure. "If you need to clean in here, you may proceed. You, er, it won't bother me."

He'd been hoping that she'd delegate all of the cleaning to the new maids he'd hired, but he had to allow that perhaps she was having trouble shifting her duties completely. Having her underfoot cleaning for another week or two wouldn't matter.

And now he was lying to himself. Daphne's presence was going to do nothing other than be a bother.

She eased farther into the room, a basket handle nestled in the crook of her elbow.

He'd seen her clean quite a bit over the past few weeks and knew more about her routine than he'd have ever thought possible, and she didn't normally carry about a basket of cleaning supplies. "What do you have there?"

A blush slashed across her cheeks as she looked down in the basket as if she'd never seen it before. "A basket?"

"I've no wish to return to cryptic evasions and secrets, Daphne." He'd also had no wish to return to the conversation they'd begun before he went to Birmingham, despite the fact that he still had questions. He didn't voice them, though, torn between wanting to know the answers and afraid that further erasure of the divide between them would make his previous calm and stable world completely irretrievable.

"No, it really is a basket." She held it up. "See? It, well, it has a book in it. Borrowed from the library. I was, um, returning it and I—"

"Daphne." He cut her off with his simple statement.

They couldn't continue pretending they both didn't know who and what she was. He couldn't pretend she was a mere housekeeper, and she was terrible at being a quiet country mouse, at least around him. Now that he knew who she was, the evidence of her genteel upbringing was obvious. It was in the way she walked and talked, the way that her quietness never seemed subservient.

Did she miss that life? Perhaps not parts of it, but being raised as a fine gentleman's daughter she would have been accustomed to books as well as the piano and every other comfort a woman of her station normally had. Then she'd lost them. He'd always considered himself a man of simple pleasures, but how would he feel if he lost access to the trappings his station provided? His shoulders rolled at the uncomfortable thought.

"You are welcome to borrow a book from the library to read on your own time," he said suddenly. "Goodness knows the library's large enough that I'll never miss it."

"Oh." Her dark gaze settled on him and once again he couldn't quite read the feelings that slid so easily across her features. It was as if she were trying to keep her heart from walking across her face but could do no more than throw a light veil over it. "Thank you. I'll, um, er, get one when I clean in here next."

"Didn't I hire more maids to do that?" William grumbled. He truly had no idea what constituted an adequately sized staff, but three women should be able to take the bulk of the menial labor workload previously accomplished by one, should they not?

"Well, yes." She cleared her throat. "They're doing a wonderful job. Excellent selection of women. I'm afraid I'm not quite accustomed to having them about yet, so I thought I would clean the library myself. I'll return later to do so."

He should let her go. He couldn't continue avoiding her if she didn't leave the room.

But she was still hiding something. He could try to convince himself that his curiosity about her was less important than putting them each back in their proper roles, but as she stood there in front of him, his urge to know the rest of her secrets ate away at everything else, refusing to be ignored.

He stood from the desk and grabbed a book. "There's no need to do it later. I was planning on reading a book. Your moving about the room will hardly be noticed once I've settled into the story. I insist that you go on about your business here."

"Right, then." She crossed deeper into the room and put the basket down by the double doors. "I'll . . . go on about my business."

William fought the need to grin as he positioned himself on one of the sofas. Her prevarication skills were atrocious. How had she survived in London?

The thought stole his grin and sobered him immediately. She hadn't survived in London. His cousin, determined to follow the family tradition of selfish debauchery, had ruined her. Which made less and less sense the longer he knew her. He'd had very little to do with Maxwell in their adult years, but she hardly seemed the sort to catch his attention.

It didn't matter. It couldn't matter. Even if William's curiosity was a consuming beast that made him want to keep her near, that didn't mean he had to give in to the desire to actually ask his questions aloud. He could continue to observe and gather the bits and pieces she doled out unintentionally until he put together the story. To ask one question would lead to another and another until he was too wrapped up in her life to ever pretend to be uninvolved again.

No, he was going to read his book and forget that she was standing at the bookcase three feet to his right.

The swish of her skirt as she left the bookcase and moved to the windows was nothing more than the sound an insect would make as it flew through the room. That would hardly be something that would pull him from his reading.

She moved to a bookcase across the room. So far away he shouldn't even be able to see the dull grey of her gown.

He shifted in his chair to ease his shoulder out of an uncomfortably binding position. The fact that it meant the other sofa was no longer blocking his view of her as she knelt near the bottom row of books was entirely coincidental.

She moved back toward the window and out of the periphery view his new position allowed. Perfect. He could focus on his book, then. Only now his shoulder was uncomfortable again.

Daphne moved about the room in an inefficient and seemingly pointless manner, straightening bookcases, adjusting knickknacks, even aligning the large globe in its carved three-legged stand so that England was facing up. Not once did she pull out a duster or a cleaning cloth. Whatever Daphne's original purpose had been in coming in here, it hadn't been to clean.

A sour taste filled his mouth, and his book suddenly felt heavy in his hands. She hadn't been seeking him out, had she? Was she hoping for another moment like they'd had at the piano? Their near-kiss should never have happened, and he wasn't about to indulge in another romantic interlude, no matter how enjoyable he'd found it or how many times he'd relived it in his mind.

Why would she want to repeat that? She was the one who'd run in the first place.

She moved across the room once more, her shoulders back, her feet gliding across the floor in a way that barely ruffled her skirts. Any aristocratic governess would be proud to have her charge perform a movement with such grace.

It was a rather unappreciated skill in a country housekeeper.

Perhaps that was what he could give her. Surely a few moments where he treated her as a lady of good standing instead of a servant wouldn't cause any harm. For just a few minutes a day she could reclaim the status she'd been born to and he could give his curiosity clearly defined barriers in which to roam free. Outside of that stolen moment, taken in the middle of the day when they wouldn't be truly alone, they would return to housekeeper and master and everything would be as it should be.

It was the perfect solution.

"Daphne," he said as he made a deliberate point to look down at his book and turn the page he had yet to read, "bring up a tea tray. And include two cups. I'd like you to join me for tea."

"Tea?" she squeaked.

"Yes, tea." He looked up at where she'd been standing but had to search her out. She was over by the double doors. Again. How had she possibly managed to keep an entire house clean? "It's a beverage, normally partaken of while having conversation. I thought we might discuss plans for the house and meals."

"Of course!" Her enthusiastic agreement almost made him drop his book. "Tea."

She glanced down at the floor and then scurried from the room.

He was not going to think about it. He was not going to wonder what kept drawing her over to the window. It didn't matter what his housekeeper did as long as she kept his household running smoothly and all of the silver stayed where it should. His curiosity was merely about her past. Not her present and certainly not her future.

A little fresh air never hurt anyone, though.

Before he could stop himself, his book had been set aside and he was standing at the doors. Everything outside appeared normal. Sunshine, with a bit of a grey pall over the tops of the trees, indicating it might rain later. A slight breeze.

Was she simply drawn to the sun, then? Why not just take a walk?

He shifted and his foot bumped the basket she'd carried earlier. She'd claimed it held a book when she brought it in. Now it held five. The one she'd started with plus one for every trip she'd made around the room.

Why did she need five books?

With a quick glance at the door to make sure she hadn't yet returned, he knelt down to see what she found so enthralling.

A General History of the Science and Practice of Music, In Five Volumes, Volume the First. William frowned. She certainly seemed to care for music, but he'd thought her more drawn to the emotion of it than whatever this book talked about. And five volumes? He glanced around the library. Did he own all of them? Because he was vastly curious to know what about music was scientific enough to fill five books.

He shifted the book to the side and looked beneath it to find *The Modern Part of Universal History*, *An Introduction to the Making of Latin*, and Euclid's *Elements Volume II* all sitting atop a thick book on algebra.

A noise elsewhere in the house had him scrambling back to the sofa and snatching up the novel he'd been reading earlier, *The Freaks of Fortune*. He'd picked it from a section of the bookcase containing multiple rows of similarly entertaining-looking books, so why had Daphne pulled such a scholastic and frankly boring selection?

A few moments later, Daphne entered the library again, this time with a laden tea tray in her hands. She looked everywhere except at him as she brought it over to the seating area. It was understandable, he supposed, to be a bit nervous. What he'd suggested wasn't normally done. Perhaps the lady of the house might have tea while discussing plans with her housekeeper, but a bachelor?

No matter. She deserved to have a bit of her dignity returned, and since he could hardly set her up in a London ballroom, taking tea with him would have to do. It was his task to restore as much of what his family had taken from her as possible.

And if he got to calm the beast of curiosity inside him while doing it, all the better.

Her hands trembled a bit as she asked his preferences and poured the tea, but her mannerisms assured him that she had, indeed, been taught this proper ritual. Once he had his tea and plate with a bit of cheese and biscuits on it, he sat back and waited for her to settle in with her own.

He drank.

She sipped.

And for the first time in his life William wished he hadn't been raised with any sense of responsibility, because he wasn't certain he'd provided her one whit of returned dignity unless it now came packaged in a thick wrapping of awkward silence.

CHAPTER TWENTY-SEVEN

Daphne gave serious consideration to gulping down the entire cup of tea so that this encounter could be over as soon as possible. Years of training she thought she'd forgotten, along with a throat that felt almost too tight to breathe, kept her taking sips that were almost too small to be termed ladylike.

"I didn't invite you to tea as a form of torture, Daphne."

She winced at Lord Chemsford's dry statement. Why had the man invited her to sit with him at all? What could they possibly have to discuss that would take that amount of time? The house was clean, and he'd never complained about Jess's choice in meals, so unless there was a party . . . *oh, Lord, please don't let there be a party.*

She cleared her throat and gently set her cup and saucer on the table before she dropped it. The presence of new staff members whom she had to converse with had already left her shaking in her boots. The only reason she hadn't retreated to a far corner and ignored them was because she had a task to focus on: dispersing and instructing them like she'd always done the children. Party guests, however, were something else entirely. She wanted to know right away if that was something she was facing. "Is there something in particular you wished to discuss? You expect more guests, perhaps?"

He waved a hand through the air and picked up a slice of cheese. "No, though we will be having a guest for an extended stay in a few weeks. Mr. Thornbury will be residing on the premises while he catalogues and evaluates the art and other items of interest. He's been doing some work at Oxford of late."

Daphne relaxed enough to swallow more than a small trickle of tea, though she put her cup back on the table immediately in case the trembling returned. She could handle a scholar. They tended to be as quiet as she was most of the time.

Nor did scholars socialize often, so there was very little chance of him knowing her. Even though she'd have preferred spending her social evenings in quiet salons and such, her London Season had consisted mostly of following Kit around wherever she wanted to go, and Kit's father had wanted her to reach as high as she possibly could up the social ladder. There'd been no professors in the mix.

If Mr. Thornbury was here to work, he might not even spend his evenings with the marquis. Daphne glanced at the door where her basket of books lay. Could she find the gumption to ask the man to tutor the children a bit? If he was working at Oxford he must know something worth teaching.

"I'll see that we have a room ready," Daphne said, running her hands over her knees. She didn't know if her palms were sweating or not, but her heart was certainly pounding and the two frequently went together.

Lord Chemsford held the cheese up and examined both sides. "Where did this cheese come from? It's delicious."

"Jess made it. Using the milk from our goats."

"Jess?"

"Your cook?" She'd forgotten that he'd been calling Jess *Cook* and the other woman hadn't corrected him.

His brows drew together, but apparently it wasn't the name change that was concerning him since he asked, "Why do we have goats? And chickens?"

She could hardly tell him it was because goats were far cheaper and easier to handle than cows and a dozen children required some source of milk. "Cheese is very important in Marlborough."

He swallowed the last of his cheese and looked at her skeptically.

Daphne wanted to crawl beneath the sofa. *Cheese is very important in Marlborough?* What sort of asinine answer was that? He was going to think her a simpleton.

"Well." He drew the word out as if he, too, wasn't sure what to say to her ridiculous remark. "I wouldn't want to offend the sensibilities of my new town."

"Of course not," she mumbled and snatched her teacup again, just to have something to do.

"Where should I have Mr. Thornbury start?"

Daphne's brain stumbled over the change in topic. She'd been imagining three or four different directions the conversation could take, and that question didn't lead to any of them. "Start, Lord Chemsford?"

"You may call me Chemsford during these teas." His lip curled in distaste for a moment. "On second thought, don't. That still sounds too much like my father. You may call me William over tea."

"Are we, er, going to be doing this often, my lord?"

"William," he insisted. "And yes, I think we are. You are a gentleman's daughter. And while life hasn't been kind to you, I can be. Each day you'll be able to leave all that behind, at least for a while."

Did he truly think a spot of tea was going to make it all better? A swirl of anger—an emotion she hadn't felt in so long that it was rather difficult to identify—gave her the nerve to say, "That sounds rather pompous." She took a deep breath. "William."

"It does, doesn't it? I didn't mean it as such." He frowned. "I suppose I want to give you back what my family took from you. And since I can't fully restore your position in this world, a bit of tea and conversation seem the least I can do. Oh, and"—he gestured around the library—"use of the library and music room."

And that was all it took for that frisson of anger to fade away.

Perhaps he didn't know how to express himself properly, but his intentions were in the right place.

Besides, he'd just offered her use of that marvelous piano she'd been missing so much. She could teach Sarah again, express the emotions she never knew how to voice or was too scared to acknowledge. She couldn't stop the smile that spread across her face, even if she'd wanted to. "You're letting me use the music room?"

He cleared his throat and avoided her gaze. "At appropriate times, of course."

Meaning no more midnight visits with music and candlelight and soft words and memories that were better than any fantasy and dared her to dream much bigger than she ever had before. "Appropriate times," she agreed. "And when the house duties are done, of course."

He didn't acknowledge her statement as he reached for a biscuit. "What art is your favorite? Where should I have Mr. Thornbury start?"

She'd never given much mind to the art. When they'd first walked into the house, the gorgeous, glorious piano had been all she cared about. "I would probably have him start in here."

"The library?" he asked in surprise. "Not the portrait room or that strange little drawing room I'm afraid to even enter because I feel like breathing too hard would make everything break?"

She coughed to cover her laugh but then gave in to the small giggle. "You should try being the one who has to dust it all. But yes, I think he should start in the library."

Mostly because it was the room with the most treasures that had remained out while the children had lived in the house. If anything was going to be damaged, it was likely to be in here. Best to start with the room in potentially the worst condition so it wasn't so obvious later on.

"The library it is, then. Probably a good idea. It will keep him out of the way of the workers on the upper floors. The garret rooms should be completed by the time Mr. Thornbury arrives, so they'll be back to working on the other rooms."

And Daphne would be out of excuses to continue living in the cottage. She would no longer have a room in the proper portion of a house. She would be living out of the way in the servant quarters. Her fall from polite society would finally be complete.

She tried to tell herself that that was actually comforting. Finally facing it would have to be better than fearing it.

They lapsed into silence again, but Daphne didn't worry over this one. She even felt relaxed enough to reach for a biscuit.

It was hard to believe that biscuits and tarts and anything else Jess felt like making appeared on a daily basis now. In years past, biscuits and puddings had been a rare treat, but now that the larder was filled with any supplies Jess requested, it was a different story.

The silence stretched until it went from comfortable to strange. Should she carry the conversation a bit? Since it had been so long since she'd engaged in polite society, and even then she'd always just sat quietly while the other women talked around her, she wasn't sure what to say. Should she ask him what his favorite art was? No, that was what he'd asked her. If she was going to pretend herself his social equal for an hour—something she had never been even at the height of her dismal Season—she could do better than mimicry. Silence was better than admitting that she had never really had any conversational skills.

"Have you traveled?" she finally landed on.

He tilted his head. "A bit. My father thought I traveled a great deal." A small smile tugged at his lips. "In reality I was over in Ireland."

"Ireland? Whatever were you doing over there?"

"It was more about what I wasn't doing. I wasn't becoming my father."

"How did he feel about it?" she asked quietly. William had cut his father out of his life by choice, whereas she . . . well, she supposed it had been a choice she'd made that had created the divide between them, but she'd never meant for it to have that consequence.

"I think he was relieved, to be honest," he answered just as quietly. "It made it easier for him to pretend his new family was the only one he had."

Daphne looked down into her cup, turning it this way and that so the dregs of tea and the small flecks of tea leaves drifted about into different patterns. Her father had been fairly young when Daphne had been born. It wasn't beyond the realm of possibility for him to have married again after she left London. He'd obviously gone on with his life and been very successful. Why not start a new family?

"Daphne."

Her head snapped up and her eyes met his. The way he'd said her name . . . it was the same way he'd said it at the piano, when she'd suddenly realized that everything was real. There was a tenderness, a strength that she couldn't replicate in her mind. She couldn't imagine anyone saying her name with that sort of caring behind it. "Does my father have a new family?"

"No." His blue gaze stayed steady on hers. "I think that he regrets what happened. I think he'd like to see you again. He's a good man."

"I know he is. He always has been." Daphne placed her cup and saucer on the tray and began cleaning up. "Thank you for the tea," she said around the sudden thickness of her throat. "But I think it best if I remember my place from now on. I'm a housekeeper."

"Daphne."

No, she would not be taken in by that again. She would not savor the way he said her name and memorize every nuance so that she could try to recall it later when she was alone. She was a housekeeper. A servant. Someone with whom her father would never associate. As much as she'd railed against the strictures of society that would force her son to pay for a sin he hadn't committed, she understood them now. A clear understanding of classes meant everyone knew their place. Hopes didn't rise up only to be crushed later.

She didn't say anything more. She simply gathered up the tea tray and left the room. As she did, a single tear escaped and for the first time in a long time, Daphne tried to stop it.

The look on Daphne's face stayed with William the rest of the day. He'd made a muck of things, and he didn't know how to make them right again.

When Cyril, the new footman, appeared in the dining room to serve his dinner, it felt so wrong that William had to bite back the urge to dismiss him immediately so that Daphne would have to deliver the remainder of his meal.

He held his tongue, though, because he shouldn't care. Yes, his attempt at a sort of peace offering had failed, but wasn't the attempt what mattered in this case? It wasn't as if he could make any sort of substantial reconciliation.

One look down at his plate revealed that at least one person belowstairs thought it mattered a great deal. The edges of the unidentifiable meat were burnt. One taste revealed salt in enough abundance to make his mouth burn.

His cook was admittedly another mystery of this bizarre house, but he'd eaten enough of her food to know that this was deliberate. She was willing to risk her position in order to make a statement about his behavior.

It showed an admirable but confusing level of loyalty. She'd been here only a few months, hadn't she? He'd been under the impression that she'd been hired soon after he sent word that he intended to live here.

He was fast coming to learn that what he thought he knew meant next to nothing around here.

He sawed through the meat on his plate, hoping that trudging through this meal would be enough penance and he could leave the entire day behind him. After chewing long enough to make his jaw hurt, he was finally able to swallow. The effort stole what remained of his hunger and he shoved the plate away, nodding at the footman that the plate could be removed.

"Shall I bring up your pudding, my lord?"

William ran a hand along his jaw. "Does it look edible?"

"Yes, actually," the man said, giving the plate a strange look. "If I may be so bold, sir, it looks considerably better than this."

Which probably meant she'd poisoned it with something that would make him miserable for the next two days. "No, I don't think I'll need it tonight."

The man nodded and cleared the table, leaving a glass of port in front of William. His motions were efficient and quiet, just as a servant's should be.

It bothered William.

Cyril left the room to return belowstairs, presumably to eat his own dinner. The servants' portions were probably perfectly cooked and correctly seasoned.

A dish of exquisitely browned baked custard landed on the table in front of him, a spoon slammed next to it.

"Food is a necessity," said a woman's voice, "but pudding is a luxury."

William looked up into the cold face of the little blond woman he'd barely seen since the first day. He didn't recall her looking so fierce before. If anything, the rare times he'd seen her she'd been almost meek.

"If I take the time to make a dessert," she continued, "I'm going to make it right."

He cleared his throat and picked up the spoon to poke at the top of the custard. "Is it going to make me ill all evening? Perhaps wracked with cramps and seizures for the next three days?"

The smile that tilted one side of her mouth looked sinister and deadly. "If I'd wanted that, I'd have put it in the sauce over the chicken. Pudding is too obvious."

William coughed and dropped his gaze. That had been chicken? He wasn't sure he believed her. "There was no sauce on the meat."

"Precisely."

She stood there, staring at him. Was she going to wait until he'd taken a bite?

He dipped the spoon in the dish and took a small bite. The perfect creamy texture rolling across his tongue gave him a moment of culinary bliss he hadn't thought he was going to get tonight.

She spun on her foot and walked to the door. "Your family has stolen enough from her. It isn't too much to ask that you leave her sense of purpose and identity alone." She paused at the door and looked over her shoulder. "But thank you for offering her the use of the piano. The harpsichord in the cottage sounds terrible."

And then she was gone.

What did she mean? He ate his pudding slowly, sifting through her words. He'd done nothing to Daphne's sense of purpose. If anything, he'd more firmly established her as the housekeeper by giving her a staff that would actually do the menial work and leave her to do the rest of it. That was good, wasn't it?

But maybe to her it wasn't. She'd been caring for this house for years. Had she raised Benedict in that little cottage? Perhaps she'd hired the children to ease the emptiness left by his going to work with Mr. Leighton.

He wasn't going to get rid of the new maids. For one thing, Mr. Banfield had hinted that the girls came from families that were in rather desperate need of money. For another, keeping an occupied house clean had to be more difficult than maintaining an empty house. The work would eventually become too much for Daphne and Sarah.

But the idea of Daphne being unsettled about her sense of purpose and identity made the defeated look she'd worn earlier make a bit more sense. He'd never seen her defeated. Even when her father had appeared unexpectedly and she'd wanted to flee badly enough to climb out a window, she'd looked determined. Even the night she'd thought herself alone as she poured out a gloomy song on the piano, she'd eventually succumbed to some innate sense of positivity.

She'd built a new life after the loss of her old one. He didn't want to destroy it. He just wanted to make it better. Obviously, he wasn't going about it the right way.

As he scraped up the last of the custard and sipped his port, he tried to do something he'd never done in his life. He tried to imagine what it would be like to be someone else.

CHAPTER TWENTY-EIGHT

There wasn't room to fit any more people around the servants' dining table. With five maids, two footmen, two grooms, three groundskeepers, one cook, one housekeeper, and one valet, it was a bit of a tight fit, but Jess refused to do it any other way. So here they sat, shoulder to shoulder, eating perfectly cooked chicken.

Well, everyone else was eating the chicken. Daphne assumed it was perfectly cooked by the way everyone enthusiastically cleared their plates. The children sat to Daphne's left and murmured amongst themselves about how good it was, while one of the footmen kept glancing in Jess's direction with a look that fell somewhere between awe and fear.

Jess, who had disappeared for a moment after making sure everyone had their food, didn't look at anyone while she ate, but a slight smile curved her lips as she chewed.

As the meal finished, she stood. "There's baked custard for everyone tonight, so if you'd like some stay seated. Eugenia and I will bring it out."

"You made dessert for everyone?" Daphne asked as Jess set a bowl next to Daphne's still-full plate.

She nodded and flashed a smile full of white teeth. "Yes. I did."

"I know we have more supplies now, but—"

"Don't worry, Daphne," she said with a glance toward the

ceiling. "He won't say a word about it. Besides, most of it is milk and eggs. We have more than enough."

"Oh." Daphne poked at her own custard and listened to the chatter all around her. The new staff members were from town or the surrounding area, handpicked by Nash to fit in at Haven Manor as best as possible. One or two of them Daphne knew by sight, but she didn't really know any of them and they had never spoken before yesterday.

It was like London all over again except with less-comfortable chairs and plain painted walls. She sat in her corner, saying nothing so that no one would send their attention her way.

Her world had been this house and the small group of people who lived in it. It had been a happy little world where she was secure and knew her place.

Now she wasn't sure she belonged anywhere.

The small room near the kitchen had once been used to hold clothing that was waiting to be mended. With twelve growing children, there was always a lot of clothing that needed attention.

Now it was empty, and Daphne had reverted it back to what had likely been its original purpose as the housekeeper's office. The new footmen, Cyril and James, had brought in a small table from the larder, and Daphne had pulled one of the chairs from the servants' dining hall. There were pencils, papers, and even a ledger book for tracking household expenses.

The ledger book was currently blank because, until today, their household expenses had consisted of food supplies for the kitchen. Now there was staff to pay, and she should probably start keeping track of the cleaning supplies they used. Right now, though, there wasn't much to put in it.

So, she sat in her new office, wondering what in the world she was supposed to do with herself. Delegating duties didn't take her long. She should probably look in on the work the maids were doing and make sure it was up to her standards. But that was something that required venturing back into the main part of the house, and she was not ready to do that.

If Lord Chemsford saw her, if he tried to make her feel better about her lowly station again, she just might forget that she'd always been the calm and happy one. When Jess had insisted on teaching everyone in the house how to defend themselves, Kit had been enamored with the lessons, even if she was not very good, but Daphne had tried to avoid them. She didn't like the idea of hitting someone or thinking about what sort of situation would necessitate her doing so. She hadn't always been able to avoid the lessons, though, and so if it came to it, she knew she could give the marquis a decent whack.

Of course, then she'd find herself in the unenviable position of being homeless. Again. Having nowhere to go once in her life had been enough, so she would stay in her new little office until this unusual urge passed.

Now she just needed something to do.

If Jess planned out meals beforehand, Daphne didn't know it, nor was Jess likely to start allowing Daphne to organize such a task. With two footmen in the house, Daphne didn't even have to go into town to do the shopping anymore.

She frowned out the little window set high into the wall of her office. When she was standing, she could look over the bottom sill across the grass and see the edge of a section of garden that was in the process of being tamed. That wasn't her domain either, was it? She knew how to milk a goat and collect eggs from chickens, but tending the garden hadn't ever been an area where she felt very confident. She wouldn't know the first thing about what to tell them to do with the lawns or the trees.

Daphne dropped into her chair with a groan. How had she been able to stand all the idleness in the days she'd been in London? Had she really been able to fill her time with taking tea, reading books, and playing the piano? Surely she'd done something else. Those last few years there'd been lessons, of course. Since she'd been without a mother most of her life, her father had brought in tutors to teach her everything from dancing to pouring tea.

Now she had time to fill her day with lessons once more, only this time it would be in preparation for teaching instead of simply learning.

She pulled the first book out of the basket she'd retrieved early this morning. There was no particular logic behind the books she'd chosen. She'd simply looked for titles that sounded like subjects taught in school. It was all she had to go on since she hadn't a clue what Kit had been teaching them before.

Two hours later, her head and neck hurt from hunching over the table, but she knew a lot more about mathematics than ever before. Even seeing letters instead of numbers was starting to make a little sense, as long as she stuck to the basic ideas.

There was something thrilling about knowing she could calculate how much of an ingredient Jess needed to make a large recipe. Not that Daphne could actually do anything with that knowledge.

Jess was bad with numbers, though, so perhaps Daphne could help make the supply list or something similar.

Using her new knowledge was different than teaching it, though. How was she supposed to show the concept to the children without plunking the book down in front of them and making them work through it the same way she just had? That hardly seemed like something they would like to do after working hard all day.

Perhaps Sarah's day could be shortened a bit with all the new maids. Some creative scheduling should free up a bit of Eugenia's time. Daphne could even lend a hand in the scullery and wash a few pots while the girl did her lessons. Reuben was a bit trickier, of course. Daphne didn't know the first thing about exercising horses, and she doubted Mr. Pasley would take kindly to her request that she be allowed to learn.

She pushed the mathematics books away and pulled out the science book. Before she could open the tome, a knock came at the door.

"Mrs. Brightmoor," Horatia said from the doorway, "Lord

Chemsford is requesting a tea tray in the plain room. With two cups."

Two cups. He expected to take tea with her again.

"Thank you, Horatia. I'll see to it." She congratulated herself on being able to say the sentence without even a bit of quake in her voice.

In less time than she would have liked, she was carrying a tea tray into what had once been the girls' bedchamber. The attached dressing room had held beds as well. The smaller bedroom next door had then become the dressing room.

Now the room was referred to as the plain room because it was, well, plain. It would soon have the added distinction of being the scene of her latest degradation.

Lord Chemsford was already in the room, standing in a small alcove off to the side.

The rattle of cups revealed her shaking hands as she crossed the room to set the tray down. Without a word she began to pour the tea. If she was going to be forced to visit with the man, she was going to make it as fast and non-humiliating as possible.

"Thank you," he said as he accepted the cup. "What do you think should be done with this room?"

Daphne paused, her own cup an inch from her face. "Done?"

"Yes. They've almost finished the garret rooms. I've asked Mr. Leighton and Benedict to move in here next. This house has been yours longer than it's been mine. I'm sure you've envisioned possibilities."

Of course she had. She'd simply never imagined being able to see them come to life. And had he called the house *hers*? Did he realize how much it meant to her?

She set her cup aside very carefully and began to talk.

William had heard Daphne speak many words in the few weeks that he'd known her. There'd been a lot of emotions threaded through them, such as worry or nerves, which had left William filled with pity or irritation—sometimes directed at her, other times at himself. But opening the door for her to share her ideas for the house had brought out something he'd never expected.

She was alive. Bright. Passionate.

He couldn't care less about what the house looked like, as long as it was presentable and not so out of date that the marquisette looked like it was faltering. But since the rooms had to be updated, he'd thought asking her opinion would be a way to break the awkwardness from yesterday's disastrous tea.

It apparently was one of the smartest ideas William had ever had.

She knew everything about this room. She knew where the sun hit in the mornings and where the drafts came through in the winter. She talked of furniture and the ways in which he might want to set the room up if he intended to have it reserved for the best guests. She even made suggestions of decorating colors and fabrics, along with art from various areas of the house that could be brought in to complement different ideas. Every word she spoke, every idea she described brought a glow to her face that reminded him of watching her at the piano.

There was considerably more going on in Daphne Blakemoor's head than she let on.

It was fascinating. Like watching a unique, exotic flower bloom with an array of colorful petals you hadn't realized were contained in the plain, green bud.

"And that's what I would do." She wound down her descriptive ramble and suddenly dropped her gaze to the teacup in her lap. She cleared her throat. "If it, well, if it were mine." Her shoulders slumped, and the vitality of moments ago seemed to fade before his eyes.

William wanted to shout in despair as her glorious confidence shriveled back into her insecurities. A few moments ago he'd been entranced by her. It was probably dangerous to encourage, but he couldn't imagine asking someone who was capable of that sort of exuberance to live in silence.

"I like it," he said, even though he'd barely grasped her idea. But he'd see the fullness of her vision once the renovation was completed. "I want you to make it happen."

"Me?" Daphne squeaked. "But, I . . . I can't."

His eyebrows lifted. "Why not? You were cleaning this entire house top to bottom practically by yourself. Now you have three new maids. Surely your time is a bit more available."

"Well, yes, it is, but . . ." She fidgeted in her seat. "May I speak plainly?"

"Please do."

"I'm the housekeeper. This isn't what housekeepers do."

That was certainly true, but why was Daphne suddenly caring about being a proper housekeeper? He tilted his head. "It isn't?"

She hesitated, just like he'd expected. "N-No," she said without a bit of decisiveness behind the word. "I'd rather think that more the job of the mistress of the house."

"I think," William said slowly, because despite his best efforts he wasn't having any trouble at all visualizing Daphne as the lady of the manor, "that you love this house."

"I do," she whispered. "You have no idea what this place means to me."

"Then you'll do right by it." He knew this was true. She would care more for every little facet of this place than anyone else he could hire to do it. "I've some modernizations I want to work in, but I'm putting you in charge of the aesthetics of the project."

"In charge?"

"Yes. I'll want to discuss ideas with you on a regular basis, naturally." There was absolutely no need for him to hear her plans, but he couldn't deny himself the possibility of experiencing her as she'd been moments ago.

The way she'd smiled while talking through her ideas. How her hands waved through the air as she described how beautiful the morning sun was when it splashed across the far wall. Her eyes hadn't dropped away from his but had held his gaze, wide-eyed and earnest.

He wanted more of all of that. It intrigued him, gripped him. Some of the same unnameable, unspeakable emotions that had run through him while he watched her play piano coiled inside him when she talked about the house. It was like a flame that entranced a person even though touching it was unwise.

It would burn him. And her. Because as much as he could see her as mistress of this house, he couldn't really see her as his marchioness. He couldn't see her in London or even at Dawnview, dealing with the masses of people and the politics and the gossip. She was too pure, despite her past—or maybe even because of it. Perhaps going through something like that showed a person the value of the other extreme.

"It will give you a reason to spend more time with your son as well," he added, just in case she needed a bit of an incentive.

"Benedict," she choked out. "Call him Benedict. Not my . . . my son."

He nodded and pushed on before she could retreat behind her walls. "Tell me what you would do in the portrait room."

That was the most ridiculous room in the house. He didn't know the people, didn't care about them, and wasn't about to haul the family portraits from Dawnview to here.

"Well," she began cautiously, as if afraid to allow herself to get caught up in her ideas the way she had earlier. "It depends on whether or not you intend to do any entertaining. With the music room situated as it is between the front hall and the portrait room, it would be two excellent open spaces for a country assembly."

"I have no intention of entertaining, and if I do it will hardly be on that grand of a scale." Balls and assemblies would never be part of his life, even when he married. He refused to marry anyone as socially connected or ambitious as his stepmother.

"In that case"—her fingers twined together as if afraid he was going to stomp all over her suggestions—"do you have any hobbies? I mean, it's an excellent room for activities. If you . . ." Her eyes darted around as if trying to come up with an idea that might possibly be something he'd find appealing. "It could be excellent for fencing, if you do that, or, well, you wouldn't sew or craft, but if there is something you enjoy doing outside, the room makes a wonderful rainy-day alternative. Would make, that is."

He leaned back, already considering the equipment he could place in the room. Fencing bags and training machines. Possibly even some of the new equipment he'd seen in a book by Friedrich Ludwig Jahn. William's German wasn't the best, but the book he'd seen was mostly diagrams, and the exercises on the pages looked interesting.

It would be a rather bizarre room for a country manor, but as far off from the rest of the house as it was, it wouldn't cause a problem.

"I think that's an excellent idea," he said.

"You do?" She blinked at him as if she'd never heard those words before.

And, honestly, if some of the ways she'd tried to keep him and Benedict apart were typical of her usual ideas, she might not have heard them. But in this case, she was on an excellent track.

"I do." He took his cup of tea and settled deeper into his chair. "Tell me your thoughts on the rest of the house."

CHAPTER TWENTY-NINE

God was making sure that one atypical behavior in the house led to another.

First, William had been mesmerized by a confident, passionate, and enthusiastic Daphne who was putting together workable and insightful ideas. Now he made his way up into the attics, chasing an even more addlepated idea than anything his housekeeper had ever come up with.

In the doorway to one of the garret rooms he cleared his throat.

The boy measuring the wall jerked his head up, saw William, and snapped into a standing position, a long, thick string dangling forgotten from his fingers. "My lord."

He blinked and swallowed before casting his eyes around the room. It was the same nervous habit his mother had and seeing it brought an inexplicable layer of calm to William's nervousness. This was why he was here. When he'd put himself in her place last night, he'd realized that what ultimately mattered to her was what was going to happen to Benedict. He was, after all, the truly innocent person in the situation William was attempting to rectify.

William stepped farther into the room. "Good afternoon, Benedict."

"I haven't had time to work on your desk yet, sir. We've been here every day. It'll be a while yet."

William waved his hand to the side. "I'm not worried about the desk. You're a talented young man, but even you can't do two things at once."

His eyes grew big and round. "Thank you, sir."

William looked out the small window across from the door, hoping for a bit of inspiration. His view of how to accomplish the vague goal that had brought him up here was as clear as the large carved stone balustrade that marched around the roof and blocked everything, save the tops of a few trees.

"What do you plan to do when you finish your apprenticeship with Mr. Leighton?"

There was nowhere to sit, so William leaned one shoulder against the window frame in an attempt to appear casual. As if he hadn't purposely climbed several sets of stairs in order to have this conversation.

"I'd like to have a shop of my own. I don't know how many people around here want to buy the type of furniture I want to make, but there are a lot of people who come through Marlborough. Some of them like unique pieces." Benedict wrapped his measuring strip around his hand a few times before unwinding it and repeating the process.

"I think with a few pieces in the right places you could have more work than you can handle," William said.

A smile eased up the corners of Benedict's mouth and his shoulders seemed to relax. "Do you truly think so?"

"You made that gaming table downstairs, right? And the tea box in the dining room?"

The boy nodded.

William nodded in return. "Then, yes, I think people will want what you can make."

And suddenly William knew exactly what to do. He'd wanted to somehow encourage and validate the boy's passions but Benedict didn't need that. He was already honing his passion, working with something he loved. What he needed was the exact opposite.

"Do you know how to run a business?" William asked.

"No, sir." Benedict's shoulders tightened up again. "I've never dealt much with money at all."

Whereas William's first book had been an estate ledger. "I'd like to teach you."

Blue eyes met blue eyes, and William had to work to keep from flinching at how odd it felt to stare down eyes the same color as his own. He braced himself for Benedict to say he wanted nothing to do with anyone connected to the father who hadn't wanted him or the employer making his mother's life occasionally difficult. Even though he didn't know Daphne was his mother, William rather believed she felt like one to him.

Instead, Benedict asked, "Why?"

An excellent question and one William wasn't sure he could answer. It was a feeling, some combination of guilt and responsibility and a desire to see a bit of balance in a world that was incredibly unjust. "Would it be enough if I just thought it was the right thing to do?"

Benedict tilted his head in thought. It was something William did, something he'd seen his father do. Probably something his cousin Maxwell did as well. William gave his head a small shake to bring his focus back to the matter at hand.

"Yes," Benedict said. "I think that would be enough." He glanced at the string in his hand and the wall he'd been measuring. "I have a lot of work to do, though. It will have to be during my break. I usually take one around noon."

And with that sort of work ethic, the boy was going to go far. William nodded. "Noon it is."

William left Benedict to his work then and went straight to the library, pulling out the various ledgers he had to see which ones would provide the best example to show Benedict how to manage a business.

He could feel the same internal thrill he'd seen in Daphne earlier welling up within him, as if God had put him right here, right now to accomplish this task. This was something he could do and do well, and there wasn't anything much more exciting than that.

Four days later, after taking tea in various rooms of the house so that she could share her ideas, Daphne finally believed it when William said that he was going to let her oversee the redecoration of the house.

Three days after that, Daphne was using her spare time to make sketches and dream up elegant but creatively useful designs for every space. She didn't know much about modern fashions or current styles, but she knew this house. It was meant to be a grand lady of understated elegance, not a London dandy tripping over whether or not his shoe buckles were the right size this year.

She took her sketchpad up to the attic, as was becoming common during the midafternoon, to toss ideas around with Benedict while he worked. Sometimes he would pause what he was doing and draw a rough sketch for a piece of furniture or share what he'd seen in other catalogues. Other times they simply talked while she put her ideas on paper, sharing jokes and little stories the way they used to.

And when he shared that he'd been learning about business from the marquis during his mid-day break, Daphne's maternal heart had melted in gratitude and she'd lost the last hold she had on her imagination.

She then stopped by the library, sketchpad clutched to her chest, knocking on the door to draw William's attention from the letter he was steadily writing at the desk. It had gotten so much easier to think of him as William over the past week.

No longer did she see her son when she looked at him. The ways in which they were different were obvious to her now. William's eyes were the same shade and shape but just a bit closer together, his nose the smallest bit narrower. He didn't possess Benedict's dimples when he smiled, and as his hair got longer and in need of a cut, a slight curl made an appearance where Benedict's hair, though the exact same shade, was perfectly straight no matter how long it grew.

No, her son was not what she thought of when she looked at William.

Her thoughts had become ever so much more dangerous.

He glanced up at her, and she cleared her throat, hugging her sketchpad even tighter. "Thank you for what you're doing with Benedict."

William nodded. "His pieces are excellent, but that will mean nothing if he can't run a business well."

Daphne shifted her weight, knowing she should leave but not wanting to do so. Only a few hours ago they'd taken tea in the upstairs parlor that had once been Daphne's bedchamber. They'd talked about the room for a while, but then their conversation had shifted to books and which of the new flowers being planted in the garden was their favorite.

"What do you have there?" William asked.

"Oh, sketches. For the dining room."

"May I see?"

Daphne looked down at the thick book in her hand. Drawing had been the only other ladylike skill she'd possessed in a level above mediocrity, but it had been a very long time since a non-family member had looked at sketches she'd made. Her arms trembled a bit as she set the book on the desk.

He glanced at the drawing before lifting his attention back to her. "Tell me about them."

So she did. Even though she'd already shared her ideas with him verbally, now that there was an image to go with it and Benedict's additional input on the furniture, she could express more detail.

After a while, she realized she'd talked so much that her throat was a bit dry. A glance at the clock revealed she'd given considerably more time to this project this afternoon than she normally allowed. "Oh. I should go. Your dinner will be late."

"Share it with me."

"What?" Daphne froze with one hand extended to collect the sketchpad. He couldn't possibly have suggested what she thought he did, could he?

"Share it with me. You can—" He paused and waved a hand through the air, lips pressed together as if he couldn't quite find the words he was looking for. "You can talk about your ideas more in the room. Looking at the drawing in the physical space would be impactful."

"I . . ." She should say no. She should return belowstairs and see to her housekeeper duties and remember her new place in life. But it was a reasonable request he was making, wasn't it? To visualize and experience the design ideas as close to their reality as possible? "Yes."

Her voice was soft and a small smile graced her lips. His mouth moved into a matching curve and they stood there, smiling stupidly at each other until the clock chimed and broke the trance. Heat bloomed across Daphne's cheeks as she scooped the pad back into her arms and mumbled something about seeing him at the table in a few moments.

And so it began. Sharing tea turned into sharing dinner. By the time another week had passed, Daphne was taking time to run down to the cottage every evening to put on her best dress while William—it had become nearly impossible to think of him as Lord Chemsford anymore—exchanged his day wear for fitted evening coats and sharply tied cravats.

He looked incredible in evening clothes. She'd nearly swallowed her tongue the first time she saw him in them.

Admittedly they still made a ridiculous pair since Daphne's best dress wouldn't even qualify for an acceptable morning dress in London, much less a proper dinner gown. William didn't seem to mind, so Daphne tried not to think about it either. At least not much. If she spent an evening adding a bit of trim on the sleeve or a new tuck in the bodice it was simply because keeping one's clothes properly mended made them last longer.

Three weeks of dinners later and she'd nearly gotten over that first jolt of attraction when she entered the room. She'd have thought they'd have run out of conversation topics as well, but they never did. Every evening started in an awkward silence and then he would ask her something simple about carpets in the upstairs corridors and that would turn into a discussion on favorite colors and flowers and animals and three hours later all they'd decided on was a rug. Sometimes he would mention the factory he was building or some of the other tasks he had worked on that day.

It was a struggle at times, or perhaps every time, to keep her mind engaged in the conversation and not let herself drift into a daydream while sitting at the table. Tonight her mind was a bit more easily focused because they were discussing the music room. She was fairly certain they'd discussed it once already, but since he'd brought it up maybe he'd forgotten.

"There isn't much I would change in the music room." Mostly because when she, Kit, and Jess had been removing their presence from the house and returning the original pieces to their places, she'd made the music room more the way she wanted it to be instead of the way it had been. "The piano is in fine condition, so any decorating should be done with that in mind. It's currently the focus of the room, and there's little reason to change that."

"Indeed." William sat back as Cyril cleared away the plates and the next course was brought in. Ever since Daphne had begun dining with William, Jess's meal preparations had become more elaborate. Now it was rare for there to be fewer than three courses.

The blonde frowned at Daphne every time she came through the kitchen dressed for dinner. After the first three times, she'd ceased reminding Daphne to be careful, which made it ever so much easier for Daphne to pretend she wasn't worried about what would happen when this idyll eventually came to an end.

She was simply his way of passing time in an acceptable manner, but he was quickly becoming what she looked forward to every day.

"After dinner, would you be willing to play for me?"

Daphne was very glad she had not yet taken a bite of asparagus. "You wish me to play?"

"Yes. If you don't mind, of course."

No, she didn't mind. She welcomed any excuse to play the piano. But the last time she'd played for him . . . Memories burned through her and brought a tinge of heat to her skin. She looked down at her plate in hopes that the curls she'd tried to fashion alongside her head swept forward enough to hide her pink cheeks.

"Daphne?" he prodded.

"I would be happy to play for you."

And tonight, when she returned to the cottage and laid her head on the pillow, she would, without a doubt, dream of playing for him on a regular basis. Perhaps even imagine playing while their children danced about, laughing and giggling. She would picture looking across the piano at him sitting in a chair by the window, smiling indulgently at his rambunctious offspring.

Very dangerous thoughts indeed.

"Excellent," he said. "It's one of the difficulties I didn't anticipate, living out here alone."

"What is?"

"Silence. The quiet is peaceful, but it's also heavy. It can leave a man feeling quite alone. I'm sure you know, since you've lived out here taking care of the house all these years."

No, Daphne really didn't know. If she were ever going to reveal the secret of Haven Manor, maybe now would be the time to do so. She'd filled the house with children and done so with her closest friend at her side. It had been anything but quiet.

"I think . . ." she said slowly, deciding the past was best left in the past but still needing to respond to his observation about the solitude. The truth was, though, that she'd felt ever so much more alone in London than she ever had out here. "I think that silence can sometimes help you find yourself."

"What do you mean?"

"Life is so busy and loud sometimes. It can be easy to have everything crowd your mind until you can't hear yourself and you forget who you are, and only see how you fit into the larger churning picture."

He sat back from the table, watching her with blue eyes that looked serious, curious, and something else that she couldn't quite define. "Is that what you did out here? You found yourself?"

"I rather think I did." She'd discovered she could do so much more than she'd imagined—and she'd imagined an awful lot. Necessity had pushed her and brought her to a place she'd likely never have gotten if she'd kept floating along with life as she had been in London.

"What about you?" she asked, dredging up the courage to turn this moment into a true conversation. It wasn't a discussion between master and servant—or even between homeowner and the woman he'd arranged to fix his house. This was two people talking without barriers and without hesitations.

"I think perhaps I'm getting there." He pushed back from the table, automatically angling his legs to avoid the grotesque gargoyles. "Shall we adjourn to the music room? It will be a nice change to take my port while listening to beautiful music."

She ducked her head and blushed again. Her musical abilities had always been appreciated but with a certain negligence, the way one appreciates a clean window. To have it expressly stated sent a pleasant glow moving through her, one that had her deciding to play one of the harder pieces in her repertoire for him.

He fixed himself a glass of port from the dining room sideboard and followed her into the music room, going straight to the chair she'd pictured him in earlier. The evening sun shone through the window, creating a beam of light that centered on the golden upholstery of the chair.

It took a moment to discern reality from her imagination, but not as long as she'd have thought. She glanced around, seeing the room as it was, with its faded and out-of-date wall coverings and its abundance of decorative knickknacks. And a real-life William sitting in the corner, smiling.

With a small smile of her own, she lowered her attention to the keys and played.

CHAPTER THIRTY

It was the best of ideas, it was the worst of ideas.

William soon found himself lost in the music the way he'd wanted to be, but he was also lost in thoughts of her, of doing this more often.

He could only see them like this, surrounded by simplicity and purpose. The problem was, he couldn't stay here forever, and she was as much a part of this house as the columned front porch.

But he was addicted to her.

When she lost her hesitancy and let her passion for life come forward, it was entrancing. Talking about the house unlocked it, but if he guided the conversation carefully, she would remain that way, letting him bask in the warmth of her zest for life. She found so much pleasure in simple things, it was a wonder she'd survived even as long as she did in London's fast-paced duplicity.

Seeing her joy over tea hadn't been enough. It was too short, too easy to escape. Dinner had been an inspired idea that he'd regretted suggesting instantly, but only until the moment they sat together at the table. He could trap her with dinner, keep her in one place long enough to relax, and then he could enjoy her company.

Every morning he told himself it couldn't continue. Every evening the idea of returning to dining alone in silence had him once again suggesting they discuss her plans over dinner instead of tea.

He couldn't care less about the plans, but he did enjoy watching her talk about them.

She always wore the same dress, but the effort she put in had him pulling out the best clothes he'd brought as well. It made Morris happy to be cleaning him up properly, but it made his and Daphne's differences stand out all the more. They'd created a sort of friendship, but it could never be any more than that.

He'd tortured himself by coercing her back into the music room. Memories were here. Memories that were certainly beyond friendly.

Her music washed over him, and his gaze stayed locked on her, watching the emotion cross her face as it flowed from her fingers.

This was madness, and it had to be stopped.

He'd received a letter from Derek Thornbury stating that his work at Oxford had finished and he was available at any time. William had put off writing back, knowing the dinners would cease as soon as the scholar arrived. But William would write back to Derek in the morning, informing him that he could begin assessing William's art at his leisure. Perhaps he'd word it so that it implied sooner was better.

Daphne bit her lip as she played through a series of lilting notes.

Then again, perhaps William should send Pasley to collect the other man directly. Tonight if possible.

More people had knocked on the front door of Haven Manor in the past six weeks than in the previous twelve years, but it still made Daphne jump every time the brass knocker sent an echo rumbling through the central halls. Every knock had ended up being a life-changing moment for Daphne, so it was with more than a little trepidation that she watched as Cyril opened the door.

The man who walked in was as far from threatening as Daphne had ever seen.

He was slightly taller than average, with a pointed chin, a pointed nose, and a flop of brown hair falling over his forehead.

He wore round black spectacles, and his brown coat and tan trousers were as nondescript as clothing could be.

And he wasn't paying a bit of attention to Cyril by the door or Daphne across the hall.

Instead, he was examining the doorframe.

"Corinthian columns on the portico and a definite Palladian influence across the front." His gaze swooped from the door across the walls. "He's got an Albrecht Dürer print. And oh, look, I do believe that's a painting by Joshua Reynolds." He stopped as his eyes connected with Daphne's. He smiled. "Oh, hello."

"Good afternoon. You are Mr. Thornbury?" She truly hoped this was Mr. Thornbury because if he wasn't, Daphne wasn't sure what to think of him.

And if he was, then he was far more threatening than he appeared. She'd known her happy bubble of dinners and conversation would eventually pop, but she'd thought she'd have a bit more notice.

"Yes." He gave a bow and another smile. "Derek Thornbury at your service. And you are?"

Now, that was an excellent question. She wasn't sure she knew anymore. "I am the housekeeper, Mrs. Blakemoor."

Every time she introduced herself now, a sliver of panic curved around her spine. William had refused to call her *Brightmoor* so she'd had to drop the name when the new servants were hired.

Now, she had only to live in fear of the day her father came back for another business visit. At that moment, though, she had bigger concerns than her father's possible future return.

She had a scholar set to rip her world apart.

"A pleasure." His gaze crawled across the walls again. "This is going to be a fascinating house to go through. Such an eclectic collection." He whipped out a small notebook and a pencil and then dropped his bag. He started walking about the room, making notes.

"Mr. Thornbury?" Daphne followed him.

"Hmmm?" he asked before he began to mumble, "Mid-Baroque. Possibly a student of Rembrandt, but not the master himself."

Daphne raised her voice and waved a hand in the air, as if she could somehow pull his attention from the wall. "I believe his lordship wanted me to show you to your room, then have you brought to the library once you'd had a chance to rest from your trip. Cyril will bring up any bags you have."

"Oh yes, excellent. Well, that won't take much time, but I would like to freshen up. Please lead the way."

Daphne shook her head and led the man up the stairs to one of the smaller bedchambers. Daphne called it the blue room because there was a giant statue in the corner of the room veined with blue.

Jess, who somehow or another always seemed to know what was going on in the house despite staying tucked away belowstairs, entered behind them with a tea tray.

"Oh, how nice. Biscuits." Mr. Thornbury took one and bit into it. "Excellent. Sugar, eggs, flour, obviously, and rosewater. Have you ever tried adding a liqueur syrup?"

Jess's eyebrow twitched, but she otherwise remained as expressionless as she always did when she wanted to appear unremarkable. "I'll take it under advisement."

"Not necessarily advisement," he said as he poured himself a cup of tea. "These are excellent traditional Naples biscuits, particularly with tea. Syrup would let them stand alone. A variation, if you will."

Jess's shoulders stiffened the slightest bit and Daphne tried not to laugh. She wasn't sure which was bothering Jess more: being told how to cook better or being told she'd done something traditional.

Best get her out of there before she decided which.

"When you're ready, sir, I'll be in the front hall and will show you to the library," Daphne said.

"Yes, thank you." He wandered over to look at the furniture. "And thank you for the tea."

"You're welcome," Jess clipped out.

Daphne pushed Jess out of the room before nearly collapsing into giggles.

"How can you possibly find that funny?" Jess grouched.

The grin on Daphne's face was wide enough to stretch her cheeks. "It isn't often someone dares to correct you," she said, rather proud that she managed to get out the sentence without actually laughing.

There was no reply as the two women walked down the stairs. At the door to the stairs leading down to the kitchens, Daphne stopped Jess, an inkling of concern worming into her. "Jess, what are you thinking?"

Jess didn't say anything, simply looked off to the side for a moment before sighing. "I'm wondering if we have any syrup."

Twin swords of guilt and relief stabbed through William when he looked up to see Derek trailing behind Daphne. It had been a bit cowardly—and possibly rude and irresponsible—not to tell Daphne he'd arranged for Derek to arrive today, but as difficult as it was to see the calm, meek mask Daphne was wearing over her emotions, it would have been ten times worse to watch it appear.

If she were truly his housekeeper, he'd be ignoring her in favor of his guest.

So that was what he did.

"Derek, welcome!" William came around the desk and extended his hand.

"Chemsford, always a pleasure." Derek ignored William's hand entirely, already looking around the room instead. His hands rubbed together with the glee of a child told he could leave a candy store with as much as he could carry.

"Have you been able to look around any?" William asked.

"Fascinating place you have." Derek ran a hand gently over the carved legs of the enormous globe. "Why didn't you mention it?"

"I didn't know about it." William considered smothering his grin, but the art scholar wasn't going to pay the least attention to other people until he'd gotten the full scope of the room, so he gave his lips permission to curve.

"A hidden treasure, then? Even more fascinating." Derek moved on to examining the desk. "I've only managed to see a few rooms. Is the rest of the house this way?"

"Some rooms are even more crowded." William nearly laughed at Derek's stunned expression. "I hope you plan on staying for a while."

Derek walked over to the bookcase and ran a finger along the book titles.

"I see you can't wait to get started," William said, allowing a slight chuckle. Once Derek had a chance to complete a basic perusal of the house, he'd be much less distracted, though not so observant as to notice the underlying tensions in the house.

He was the perfect choice to bring much-needed balance to the house and the controls William very much needed in place.

Derek moved farther down the bookcase. "This collection has just been sitting here? Unappreciated? Unused?"

William started to say yes, but something stopped him. A memory. One that had occurred a time or two over the past few weeks. He still remembered the odd choices Daphne had made selecting books. He'd noticed that same basket in the corner by the door a couple of times since then.

The library might not have been sitting as dormant as he'd once thought. "Whether it was or wasn't, we're here to enjoy it and use it now," William finally answered.

Derek nodded and started murmuring to himself about titles, occasionally opening a book to check the publishing date.

"After dinner I'll take you on a tour of the house. Then tomorrow you can start right here in this room. I've got pens, ink, and the type of ledger you requested all ready for you."

Derek gave a jerk and then looked up at William. "I'm sorry, what? Oh yes. Dinner. And a tour. Yes, it's best to start fresh tomorrow and make a system."

William turned to Daphne, who was still standing in the doorway, watching Derek with open amusement. He couldn't blame her. Within a day or two he'd appear considerably more normal, though he'd still be spouting off facts about things one didn't even know had facts to learn.

"Please see that the table is prepared for dinner, Da, er, Mrs. Blakemoor."

"I'll have the table set for two, my lord," she said softly, her gaze tucked somewhere beyond his left shoulder.

Irrational pain hit his chest. This was what made sense. There wasn't a future for him and Daphne. Better to cut it off before either of them started thinking in ways they shouldn't. And definitely before either of them started doing things they shouldn't.

He had indulged himself with the impossible, but it was time to return to reality.

He'd brought in a chaperon.

While Daphne had no doubt that Mr. Thornbury was there to do a job, he was also there to put Daphne back in her place. She'd dared to try to return to a status she'd once taken for granted, and William, no, *Lord Chemsford*, was reminding her that it wasn't a climb she was allowed to make.

"I suppose there's some comfort in the fact that he couldn't do it himself. He had to arrange a visitor to get me to go away," Daphne grumbled as she walked into the kitchen.

"Did you say something?" Jess asked as she helped Eugenia finish the dinner preparations.

"Nothing important," Daphne said with a sigh. She started to collect the dishware needed to set the table for dinner.

"Eugenia can do that," Jess said. "It's time for you to go dress for dinner, isn't it?"

"No." Daphne swallowed and clutched the plates closer to her chest. "You'll be happy to know that I'll be returning to my proper seat this evening."

Jess was well within her rights to say *I told you so* at the moment, given that she'd tried to warn Daphne nothing good would come of these dinners, but she didn't. Instead, she stood there, watching Daphne, looking *through* Daphne, the spoon in her hand slowly dripping onto the table.

Without a word she reached for the recently emptied pot and started pouring the cooked vegetables back into it.

Laughter bubbled up in Daphne's chest as she set the plates back onto the table and rushed around to keep Jess from putting the food back over the fire. "You don't have to burn his dinner simply because he remembered who he was and who I was."

"Who you are?" she asked in a hard voice, but at least she didn't shove the pot into the flames. "Who would that be, Daphne, because I'm fairly certain you are the same person you were last night, and if he was willing to have you at his table then, he should be willing now."

"It doesn't work that way." Daphne took the pot from Jess and scooped the vegetables back into their dish. "I'm the housekeeper."

"You're a *person*. Believe me, I've known every class of person possible and the only difference is the clothes they wear and the houses they live in. Those things had no bearing on if they were good or bad, generous or greedy, thoughtful or cruel." She placed the meat on a platter and didn't bother to make sure it looked nice. "I was beginning to hope that he could see that and be . . ." She faded off and stabbed a knife into the ham.

"Be what?" Daphne asked.

Jess braced her hands on the table and turned her blue eyes in Daphne's direction. Her mouth was pressed together, the corners turning down in an expression that looked like the sadness that remains when anger fades away. "I thought he could be the one to show you that you mattered."

Daphne turned away and scooped up the plates again. "I know I matter."

"Do you?" Jess asked, taking a moment to rearrange the ham on the platter.

"Of course I do," Daphne said. She told the children all the time that they mattered. It would be the worst thing in the world if they thought where they'd come from made them less in God's eyes. Even if they lived their lives as servants or in trade, God considered them worthy of love.

She was sure of its truth right down to her bones.

Why would Jess question if Daphne knew it?

When Daphne finished arranging the table for dinner, it looked the same as it had every evening for weeks. Only the second place wasn't for her.

That was life. That was how it worked. They couldn't all be lords and ladies of the manor and they couldn't all be farmers. It took a variety of people to make the world turn, and that was good. She would hate it if everyone were forced to be the same, live the same, act the same.

Just imagining Benedict being told that he couldn't work with wood because he had to be a farmer made Daphne feel ill. Or Sarah being told that she had to stop practicing music because not everyone could play like she could. No, it was good that people were different. God saw value in differences.

But Jess saw more than she said and she didn't speak unless she was sure. So why would she say such a thing?

As Daphne stood in the dining room, pondering Jess's words, she caught a glimpse of herself in the mirror over the sideboard. Daphne didn't often look in mirrors in either a literal or figurative manner. As long as her hair was all caught up and her face free of smudges there was no reason to look closer.

Life had changed her. She was a far cry from the woman who'd walked through that front door twelve years ago, and even further from the girl who'd held up drawing room walls all over London.

That girl had been happy to watch life pass her by. She'd had her friends—well, her friend—and standing to the side had never bothered her. She would speak to those around her, smile at everyone who passed, then go home and dream about what her future could be.

Daphne still dreamed, but not about her future. She would imagine scenarios, explore the might-have-beens, but never did she truly think there was anything better waiting for her tomorrow. Any future hope had been placed on the children. If they went on to be successful and live full lives, that was all she needed.

At least it had been.

What about when the children were gone? What then?

Daphne smoothed a hand over her skirt. *What then?* was an excellent question. Somehow, when she'd buried her past, she'd buried her future right along with it.

If she faced the pain and dug up those memories, took time to remember where she'd come from, really looked to see the direction her life had taken, perhaps she could see where that path might actually lead instead of filling her mind with unattainable dreams.

It was easy to recall the recent years, with the children and the work of Haven Manor trying to save women and children from a fate worse than what Daphne's had been.

The memories from the year before weren't too difficult to remember either. Just Daphne and Kit in a borrowed house on the edge of Marlborough, living on charity and what they could make doing a bit of mending. But they had a beautiful baby boy and the money that should have been their dowries to create a future, once they determined what that was.

But parts of those days had been bleak, like having her father rip her from his life or the tumult of emotions that cut at her as she came back from the dark for the sake of her child, smiling wider than she was ready to because Benedict and Kit needed her to be the happy one.

Daphne suddenly felt weak and she collapsed into a chair by the table, cracking her knee against the head of one of the gargoyles and sending a shooting pain up her leg. As much as it hurt, it was rather convenient, as she could blame the sudden burn of tears on the physical pain.

Much better to blame the gargoyle than decade-old memories.

With the heels of her palms pressed tightly into her eyes, Daphne admitted something she'd never even considered.

She'd died the day Benedict was born.

That first night she'd lain in bed, looking over the edge at the little bundle wrapped so carefully and lying in an old wooden cradle. His perfect cheeks, the adorable pucker to his mouth, the soft mewls he'd made in his sleep. God had given her a precious gift, despite her mistakes. From that moment on, it had become all about making sure that little boy knew God loved him even though he'd come from a poor decision.

Daphne didn't exist anymore, and what she wanted didn't matter.

But without Benedict, without the children, what did Daphne do now? What would happen to her? How did someone learn to live after denying themselves for so long? Did she even deserve to make her way back to such a state?

A sound from the next room sent Daphne scrambling from the dining room. The last thing she needed to worry about right now was what Lord Chemsford thought of her. She wasn't even sure what she thought about herself.

CHAPTER THIRTY-ONE

William should not have been able to identify individual people in the work yard from a window three floors above the ground.

He also shouldn't have been spending his time standing in the chapel because it was the only room in the house with a window from which the servants' work yard could be seen.

Yet here he was.

And there she was. A small figure draping linens over the line to dry. Over the weeks he'd known her he'd seen her dresses—all six of them—and learned all her movements.

He knew it was her.

This was the most he'd seen of her in the three days since Derek had arrived. Their interactions had been on the verge of companionable and now they had been reduced to distant professionalism. Very distant. Only-through-other-people sort of distant.

It was what he'd wanted, to put that distance between them again, to establish their roles.

But now that he had it, he didn't like it.

"Chemsford?"

"Yes?" William didn't turn around while acknowledging Derek's arrival and statement. He was too busy watching the slight sway in Daphne's movements. What song was she humming? One she'd played for him?

"In the library, you have an exquisitely carved chess set."

"Yes, I know. It's missing a pawn." It was a shame. It was one of the most unique chess sets he'd ever seen.

"Yes." There was a shuffle of feet, as if Derek were pacing across the back of the chapel. "Strange, isn't it? For a house that's been standing empty? Items don't tend to go missing when all they do is sit."

William turned from the window to see Derek not pacing but merely shuffling his feet back and forth while he clasped his hands together with an earnest look on his face. He almost looked excited. Over a chess set? Perhaps it was more than simply pretty.

"What is the chess set?" William asked.

The other man looked a bit startled. "It's simply a chess set. Very nicely carved and of a rather unique design, but there's no marks on it that would indicate it as something out of the ordinary. But I thought perhaps in the process of new inhabitants the pawn had fallen, so I've been searching the room this morning."

At this rate, Derek would be lucky to finish cataloguing the library by the end of the year. "Did you find the piece?"

"What? Oh yes," Derek answered. "It had rolled under the desk, in that carved opening beneath the drawers."

And he'd felt the need to find William and tell him that? The past two days, he'd stored up news of his more interesting discoveries and shared them over dinner. "Good."

"But there was something else under there, too, Chemsford, and I think you'll want to see it."

Why hadn't the man led with that? Whatever Derek had found, if it was enough to send him into some sort of fit like this, it might just be enough to take William's mind off Daphne. She was an impossible problem that didn't seem to make sense. Everything was just the slightest bit wrong. Or maybe he wanted it to be because it gave him an excuse to think about her more.

"Lead on." William gestured for Derek to go back toward the library and then followed close behind.

A ledger covered in tufts of dust and smudged with dirt on the bent green cloth–covered corners was spread out across the desk in the library. Neat lines and columns marched across the page, but from this distance William couldn't read the words.

"What is it?" he asked as he rounded the desk.

"A ledger."

William stopped and gave Derek a look that, hopefully, told the man he wasn't quite that thick.

The scholar cleared his throat. "Yes. Well, it appears to be quite different from the rest of the house accounts, which were in that cabinet over there and all bound in a similar-colored leather. And while the other account books hold very helpful recordings of art purchases and the like, this, well, this seems to contain mostly household expenditures."

So much for the distraction he'd been hoping for. The household accounts of an eccentric hermit weren't likely to hold William's attention for long. "He probably kept separate books for his house and his art." William glanced at an entry for a purchase of coal. "It's rather obvious he cared a great deal about his collection."

"Yes, but look at the date."

The excitement was back in Derek's voice and hope sprouted wings once more as William dropped his gaze back to the book. "November 1809."

A time when the house had supposedly been empty but for Daphne's care, being kept from degeneration. William flipped back a page in the ledger. "Have you looked through this?"

"Of course, but I'm afraid it doesn't make any sense. I would think it had somehow come from another estate except that I found a book of sketches of the house labeled as *Haven Manor*, and that is the name in the front of the book."

Derek came forward and flipped to another page. "There's the sorts of deposits one would expect to see, well, if this had been a working estate."

Entries for goat cheese, goat milk, and eggs marched down the page. The sorts of items one might sell if he or she had a large flock of chickens and a herd of goats. "Yes," William said slowly. "I think this ledger is for here."

A moment of silence met William's declaration, but soon Derek was moving through the pages again. "Normal household expenditures," the man murmured before stepping back from the book with a look of curious frustration. "And not a single listed wage."

"Not even a housekeeper?" William's brows scrunched together. Surely Daphne hadn't been caring for the place with only a roof over her head in return.

"No. But over here"—Derek flipped a page over—"there are sizable deposits made next to people's names. All the same amount and at the same time. Two for each person."

"Alice, John, Blake, Reuben." William's voice got tighter as he continued down the list. "Eugenia, Sarah."

He knew those names—well, some of them. And the amounts next to their names weren't small.

He'd wanted a distraction, something big enough he'd be forced to give it his attention. He'd gotten it. But he didn't think it was going to help him stay away from Daphne.

Likely quite the opposite.

She'd known it couldn't last forever. He would eventually insist that she stop avoiding him. The note on her desk when she returned from hanging linens proved he'd reached the end of his patience. She glanced at the note one more time.

I need to meet with my HOUSEKEEPER.

The implication was clear. She was not to send Horatia or Cyril as she'd been doing. If she were honest, he'd allowed her to do so for longer than she'd anticipated.

She paused in the antechamber to the library, standing in the shadows to get a feel for the situation. He was sitting at the desk, hunched over a book, occasionally writing something on the paper set to the side of the desk.

This wasn't the first time she'd seen him like this. He actually spent a great deal of time working through papers, ledgers, charts, and other tasks she had no idea went into the management of a title's holdings. There was something appealing about his attention to detail and responsibility.

But she didn't know what it had to do with her.

Behind him Mr. Thornbury paced. Occasionally he would reach over and point at something in the book on the desk. Lord Chemsford would nod and make another note.

Daphne lifted onto her toes and raised her chin to see if she could determine what they were looking at. From its size she would guess it to be some sort of ledger. She could do ledgers. She'd been studying her maths, after all.

"You wanted to see me, my lord?" she asked, stepping into the room.

"How long have you been caring for this house, Mrs. Blakemoor?" Lord Chemsford asked without looking up.

Daphne frowned. They'd been over this. Repeatedly. "Twelve years, my lord."

He crossed his arms on the desk and looked up at her. "And how long have you been *employed* to care for the house?"

Her gaze dropped from his and fell back onto the book on the desk. Now that she was a few steps closer she could see more details, and the familiar green cloth, though dirty and obviously neglected, sent her stomach plummeting into her toes. She knew that book. And while she could honestly say she hadn't written any of the entries, she was all too aware of what it contained.

How had he gotten his hands on a Haven Manor ledger?

Mr. Thornbury reached over and pointed at a page. "There's another set of strange deposits."

"Yes, I know." Lord Chemsford glanced down at the pages and then back at Daphne. "Tell me about the goats, Daphne."

"We're using Christian names again, are we?" Daphne bit out, fear and anxiety pushing her to find some way of putting him off, of delaying what was now inevitable. Jess would have been rather proud of the attempt.

"I wasn't aware we'd stopped."

Apparently her diversion had worked. But now she didn't know what to do with his attention. "I believe it leads only to confusion, my lord."

He rose and came around the desk to lean against it about a foot away from where she was standing. "Not as much confusion as the goats bring."

Daphne's face screwed up in confusion. They were going to talk about the goats? Not the children? Not the payments their parents had made so that Kit and Daphne could raise and hide their illegitimate children? "Goats?"

"Yes. Goats. When I inherited my father's properties, my solicitor very expressly told me that the estate hadn't generated one shilling of income in the entire time Father owned it. In fact, other than the allotment of basic caretaking funds that were sent and acknowledged each quarter, he had no records of this property at all."

He gave her a moment to respond, but what could she possibly say? Yes, the goats had been at Haven Manor for years. They'd milked them for not only their own use but to make cheese to sell at the market and provide funds to care for the children.

"I'm assuming there are more ledgers somewhere."

There were definitely more ledgers. An entire stack of them in the corner of her bedchamber at the cottage.

She pressed her lips together and folded her hands in front of her. If ever there was a time to think before she spoke it was now. "I don't suppose you'd tell me where you found that."

"Under the desk," Mr. Thornbury said, coming around to be part of the conversation. "Wedged beneath a drawer. It was quite dusty down there."

Of course it was. There was little point in getting down on her belly and cleaning the short gap beneath the drawers.

Or she'd thought there was little point. Apparently there'd been a ledger-sized point.

"I believe Daphne and I can handle this discussion, Derek.

Perhaps you could begin seeing if there's anything interesting in the portrait gallery?" Lord Chemsford, who was apparently still supposed to be William despite the fact that she wasn't allowed to dine with him anymore, didn't break eye contact with Daphne while he spoke.

It made it impossible for Daphne to look away either.

Derek collected his ever-present notebook and left the room.

Daphne felt a pang of envy at the ease of his exit. She had a feeling it wouldn't be quite such a simple matter for her to walk from the room.

"Shall we drag this out question by question?" William asked in a voice so calm it felt deadly. "Or would you simply like to tell me what's been going on at Haven Manor?"

She couldn't stop herself from wincing. "You know the name?"

"Derek found a sketch labeled such." He reached back and tapped the cover of the ledger. "It's also written on the front page. Along with the year 1809."

1809. Daphne tried to filter through her memory to remember who all was in residence in 1809. By then they'd started having the babies live with wet nurses for the first year, so Alice wouldn't have been here yet, but she would have been in the book.

Daphne wanted to speak, she did. But when she opened her mouth there were no words. She didn't know what to say. Every time she'd imagined this moment of discovery, he'd been angry. He'd blustered about like her father had when he learned she was with child, making damning comments about how her life was over and everything they'd worked for was in ruins.

Never had she considered this calm curiosity, though perhaps she should have. William had never shown an inclination toward rage.

"Daphne," he said on a sigh. She understood why he was frustrated, but he didn't understand that she just truly didn't know where to start.

"I don't know what to say," she choked out in a rushed whisper. "Twelve years is a lot of information."

His blue eyes met hers in a few moments of silence. When he

spoke again, he voice had lost the edge of frustration and returned to firm curiosity. "Question by question, then. We'll start with the goats." He turned the book so he could read it from this side of the desk. A clump of dust drifted onto the floor as he flipped through the pages. "Cheese and milk?"

"Yes," Daphne said before taking a deep breath and plunging on. "Mostly cheese. We didn't have a good way to transport the milk, so what we didn't drink got made into cheese."

"And the money from the cheese went to . . . ?"

Daphne frowned, rather embarrassed to have to admit she'd never paid much attention to the money handling of Haven Manor. "I wouldn't know. I didn't keep the books. I assume that was how we paid for coal and the foodstuffs we couldn't grow or provide ourselves."

"Have a seat, Daphne, before you fall down. You look pale as death."

Did she? That would explain why she felt so cold. He tucked the book under one arm and led her to the sofa with the other. Once she was seated, he sat across from her and put the ledger on the tea table between them.

"Who kept the books? Jess?"

The idea of Jess keeping the books was enough to break Daphne out of her frozen trance. Numbers were probably the only thing that struck fear into the woman. Books in general made her a bit nervous.

A giggle mixed with the tension and fear inside her until it burst forth in an uncontrollable fit of laughter. Not delicate laughter, but the kind that required Daphne to fold herself over her legs to try and catch her breath while tears threatened to trail down her cheeks.

Once she finally caught her breath, she wiped away the moisture clinging to her lashes. "No, I can assure you that Jess did not do the books."

Taking a deep breath, Daphne ran sweaty palms across her skirt and tried to remember that she'd done the right thing with Haven

Manor. Or thought she'd done the right thing. She'd been *trying* to do the right thing, even if the mess she was currently in meant there'd been more than one decision made in the past dozen years that wasn't entirely forthright.

"We might want to ring for tea, W-William." She stumbled over his name but pressed on, trying to cling to the delicate friendship they'd been forming. She was going to need it to confess all without fainting. "It may take a while to answer your questions."

CHAPTER THIRTY-TWO

Daphne was beautiful when she laughed. It brought out that hidden passion that had lured him into asking her to dine with him, only it came with an edge of joy that made her almost irresistible.

He had to resist, though, because this discussion was obviously serious. He thought he could guess most of it. Or at least some of it. What he was thinking didn't make him angry. Instead, it brought a sense of relief that several mysteries might finally be solved.

But she really was beautiful when she laughed.

It wasn't just the way her face changed, though the laughter made the apples of her cheeks glow. The dimples that formed deep on each side of her mouth drew his attention and made him remember every moment of that night in the music room. The laughter then had seemed to free her somehow. In that moment he'd been behind the wall she kept between herself and the rest of the world.

He'd thought she'd let down her guard before, but now he could see how much she'd been holding back.

With a happy sigh, she let her mirth fade into a smile that dropped but didn't die when she looked down at the book between them. She leaned forward and flipped to the front page filled with bold, decorative words. *Haven Manor* was written in beautiful curving letters, vines and swirls surrounding it.

"I did this every year," she said, tracing a finger over the vines. "Kit always laughed at me and told me I was ridiculous, but I did it anyway. I suppose it was my way of hoping the year would be a good one."

He'd seen that happy trance before, the night he'd found her playing the piano. As lovely as she was, he couldn't leave her in it. It was time she laid out all the answers.

Especially since a brand-new name had just been brought into the mix. "Who is Kit?"

"A friend," Daphne said, not entirely losing the hazy look from her face. "She left London with me when my father kicked me out. We ended up here."

"*Here* being Marlborough?" he asked.

She nodded. "Mrs. Lancaster took us in."

"And then Mr. Banfield placed you here?" William was under no illusions that the solicitor hadn't been aware of everything that was going on.

The documentation sent about the supposedly empty property had been much too neat and thorough for anyone to question anything about his handling of the house and grounds.

It was admirable how well it had been done. If he hadn't decided to live in whatever property his father had occupied the least, they might have been able to go on as they were for another dozen years.

"Where is Kit now?" Because she certainly wasn't here. Although she kept a very neat set of books. He refused to acknowledge the relief he felt that the unknown Kit was a woman.

"On her wedding trip. She got married a few months ago."

And the surprises continued to come. "To whom?"

The vacant look left Daphne's face, but she still gave a dreamy sigh before answering. "Graham. Lord Wharton." Her face tightened as she thought for a moment. "He's a baron, I think, though it's just a courtesy title. He's the heir to the earldom of Grableton."

And there went any idea that he was starting to get a grip on what had been going on. "Perhaps we should simply go back to 1809 and work our way forward."

"We should probably start a little before that," Daphne said as she rubbed her hands along her skirt. "Kit, Benedict, and I moved into Haven Manor in 1804, after all."

And then she started speaking.

And the story she told left him silent in shock.

Two women determined to help those with no way to build a future if their reputations became ruined, desperate to save the children from being left in the gutter or worse. They'd built a home for those children, given them a family. Then another woman had joined them and their family had grown.

And with each new piece, details that had been bothering him for months were explained.

Rows of beds that accidentally left marks on the wall as children wiggled in their sleep. Goats and chickens to feed fifteen hungry mouths and provide income.

"These are the children's names?" He ran his finger down the column. "What are the large sums beside them?"

Daphne's gaze dropped to her toes for the first time since she'd begun telling the story. "Payment. From the parents. We put away whatever we could, hoping to be able to give it to the children to buy apprenticeships or start life on their own. A lot of it went into simply living, though. It's expensive, maintaining a house such as this."

"And you didn't want to ask for additional money when there were repairs to be made, like the roof."

Daphne nodded. "But then Graham—Lord Wharton—came along, and he had a new plan. They're finding families for them now. The children. That's why many of them aren't here anymore. They've been taken in, mostly by farming families. Not the older ones, though. They don't . . . Nobody wanted them."

Suddenly Daphne pushed to her feet, words and emotions seeming to pour from her entire body. "I'm sorry. I'm so sorry. We shouldn't have used your house without permission, but if I had to do it over again, I would because each and every one of those children deserved to know that they were precious, no matter how they'd been born. It wasn't their fault."

William knew he should stand, should have stood as soon as Daphne found her feet, but his muscles weren't quite working properly. He was too much in awe of this woman. Everything she'd done, everything she'd built.

She hiccupped. "It wasn't his fault. It was mine. My fault. And I was so afraid that life would make him pay for it."

Words continued coming in a babble he couldn't quite catch, though he had a feeling she'd moved on to talking about Benedict specifically instead of the children in general. And William couldn't pretend anymore that he didn't find this beautiful and unbelievably capable woman appealing.

"And then you were here."

When had she started talking about him?

"I didn't want you to meet him, I thought you'd throw him out, try to make him go away, but you didn't. Everything you're doing for him, the furniture orders, the business lessons, it is incredibly nice of you, but then, you're incredibly nice. That's one of the things I like about you."

The babbling turned incoherent then, but he caught a word here and there, enough to know that she found him appealing as well and had been suffering as much as he had these past few days since Derek's arrival.

And all of the reasons he'd told himself why he and Daphne were a horrible match didn't seem to matter much anymore.

He stood, intending to go to her, but his movement broke her free of whatever rant she'd been caught up in and the shock on her face told him she'd revealed far more than she'd intended.

She was going to run.

If she left now, she'd go stuff these feelings under a pillow somewhere and rebuild her wall higher and stronger than before. He might never find a way through it again.

And since the new admiration had made his feelings grow past the point of being able to be stuffed anywhere, he rather hoped he could convince her to keep hers out in the open as well.

William stepped sideways to block her way around the couch and she ran into him with such force that he had to shift his feet to maintain his balance. Her balance was a far more lost cause so he wrapped his arms around her and pulled her close until she had her footing back. He allowed his arms to drop, but he didn't move. There was ample room for her to step back and a clear path behind her to the door, but he hoped, prayed, that she didn't really want to run from this.

Whatever this was.

She straightened her shoulders and slid back a half step. Close enough he could still touch her. Close enough that he could still hold her.

If she would let him.

"What do you want from me?" she asked softly.

What did he want? For so many weeks it had been the truth, but now that he had it, he wanted more. He wanted to know *her*, not just her past. He wanted her to be someone he could court, someone who would happily build a quiet life with him.

More than any of those, though, he wanted to know with complete certainty that he wasn't alone in this infatuation. He didn't want to be the only one staring at the ceiling every night, wondering what he could have done differently that day.

"I want you to stop running."

"I've a house to care for."

"I can hire another maid."

She frowned at him. "You've already hired half the county."

He scoffed. Did she even know how many people lived in Wiltshire? "Hardly. Still, I'm sure there's another young woman in need of work."

"But why?"

"Because I can't stop thinking about you." He lifted a hand slowly, watching her face while she watched his hand. When she didn't move away, he brushed a curl gently from her cheek.

"Even before now, before I learned you aren't who I thought you were."

A half-smile preceded a short laugh, and she dropped her gaze to the floor. "You weren't expecting your housekeeper to be the shamed daughter of a gentleman, hiding out in the country, raising her secret son and a dozen other illegitimate children in your house without permission?"

The hand that had gently brushed her hair back forced her chin up so that she could see the sincerity in his face. "You are not shamed, ruined, or any other of those horrendous adjectives you probably wear like an apron. I've never seen a woman with more honor. You have lived your life for the care of others and discarded all the luxuries you knew before so that they could live."

His other hand rose so he could cradle her face, thumbs lightly stroking her cheekbones, ready to catch any tears her glistening eyes were threatening to produce.

But she didn't cry, didn't even sniffle. And she didn't pull away.

He took a shaky breath. "I want you to know, Daphne, that I'm here, right here in this room with you right now because I want to be. You realize that, right?"

Her brows pulled together. "Why would you ask that?"

"Because this time, when I try to kiss you, I want there to be no question that it's real."

He paused for a breath, watching her face, her eyes, seeking a sign of panic or fear. He was aware, all too aware, of how vast a gulf stood between them socially. As far as the rest of the world was concerned, he held all the power in this room. What they didn't know was that right now he was at her mercy. She could tell him to leave and he would. He would probably pack up his residence and move it elsewhere because he couldn't imagine this house without her, and he didn't want to have to see her without him.

She blinked. Her lower lip curled into her mouth for a moment, then returned, glistening a bit. A deep breath caused her shoulders to slowly rise and fall.

But she didn't leave.

She didn't break eye contact. Even as he lowered his head.

His own eyes slid closed as his lips neared hers and time seemed to stop. Her breath brushed his lips first, then her lips were under his.

Time didn't matter. The urge to pull her in, make her part of him was overwhelming. His hands slid from her neck to her shoulders and when he felt the gentle press of her hands against his sides and the shift in the pressure of the kiss as she lifted onto her toes, he couldn't stop his arms from circling her fully and pulling her close.

This kiss was more than he imagined, more than he'd dare to dream. He'd never have thought that caring about a person could have such an impact in how a simple kiss affected him.

Not that this kiss was simple anymore. They'd left that behind when he'd eased her forward and pressed their bodies together.

He tore his mouth from hers and buried his face in her neck, pressing kisses along the edge of her worn muslin collar. Her breath rushed past his ears as his own sawed in and out of his lungs, desperate for more of that scent that was so uniquely her. Her hands lifted to his shoulders and her fingers pressed in, trying to pull herself closer.

He could have more. They could have more. She might not know it yet, but he wasn't letting her go. Not now, not when she'd let down her guard enough to show him that she was as swept away by the overwhelming feelings as he was.

It wouldn't be her first time. Nor would it be his. They could take a bit more, share a bit more, and not be crossing any line they hadn't tripped over before.

But that wasn't the point.

William crushed Daphne to him as he turned his face away from her neck, laying his head on her shoulder as he tried to fight his way through the fog in his brain that would convince him he could have everything he wanted right now.

And he probably could.

She was shaking as much as he was.

But she deserved more. They deserved more.

Love, if that's what this was, deserved more.

It deserved more than passion, more than a moment.

It deserved a lifetime.

And the fear that he wouldn't be able to find a way to make that happen wasn't an excuse to take what he could now, even if it would be freely given.

He held her, simply held her while their breath slowed its frantic pace. Once Daphne realized what had happened, what could have happened, she was going to be wracked with guilt and he didn't know how to fend it off.

So he held her, hoping maybe a few moments of connection that weren't so charged would tell her that she meant so much more to him than any fleeting physical pleasure could bring.

Then she stiffened in his arms.

He turned his face to press back into her, his nose buried in the curls he'd knocked loose. He whispered in her ear, "Don't. Please don't. " He took a deep shuddering breath. "Please don't regret that this exists. I—I won't kiss you again until we figure this out, but please, please don't regret what we make each other feel."

He waited, arms wrapped tightly around her, until she relaxed ever so slightly and nodded. Her hands brushed against his shoulders in a light caress as he opened his hold and took a step backward.

So many emotions warred on her face that he couldn't read her expression. She might not even fully know what she was feeling right then. He knew he couldn't make sense of everything that was hitting him. Between the revelations and the kiss, his mind was swimming with new ideas and sensations. All he knew at this moment was that this was a woman he wanted in his life, and it had been a long time since he'd wanted anyone to be a part of his life.

Unfortunately, caring for her didn't make the rest of the problems facing them go away.

"I think . . ." She cleared her throat and tried again. "I think I'll go see to the . . . house."

He nodded and she turned and walked toward the exit. She paused in the doorway. "This can't happen again."

Yet, William silently added as she disappeared into the antechamber. He'd agree to being careful and slow for now, but he couldn't imagine a future that didn't involve him and her exchanging vows and making sure *this* happened for the rest of their lives.

CHAPTER THIRTY-THREE

For the first time since the extra maids and footmen had invaded her home, Daphne was thankful they were there. It meant she could abandon the house into their care for the rest of the day. Given the way she'd been hiding for the past few days, it was entirely likely no one would even notice her disappearance.

She returned to the cottage and readied herself for bed despite the fact that the sun was still above the tops of the trees.

He had kissed her.

She had kissed him back.

And she had very much enjoyed it.

Crawling into bed, she pulled the covers up over her head until she was encased in a world of shadows where the only sound was the muffled rasp of her own breathing. She inhaled the crisp scent of the freshly washed linens and tried not to think.

It had been fourteen years since she'd been kissed, although she wasn't sure the two instances should be compared. Kissing William was nothing like what she remembered of kissing Maxwell Oswald. Her memory was hazy, of course, but she knew the kiss with William had been more powerful, more emotional, more everything.

It didn't escape her notice that he was the one who stopped. Not her. He was the one who'd pulled away, who'd hauled them back into reality, who'd managed to keep a hold on his senses. Not her.

A part of her had been holding on to the knowledge that he'd considered the possibility Benedict could be his to convince herself the real William wouldn't live up to the one she imagined. But whatever his sensibilities had been all those years before, they'd obviously changed. Real live William had grown from his past and put a stop to something she could only hope she eventually would have stopped as well.

What did that say about her?

He seemed intent on pursuing her. Could she let him? Could she trust herself to keep her head on straight while actually contemplating a future with William?

If she couldn't, she was better off alone.

If.

What a very large word *if* was. Because *if* was all about choices, wasn't it? *If* she went to the party in Kit's dress. *If* she was going to do whatever it took to keep her baby alive and well and with her. *If* she was going to devote her time and life to raising children.

Those choices had been easy to make. It was so much easier for Daphne to make it about other people. Even then she hadn't always been able to follow through. Despite her best intentions, she always seemed to fall a bit short.

Maybe that's why it felt so wrong to make a decision that might benefit herself. Did God want that for her? It seemed like an awfully big gift to be giving someone who had required such a large allotment of forgiveness already.

A sudden pressing weight on Daphne's chest woke her from her fitful sleep and had her attempting to rip the covers from over her head as a scream tried to claw its way out of her throat. Finally she got the blanket off her face, and breath rushed in and out of her chest like a set of bellows.

It took a few moments for the panic to clear from her vision and her eyes to adjust to the lantern light filling the room, but finally she was able to make out Jess, sitting atop her, a smirk on her face.

"What happened?"

With a groan Daphne dropped her head back onto the pillow

and gave serious consideration to covering it with the blanket once more. She settled for closing her eyes. "What do you mean?"

"You're down here hibernating like a bear while he prowls the house like a wounded lion."

Daphne lifted one eyelid and frowned at Jess. "We don't live in the jungle."

Her eyebrows drew together. "I don't think bears live in the jungle."

"Surely there's some form of bear that lives in the jungle." This was good. Daphne would come up with fifteen dozen remarks about bears if it was a topic that would successfully divert Jess.

She should have known better than to hope for that, though.

"As neither one of you are actually animals, I don't think it matters." Jess shrugged. "He brought his own plate to the kitchen."

"What?" Daphne sat up so fast she actually managed to dislodge Jess from her perch. The blonde had to scramble not to end up in a pile on the floor.

"After the last course," she said, straightening her dress once she found her feet, "he brought his plate down. Made a point of speaking to Eugenia for a moment. Sarah said he asked her how her day was while she was cleaning earlier. How much would you like to wager the man also wandered outside to chat with his stable boy?"

"He found a ledger," Daphne mumbled as she pressed her hands into her eyes. "He knows about the children."

Jess's bemused attitude dropped away as she looked at the stack of ledger books in the corner of the room. "He knows? Was he angry?"

"No." Daphne rubbed a hand over her head. She'd been so focused on the kiss and what it meant that she'd forgotten about the revelation of the children. But the fact was, he hadn't cared. He'd been . . . relieved? "I don't think it bothers him at all."

"Well, I suppose we can thank God for that favor." Jess leaned on the dressing table and crossed her arms over her chest. "What has you so upset, then?"

Daphne might as well tell her. It would save Jess the time and energy required to wear Daphne down. And she would. Somehow Jess always knew how to trap Daphne into saying whatever exact thing she was trying not to say. "He kissed me."

Jess fell silent, head cocked to the side as she considered that information. Her lack of reaction—not that she ever really had uncalculated reactions—made Daphne nervous. Finally, Jess asked, "Was it any good?"

"What?"

"Did you enjoy it?"

Daphne's mouth dropped open. "What does that have to do with anything?"

"If you hated it and want nothing to do with him, then that requires me to have a different plan than if you liked it and don't know what to do with yourself now."

Daphne pulled her legs into her chest and wrapped her arms around her knees. Would it be too obvious if she dove back under the blanket? Probably. "Why do you need a plan at all?"

Jess blinked at Daphne. "I always have a plan."

"So what plan have you been acting on since Will—er, since he got here?"

A crooked grin slowly spread across Jess's face. "William, is it?"

"As if you didn't know he's been William for weeks now," Daphne grumbled. "Just answer the question."

Jess moved to the screen in the corner of the room to prepare herself for bed. "At first I was thinking of ways to get the children out, if necessary." She poked her head around the screen. "Then once it was obvious their positions were somewhat secure, my plans turned to getting you out."

"Me?" Daphne's grip on her knees loosened. "Why me?"

"Because . . ." Jess's voice faded away as she pulled her head back behind the screen.

Daphne placed one foot on the floor, ready to charge back there if the woman didn't finish her sentence.

Fortunately Daphne didn't have to launch an attack on her friend because Jess started speaking again, though her voice was quieter. "Because I'm worried about you. You still have a lot of life to live, and I don't know what will happen to you without the children."

Daphne was touched to know that when she'd been worried about whether or not Jess even intended to stay, the other woman had been thinking of Daphne's future.

"I can be a housekeeper." She could. She was getting better at it every day. One day she might even be happy as a housekeeper. Wasn't it simply caring for people in a different capacity?

Jess came out from behind the screen and sat on her bed, facing Daphne with a serious expression. "You can be a housekeeper but not a marchioness?"

A harsh laugh escaped Daphne's lips. "Even when I was in London I didn't have visions of being a marchioness. Why would I think that now?"

"Because he's William," Jess said in a firm but quiet tone. "Because you're changing into your best dress to eat dinner with him. Because he isn't angry about the children. Because he kissed you. Because when reality forces the two of you to finally decide what crazy dance you are doing you could end up hurt and I don't know what will happen to you without the children to pull you out of it."

There was too much truth to Jess's statements. "You're right," Daphne whispered. If it hadn't been for Benedict, she'd have never found the courage to pick up the pieces of her life and rebuild. If she shattered again, she might not survive. "So I'll be safe. I'll be nothing more than his housekeeper. And," she added with determined emphasis, "I will be happy about it because it's a far better lot than most women in my position would have found."

Jess snorted as she fluffed her pillow. "Right. One question, though. Will you still be happy when you're his wife's housekeeper?"

Before she could stop it, Daphne's lip curled in distaste. Could she serve the wife of a man she'd kissed, of a man she'd had more than one fantasy about?

Could she survive living under the same roof as the woman who could take on all the aristocratic duties Daphne couldn't possibly consider filling?

Not without a great deal of agony, no.

"That's what I thought," Jess said. "And I suppose that answers the question of whether or not you enjoyed the kiss."

Daphne huffed and threw her pillow at the other woman.

Jess tossed it back with a laugh. "I've never believed in wishing something had been done differently, so the situation is what it is. You need to decide what you want and I'll help you. We can make it so that he runs into you constantly. The man already likes you well enough to kiss you. Mere proximity might send his feelings the rest of the way over."

"I don't want to manipulate him into loving me," Daphne grumbled.

"It's not manipulation. It's creating opportunity."

Daphne groaned and punched her pillow back into place. "You, my dear friend, are frightening."

"I try," Jess said and blew out the lantern.

The dark didn't keep her from speaking. As moonlight crept across the ceiling, Jess said, "You need to decide what you want, Daphne. Because he's deciding what he wants. And I can guarantee you that once he decides, he won't be above creating his own opportunities to convince you."

"You say that as if you already know what he's going to choose."

"The man hauled the most annoying person in England into his house to be some sort of wall between the two of you, and the first chance he got he scaled right over that wall and kissed you. He may not have admitted it, but I think his intentions are obvious."

Part of Daphne wanted to defend Mr. Thornbury, but she had far more pressing matters to consider as the quiet that fell over the room refused to fall over her mind.

For once, for one night, perhaps the first night in years, she didn't lie in bed imagining some other life.

She made herself consider everything she'd done—the distant past, the choices made—and she didn't play an internal game of *what if* and she didn't pretend anything had gone differently than it had. What she was reminded of was that, at some point, *she* had stopped truly existing. She'd been a mother, a caretaker, a friend, a teacher, but all of those were who she was for other people.

Who was she when it was only her in the room? She glanced across the room at the lump in Jess's bed. Well, only her in the room figuratively speaking.

This was her life.

What would it mean to actually live it?

CHAPTER THIRTY-FOUR

Daphne put on her ugliest dress the next morning.

Not that there was any chance she'd attracted whatever amount of William's attention she had with a stellar wardrobe, but she hoped the printed muslin with the orange flowers that had faded to some sort of sickly yellow and had two inches of entirely non-coordinating fabric tacked on to the bottom hem would repel him for a little while.

It wasn't an appropriate dress for a housekeeper, but kissing the master of the house wasn't appropriate behavior either, so she doubted it mattered.

Once up at the house, she noticed the servants' rooms on the lower floor had been emptied. She'd known the garret rooms were near completion, but she'd completely missed the staff moving into them.

There was no reason for her to remain in the cottage anymore. Jess's admonishment that Daphne decide what she wanted pressed on her harder than ever. If she were going to be a housekeeper, this was the moment to decide. She would give up having her own home, her own space with her remaining children underfoot. Her room would become part of her pay. Nothing would be hers.

Not that it was really hers now, but it still *felt* like it was.

The truth was, if she married William, she'd bring nothing. She didn't even have a dowry or a proper wardrobe. There was nothing to offer but herself.

That didn't seem like quite enough.

She managed to avoid William throughout the morning, resorting to hiding in her office when it started to rain in the middle of the day. When did he expect an answer? Had he ever really asked her a question? It was imperative that she make her own decisions without his sharp jawline and bright blue eyes muddying the matter.

And without the plain walls of the housekeeper's office closing in on her.

She slipped quietly up the stairs, avoiding the maids who were replacing the partially melted tapers in the candle holders so they would be fresh if used that evening. When Daphne and the children had lived here, it was a simple matter to go retrieve a new candle when the one you were using became nothing more than a pile of wax and a burned-out wick.

That wasn't the case anymore.

Keeping an eye and an ear open for William, she made her way to the chapel.

She'd spent most of her mornings here when she'd lived in the house. After waking, she'd slip through the children's rooms and into the quiet solitude of the chapel. No one else went there except for the weekly family gathering, but Daphne loved the beauty of the room too much to limit its use that way.

For Daphne, it was a refuge.

The room was dark now, with the rain clouds rolling in and obscuring the sun, but Daphne didn't mind. She knew what it looked like when golden light streamed into the room and lit on the Bible in the center of the carved altar.

Just closing the door behind her made it easier to breathe. Lowering herself onto the back bench cleared a bit more of her mind.

It was here she'd first found forgiveness after Benedict was born. It was his second birthday, and she'd sat on this very bench and sobbed. She'd poured everything out. Everything. Her fears, her insecurities, her guilt. She'd held nothing back.

And God had forgiven her.

But somehow, when she'd poured everything she was out to God, she'd forgotten to pick any of it back up.

Everything Daphne did, everything she had become was in relation to someone else. It was as if Daphne didn't exist if someone else wasn't in the room. Whenever she was alone, she escaped into her imagination. When had she started doing that? What used to be an occasional tactic to handle social interactions when they became particularly terrifying had turned into an escape from reality that was almost more of a prison.

How much had she missed because she didn't want to be alone with herself?

Was it possible that while God had forgiven her, she'd never quite forgiven herself? She always told the children that God had made them special, in His image, to be exactly who they were. God didn't make mistakes or have accidents.

But it was possible she'd been believing that truth for everyone but herself.

Jess was right. "God," Daphne prayed on a groan, "I'm so tired of saying that sentence. Could you provide your next revelation through someone else, please? Anyone will do."

The door behind her opened and she felt who it was without looking back. She didn't know how he'd found her when she'd told no one where she was going, but he had.

He didn't say anything as he lowered himself to sit beside her on the bench. At least six inches of space was between them, a proper distance by any standard, but she could still feel the warmth emanating from him, making the hairs on her arm stand up.

"Seeking God?" he asked after several silent moments.

Daphne tilted her head and looked at the altar, considering his question. "Seeking myself, I think."

"I don't think the two are mutually exclusive."

He fell quiet, waiting for her to answer. Daphne wasn't sure she could. "I think," she managed to whisper as she ran her hands over her lap and let the softness of the fabric ground her in the present, "I don't quite know who I am anymore."

"Who do you think you are?"

"A caretaker, a mother of sorts. Perhaps a friend. More recently a housekeeper. But I don't know who I am when no one else is in the room."

He was silent for a while. His soft, steady breathing and the pounding of her own heart filled her ears, the rush of blood proving she was alive. Perhaps if she went back to where she lost herself in the first place, the last time she'd known who she was, she could figure out who she'd become.

"I never had many friends," she began. The deepening shadows made it easier to be honest. "Only one, really."

He'd been looking at the altar and when she spoke his face swung in her direction. "When?"

"In London. Growing up." She gave a short little laugh. "Ever. People . . . frighten me. New people, anyway."

She fell quiet and so did he. Did she have the courage to say what it felt like she needed to say? What if she told him and he walked away? What if he didn't care for her anymore?

A deep breath stretched her chest until it was almost painful. If what she said made him leave, then he hadn't really been seeing her either. And if finding herself meant losing whatever this was that they were on the verge of experiencing, it was a loss worth taking.

"I literally wasn't myself that night." Her tongue felt thick as she stumbled over the words. "I mean, yes, I felt like another person wearing a mask and a wig and a dress from another century, but it was more than that. I was actually pretending to be Kit. I was living her life. The idea had been scary at first, but she was convinced people needed to think she'd been at that party, so I became her."

She looked down at her toes. "Despite going everywhere with Kit, I'd never experienced her life. I'd never received attention like that before. Nothing seemed real, so somehow, it didn't frighten me."

William blew out a harsh breath but didn't say anything.

"Part of me blames him, but I don't think he meant for it to . . .

to . . . happen like that." Daphne paused to dash away a tear. Even after all these years, after begging for and receiving forgiveness, she still felt a bit of shame for her actions that night. While she certainly hadn't known what she'd been doing, she'd encouraged Maxwell Oswald every step of the way.

Sliding out of that ballroom had been an exciting adventure. Kissing him had been a new experience.

And an enormous betrayal of the friend she'd been claiming to help.

"I think I gave him an opportunity he hadn't expected and he took it."

"That doesn't make it right," William growled.

"It doesn't make him wrong either," Daphne answered. "At least, not the only one who was wrong."

"Why didn't you tell him? Tell anyone?"

This was the difficult part, where the blame and guilt shifted solely onto her own shoulders. "He was already married by the time I knew there would be . . . He was married by the time I knew there were consequences. I refused to tell my father who he was because there was nothing that could be done at that point. He kicked me out. Since I'd been pretending to be Kit, her reputation was in ruins as well, so she left with me. We ended up here. Then the children gave me purpose."

The tears came faster now and she let them fall, just like she always did. They splashed onto her lap, making the faded pattern look even murkier. "Without them, I don't know who I am."

His hand slid across the bench and covered hers. "Can I tell you who I see?"

She lifted her watery gaze to his. His face didn't look anything like what she expected to see. His gaze was soft, his mouth curved into a gentle, caring smile.

"I see a strong woman who didn't let a mistake take her faith or her future. I'm a little in awe of you, if I'm honest. Because I've never even considered helping others if it required a sacrifice from me. You still love life. I can see it when you play the piano, when you guide Eugenia and Sarah, even the way you direct the new maids and sing when you wash linens."

Daphne blinked. He'd heard her singing? "I only sing when I hang them to dry."

"It's possible I've ridden by the area in the afternoons."

A smile broke through the tears and she wiped her cheeks dry.

He wasn't finished, though. "I see an incredible woman, but it doesn't matter what I see. It matters what you see. And I think you've forgotten something."

"What?"

"There's life after forgiveness."

Such a simple concept. It seemed like such an obvious truth, but sitting there, Daphne knew that she'd missed it.

She did love life. But she loved this day, this moment. She took whatever came and said it was what she wanted.

But was it? If she could *choose* instead of simply letting it happen, what would her life be like?

"When my mother died," William said, "I did things I'm not proud of. In that respect, I don't know that I'm any better than my cousin. When I came to my senses, I hated who I had become. I let my father think I was traveling the world, but I only went as far as Ireland. Over time, I realized I needed to not just change my ways but ask God to forgive the old ones." He took a deep breath and squeezed her hand. "Forgiveness is an interesting thing."

"How so?" Daphne asked.

"Unlike a lot of other things in life, it's easy to ask for and hard to accept." His hand, still covering hers, shifted until he could twine his fingers through hers. "I like you, Daphne. I don't see a mistake when I look at you. I don't see your past, any more than I see mine when I look in the mirror."

"But I bungled so badly."

"Who hasn't? Some of us are simply able to hide our bungling easier than others."

Daphne didn't speak. She looked down at their joined hands and the story told by their linked fingers. She had calluses and one of her nails had cracked and torn to the quick. They were so very different. In more ways than she could begin to count. "That kiss—"

"Was not a bungle."

She lifted her gaze to his, prepared to refute his claim, but where before his features had been soft and welcoming, there was now a hard glint to his eyes and a firm set to his jaw.

"I'll agree to it not needing to be something we repeat in the immediate future, but that was not a bungle." He swallowed hard. "You will not put it in the same room as being taken advantage of or coerced or being swept away or however you need to phrase what happened before. It's not the same."

It hadn't felt the same. She'd known where she was and who he was the entire time. And her heart had been delighted in the identity of the man on the other side of the kiss. It had been wonderful because of him—not because of what she'd imagined could come next.

"Please," he said.

She gave him a quick nod and a smile while squeezing his hand. "What do we do now?"

His other hand reached across and clasped their joined fingers. "You take your time. I already see you, flaws and perfections alike. You need to see yourself. Because if we do this, we need to both be present. It will be real, Daphne, not some secret dancing in the dark."

"Real life has consequences," she whispered.

"So does dancing in the dark," he answered. "Everything you choose to do leads to another set of decisions. That's called living."

"When did you become so wise?" Daphne asked with a smile.

"When I decided to take each and every decision that came my way and go the opposite direction my father would. It was the only way I could think of not to become who he was. I never realized until then how many choices I made every day."

She laughed, but the humor didn't last. What he was suggesting wasn't a simple decision. She knew enough about life, about the aristocracy, about London to know that she would not be easily accepted. Kit had married the heir to an earldom and in the last letter she wrote before they went on their honeymoon trip, she'd bemoaned the stares, the whispers, and the general dislike of an impertinent upstart stealing one of the most eligible matches around.

And Kit had the ability to talk and charm and hold her own in a crowd.

Daphne would get slaughtered.

She glanced up to see William's mouth pressed into a thin but determined line and knew he was thinking the same. He was admitting she wouldn't be a very good aristocrat.

Never would Daphne have thought brutal reality would be so appealing, but knowing he saw her as she was and life as it was and wasn't willing to hide from it, that sort of strength was something she wanted to cling to desperately.

But she had to find it in herself as well. She couldn't just use his.

CHAPTER THIRTY-FIVE

People were funny creatures. What was easy for one person could be an insurmountable obstacle for another.

It was simple for William to see Daphne, who she was, who she could be. Any woman who could do what she'd done—start life over the way she had, learn to do laundry and care for children and who even knew what else—well, that was a woman who would stay by a man's side through anything.

After watching his father abandon others in his life at the first indication of difficulty, someone who wasn't afraid of hard work was more than a little appealing.

He should have told her about his father in the chapel that morning. He should have talked about *her* father in the chapel, since it was too late for him and his father. William would never get that chance.

Her father was still alive, though. If he sought her out to talk about him now, would she see it as pressure or see it as he intended, as a reminder of one more issue she needed to consider while on this soul-finding mission of hers?

If he started basing decisions on how he thought she'd react, he'd go mad. His intentions were good and as long as he conveyed it that way, she'd understand.

Wouldn't she?

There was only one way to know.

It took him twenty minutes to find her, as she wasn't staying in any one place but seemed to be flitting about the house like some sort of distracted cleaning nymph. Horatia said she tucked in the corners on one half of the bed linens before moving on to sweep the stairs. Derek said he saw her briefly in the portrait gallery, where she dusted three picture frames before rolling up a rug and dragging it to the back porch. Cyril had brought the rug back inside since it was currently raining but had no idea where Daphne had gone.

Finally, William caught her as she was running a polishing cloth over the tables in the front hall.

"Daphne," he said, catching her by the arms to hold her in one place. "What are you doing?"

"Thinking. I can't seem to focus on any one task at a time while also thinking about everything else, so I've been moving about." Her face screwed up into an adorable frown. "Do you think Jess has cooked the bread yet? There may be pots in the scullery that need cleaning."

William laughed. He tried to smother it, but there was no keeping it in. How very different they were and how glorious it was.

"I wouldn't know about the pots," William said, "but I did think of something I wanted to tell you."

Her face cleared and her full attention landed on him with enough force that he sucked in a sharp breath between his teeth. So many times when he'd been talking to her before, she'd been distracted. He recognized now that it was a combination of her guilt and her secrets, but with that removed from between them, her gaze was clear.

And fully on him. She might be a bit flighty in other areas, but it was clear that when it came to people she cared about, she could home in like a sniper. He'd seen it with her dealings with Benedict.

To be given that same consideration was humbling. And energizing. "It's about your father."

Her frown returned, but her gaze didn't drop from his. "Is he making another trip here?"

"Eventually, yes, but that's not what I wanted to talk to you about." He took a deep breath. This was only going to work if he exposed a bit of himself, if he told her why he thought this decision mattered. "I wasn't ever close to my father."

Her hand lifted to cup his cheek and he felt the touch to his soul. No one had really shown him physical affection since his mother. No one who really cared about him, anyway. Perhaps that was why he was having such a difficult time releasing his grip on her arms.

"Did you fight a lot?"

"No. Probably worse than that. We ignored each other." William took a deep breath and plunged on. "My mother was an advantageous marriage for him. She brought money and old connections. They only met one time before they married and that was in the presence of her entire family."

He rubbed his hands along her arms, feeling the warmth of her beneath the ugly faded fabric. And it was incredibly ugly. Possibly the ugliest dress a woman could own.

He'd rather think about her dress than his parents, but that wouldn't help anything. "My mother thought him a wastrel, my father thought her a moral braggart. Neither was exactly wrong, but not completely right either. Mother had high standards, but she also had a great deal of loyalty and a sense of honor, which was why she married my father in the first place. He wanted to live in London, near his club and other social gatherings. She wanted to spend more time in the country, doing charitable works in the area and raising a family. They put up with each other long enough to have me, and then my father walked away."

"What did your mother do?"

"She raised me. Most of the time we acted like he didn't exist. He would come home, berate me however he could for two weeks, spin glorious tales of all the fun he was having in London without us there to weigh him down, then he'd leave again."

"That's awful."

He had to agree with her. While it had seemed terrible as a child, looking at it through the eyes of an adult made him angrier. That his father hadn't been able to put his pursuit of pleasure aside long enough to be a father to his heir was reprehensible. That his mother had been too stubborn to search for a compromise wasn't much better.

"The point is," he said, "my father never felt a bit of remorse for our separation." He took a deep breath because this was where he was afraid he'd lose her. "Your father does."

She blinked up at him, and her face dropped all expression. He knew well enough now to recognize that blankness meant she felt too much. "He does? How do you know?"

"He mentions regrets, gives advice, talks about taking time to think so that he knows he can live with his decisions." William licked his lips. "I want you to consider it. I won't tell him you're here without your permission, but, Daphne, I'm going to be working with him on this new factory. If you . . . If I . . . If *we* . . ."

"I understand."

There was a fine trembling beneath his hands. Was the fact that any sort of future with him was going to include her father going to make her walk away? Would he never again get to hold her in his arms or listen to her play?

He shook his head. He was getting lost in a future that might be. Perhaps he was picking up her habits. Not that it would be a negative to not be quite so obsessed with facts and figures, but he didn't want to get lost in possibilities and miss opportunities.

"I'll think about it," she said. "Do you—"

Her sentence was cut short by a sharp knock on the door.

Daphne swung her head to the side. "Were you expecting someone?"

"No," William answered as he started for the door.

Daphne cut him off with a hand to his shoulder. "What are you doing?"

He blinked down at her and then looked at the door. He'd been going to answer the door. He'd never answered a door in his life. Living in this strange house had definitely gone to his head.

With a bow he waved Daphne ahead of him. "After you, of course."

She rolled her eyes and smiled. That felt like such an accomplishment after the tears of this morning, and he smiled in return.

Her smile didn't last as she opened the door.

His didn't either.

Because standing on his front porch, framed by the rain sheeting down beyond the portico's shelter, were his stepmother and her son.

Daphne knew the woman at the door. Well, she knew who she once was. The chances of a woman like Miss Araminta Joysey remaining unmarried for fourteen years were nonexistent.

Miss Joysey hadn't been someone Daphne saw very often, usually only when Kit managed to finagle an invitation to a ball or party far above their normal social circle. Those times had been enough, though, to see that Miss Joysey was only nice to those who could gain her something.

And Daphne had never been one who could help anyone attain anything.

So while the woman stood in Daphne's doorway, looking her up and down as if someone had left a pile of garbage in the foyer and asked her to clean it up with her bare hands, the chances of her actually remembering the two or three encounters she'd had with Daphne were zero.

With a blink, the woman dismissed Daphne and tilted her head to look over Daphne's shoulder.

Daphne's tongue seemed to swell in her suddenly dirt-dry mouth. She was supposed to say something here. That was her job, after all. She finally managed to croak out a very pitiful, "May I help you?"

"Yes." Araminta's cultured voice was smooth and rich in comparison with Daphne's stuttering. "You can let me into this house and then bring tea."

"What are you doing here?" William appeared at Daphne's

shoulder but didn't touch her. Given the way he'd been rubbing her arms and holding her hand every time he'd seen her today, the absence of that touch when he was so close left her cold. Even as she understood he couldn't do anything in front of this woman while they were unsure where they stood—and probably wouldn't even do anything in front of her if their relationship were settled—the moment sent a pang of unease through Daphne. Regardless of William's pretty words, he was still very aware of the gulf between them.

"You invited Edmond at the end of the term." She waved a hand at the boy beside her. "Here he is."

"And here you are," William said, his voice flat.

"If I go visit anyone else yet, it will look bad. Are you going to move aside and let me in, Chemsford?"

It was the title that finally broke through Daphne's stupor and got her moving. She let go of the door and stepped to the side, carefully avoiding touching William or making eye contact with the other woman.

If Daphne were a gambler, she would bet Araminta was the stepmother who had sent William over the edge after his mother's death. Edmond would be the half brother who shared Benedict's age and part of his lineage but whose life had been ever so different.

A bite of jealousy attacked Daphne from out of nowhere. She'd never been envious of girls like Araminta, other than their ability to greet their hostess for the night without having to practice the words fifteen times in the carriage on the way over. But on her son's behalf, she was more than capable of feeling the emotion.

What was Daphne supposed to do with these people in the house? What did William expect of her? Both of their roles were muddled. Did he expect her to go back to acting the perfect, unemotional housekeeper? She hadn't been good at that even before they'd kissed.

Jess would know what to do. She'd survived a dangerous world by pretending to be people she wasn't. Surely she could help Daphne be some other version of herself.

Feeling a bit bad about abandoning William to the mercies of a woman he couldn't stand, she fled down the stairs to the kitchens, almost tripping on the bottom one.

Jess wasn't in the kitchen, but angry voices were coming from one of the small storage rooms where they stored utensils and dishes.

"I don't care what you think you saw, you can't just come down here and start moving things around in my kitchen." Jess's voice was low and cold.

Daphne rushed a little faster toward the storage room. If Jess was that angry, whoever she was talking to might be about to find a knife skewering their shirt to the wall whilst they were still wearing it.

"But the platter I saw last night could very well be a piece of Iznik pottery. If there's more of that here, it would be an extraordinary find." The other voice was Mr. Thornbury. The last time Daphne had seen him he'd been scribbling in his notebook in the portrait gallery. When had he come down here?

"Then you can come find them sometime when I'm not preparing a meal because I do not need these dishes spread out across every available surface."

Daphne got to the door of the storage room and saw Jess with her arms crossed over her chest—no knife in sight, thankfully—and her eyes narrowed into thin, angry slits. Derek Thornbury was across the room from her, a plate in each hand and three more in a stack by his feet.

He angled his head and gave Jess a blank look. "But you're never not preparing a meal. You never leave this kitchen."

"Sounds like you have a problem," Jess said.

He considered the plate and then set it and the rest back on a shelf. "I'll ask Lord Chemsford to request a particularly simple meal. That way your time in the kitchen will be lessened. You'll get a bit of a rest and I'll get to look at the plates."

The grin that spread across his narrow face was that of a little boy expecting everyone to be proud of his problem-solving skills.

Jess muttered something in another language. Daphne thought it might be Italian, but she wasn't entirely sure.

Bizarrely enough, Mr. Thornbury answered in the same language, though his words were very stilted compared to Jess's easy flow of words. A flush stole up the petite woman's neck.

When was the last time Jess had blushed?

Everything about the entire encounter was strange and Daphne wasn't sure she could handle more tension right now. She looked at Mr. Thornbury, then at Jess, and blurted out, "I just opened the door to a prettier version of myself."

Both people in the storage room swung their gazes in her direction, the foreign words dying on their lips.

"I'll be back when that meal has been arranged," Mr. Thornbury said, shuffling out of the room with his gaze averted.

Jess didn't say anything until the man's steps could no longer be heard echoing in the stairwell.

"Do you want to repeat that?" she asked.

Daphne hadn't even realized what had bothered her so much about Araminta's presence—aside from the fact that it was another intrusion, of course. "She has dark hair and dark eyes and she's my height and my age and her dress looks like it was made sometime this decade and her skin has obviously never been submitted to the sun while working in a garden or hanging laundry."

"And she's on the porch?" Jess asked.

"I don't know where she is now, but I doubt it's the porch. William either sent her away or invited her in."

It was to Jess's credit that she didn't take the opportunity to tease Daphne about the use of William's Christian name. Instead, she tackled the problem at hand. "Who is she?"

"Miss Araminta Joysey. Well, she used to be Miss Araminta Joysey."

"Then she's the current Lady Chemsford."

Daphne blanched. One knee locked while the other gave way and she careened sideways into the doorframe. It was one thing to suspect and another thing to know. "His stepmother is the same age as I am. I don't want to be old enough to have married William's father."

"You're old enough to have married his grandfather, if the man had been alive and unattached. The old aristocrats marry the young blood every year." Jess gently guided Daphne back to the kitchen. "You'll need to take up some tea."

"I'm not taking it." If William saw Daphne next to Lady Chemsford again, he would realize how wrong they'd been to even consider a future together. That was who Daphne would be following if she married and accepted the title?

The situation was even worse than Daphne had imagined. Did they allow marchionesses to stand in the corner, wearing dresses just fashionable enough to be ignored?

She nudged Jess in the shoulder. "You take it."

Jess nudged back, hard enough to send Daphne turning on her heel and catching herself. "I'm not about to risk her having seen me or some other such nonsense because you think she has better hair than you do."

"And clothes," Daphne mumbled. "I'll send Sarah."

"She's in your office."

Daphne blinked. "My office? Why?"

"Because you told her to take an hour and study some of those books you brought down. But by all means, interrupt her. I think she'd thank you."

Jess returned to the storage room and came out with a tray and dishes. "Has it occurred to you," she said as she plopped the tray on the table, "that everyone has better clothes than that dress you chose to wear today? If that ugly thing hasn't bothered him yet, seeing it next to a traveling wool isn't going to either."

Jess was right. Again. But Daphne didn't want to go back upstairs. She would give almost anything not to have to deal with that situation.

Was she even willing to abandon the idea of William?

His world outside of Haven Manor was filled with people like Lady Chemsford constantly having tea and interrupting others' lives because they could.

If Daphne couldn't handle a woman like that, how could she ever hope to stand by William's side?

CHAPTER THIRTY-SIX

The rain continued the next day. It was the sort of rain Daphne knew from experience was going to last for days on end.

So they did what she'd been avoiding. They all moved into the house.

Jess made a run down to the cottage for clothing and supplies, and soon the housekeeper's room Daphne had tried to forget existed held her clothes, her brush, and most of her other personal necessities.

She'd moved in.

As expected, the next day brought more rain, and the day after that even more.

It was that soaking sort of rain that made even stepping out onto the porch a drenching experience. So everyone stayed inside.

Everyone.

Daphne spent each day trying not to drop whatever she was carrying as she went about her duties with arms weak as wet linen and lungs that could never quite seem to fully inflate.

She spent each night lying alone in her bed in the housekeeper's room, holding her pillow over her face because even though she let the tears come, they refused to be silent. Eventually she would fall into an exhausted sleep that never left her feeling rested.

The house, which had never seemed too small to her before,

now felt like the most confining space she'd ever been in. Lady Chemsford's lady's maid, a horribly snippy woman named Miss Partridge, made Mr. Morris's early days in the house a faraway dream. Her requests only added to Daphne's burden, mostly because Daphne hadn't the slightest idea how to accommodate them.

Haven Manor was not equipped to entertain ladies. As far as Daphne was aware, it never had. There were no painting supplies or embroidery needles. While there had at one point been an extensive collection of quills for doing paper-filigree work, all of those had been taken down to the cottage. Even if Daphne had been inclined to find a way to transport the paper through the rain, she wouldn't have. Those quills had been used by her beloved children.

There were no cards, and while Edmond and William engaged in several games of chess, Lady Chemsford was not so inclined. Her boredom sent her strolling through the halls until Daphne spent every moment in a sense of heightened anticipation that she would turn and find the woman standing like a specter sent to warn Daphne of her possible future.

If Daphne had only had to worry about herself, it would have just been mild agony. But the rain had trapped Benedict at the house, too, when Mr. Leighton had taken the wagon back to his shop to load it up with more moulding.

Daphne, Jess, and Benedict knew this type of rain well enough to know it would have made the river flood. The bridge from Marlborough was going to be impassable for days.

The boy had taken to whittling wooden figures in the scullery since it was the only place Miss Partridge wasn't likely to go. After three days, he'd created a small army of people who largely resembled Daphne, Kit, and the other children. It was enough to rip a mother's heart to shreds.

"The tray is ready." Jess wiped sweat from her brow with her sleeve and sighed before turning back to the bread dough that had been set aside to rest.

Daphne glanced around but quickly realized the maids and

even the footmen were nowhere to be seen. Unless she wanted to send Sarah or Eugenia with the tray, she was going to have to take it herself. Even if going up into the main house had started making her feel ill, she wasn't about to subject her children to Lady Chemsford's toxic presence.

"I'll take it."

She scooped the tray from the table and started up the stairs. It was a short walk to the library. She'd be back downstairs before her heart had a chance to stop.

Edmond and William were bent over the chessboard, talking in low tones. Daphne crossed the room and set the tray on a table next to them.

"Please tell me there's something other than blackberry scones today," moaned Lady Chemsford from the sofa across the room.

Daphne nearly dropped the plate she'd been arranging. How had she not noticed the other woman in the room when she'd walked in?

Lady Chemsford crossed the room and frowned at the food offering. "How can you live out here, Chemsford? This place is dreadful. Edmond, we're leaving as soon as this horrid rain ceases."

"You can't," Daphne blurted.

Three sets of eyes swung her way. Edmond's looked merely curious, while Lady Chemsford's were narrowed slits. William appeared as lost as Daphne felt in this whole situation. Despite what some of the books Kit used to talk about said, it didn't look like love could actually conquer all.

"Why not?" Lady Chemsford bit out.

"The rain, my lady." Daphne swallowed and ran a dry tongue across her lips in a futile attempt to wet them. "When it rains this much, the bridge between here and Marlborough tends to flood."

Daphne braced herself for the woman's disapproval. When it turned on William instead of Daphne, it still hit like a punch in the stomach. "Your father would never have let himself be in a place that could leave him so easily cut off from the world. You are a marquis. People need to see you, know you. How can you establish the title if you can't actually get to anything besides a cow and a tree?"

Part of Daphne wanted to rush to William's defense, but the other part of her, the part that was insisting on being realistic about her future, agreed. How indeed?

"Goats," William corrected as he dropped his gaze and moved his bishop. "I have goats. Not cows. And the title is already established. I received my writ of summons months ago. My Parliament seat is secure."

This woman couldn't have arrived at a worse time. He couldn't boldly claim Daphne in front of her because Daphne had never gotten a chance to decide if she wanted to be claimed or not. And every day that went by without him having a chance to talk to her or spend time with her felt like a knife to the heart because he knew he was losing her. He could see her struggle in having Araminta and Edmond in the house, stealing away the security these walls had brought her.

"The title is more than Parliament. You've an obligation to show others the proper way to live." Araminta picked up a scone and frowned at it. Since William knew Jess hadn't sent up anything that wasn't perfect, he could only assume Araminta was upset about not being able to find fault with anything other than the choice of fruit.

"Perhaps I think others should burrow themselves into the country for a while and gain some perspective. It might even do you some good, Araminta."

William stared at the chessboard, hoping Edmond would make a move, but a glance up revealed the boy was looking from his mother to William and back again, with eyes wide enough to show white around the brown centers. Had he never seen anyone not immediately give in to his mother before?

"How can this place possibly do me a bit of good?" she grumbled. "There's nothing to do here."

"Read a book." Since Edmond wasn't making a move, William couldn't really continue staring at the chessboard, so he turned his attention to the tea tray instead.

"I was reading a book. It was dreadful. This place is dreadful."

William looked up, surprised Daphne was still standing a few steps away. He'd have thought escape would have been her priority. She looked pale and pinched, and her eyes had that glazed look she'd worn when he first arrived. Worry crept in, crowding out other thoughts. "You're in an incredibly well-stocked library, Araminta. Pick something else."

Then he stood, intending to go to Daphne, no matter what the others would think, no matter what Daphne would think. She wasn't well and he refused to sit by and not see to her care.

But his movement shook her from whatever had been holding her there, and she fled the room before he could do more than look in her direction.

"At the very least," Araminta said as she returned to the sofa and her book that was terrible but apparently not terrible enough to exchange, "you should live somewhere that can provide a decent staff. Yours is deplorable."

Daphne had thought the worst part about moving into the housekeeper's room was going to be the sense of loss not having her own space would bring. It wasn't. It was having the space completely to herself. Jess was in a room on the other side of the kitchen instead of a bed on the other wall. The girls were three floors away instead of right across the landing.

There was no one to talk to, no one to tease. No one to be strong for.

Restless, Daphne left her room and picked her way through the quiet house to the back porch. She'd tried to resist the lure of the porch, but every night she found herself there again, even when it was raining.

When they'd lived here, it was a nightly tradition for Kit and

Daphne, and then Jess as well, to meet on the porch and watch the moon reflect on the lake at the bottom of the hill. They'd talk about the children, about life, about everything. They'd shared secrets and become family.

She'd missed this porch. She missed Kit. That was difficult to admit since she was truly happy for her friend, but Daphne missed her. Kit had been the one constant in Daphne's life, the person who was always willing to stand between Daphne and the rest of the world.

Sometime after dinner, the rain had finally stopped, leaving the view before her glistening in the moonlight. Fresh and full of promise and empty of people.

The door opened behind her and Daphne jerked to the side, hoping to step into the shadows before someone found her, but it was William who was joining her.

"How did you know where to find me?" she asked.

"Jess slipped a note under my plate." William walked over to join her at the porch railing.

They stood shoulder to shoulder, looking out at the moon, neither of them speaking. Probably because they both knew what needed to be said but didn't want to be the one to say it.

"They aren't all like Araminta," he finally said.

"They don't have to be." Daphne swallowed, trying to remove the lump in her throat. This was not the moment to cry. This was the moment to be strong. "I'll always be thankful to you, though. You showed me I wasn't living my life. I was simply existing."

"What are you saying?" William turned and leaned his hip on the rail.

"I don't know." She couldn't do it. She couldn't tell him good-bye yet. This wasn't going to work, though. Instead of a sparkling jewel on his arm when he went to London, she'd be the weight that pulled him down.

This afternoon in the library, as she'd stood frozen to the floor, she thought she'd been ready to tell him good-bye, but here, with the night and the peaceful quiet, she wasn't as sure that it was the right choice.

"Don't give up yet," he said, reaching a hand out to run the back of his finger along her cheek. "There's time. Araminta won't stay here forever. She'll probably leave as soon as the bridge clears. Then we'll take some time."

It wouldn't change the answer, but Daphne was selfish enough to want that time.

"I've never felt like this, Daphne, like I would stop the whole world for another person." His words were whispered, but their impact was enormous. No one other than Kit had ever wanted to put Daphne first. Even Kit had eventually traveled her own path, a path Daphne couldn't follow.

William ducked his head a bit so he could look Daphne in the eye. "I want you to know that the only reason you haven't dined at my table this week is because I didn't think you were ready. I want you there, Daphne, and I'd have sent a tray to Araminta's room if she couldn't handle it. But I'm not going to do that to you without your approval. I see you, Daphne. Don't think I'm waiting for you to turn into someone else because I'm not. But I'll never make you do something you don't feel you can handle."

But she wouldn't be what he needed. "You are a marquis," Daphne whispered. "People need to see you, know you."

"Do not quote that woman to me. I have never wanted anyone like Araminta. Ever. All I want is a woman at my side who cares about me and the same things I do."

"But she's right. People need to see you. Your people. If I stand by your side, they'll see me, too. I don't think I can do it, William."

It had been such a lovely concept, life after forgiveness, but it was too late for her. She didn't know how to live anymore. "These past three days have been some of the hardest I can ever remember. I can't eat, I sleep only when I'm exhausted." A sob broke through her restraint, and the rest of her words were broken by hiccups and gasps as her chest heaved and the tears flowed. "And that's here, in my own home. I don't know what to do in front of her, I don't know what to say. I was never very good with people and now what little skill I had is lost."

"You can relearn." He pulled her close to him, and she buried her face in his chest, soaking up his warmth.

She tried to speak, tried to form the words to say good-bye, but all she could do was weep. He held her as her shoulders shook and her body trembled and she cried—not just the tears that managed to overflow the walls she'd built in her heart, but the ones that had lain trapped inside. She cried until she didn't even know what she was crying about anymore.

And then there was nothing.

She woke up in her own bed, somewhere in the early hours before everyone else was awake. Jess was in a chair in the corner, her head leaned against the wall, chest rising and falling easily in sleep.

And Daphne knew. When the bridge cleared and Araminta left, Daphne was going to be right behind her.

CHAPTER THIRTY-SEVEN

For the next two days, William ignored Araminta. The more she complained, the farther away he stayed. He took Edmond and Derek and began packing up the items in the glass drawing room. While Derek scribbled in his ledger, William and Edmond wrapped the various articles in old linens and placed them in crates that had been found in a storage room.

Daphne didn't deliver any more trays.

He didn't go out onto the porch again. He was too afraid the next time they spoke she would say the words that killed his hope.

"What are you going to do with this room? Oh, that's a Ming vase. You should put that on display somewhere." Derek wrote another line in his ledger, and Edmond added the blue-and-white vase to the small pile Derek had declared too precious to store.

William wasn't sure he liked them any better than the other pieces they'd put away, but there was a table in the saloon that would easily hold whatever Derek wanted left out. Daphne could always crate them up later if they didn't fit with her vision for a particular room.

"A billiard room," William declared as he carefully picked up the next piece. "If this rain has taught me anything it's that I need a few more indoor amusements around here."

"That would certainly be convenient, if you intend on spending more time here. It's rather removed, though, for a marquis," Derek replied.

William really wished people would stop telling him that. It was almost as if God himself was trying to remind William of his obligations.

Maybe He was.

That didn't mean William had to like it.

William didn't join her on the porch again, even though Daphne continued going out each night. The moon was starting to shrink now. In a few days there'd be nothing but stars in the night sky. Then the moon would grow again and the cycle would repeat. Time. Moving on the way it always did. Always would.

Even though the rain had stopped, she hadn't moved back down to the cottage. She was done lying to herself. For as long as she was here, she would be the housekeeper. She couldn't pretend to be the mistress of a home.

When the door opened behind her, she dug her fingers into the stone railing before turning her head. But it wasn't William stepping out on the porch.

It was Benedict.

"Ben," she said, reaching over to run a hand through his hair the way she'd done when he was younger. "What are you doing out here?"

"Looking for you. The bridge should be passable tomorrow, so I'll be going back. Mr. Leighton's probably been able to do a lot without me there, but I should get back to work as soon as I can. I don't want him to think I'm more trouble than I'm worth."

Daphne rather thought Mr. Leighton would soon be willing to pay for the privilege of being a part of Benedict's brilliant future, but she kept that to herself. A little humility would do the boy well if his designs became as popular as she thought they would. "I'm sure he understands. He's seen the bridge flood before."

Benedict nodded and then sat on the steps. "I've been lying in bed the past few nights, thinking one thing over and over. I did what you always said and I talked it out with God, even sat across from an empty chair like you do sometimes and pretended He was sitting there."

Daphne swallowed, tears burning the edges of her eyes. As far as legacies went, that was a rather nice one to be leaving her son. "And?"

"And the question didn't go away." He swallowed hard. "And I think you know the answer."

Dread pooled in Daphne's gut as she lowered herself onto the step next to him.

Benedict rubbed a hand along his neck. "I understand my . . . well, my father, I understand him not coming. I've been in Marlborough a few months now and I've seen some of those dandies coming through from London. Some of them are more interested in making sure their boots are shiny than ensuring the proper fit of their horses' harnesses. I guess I'm kinda thinking my father was like that."

Maxwell Oswald had never truly been a dandy, but he'd certainly been more concerned with power and social prestige than the well-being of anyone else, so the assessment was close enough.

"But I have to know"— Ben's voice grew raspy—"who was my mother? Why did she leave?"

Daphne's heart cried to tell him the truth, that his mother loved him enough to give up everything for him. But she couldn't. Instead, she said, "A woman on her own is very vulnerable, Benedict. If she hasn't the means to live on her own or the protection of someone who will support her, she has nowhere to go but the poorhouse."

"They buried a baby last week." Benedict scuffed his foot and kicked a pebble down the steps. "I see things like that now, living in town."

The image stabbed Daphne in the heart. "We created Haven Manor so that you and Sarah and Reuben and the rest of them wouldn't be that baby. We couldn't save them all, Ben, but we did what we could."

"Why? Why keep taking us in?"

Daphne smiled and cupped a hand around Benedict's cheek. "Once your house is full, what's one more? There were always hands to help and food to eat, though we all grew a bit tired of turnips."

"Why me, then? I was the first one. Why did you take me in?" The moon, waning though still bright, threw shadows across his face, deepening the strong lines and making him look older than his thirteen years. "Who was my mother? Because you took me in to save her, didn't you? It wasn't about me. It was about her. She pushed me away. And now I'm being pushed away again. Lord Chemsford has been nicer to me than I could have ever expected, but I know he doesn't want me abovestairs right now. He doesn't want to have to explain me. I know why he'd shove me away. But I need to know why she would."

What could she tell him? Would the truth help him or hurt him? And what about Sarah and Eugenia and Reuben, the ones who hadn't yet reached the point of making a life for themselves? What would the truth do to them?

"I came here for you," she said quietly, deciding to go with the truth that truly mattered. "Whatever you may think, I want you to know that. You are all I was thinking of when I committed to raising you and other children like you. I love you more than I have ever loved anything in this world."

He leaned sideways and buried his head in her shoulder. She tried to wrap her arms around him, but he'd gotten so tall that the position was awkward and she had to settle for one arm across his shoulders.

"Who was she?" he asked. "I have to know. I don't want any more surprises, I don't want to wonder. I just need to know so I can nail it up and move on. I want to stop thinking about it, Mama Daphne."

And because she would do anything for her son, she told him. "It was me."

His head snapped up and he looked at her. She wanted so badly to tear her gaze from those blue eyes, but she made herself stay steady. "I am your mother."

He jolted up, stumbling in the process. She reached out a hand to catch him, but in moments he was safely at the bottom of the stairs.

And then he ran.

The chaos in Daphne's heart was matched by the upheaval in the house the next morning. Lady Chemsford was insisting on departing as soon as possible. Edmond declared he wanted to stay, while Lady Chemsford said she couldn't leave her son in such a mudhole.

Mr. Thornbury was moving glass and ceramic pieces to every room in the house, and no one was quite sure what William was trying to do, but he was getting in everyone's way.

Since Daphne still held the title of housekeeper, it meant sorting out the entire mess fell to her.

It should have been Daphne's worst nightmare, but it wasn't. All she had to do was arrange her people in all the right places to make sure everyone had the help they needed. She directed the retrieval of Lady Chemsford's trunks and the preparation of her carriage. She stationed maids throughout the house so anyone who needed help wouldn't have to look far.

Little by little, she brought control to the chaotic morning. The only issue she couldn't resolve was the ongoing fight between Lady Chemsford and William over whether or not Edmond was staying.

The first loaded trunk was being brought into the front hall when the front door flung open, breaking Daphne's composure into bits.

Kit, dressed in a gorgeous dark blue traveling dress and flower-bedecked bonnet that framed the enormous smile on her face, strode in only to stop dead when she saw Cyril setting the trunk down. "Oh dear."

Her new husband, Graham, followed her through the door. "What is it?"

Their arrival was going to add a new wrench in the works, but for the moment Daphne didn't care. She was so happy to see her friend. With a squeal, Daphne rushed passed a gaping Cyril and wrapped her arms around her friend.

Once the hugging ended, Daphne stepped back and looked at the two of them. Kit had never appeared happier, even when she'd been pushing her way into London society before their lives had taken a drastic turn.

"I think," Graham said, casting an eye about the front hall, "Mrs. Lancaster has misinformed us. She said the new owner was out."

"Then Nash told us it was complicated with the new owner. He didn't correct her about him being in residence, though." Kit bit her lip. "Is he here?"

"Oh yes," Daphne whispered with a wince. "And the thing is, the new owner—"

"If I were to make a guess, I would have to assume you're Kit."

Daphne glanced over her shoulder to see that William had come to the door.

Kit's loud gasp was followed by Graham's low chuckle. "I think, my dear, that Nash wanted us to be as surprised as he was." Graham stepped forward. "Lord Wharton. I don't know if you remember me from Harrow. I was a year or two behind you."

"I remember you. And to save all of us any unpleasantness, I can assure you I have already met Benedict." He glanced back into the house. "I believe he's around here somewhere, but there are other guests in the house at the moment whom he's been avoiding. Won't you come in?"

Daphne could have told them Benedict was not, in fact, on the property anymore, as he'd run off into the woods the night before. The moon had cast enough light and he knew his way well, so she assumed he was safe. That didn't mean she wasn't worried about him, though.

"What is going on here?" Kit whispered in Daphne's ear.

"More than I can tell you right now," Daphne answered. "But you can assume he knows everything. His other guests, however, do not."

"Oh." Kit twined her fingers with Daphne's as they all stepped farther into the front hall so Cyril could close the door.

Lady Chemsford strode in, grumbling about how slowly her luggage had been retrieved.

Daphne dropped Kit's hand and stepped away, resuming a housekeeper's proper placement. Kit frowned in response, but thus far Daphne had managed to remain just beneath general notice, and she aimed to keep it that way. Looking chummy with the new Viscountess of Wharton wasn't likely to do that.

Lady Chemsford went from frowning to simpering in an instant. "Lord Wharton. I had no idea you were acquainted with Chemsford."

"Old schoolmates from Harrow," Graham said with a slight bow. "My condolences on the loss of your husband."

He hadn't given the same condolences to William, but then, Graham always seemed to know what other people needed to hear. It was one of the reasons he was so good at finding families that wouldn't hold the by-blow birth of a child against them.

As the group discussed the now-passable nature of the bridge, Daphne decided to see to the remainder of Lady Chemsford's trunks. With Kit here for a visit, Daphne wanted the other woman gone as soon as possible. Before Daphne could exit the front hall, though, a knock sounded on the front door.

"Apparently we weren't the only ones waiting for the path here to become clear," Graham said as Cyril moved to answer the door.

Daphne told herself to keep moving, that it didn't matter who was at the door because it was sure to be someone to see William. But life was turning into a small world, and so she looked back, needing to know if the new arrival was someone who might know her. With Kit on the premises, it was far more likely someone might notice Daphne.

Or it might be the only other person besides Kit who would recognize Daphne anywhere.

Her father was standing on the threshold.

There was no way he wasn't going to notice Kit's attendance.

"Hullo there!" Papa said cheerfully. "There was an update on the factory and I thought I'd bring it to you myself. I took the stage in and had to wait because the rain covered the bridge. Fortunately, I ran into your cousin at the inn, and he was coming this way and gave me a ride."

Daphne's legs nearly went out from under her. Kit gasped and scrambled across the room. Graham went to join William in creating a wall of bodies. Lady Chemsford gave Kit and Daphne a strange look as Kit steered Daphne in a circle, intent on going down the stairs to the kitchens. Only someone else had just come up those stairs because Benedict ran into the room and threw his arms around Daphne.

"It doesn't matter," he whispered in her ear as he squeezed her tight. "I got all the way to Mr. Leighton's last night and realized the only person I wanted to talk to was you because you've always been my mum."

"My goodness!" Araminta cried. "Who is that?"

Benedict stepped back but kept one hand on Daphne's shoulder as she turned to face the front hall.

Daphne's heart pounded and her breath came in short, small bursts until her lips began to tingle and a dimness crept across her vision. She could see her father clearly enough, though, as everyone turned to look at Lady Chemsford.

Then another man, with a beautiful woman on his arm, stepped in behind her father, and it was the sight of Maxwell Oswald that finally did her in. Those short, harsh breaths came faster and faster until she wasn't sure she was actually breathing at all.

"I don't think we're going to have enough guest rooms," she choked out.

And then she fainted.

CHAPTER THIRTY-EIGHT

William wasn't sure who to handle first: Araminta, Mr. Blakemoor, or his wastrel of a cousin. When Daphne's legs gave way and Benedict scrambled to catch her, the question was answered.

He strode across the room and picked her up, holding her tightly to his chest. She was breathing now and a bit of color was returning to her face. He glanced around the room at the various expressions ranging from outrage to surprise to mild panic. Perhaps it was best if she didn't wake up too soon.

Everyone trailed behind him as he carried Daphne into the drawing room off the front hall and placed her gently on the sofa. Kit was there immediately, kneeling by Daphne's head and brushing the hair from her face.

Benedict knelt beside Kit, while Graham stepped behind and placed a hand on each of their shoulders.

Mr. Blakemoor slowly approached the sofa, looking at the daughter he'd thought he'd lost. He braced one hand on the back of the sofa and reached the other down to clasp Daphne's cold fingers. "Daphne? My Daphne? Oh, my sweet girl."

A slight burn hit the corners of William's eyes. He'd known this reunion needed to happen. But it probably shouldn't have happened in quite this way, because everyone else had trailed into the drawing room as well, and they weren't nearly as happy.

Araminta pointed one long finger at Benedict. "Who is that boy?"

Maxwell snorted and wore a look of complete superiority. "Isn't it obvious? The perfect, self-righteous Lord Chemsford has a son."

"Actually," William bit out, "he's your son."

Kit groaned and dropped her head to the sofa next to Daphne's shoulder.

"Probably could have stated that a little gentler," Graham whispered.

"Probably shouldn't have said it at all," Kit added.

They were both correct, but there was nothing William could do about it now. The truth was, he was through being delicate. This was his home, and of all the places he should have control it was here. But he was losing the person who mattered most to him because he was trying to be perfect for everyone and he was tired of it. A glance at Benedict's pale face made him wish he'd held on to aristocratic diplomacy a bit longer, though.

Then again, if William had been more direct and actually answered his cousin's missives, the man probably wouldn't be here now.

"He's not mine," Maxwell shouted, stepping forward. "I don't have a son, I've never—oh." His words came to a crashing halt as he got close enough to see over the edge of the sofa and identify Kit. "I assume he's yours, then."

Kit glanced up at William, then Graham, before setting her mouth and borrowing William's line. "Actually, he's hers." She nodded her head toward Daphne.

Graham groaned. "Really, dear?"

"As if everything wasn't about to come out in the wash right now anyway. We might as well get it over with while she misses the worst of it."

The woman who had come in with Maxwell gasped. "What? When were you with her? Who even is she?"

"That's my daughter," Mr. Blakemoor growled. Then he looked

at Benedict, his eyes glazed. "And that's my grandson. Who are you?"

Jess slipped into the room with a bottle in her hand and tried to ease around the crowd. It was a bit difficult. The drawing room hadn't been designed to hold this many people standing around one sofa.

"I am Mr. Maxwell Oswald," he said, puffing up his chest. "And I have never seen that woman in my life."

Lady Araminta stepped in. "Are you calling the Marquis of Chemsford a liar?"

Kit sprang up from the floor and rounded the sofa, fists clenched. "She was in my costume when you set out to ruin me, you monster." She started to swing her fist, but Graham wrapped an arm around her and held her back.

"No, I rather think she has the right idea." William went around the other end of the sofa, his own fist clenched. He'd never hit a man before but this seemed a prime first opportunity.

Araminta screamed, but Graham was there again, one arm still around his wife's middle as he grabbed hold of William's arm. "I don't think this is the answer."

Then the sickening thud of bone to flesh followed by Maxwell's howl of pain had everyone turning to see Mr. Blakemoor shaking his hand out and Maxwell cupping his eye.

"Well, then," Graham said as he let his captives loose.

"It wasn't supposed to be her," Maxwell moaned and then pointed at Kit. "I thought it was her."

Graham sighed. "Don't make me want to hit you, too. It wouldn't take much at this point."

"Why me?" Kit asked, leaning into Graham's side. "Why did you want to ruin me?"

"It was just supposed to be your reputation." Maxwell shrugged as if what had happened was as inconsequential as tripping over a torn hem during a dance.

William growled and stepped forward. The hand Graham placed on his shoulder wasn't all that heavy and William could have easily stepped free of it, but it was a reminder that punching the man wouldn't change anything.

"That doesn't tell us why," William said instead, straightening his coat with sharp jerks.

Maxwell glanced at his wife. "She hated Katherine. Said the only way she would marry me was if I put her in her place."

Charlotte, who had up until this point been trying to stand to the side, gasped. "You can't blame this on me."

Kit crossed her arms and stepped forward. "What was it you told me? That you'd made a bet with Maxwell about women who married and women who dallied?"

Charlotte blanched a bit. "I might have been young and foolish. But weren't we all? I never meant for this to happen. I just wanted you to step back down where you belonged."

In the next moment, a pillow came flying across the room, tassels fluttering as it connected with Charlotte's head and shoulders. She screamed and ducked to the floor as everyone's attention swerved once more.

Jess was calmly walking away from a now-pillowless chair, bottle of smelling salts still in hand. As she made her way to the sofa and uncorked the bottle, she looked around at all the faces and raised her eyebrows. "It was that or the vase."

Kit's snicker broke the silence, but no one else said anything as Jess knelt and waved the smelling salts beneath Daphne's nose.

Those beautiful brown eyes blinked open, and William rushed back to her side, supporting her head as she lifted it and looked around the room.

"I think," she said softly, "that I'm going to be sick."

The water cooled Daphne's neck as Jess changed out one cloth for another.

After her declaration, Kit and Jess had swooped in and escorted Daphne from the room, one under each arm. William had wanted to follow, but Kit had told him there were other people who needed to be dealt with right then. Benedict had followed them down to the kitchens but stayed out of the way.

"I think I'm well now." Daphne slid the cloth from her neck and used it to dab her face. "Physically, anyway."

"What do you want me to do?" Kit asked, rubbing one of Daphne's hands between her own.

"I don't . . . I can't . . ." There were so many people. People in the house, in the kitchen, on the estate. Everywhere, there were people. How was Daphne supposed to think straight with so many people around? How could anyone think like that?

Jess slid a cup of tea in front of Daphne. Kit moved toward a basket next to the hearth to grab a couple of Naples biscuits.

"Not those," Jess said. "I'm taking those out to the goats."

Kit frowned at the treat. "Why? What's wrong with them?" She took a tiny nibble of one and then groaned. "What is wrong with *you*? You can't feed those to goats." She snatched the entire basket and brought it over to Daphne. "Try one of these."

Thankful for the distraction, Daphne took two of them before Jess grabbed the basket and chucked the remaining ones into the fire.

Kit whimpered.

Daphne bit into the biscuit, but instead of the hard crisp she was accustomed to, her teeth sank into it and gave her a mouthful of something that seemed more like a cake. She chewed on a moan and swallowed. "That's fabulous. What did you do?"

"Added syrup," Jess grumbled. "And you're both wrong. It made them completely terrible."

Daphne couldn't hold back the snicker.

Kit shoved the rest of her biscuit into her mouth. "Clearly there's a story here," she said around the crumbs, "and I'm sure I want to hear it, but it made you smile again, so I really don't care what it was."

"Mama Daphne?"

Daphne looked over to see Eugenia, Sarah, and Reuben hovering by the kitchen door. "You heard?"

Sarah nodded, her eyes wide, those thick dark lashes standing out starkly against her fair skin. "I think everybody heard."

That was not what Daphne needed to hear. She groaned and dropped her head to the table.

"No, no, no." Kit pulled on her shoulder and got her sitting back upright.

Daphne knew Kit had the right idea, so she straightened up and made a gesture to welcome the children forward. Then she waved Benedict over as well and wrapped her arms around the lot of them. "I don't regret a single moment with you. I love all of you."

Arms twined around her, the children grabbing on to her wherever they could reach.

Even this felt overwhelming, telling Daphne what she truly needed was to be by herself. "Kit, did you bring your carriage out here?"

"Actually, we brought Nash's wagon. Our carriage cracked an axle on the way into town."

That was good. It wouldn't take long to hitch up, and she wouldn't have to take a coachman with her.

"I can hitch up Balaam," Reuben said as he pulled out of the mass of bodies swallowing Daphne.

"I'll drive you back," Benedict added. He glanced over at the door of the kitchen and the stairs beyond. "I'm not staying here."

Daphne didn't blame him.

"I'll pack you a bag," Kit said, easing up from her stool.

Soon Eugenia was wrapping up bread and cheese as if the trip were longer than a mere two miles, and Sarah busied herself repairing Daphne's topknot. Jess changed out Daphne's cloth for a cool one again. It was wonderful to have friends who cared about her.

Kit brought in Daphne's satchel and set it on the table. "I know you want to be alone, but you might want to go to Mrs. Lancaster's shop instead of her house. We, uh, that is, Graham and I brought a woman with us. I don't want you to worry about that right now, I just wanted you to know where she was staying."

Daphne nodded and took her bag. She hugged Sarah and Eugenia one more time. The last thing she wanted was them to feel bad about anything. Kit and Jess would simply have to make sure that didn't happen. Then she went out the kitchen door to find Benedict pulling the wagon over. Balaam the donkey brayed at her as she climbed in, and then they were rattling slowly down the lane and away from the house.

Part of Daphne wondered if she'd ever be back.

A rickety wagon usually wasn't where a mother-son relationship started, but with a two-mile trek and a world of confessions between them, Daphne knew it was either clear the air or throw herself off the wagon.

"Can I ask . . . I just want to know why," Benedict said as he stared straight ahead, hands gripped on the reins.

That was a fair question, though it had no good answer.

She told him what she could, twisting her fingers into her faded skirt as she spoke. After telling him about her and Kit's intention to start a family, she explained her reasons. Right or wrong, they'd been what she was thinking at the time.

Benedict said nothing as he guided the donkey down the narrow lane.

Finally Daphne had no more words, though it felt like the explanation of something so important should take longer. Her decision had been simple, though, even as the consequences were never-ending.

As they crossed the bridge and the edges of Marlborough came into view, Benedict gave a gentle shake of his head and finally spoke. "Adults can be so stupid." He gave her a crooked grin. "I'm glad you loved me enough to stay."

"What you said back there, in the house . . ." Daphne said, watching Benedict's profile. "Did you mean it?"

The boy nodded. "You've always been my mother. I can't think of anything I'd have had you do differently."

Daphne had been so afraid that her boy would think he'd ruined her life, and he might one day think thoughts like that. But right now, they were moving on, healing. If that was the only good thing to come out of this crazy day, it would be enough.

CHAPTER THIRTY-NINE

Two small rooms above a grocer's shop in the middle of town, and Daphne breathed easier in them than in a large four-story house. She stood in the bedchamber, looking out over the street while Mrs. Lancaster and Benedict talked softly in the other room. Daphne had tried to tell Benedict to go back to Mr. Leighton's, but he'd refused, saying he was the man of their family and he was going to make sure she was well before he left.

It had been adorable and endearing, so she'd let him stay.

She'd closed herself off in this room an hour ago and had been standing at the window ever since. Her breathing was coming easier now, and her heart wasn't beating hard enough to be painful anymore. Nothing was tingling and her vision was clear.

And she had an answer to the question. There was no way she could marry William. Though he had not outright proposed to her, she had to assume that was his intent because he was a good, honorable man with no intention of repeating his past mistakes. If it were only him to consider, she'd jump in. But he was a marquis. And Daphne simply could not be what she'd known titled ladies to be. Even the good and kind ones.

She took a deep breath. As painful as the decision was, having made it seemed to lift a burden off her shoulders. Laughter greeted her as she walked into the other room. A small fire crackled in the fireplace, and Benedict and Mrs. Lancaster sat at a small table, playing a card game.

"There now, you see, boy? I told you she just needed a little bit of time. Your mother's a deep one. Solitary. She needs a bit of space every now and then."

Daphne joined them at the table and fiddled with one of the cards. Mrs. Lancaster had probably gotten the boy to tell her everything that had happened at Haven Manor by plying him with candy and tea and that sweet smile of hers.

"Are you going back?" Mrs. Lancaster asked as she played another card on the table.

"No," she said. She knew she couldn't be around William and not give in. From the safety of Haven Manor she would believe she could handle it, but as this week had taught her, she couldn't.

"I've been wanting to get some help in the shop," Mrs. Lancaster said. "You may not know this, but I'm getting older. Someday I'm going to need someone to take over for me."

"I'll think about it," Daphne said. How awful would being a shopkeeper be? People in and out, constantly on display right in the middle of High Street. Could she do it? She might have to. She had, hopefully, a great deal of life left to live. She couldn't survive on charity. And she already knew she was a horrid housekeeper.

She glanced up to find Benedict staring at her, a question in his eyes and too much maturity on his face.

A knock at the door had Daphne groaning. "No more knocks. No more knocks, no more doors. I forbid anyone from ever visiting me again."

Mrs. Lancaster chuckled as she crossed the room to answer the door. "May I help you, sir?"

"I'm here to see my daughter." There was a brief pause, during which Daphne lifted her head and stared at the door in disbelief. "And my grandson, if he's here."

Benedict whimpered, and Daphne blindly reached her hand out to him while still staring at the door. He clutched it so hard she could feel all his calluses that had built up over the years and the strength that had come along with them.

The door opened wider and then suddenly there he was. Her father. She wanted to run into his arms, she wanted to run away, she wanted . . . Oh, she didn't know what she wanted.

"I'm sorry, Daphne," he said, hat clutched in his hands. "I'm so sorry. I never should have let you leave. I should never have tossed you out. I stayed mad for so long. And then I got your letter and learned you kept the baby, and I got angry all over again and threw it in the fire before I could finish it. I don't even know what I was angry about anymore. I'm not a perfect man, Daphne, but for some reason I thought I was. I've learned different since then, and I'm hoping you can forgive me."

He came over and sat at the table. Daphne's lips moved, but she couldn't find any words. This was something even she'd never imagined. She'd pictured seeing him again, of her being worthy, but never this bare apology.

"I'd be pleased to meet this young man, if I can. By all accounts you've done something remarkable with him. And with the others. There's a man back at that house who you've impressed very much, Ace."

"Papa," Daphne whispered. And then she was there wrapped in his arms. He still smelled of cigars and lemon drops. It was wonderful. "I've missed you, Papa. And I forgave you a long time ago."

Finally, they separated and she sat back in her seat to smile at her son. "This is Benedict. He's going to be the best furniture maker in the country."

"Exciting day," Graham said as he stepped out onto the porch where William was sitting on the steps, staring down at the cottage. "Here."

William took the glass Graham extended and sipped it before setting it on the stone beside him.

"So you were here"—William swept his arm in a circle, indicating the grounds—"when it was full? With children?"

Graham nodded. "For a while. It was something to see. The portrait gallery was their rainy-weather playroom. That's where I first saw Benedict. I thought he was yours."

"I don't blame you." William took another sip. "For a moment I thought he was mine."

The men sat silently for a few moments. Graham swirled his drink, looking into the small whirlpool it created. "It's good work they do. Thankless and not very popular, but good."

William's eyebrows lifted in surprise. "I thought it was over, as the children have gone to families or are preparing for jobs. Kit can hardly raise other children if she's married to a future earl."

Graham watched William for a moment and then shook his head. "Sometimes I forget not everyone was raised with a man like my father. For England's sake I wish my father could raise all the future title-bearers."

William snorted a laugh. "That would be a crowded house."

A grin crossed Graham's face. "I wish all title-bearers were like my father, then." He sighed. "Having a title doesn't mean your purpose is defined for you. It is possible to be noble and still give of yourself. Yes, there are responsibilities—and you've already got them, whereas mine are hopefully many years down the road—but if that's all you are, then you're missing the point."

Graham stood and walked a few steps down so he could lean on the railing and still be eye level with William. "My father taught me to be a good man first and a good earl second. Kit's helping me do that. Just because they've stopped taking in children doesn't mean there aren't still women to help."

"What if a woman wants to keep her child, like Daphne did?" William couldn't imagine Daphne walking away from Benedict. It would crush her.

Graham sighed and finished his drink. "There's a woman at Mrs. Lancaster's house right now. Kit and I brought her into town with us. She embroiders like a dream, but she nearly burnt the house down trying to make soup. Think about the women you know, Chemsford. Even Daphne. What skills do they have to support themselves and a child? Who's going to hire them?"

He could. William drained his own glass as the idea took root and started to bloom. He could hire them. The woman might not have been able to make soup, but she'd been willing to try. That had to mean something, right? When Daphne came back, he'd tell her his idea. She knew the situation these women were in, would know if his idea was even viable.

All he needed was for her to come back.

Morris was in the middle of tying William's cravat when the sound of a wagon came through the open window. William jerked away from the valet and ran down the stairs, ignoring the flapping ends of his cravat until one slapped him in the face. He tied a hasty knot and tucked the ends inside.

He cut through the library to get to the side of the house where the path wound around to the servants' door. There he found Benedict and Mr. Leighton unloading carved sections of moulding. There wasn't, however, any sign of Daphne.

Mr. Leighton clapped a hand on Benedict's shoulder and then carried his load inside, leaving William and the boy beside the wagon.

The young man's shoulders went back and his head went up. Then he jerked his cap off his head and stuffed it in his pocket, leaving a tuft of blond hair sticking up in the back. Had William looked like that as he learned how to be a man? Had he stood like that on those excruciating visits home when his father would examine his grades and sporting accomplishments before inquiring about his friendships and connections? The glimpse into the past was more than a bit disconcerting.

"I took my mother back to town yesterday."

William nodded. "I heard. I'm glad you were able to take care of her."

"If I may, my lord, I'd like to ask a question."

As difficult as growing up had been for William, he'd always known his place in the world. He'd always known that no matter how awkward he was or how much he blundered, he would one day be the marquis. This boy had no such assurance, yet here he stood, confident and forthright. "Go ahead."

"Did you do something to her?"

William slid back a step in surprise. "What? No. I would never hurt her."

At least, not intentionally. Their journey had not been easy, though.

"She loves this place. I know yesterday there was a lot to take in, but she's never run before. I'm just wondering why she's running now. I'm worried. If she doesn't come back, what will happen to Sarah, Eugenia, and Reuben?"

The bottom fell out of William's world. "What do you mean if she doesn't come back?"

The boy shuffled his feet and his gaze dropped before snapping back up, along with his posture. "Mrs. Lancaster offered her the store and she's thinking about taking it."

Daphne had been a bit of a disaster as a housekeeper, but she'd managed. "She'd hate being a shopkeeper," he murmured.

"I know," Benedict said. "And I think you might be the only one who can stop her."

He rode his horse into Marlborough, then went straight from the stable to Lancaster's.

Inside, three customers stood around the counter. Mrs. Lancaster moved back and forth, smiling, talking, and filling shopping lists. There was no sign of Daphne.

"Good morning," Mrs. Lancaster called to him with a smile.

"It's a busy day. I'll be with you in a moment. You just wait at the end of the counter there."

His eyebrows raised as he went to the end of the counter. She didn't seem to be telling anyone else where to stand.

"Good day, Mrs. Roth," she greeted another customer. "I say, quite a spell of rain we had. Washed all sorts of things onto my walk. I spent so much time sweeping I never made it home last night. Stayed in my upstairs rooms instead."

William didn't watch the interaction but kept an ear on it. Was it possible Mrs. Lancaster was talking in some sort of secret message, like she and Daphne had done the first time he'd been brought in here? If so, what was it? The rain had washed something up and she'd swept it off? Had she sent Daphne away?

No, that didn't seem right. He hadn't spoken to this woman much, but Daphne had talked about her a lot, and sending anyone away didn't seem like something she'd do. There was something else, then. Mrs. Lancaster said she'd stayed the night. Had Daphne stayed the night? Here?

"There you are, Mrs. Jenkins. I'm glad to see you. Those spices just came in yesterday. You wouldn't want to miss them."

"You always have exactly what I need, Mrs. Lancaster. I'll be back next week." The other woman waved as she left the store.

Now William was all but positive Daphne was above the store. He just needed to figure out how to get there. He pushed away from the counter and looked at the myriad of goods.

"While you're waiting, my lord, you may want to look at the barometers in the back of the store. They'll help you predict when the next rain is coming."

"I'll do just that. Thank you." He nodded to Mrs. Lancaster and the other women waiting to be helped and then turned toward the back of the store. On a shelf sat two barometers. To their left was a door.

As quietly as possible, he slipped out the door and found himself at the bottom of a set of stairs. His heart beat harder as he climbed them. What happened when he got to the top of these stairs could be the best or worst moment of his life. It all depended on whether or not Daphne came back.

He knocked on the door. It was a few minutes before it opened, and then he saw Daphne standing there. His impulse was to gather her into his arms and never let go, to claim her strength and hope and imagination as his own for the rest of his life.

"Daphne," he said, curling his fingers into the legs of his trousers to keep from reaching for her. "May I come in?"

CHAPTER FORTY

Daphne wanted to say no, he could tell. But it was probably much easier to plan on saying no to him than it was to actually say it. She opened the door farther and waved him into the room.

"My father will be coming back over in a bit. He's staying at the inn, but we're eating dinner together."

"I . . . that's good. You should get to know your father again." William rubbed his hands on his trousers.

She sat in one chair and he sat in another. The room was simple and plain. He wasn't sure he'd ever deliberately gone into anywhere like this.

"Kit and Graham told me more about what you did—do—for the women."

Daphne shrugged and picked at her skirt. "I've always done this for the children."

William's brain, which had been running ahead with ideas ever since he'd talked to Graham yesterday, stumbled to a halt. "What do you mean?"

"I did it for Benedict. When we first started, Kit was thinking about the women, but I just thought about the children."

William tried to reconcile everything he knew about Daphne, about Haven Manor, about the children, and the women, but it didn't make sense. "Why?"

Daphne looked up, a deep line between her brows. "What do you mean why?"

"Kit wasn't the one who'd been through it. She couldn't help those women. Not the same way you could."

Her confusion cleared and she blinked at him. "I couldn't do that."

"Maybe not before, since you weren't telling Benedict, but what's stopping you now? Daphne, you've come so far. You know forgiveness. You know what it's like to be scared."

"And alone," Daphne whispered. "It's so very, very lonely. Even though Kit was with me and I'd separated myself from people most of my life, I'd never felt so alone."

William bit his tongue so hard he tasted a bit of copper. He wanted to press her, to ask her how it would have been if someone had come alongside her and told her they'd felt the same way. But Daphne didn't need that. She needed to reach the conclusion on her own. He realized that now.

He'd pressed her every step of the way once he'd grasped the idea of courting her. He'd looked at the issues, weighed them, decided he was strong enough to face them, and gone after what he wanted. He'd never given Daphne a chance to catch up.

Was it any wonder that she'd run?

He didn't know how long they sat there. He glanced around for a book but found only a deck of cards, so he moved quietly over to the table and started playing a game of patience.

Eventually, she looked up. "Do you know how wonderful it would have been if someone I could actually believe had held me and said, 'I understand'?"

William slid the cards to the side and folded his arms on the table. "No, I don't. But I'd like to, if you're willing to tell me."

She didn't think she'd be making this walk again, but here she was, cutting through the woods to Haven Manor. William was on one side, leading his horse behind him, and her father was on the other. As they walked, she pointed out trees she liked that had grown larger over the years she'd been taking this path, and told them stories of her favorite moments at Haven Manor.

The sun was starting to sink as they approached the house. Benedict was harnessing the donkey to Mr. Leighton's wagon, and a huge smile cracked his face when he saw her. He gave a nod to William, then returned to his task.

Instead of going in the kitchen door, William turned the reins of his horse over to Reuben and then took her around to the front door. Daphne paused at the bottom of the stairs. "I can't go in there."

"Why not? I assure you Maxwell and Charlotte will be leaving tomorrow, but they should be easy enough to avoid for one evening."

She shook her head. Could the man have truly forgotten the way it worked? "I'm the housekeeper, William. I can't go in the front door."

He frowned. "Then don't walk in as the housekeeper."

She gasped. "Are you dismissing me?"

He tilted his head in her direction, a disapproving expression on his face. "You are a gentleman's daughter." He pointed at her father, who looked between the two of them in silence. "If he gets to come in the front door, so do you."

Papa chuckled. It was such a wonderful sound, one she never thought she'd hear again. Maybe it wouldn't hurt to pretend that's who she was just one more time. She took one of her father's arms and one of William's and they walked up together.

Kit was pacing the front hall when Daphne walked in. Her sigh when she saw Daphne could have been deep enough to make the curtains across the room flutter. "Good. You got her back here."

Daphne narrowed her eyes. "You're the one who helped me leave."

"I know. And every time I tell you to do something it goes wrong, so stop listening to me."

This time the laughter came from everyone in the room. It set the tone for the evening, and Daphne couldn't remember a better night. A dinner tray was taken up to their unwanted guests, and Jess was convinced to eat in the dining room with the rest of them.

Kit pitched in to help clean up and soon everyone was turning in. Daphne brushed out her hair and changed for bed, but the night felt incomplete.

Kit was already sitting out on the back porch when Daphne arrived. They sat on the steps, staring out at the water until Jess joined them.

"You know you'd make a terrible shopkeeper," Jess said as she sat on Daphne's other side.

"Jess!" Kit gasped. "You can't just say that to her."

"Why not? It's true. Too many people."

Daphne didn't say anything as her friends squabbled. She just stared into the dark and smiled.

Finally, they quieted, and Kit lay her head on Daphne's shoulder. "Do you want to know what I realized when I went back to London with Graham?"

"Hmmm?" Daphne murmured.

"I'm not the same person I was. Somewhere along the way I changed. I think you have, too."

Of course she had. She'd had to. She'd had to be strong for her son and the other children, had to be happy so their situations didn't throw a dismal gloom over their lives. She'd had to learn skills she never thought possible. She had to change to survive.

"I know if you were back in that ballroom now, it would be different. Despite your imagination, I think you'd have seen who he really was."

"If she didn't faint first," Jess said in a low undertone.

They all laughed, but Daphne thought it through and realized there was truth to that. She'd fantasized about William, yes, but not when he was there—or at least not when she'd known he was there. Unlike with Maxwell, she'd seen William as he truly was: confident, and yes, a bit arrogant, but that came with being raised with a title around his neck. She'd seen his sense of honor and willingness to make something right. But she'd seen those traits over time because they were really there, not because she'd wished them there.

"You know something?" Daphne smiled and leaned her head on top of Kit's. "I think you're correct."

There was a carriage out front.

Daphne stood in the music room, watching the footman secure the trunks.

If she didn't do it now, she'd never have another chance. Would she always wonder? Perhaps. But the past was a weight to make her sink or a foundation to build her life upon. If she were going to build a new life, she needed to cut the ties to the old one.

Majestic music played through her mind, spurring her on as she opened the door and stepped into the front hall.

He was there, with his wife, preparing to leave.

He held his cane in one hand and his hat in the other while he frowned in her direction. "What do you want?"

With that attitude, an apology was probably out of the question. "I wanted to see you," she said, thankful her skirt could hide her suddenly shaky knees. "And, I suppose, I wanted you to see me."

"Why?"

"Because I don't want to think about it anymore."

"Wouldn't that be nice." He frowned at her again but then opened the door and told his wife to wait in the carriage. And she went. Daphne rather wondered about that. Her husband was in the same room as a woman he'd had a child with and she walked away without a word.

Mr. Oswald closed the door behind his wife and then ran a hand over his face. "I didn't know."

"I know that. I also know it wouldn't have changed anything. You were already married and likely wouldn't have believed me anyway."

"Probably not. So what is the point of this tête-à-tête? The boy doesn't need my money when he's got his lordship sponsoring him."

Daphne cocked her head to the side. "Does it bother you?"

"Yes, greatly. I've had to spend two days trapped in a tiny room while my horses rested enough for me to leave."

At that moment, all Daphne felt was pity. The bedchamber they'd been in, while hardly large by aristocratic standards, was far from tiny. But more important, he couldn't see what he'd done wrong. "You deliberately set out to ruin a woman's reputation because of a bet. No, you didn't know it was me. Would you be sorry if it had been Kit? Did you even consider waiting to see if your evening had consequences beyond social ruin?"

He looked away, staring at some art on a faraway wall for several minutes. When he turned back, he seemed tired and considerably older than the past fourteen years should have made him. "No. I didn't consider it. And while life may have gone rotten for you awhile, it looks like you're coming out on top. You'd have never caught the eye of a marquis otherwise. We all saw him rush to your side, so there's no sense denying it."

Somehow, because her life was taking a turn for the better, he felt that excused everything he'd done? "Why are you here?"

"Because I have nothing of my own. My father is the second son of a title that has now passed beyond his generation. My choices are to live off the kindness of others or find myself a hovel and a job."

"So you came here . . ."

"To borrow the house in Bath for the Season. Obviously that's not going to happen now, so we'll have to spend the summer in London. Does that make you happy?"

Daphne realized she didn't care anymore. She'd wanted to stand tall while she faced him and she'd done that. He'd been surprised by this. Perhaps, like her, it took time for him to really comprehend something. If so, maybe one day he would return and apologize. If not, she didn't intend to live her life waiting for it.

"I find it doesn't make me happy or sad. As you said, life has moved on, and so have I." She walked over and opened the door for him, mostly because she wanted the pleasure of shutting it behind him. "I don't know if this matters to you, but it matters to me. I forgive you. But I won't be a bit disappointed if I never see you again. Have a nice journey."

He grunted, plopped his hat on his head, and walked out the door. Daphne shut it, perhaps harder than necessary, but with a satisfied grin on her face.

CHAPTER FORTY-ONE

Daphne walked into the library, smiling widely, and William promptly forgot each and every number on the factory report in front of him. He dropped the paper on the desk and stood to greet her, an answering smile spreading across his own lips.

"I thought you would want to know your cousin left," she said.

William nodded, tension he hadn't realized he'd still been holding seeping from his shoulders. "I know it's hypocritical of me to be angry at him, but I can't seem to help it. I don't want him in my house or anywhere around you."

"It's still new for you. And him, too, I suppose." She sat in the chair in front of the desk, the picture of calm serenity. "I've had fourteen years to think about it. I thought I'd moved on, but apparently something in me needed to see him again. I think, for me, it's all finally over."

"I'm glad to hear that." More than glad. Maxwell was family and could only be held so far away. If William wanted to keep Daphne in his life, Maxwell would eventually show up again.

That was the last thing he wanted to talk about now, though. "I ordered a billiard table. I would have asked Benedict, but I didn't want to wait that long. I've asked him for enough pieces of furniture to keep him busy for years."

Daphne laughed. "I think he'll understand. Particularly if you teach him to play."

Her easy, relaxed manner made his heart soar. Even when they'd been having dinner together, she hadn't been this open with him. This was the true Daphne. Despite the fact that she had so little to her name compared with him, she didn't seem to mind. Life was what it was and she was who she was and he'd never seen anything more beautiful.

She didn't seem to notice the trail his thoughts had taken because she kept talking. "Do you remember what you said about sharing my story with the women? I think I'd like to talk to the one Kit and Graham brought to Mrs. Lancaster's house. It's going to be difficult for her, and I suppose I want her to know someone else has been there." She took a deep breath and grinned at William. "I know I've been going to town a lot lately, but I wanted you to know that this time I'm coming back."

"I appreciate the information." William's breath sped up as he shifted his position in his seat. "I have a better idea. Well, perhaps not better, but a different idea."

"Oh?"

"Bring her here."

Daphne's mouth dropped open. "Here? You want me to bring an upper-class woman attempting to hide her condition from the world to the home of a marquis?"

When she phrased it that way it did sound a bit topsy-turvy. "Yes. But not here, exactly. I thought you could bring her to the cottage. It's private, she would have a bit of independence, and you could teach her skills so that if she wanted to keep her child, she would have the option of stepping down from society and making a different life."

She blinked at him but didn't tell him no.

William hoped that was a good sign. He plunged on. "She could work up at the house, learning skills like laundry and cooking, but still not be a servant. If you had more than one woman at a time, the new one could learn from the previous one. This way you'd always have somewhere for them to go. Even when there are guests here at the house, they aren't going to meander their way down to the cottage."

He stopped talking and she just kept staring at him, occasionally blinking, her face taking on that blank expression that indicated she was feeling too much and didn't know what emotion to land on.

"What do you think?" he finally asked.

"That's . . . I . . . You want the women here?"

"If you think it would help them." Honestly, William couldn't see how it wouldn't. Options were the one thing these women didn't have. It was something he could help Daphne give them.

"I don't know what to say," Daphne said, her voice a bit rough. "That you would even make such an offer . . . but even if they know how to survive, they'll never find work with a young child in tow."

William took a deep breath. He'd been working with her father on this idea all morning. Would she like it? He turned the paper around and pushed it across the desk. "Look at this. It's only an idea right now, and there are a lot of details still to work out, but this is my factory."

Daphne leaned forward to look at it, obviously happy to move on to what she thought was a change of subject. "It's lovely."

Her sweetness made him want to circle the desk and wrap her in his arms. He had to finish showing her his plan first, though.

"And this"—he pointed to a rectangle set just over the rise from the dale where the factory was being built—"is going to be a dame school. For the women who want to come work for me. You see, it's not a normal factory. We'll be making buttons, brooches, buckles, and hairpins. It's a lot of metalwork but also a lot of decorative work. That's something they could learn to do, as most of them have been learning it in some form for most of their lives."

Daphne blinked at him again, the smile dropping from her face to be replaced with a look of utter shock. "A dame school? You're going to hire someone to watch the children of your factory workers?"

"Yes. Well, it wouldn't only be for your women. I'm sure there are people in Birmingham who could use it as well, but I have to admit, it was you who made me think of it."

He flipped the paper back around to face him, making a note to ensure the windows faced away from the factory to dampen the noise as much as possible. Suddenly Daphne was up and around the desk and wrapping her arms around him.

Whatever he'd been writing didn't matter anymore. His pencil clacked against the desk as he dropped it in order to wrap his arms around her in return. He pulled her as close as he could with her standing and him sitting, savoring the feeling he'd been so afraid he'd lost. He rose to lean against his desk, taking her hands in his. "Am I to assume that's an approval?"

"Yes," she said, smiling. "I approve. I'll have to talk to Kit and Graham. A permanent place to bring them makes it all so much easier." She dropped her forehead to his chest and took a deep, shuddering breath. "I can't believe you care about this."

"I care about you. And knowing this matters to you, knowing I can help make life better for someone else . . . it feels better than I imagined. Doing it *with* you would make it even better."

Her smile fell and she bit her lip. "William . . ."

"I know. I'm trying not to pressure you. So much has happened in the past few days, but when I had this idea, I couldn't wait to share it with you." He paused, bracing himself for her reaction to what he was going to say next. "But you know this only works if you're part of it. You are the one who is going to be able to help these women in ways no one else here can."

William's fingers curled tighter around hers. He'd have their banns announced tomorrow if he could. He'd drive to London to acquire a special license. All she had to do was agree. "I wish you could see what I see, the way it could be."

She took a deep breath and squeezed his fingers. "Tell me."

"I know you'd love Dawnview Hall. There are people on the estate, tenants who haven't seen anyone really care about them in a long time. I want to change that. *We* can change that. It's not a difficult ride here from there either, whenever you feel the need to be here to help someone. It's an even easier ride from London. We could spend most of the summer here."

The more William pictured it, the more excited he became. He was nearly bouncing as he saw his life unfolding in a way he never would have dreamed. "When we go to London, you could meet with the committee Kit told me about, the one that helps identify the women who need you. I have friends whom I've been holding my distance from, whom it would be nice to spend more time with. And I'd like you to meet them. I've never enjoyed balls, but as much as you love music, I'd love to take you to the opera."

He had to pause for a moment as his breath ran out in his excitement. But when he looked at her, all the air he'd regained was lost.

She did not look happy.

She looked terrified.

She was pale, and her arms were pulled in as tightly to her body as she could get them, poised to run as soon as he gave her an opening.

"Daphne?"

"I can't do that. I can't . . . that's too many people. I wouldn't know what to do or say. No one knows me. They'll stare and talk. Even if they don't know about my ruin, they'll know I'm older and they'll wonder and they'll ask questions. I thought I could, but I can't. All the people . . . I . . . I can't." She pulled her hands out of his grasp and clutched them to her chest.

William had rushed her again, pushed her before she'd come to the realization on her own that she was stronger than she'd been before, that she could pick and choose her battles this time. He'd hoped his excitement would be enough to ignite hers, and maybe it was. But it wasn't enough to overcome the fact that groups of people scared her on some elemental level.

At least she'd liked his dame school idea. He'd tell Mr. Blakemoor to move ahead with the plans. Regardless of what happened between Daphne and William, those women would need his factory and Haven Manor.

Daphne didn't run. She wanted to, but she didn't. She managed to avoid William, while somehow maintaining her strange role that fell somewhere between guest and housekeeper. After two more days, her father left, with the promise to write regularly and visit often.

She'd shared the idea of bringing the women to the cottage and teaching them life skills with Jess and Kit. Both thought the idea a brilliant step forward. There was some work to be done, parts of the cottage to clean out and repair, but it wouldn't be long before they could bring Martha, the woman currently living with Mrs. Lancaster, to her new temporary home.

The billiard table was delivered.

A full week came and went.

And every day she'd take a moment to remember the conversation in the library, to see if maybe time would make it scare her less.

It didn't.

And because it didn't, it meant Daphne was once more searching for ways to avoid going up into the main house. Working in the kitchen was the easiest answer, so she pulled out the dough Jess had set to rest earlier and prepared to knead it.

"Get your hands off my bread dough," Jess growled.

Daphne grinned and backed away, hands raised. "But you don't have a scullery maid anymore. Kit went into town yesterday. She said Eugenia is flourishing with Mrs. Lancaster. They're competing to see who can be happier than the other and which one can actually talk a customer into a stupor."

"I'm glad. It's good for them both." Jess put down the knife she was using to cut up an already-cooked loaf. "That doesn't mean you can touch my bread."

With a huff, Daphne crossed her arms. "What do you need me to do, then?"

"Get a project."

"What?"

Jess swiveled, hands on her hips. "Get a project. You are always easier to live with if you are helping make something happen for someone else. So please, for everyone's sanity, go fix somebody."

"Is that true?" Daphne had never considered it, but the statement felt comfortable.

"You've never noticed that? If you have a task to do, particularly one that helps someone else, you couldn't care less how many people are around you." Jess took the bread dough Daphne had been about to knead and began punching it.

Daphne didn't complain that Jess was now doing the very thing she'd been about to do. "But I've had tasks to do here and the arrival of new household staff made me nervous."

"Changing the linens on a bed is entirely different than changing someone's future. One is boring. The other gives you purpose. You can hardly compare the two."

Daphne opened her mouth to argue, but a little curl of hope had her shutting it again. Could Jess be right—again?

"I'm going to town," she announced. It was time she actually put her lovely new plans into motion instead of waiting for them to wither away and leave her with nothing.

Jess looked up. "Why?"

"To visit Martha."

CHAPTER FORTY-TWO

William ran a hand across the green baize of the newly delivered billiard table. The gentle scrape of the covering reminded him of Daphne and her dresses that had been washed and worn until they bore the comforting softness of an old blanket.

Who was he trying to fool? Everything in this house reminded him of Daphne. They'd talked and planned every inch of this house. This room, though, had been William's idea, his plan. Seeing it in reality gave him a strange sort of thrill.

Derek still grumbled about the amount of art William was slowly putting away, but he couldn't continue to live in an overabundance so great that he couldn't enjoy any of it. Perhaps he could open an art museum in Marlborough and entertain aristocrats as they came through town. He'd appoint Derek the curator.

William pulled a mace from the cherrywood rack on the wall. The rack matched the wainscoting that ran along the bottom of the wall and made a pleasant contrast to the smooth blue walls, where there now hung a few carefully selected paintings, including one of a strange dog he would swear appeared to be smiling.

The entire place was comforting, inviting. Home. He liked it here at Haven Manor. It was, perhaps, a bit small by aristocratic standards—Dawnview Hall was probably four times the size—but he liked it. He didn't rattle around in it with more space than anyone reasonably needed, unless they were trying to show everyone else how important they were.

In fact, he was fairly certain there were rooms in Dawnview Hall that he'd never seen before. Not so with Haven Manor. He'd even seen the washroom and the kitchen larder.

And he'd been intimately involved in the discussions and plans for every one of those rooms. By the time renovations were complete, there would be a part of him in every room in this house.

He wanted this to be hers as much as his. That wouldn't happen unless she was his wife.

It had been a week. For an entire week she'd acted as if the conversation in the library had never happened.

She wasn't ready. She might never be ready. Maybe she would marry him if he agreed to live here all the time, but that wasn't realistic. They both knew he couldn't run a marquisette from here. Already there were matters that needed his attention and had been delayed because of the distance of Haven Manor.

No, he couldn't stay here, and he refused to have a marriage like his parents: strangers who shared a child, drifting apart until they grew to hate each other.

He could never hate Daphne, but he could become bitter that she accepted him but not his heritage. That she always made him leave her here, living her own life that he was welcome to visit on occasion.

Part of William wanted to rail at God for showing him something he couldn't have. The truth was, though, being with Daphne, learning to love Daphne, had made him grow as a person. He wouldn't trade that for anything. Even if it meant the future he'd been so excited about a week ago was slipping away and a new one was taking its place.

One where he waited for Daphne forever.

Did she even love him the way he loved her? She'd never said it. Then again, neither had he. But he'd offered her everything he was and she'd said she couldn't do it.

Araminta and Edward had already left, and Kit and Graham

were planning to leave tomorrow. William had already given his blessing for Haven Manor to be a place of refuge for the women. Whether Daphne married him or not, what she was doing was good. William wanted to be a part of something good.

But perhaps the best part he could play was to remove himself. He could go to London or Dawnview Hall or one of the other estates now under his care. There was no real reason he needed to keep a presence here. If Morris started packing now, he could leave soon after Kit and Graham.

Haven Manor could be Daphne's home once again.

Daphne was shaking as she walked into the room to visit with Martha. Within a few moments, though, it didn't matter that Martha was a stranger. She was a woman who needed Daphne, and that was all it took for Daphne to willingly and without qualm share personal details with the terrified young woman.

Martha had shared very little in return, but there was no mistaking the look of relief on her face and possibly even the hint of excitement when Daphne had assured her there was a cottage just outside Marlborough where she could stay. Where she'd be able to walk outside freely without worry.

They talked for a long while, Daphne sharing her story and the new plans and possibilities Haven Manor was going to provide. Mrs. Lancaster kept a pot of tea available, as well as plates of meat, cheese, and biscuits. It was late by the time the conversation ran down. Too late for Daphne to return home.

And then she became uncomfortable.

Without the focus of how she would help Martha, Daphne didn't know what to say. Despite the fact that she remembered how incredibly tired she'd been while carrying Benedict and worrying about the future, she was convinced every one of Martha's sighs was condemnation from the other woman. It didn't make any logical sense, but Daphne's churning middle didn't seem to care.

She lay stiffly on the second bed above the shop in Mrs. Lancaster's upper rooms, waiting for the first vestiges of daylight to appear so she could make her escape.

The town was barely stirring when she made her way through it the next morning. The few people around moved with purpose and had no interest in exchanging more than a polite nod. She was able to escape her little town without having to converse with anyone.

At the bridge on the north side of town, she encountered Kit and Graham's carriage. They were on their way to Bath to visit his parents.

She talked with them easily for several minutes, informing them of her talk with Martha and then wishing them a pleasant journey. Why couldn't she see everyone else the same way she saw her friends? Weren't all of them simply people?

"We've plenty of time to turn around and give you a ride back to Haven Manor before we go. A short delay won't keep us from reaching Bath today," Kit offered.

"No," Daphne said, climbing out of their carriage to resume her walk home. "I'm glad I got to see you before you left, but I think I'd like to walk."

As she continued on her way, a ridiculous sense of relief that it was them en route to the resort town and not her flooded through her.

What did that mean? What did her conversation with Martha mean? It felt like she had learned a great deal about herself in the past few hours, but she wasn't entirely sure what and had no idea what to actually do with it.

The answers didn't come to her as she walked through the woods.

They didn't hit her when she saw the lake.

She refused to return to the house without them, though, so she plopped herself in the middle of a glen full of purple flowers.

She was not going to run. She was not going to hide. She was going to sit here, face reality, and make a decision.

For once she was going to choose to be strong instead of being forced into being so. The strength of necessity had been good and welcome when she'd brought Benedict screaming and wailing into the world with a future more uncertain than a field mouse's. Then she'd had no alternative.

Everyone thought her strong to raise the children at Haven Manor, but she had to admit to herself that doing so had been more of an escape than anything else. She loved the children, loved every moment of raising them, but she'd been excessively thankful for the need to hide them because it meant she could hide with them.

Daphne was finished hiding.

Well. Maybe not *completely* finished. Large groups of people were never going to be something she could handle easily, but she'd learned recently it was possible to widen her circle. She even shared a joke with Horatia the other day. How far could she expand it if she took it one step at a time?

Daphne had a very good imagination. Maybe she could imagine herself in the scenario he'd painted. So what if she'd never tried to dream up something that could actually happen? It couldn't be that different a process.

With a groan of frustration, she dropped back into the field of bluebells carpeting the glen. Taking charge of one's life was hard.

Wouldn't it be nice if William were to cross this field right now? If he said he refused to accept her refusal and laid out all of the ways they could fix everything?

Daphne sighed. That would be delightful. He could take her in his arms and give her one of those glorious kisses and tell her . . . tell her . . .

With a frown Daphne sat up. What would he tell her? Why couldn't she picture it?

Perhaps because for the first time in a very, very long time, what was said mattered. This wasn't some pleasurable mental escape that she could shrug off with a smile. This was reality. She actually wanted this dream to happen.

William was a man of honor. He would respect her decision and walk away if she continued to tell him no. But if she could dream up what she wished he'd offer her, would she find a way for them to be together? Would she be able to tell him yes?

She plucked a handful of flowers and picked at them while she considered her options. It was easy to visualize William sitting across from her. It was ridiculously easy to visualize William anywhere these days.

But what did she want him to say? If he were to make another offer, build his case once more, what would she accept?

I can manage the marquisette from here. There won't be any reason for you to ever leave Haven Manor.

No. Daphne shook her head and threw the handful of bluebells away in a shower of mutilated petals. William would never say that. And she wouldn't want him to. Part of what she loved about him was he took his position seriously. He wanted to be a responsible nobleman, take care of his people and his country. That required attending Parliament and visiting his tenants.

Providing an heir.

Daphne flopped back into the flowers and pulled the brim of her bonnet down until it covered her face. Physical pain sliced through her chest at the thought of him marrying someone else. But he would have to. Every night for the rest of her life, she would lie in bed and wonder if this was the night when he met the woman who would accept the life Daphne had rejected.

No.

That was an absolutely miserable future and one Daphne refused to choose.

She pushed herself up and began to pace, her mind whirling but not landing on anything.

She didn't actually know how to make a decision.

What a scary realization.

"Lord," she murmured, "I'm going to need a bit of help here."

She scrubbed her hands down her face. A starting point. That was all she usually needed when she let her mind drift away. Once she had a starting point the rest would all unravel like a poorly knitted blanket.

William was a marquis. He had a job to do. He would have to go to London at least part of the year.

Perhaps he could go without her? It wasn't as if every man brought his family to town, was it? Yes, his parents had lived separately, but it sounded as if they'd done that year round. If Daphne came to Haven Manor while William went to London, it would be a simple stage ride for him to come see her.

Or for her to go see him. She wouldn't mind the opera. Or perhaps a visit from a close friend or two, once she got to know his friends. Especially with him at her side. It wouldn't be like before, where she stood in a corner on her own, expected to make witty conversation and social connections. She'd be with William. He could do the talking and she could just be with him.

She could spend a few days in London and then go back to Haven Manor to rest and breathe. Check on the women.

He said Dawnview Hall was huge. She could allot herself a private space, away from people. He could have whomever he needed at the house without her having to be around them all the time. Then she'd be able to see the women working in his factory. She could visit the children in the school he was creating.

She imagined it, saw how it could be. She could definitely do it. And she thought she might even . . . like it?

It wasn't the way any normal aristocratic marriage worked, but then again, William had shunned most of what was considered normal aristocratic behavior, so he probably wouldn't mind that so much.

She grabbed up another bunch of flowers and fiddled them into shreds while she paced and thought and dreamed up her perfect reality. She was going to make this work.

CHAPTER FORTY-THREE

What had once been a riot of overgrown gardens, lawns, and tree copses was now a beautiful array of manicured lawns and carefully edged nature walks surrounded by a wild wood. It was amazing what a little time and attention could do.

This was a place where he could truly learn to be at home.

Which made his imminent departure unfortunate.

Would he ever see these lands again with the lake, the bridge, and the interesting collection of outbuildings? It was unlikely. If he allowed himself to return, he'd come back again and again, hoping this time Daphne would choose to join him. That hope would turn into an anchor that would eventually sink him. He'd never find a wife if he entertained the notion that Daphne would one day change her mind.

He couldn't do that. He had a title to consider. If he didn't . . . well, if he didn't, there wouldn't have been an issue in the first place. He'd gladly ensconce them both here, raising a little family in their own little world.

But he had a responsibility to England to provide a good and noble heir to the title. And while he still held out hope that Edmond would grow into a mature, capable, good-hearted adult, he wasn't willing to gamble the future of his country or the people in his care on his abilities to erase his father's legacy from the boy.

It made him nauseous just to think of marrying someone other than Daphne. That was all the more reason to stay away from here. It would take time before he could see to his duty. He knew he was likely going to have to marry a woman he didn't love, but he refused to do so while actively loving another. Once Daphne was nothing more than a painful memory, he would be able to consider marrying another.

Not today. Not tomorrow either. But eventually.

He turned his back on the view and reentered the house. There were things here he wanted to commit to memory, no matter how painful they might be. Benedict had surprised him this morning by bringing a brand-new dining table with him in the work wagon. William moved into the dining room and trailed a hand across the polished surface, admiring the clean lines and lack of knee-crushing extensions. There were still gargoyles, though. Delicate ones no more than three inches large carved into the tops of the curved legs.

He dropped into a chair and ran a finger idly over the grinning, winged creature staring ahead, seeing nothing.

"There are loaded trunks in the front hall." He turned to find Daphne standing in the doorway, cheeks flushed, mouth set in a grim, determined line.

"Yes," William said, drinking in his last sight of her much like he had the grounds moments earlier. "I'm leaving."

"When will you return?"

He shook his head. Once he said these words, everything would be done. Final. "I'm not."

She entered the room fully and sat in the chair around the corner from him. The shadow of her hands on the table pained him. He could reach out and take her hand. One more time he could feel the texture of her skin, the rough and the soft that was uniquely Daphne.

He could. But he wouldn't. There wasn't any reason to put himself through the torture.

"Keep as much of the staff on as you need to keep the house in its current state," he said. "Bring the women here. Help them, teach them. If I'm not here, no one will have reason to visit. They'll be safe."

Her fingers knotted together on the tabletop. "I was thinking," she said softly, "about what you said, about the way you saw the future."

He grunted a confirmation that he'd heard her. He didn't need a reminder that his dreams would always remain unattainable figments of his imagination.

"And I was wondering if it was open to a little . . . adjustment."

William gave his eyes permission to seek out hers, to gaze at her face like they longed to do. "What sort of adjustment?"

"I'll never be able to handle large groups of people. London for weeks on end would make me ill, but you don't socialize much, and I think that if we ease into it slowly and I have you by my side, I could learn to live in your world."

William's breathing stopped as the hope he'd tried to kill flared to life as she spoke. His hand slid across the table to wrap over hers while she laid out her thoughts. A slow introduction to his friends until her comfort circle widened. Carefully managed time in London. Specific tasks for her to accomplish whenever she needed to interact with the tenants at Dawnview. Using the cottage here at Haven Manor to help the women.

She turned her hand over and locked her fingers with his. "I know you're scared we'll end up like your parents, but the truth is, William, as much as I love you, I really like being by myself sometimes. It wouldn't be typical, but I think we can make it work."

William's brain was still stuck in the mire of shock and surprise at her meticulously thought-out compromise, but his body had understood everything because he was rising from his chair, walking to her side, and pulling her into his arms.

He blindly groped for her head to pull her into an awkward kiss. In his exuberance, he missed completely, his lips instead connecting with her cheek. He scattered kisses across her face, making her laugh, until finally his lips settled against hers.

It wasn't long before he was having to remind himself that they weren't married yet, and he hugged her close, resting his chin on her head as they gently swayed together.

"Did you say you love me?" he asked roughly.

"Yes," she mumbled into his chest before tilting her head back to smile up at him. "Is that the only part you heard?"

"No," he said, his answering smile so wide his face hurt. "I also heard a woman who put her powerful imagination to good use and came up with a solution I'd have never considered."

"I'm assuming the offer to be mistress of this house is still open, then? You agree with my proposal?"

"Now that you've agreed to fill it, the position is permanently closed," he said, surprised by the gruffness in his own voice. "And by proposal I assume you meant you were going to marry me, didn't you?"

"Things would be rather awkward if I didn't. Particularly if we have children."

He gently helped her back into her chair before seating himself in his again. There would be time for holding each other later. An appropriate time. They'd both done it wrong before. He was going to make sure they did it right this time.

Not having some form of connection with her drove him crazy, though, so he joined their hands across the table once more. "All I ever wanted was to be someone other than my father. I thought my parents' problems were all his fault. But maybe it wouldn't have mattered if my mother had come to London more or if my father had stayed in the country more because they never loved each other."

William took a deep breath. "Your plan is going to be difficult and it's going to need adjusting along the way. But a complicated life with you by my side is better than anything else I could ever find."

"I'll never enjoy society," Daphne said. "They'll never really accept me."

William grinned. "I've never really accepted them. I think you'll find my friends a bit different from the people you remember from your Season."

Daphne licked her lips. "There is one more thing."

"Name it." He'd give her the world if she just agreed to stay in his.

"I may have to insist on Araminta moving into the dower house."

William laughed. "Consider it done." Because it already was. He'd sent word last week for her to begin making preparations. "I love you, soon-to-be Lady Chemsford."

Daphne paled and drooped against the back of her chair. "I'm going to be a lady."

William partially rose and leaned over to place a gentle kiss on her lips, taking care to keep it quick and soft. "You're going to be my wife."

Three weeks later, Daphne stood in the back of St. Mary's, getting ready to say the vows that would make her a marchioness. She'd thought her life reclusive and empty until she saw how many people were standing in the church.

Kit and Graham were standing in one row, Jess on one side of them and Daphne's father on the other. Tears rolled unchecked down her father's face as he smiled in her direction.

Behind them were Nash and his wife and their four children.

Across the aisle was Mrs. Lancaster with one arm around Eugenia and the other around Sarah. Reuben was next to them, standing tall and proud. Working in the stable agreed with him, as he looked less scrawny than he had a few months ago.

Daphne felt the small prick of tears behind her eyes. Sarah would be leaving them soon. William had gotten her a position as a parlor maid in a music master's house, and use of the piano had been included in the job offer. The young woman was as excited for the adventure as Daphne was nervous.

"You can stay at Haven Manor, you know. We can hire a music master," Daphne had told the girl.

She'd wrapped her thin arms around Daphne and shaken her head. *"It's time we all start our new lives. You're going to be teaching unfortunate women how to live on their own and survive in this world. Consider me another success story. I'm ready, Mama Daphne. I'm ready to live my life."*

There would be more success stories. Jess was already deciding what sort of lessons the women were going to get when they came to live at the cottage. She'd never admit how much she'd come to care about helping the women, and her methods would never be what anyone deemed gentle, but Daphne couldn't wait to see what sort of strong women these new relationships would produce.

Mr. Leighton smiled at Daphne from his pew, bringing Daphne back to the present. A handful of families sat with the Irishman, families of men who had occasionally helped out at Haven Manor over the years.

Even one of the families who had taken in one of Daphne's young charges had come back. Seeing young Alice bicker and play with her new siblings nearly sent Daphne's prickle of tears over the edge.

Mr. Thornbury seemed delighted with the festivities as he sat beside two of William's closest friends who were in attendance. They were staying at an inn, but she and William had dined with them several times and now she could look their way without shaking.

Then there was Benedict. He stood at her side, despite convention, smiling and wearing a brand-new custom-tailored suit. "Are you ready?" He swallowed. "Mother?"

She was never going to make it through this day without crying. "I'm ready."

Her son walked her to the man who would become her husband before kissing her on the cheek and going to sit beside Kit.

She barely remembered the vows, knowing the words didn't matter. Her heart and future and everything she was belonged to William. And he belonged to her.

A joyous cheer went up from the collected crowd as Daphne and

William were declared husband and wife. Friends and family surged around them, not waiting for the rest of the traditional ceremony.

Daphne swung from friend to friend, marveling at the number of people who were around her and the attention focused on her, and yet she didn't feel the need to hide.

She wrapped her arms around Kit and hugged her with all her might. "I wouldn't be here without you."

Kit hugged her back briefly before giving her a punch on the shoulder. "I think we can all agree you're stronger than you thought you were—than any of us thought you were."

Daphne looked to Jess to see if she was going to join in the teasing, but the smaller woman wasn't watching them. She was looking toward the back of the church.

"Jess?" Daphne asked. "Is everything all right?"

She blinked a few times and then swung her gaze back to Kit and Daphne. "I thought I saw . . . someone for a moment. And yes, I think any woman who can convince a man to actually see that he's completely wrong about something is impressive."

Her glare drifted across the church to land on Mr. Thornbury. Daphne couldn't hold back a giggle. "I thought the problem with Mr. Thornbury was that he wasn't wrong."

"Mr. Thornbury is irritating," Jess returned. "Isn't it time we all went back to the manor? Horatia was overseeing the last of the food preparation, and it should all be ready by now."

Once at Haven Manor, the guests ate and laughed. Children played on the lawn. Eventually they trickled away, returning to their own homes.

Darkness rolled in, and that night, when Daphne lay in bed, her new husband curled at her side, she didn't have to dream. Nothing she could imagine could possibly be better than the reality she was living.

Acknowledgments

While I am intimately aware of the dangers of an overactive imagination, there was a great deal of the rest of Daphne's life I have never experienced.

I want to thank the men and women who shared their stories with me. The ones who opened their hearts, showed me their scars, and bled their stories into Daphne and William.

You are strong, my new friends. You are an inspiration. I hope Daphne shares your story in some small way and maybe spreads your strength to someone who needs it. I hope William inspires someone to begin anew with a sense of purpose.

God bless you all.

Kristi Ann Hunter is the author of the Hawthorne House series and a 2016 RITA Award winner, an ACFW Genesis contest winner, and a Georgia Romance Writers Maggie Award for Excellence winner. She lives with her husband and three children in Georgia. Find her online at www.kristiannhunter.com.

Sign Up for Kristi's Newsletter!

Keep up to date with Kristi's news on book releases and events by signing up for her email list at kristiannhunter.com.

Also in the Haven Manor Series...

Forced to run for her life, Kit FitzGilbert finds herself in the very place she swore never to return to—a London ballroom. There she encounters Lord Graham Wharton, who believes Kit holds the key to a mystery he's trying to solve. As much as she wishes that she could tell him everything, she can't reveal the truth without endangering those she loves.

A Defense of Honor, Haven Manor #1

More from Kristi Ann Hunter!

Lady Georgina Hawthorne has kept a secret her entire life. She must marry during her debut season or she could lose everything—and Colin McCrae is not her idea of eligible. But as their paths cross, their ongoing clash of wits has both Georgina and Colin questioning their priorities.

An Elegant Façade
HAWTHORNE HOUSE

After a night trapped together in an old stone keep, Lady Adelaide Bell and Lord Trent Hawthorne have no choice but to marry. Dismayed, Adelaide finds herself bound to a man who ignores her, as Trent has no desire to connect with the one who dashed his plans to marry for love. Can they set aside their first impressions before any chance of love is lost?

An Uncommon Courtship
HAWTHORNE HOUSE

The Duke of Riverton has chosen his future wife using logic rather than love. However, his selected bride eludes his suit, while Isabella Breckenridge seems to be everywhere. Will Griffith and Isabella be able to overcome their pride to embrace their very own happily-ever-after?

An Inconvenient Beauty
HAWTHORNE HOUSE

BETHANYHOUSE

You May Also Enjoy . . .

As England plunges into war, Barclay Pearce uses his skills as a thief to help his nation. But upon rescuing Evelina Manning from a mugging, he begins to wonder what his future might hold. When her father's invention gives England a military edge, the whole family is in danger—and it may just take a reformed thief to steal the time they need to escape it.

An Hour Unspent by Roseanna M. White
SHADOWS OVER ENGLAND #3
roseannamwhite.com

In the aftermath of tragedy, Grace hopes to reclaim her nephew from the relatives who rejected her sister because of her social class. Under an alias, she becomes her nephew's nanny to observe the formidable family up close. Unexpectedly, she begins to fall for the boy's guardian, who is promised to another. Can Grace protect her nephew . . . and her heart?

The Best of Intentions by Susan Anne Mason
CANADIAN CROSSINGS #1
susanannemason.com

Much has happened in Ivy Hill, and while several villagers have found new love and purpose, questions remain—and a few dearly held dreams have yet to be fulfilled. When a secretive new dressmaker arrives, the ladies suspect she isn't who she claims to be. While the people of Ivy Hill anticipate one wedding, an unexpected bride may surprise them all.

The Bride of Ivy Green by Julie Klassen
TALES FROM IVY HILL #3
julieklassen.com

CPSIA information can be obtained
at www.ICGtesting.com
Printed in the USA
LVHW091124201019
634737LV00007B/94/P

9 780764 233128